In a Land of
Smuggling, '
that Lead

David DeLuca: The former Boston street cop turned counterintelligence team leader is just back from Iraq when he's sent to southern Arizona. His job: find a missing female Army sergeant who may have stolen military secrets—or find out who might have abducted her . . .

Cheryl Escavedo: With top clearance to work at the heart of America's classified nerve center buried in Cheyenne Mountain, the beautiful sergeant leaves behind a trail of mystery. Her commander is sure she stole vital information. But DeLuca suspects something worse than treachery . . .

Colleen MacKenzie: Smart, sexy, and fluent in enough languages to go anywhere posing as anything, she becomes DeLuca's Team Red point woman when the hunt leads to a Mexican porn and drug dealer—teamed with a Russian crime lord . . .

Sami Jambazian: He is a vital member of DeLuca's Team Red—especially for this mission. Because when the case crashes into the world of UFO fanatics, Sami has one thing in common with the crazies: he's seen a UFO with his own two eyes . . .

Dr. Gary Burgess: A Ph.D. at sixteen, the brilliant physicist quits his work and disappears, convinced that the U.S. government is using his research to create a horrific, space-based killing technology. And DeLuca thinks the vanished genius might just be right . . .

Also by David DeBatto and Pete Nelson

CI: Team Red

CI: Dark Target

DAVID DeBATTO
and PETE NELSON

WARNER BOOKS

NEW YORK BOSTON

Cover design by Jerry Pfeiffer
Book design by Stratford Publishing Services

Warner Books

Time Warner Book Group
1271 Avenue of the Americas
New York, NY 10020
Visit our Web site at www.twbookmark.com

Printed in the United States of America

First Printing: February 2006

10 9 8 7 6 5 4 3 2 1

To my son, Christopher,

Thank you for heeding my advice and enlisting in the Air Force instead of the Army!

To Pete Nelson,

You are truly amazing. I pray that the "CI" series continues for years just so I can continue to work with you my friend.

To Dan Ambrosio, for having "that vision thing."

—David DeBatto

Pete Nelson would like to acknowledge the kindness, generosity, assistance, and expertise of the people without whom this book could not have been written. That includes, of course, first David DeBatto, my co-author, but also the other people I harassed on the telephone or via e-mail, including Hugh O'Doherty, Dave Elliott, Jack Brehm, Robert Borth at NORAD, and Major Karen "Jack" Magnus, Director of Public Affairs with the 22nd Air Force. Thanks to Carolyn Gear for making sure my Spanish translations made any sense at all, and thanks to Kevin Downey, cave photographer extraordinaire, for helping me navigate the underground passages. Thanks to Dan Ambrosio for his edits and thanks to my wife Jen for all her help and patience. Final thanks to my son Jack for not pulling my laptop off the table by the power cord.

—Pete Nelson

Chapter One

THE GIRL RAN, LEAVING THE JEEP BEHIND. She'd switched cars, abandoning her Civic at her uncle Henry's trailer after parking it in a grove of cottonwoods, though she doubted the trees would conceal it for long. She'd teased her uncle about owning a Cherokee (they were Cocopah) and told him he was a fool to leave the key in the ignition, abandoning the vehicle for weeks at a time while he traveled the country, but she'd been glad to find the old car gassed up and ready for use. She'd been wearing night vision goggles to drive with the headlights off, and was in the middle of nowhere, ten miles short of the Mexican border, on a dirt road the locals called Camino del Diablo, so rutted and eroded with deep corduroylike ripples that she couldn't make much better than twenty miles per hour, when it just stopped. It could have been simple mechanical failure. The Cherokee had more than two hundred thousand miles on it.

She turned the key. Nothing happened. She pounded on the dashboard. She tried to turn the headlights on and off, but the headlights didn't work, nor did the radio. When she checked the fuse box, she discovered that all the fuses had been tripped. The spare fuses in the glove box were blown as well.

She left the NVGs on the seat and ran, out of breath, across the floor of the desert. She was headed for Spirit Mountain, pausing to consult the topo map her friend had e-mailed her. Her ancestors had taken refuge there. Perhaps she could, too. Her goal was a place her friend had called the Ano Kayai, the Village of Eagles, an ancient Anasazi cliff dwelling beneath a red rock overhang, her friend had said, a ruin picked over by pot thieves and of little further interest to archaeologists, last occupied by mushroom-eating hippies in the sixties, but it was still holy, and she'd found herself praying a lot lately—perhaps it would protect her. If she could reach it before daylight came, she might be safe. They might not find her. The evil ones. The ones her uncle had warned her about. Her boots dug into the sand where it gathered in wind-blown drifts, her heels clattering across the hard-baked *caliche* where the wind had scoured the sand away. She navigated between the saguaros and the ocotillos and the jumping cholla by the light of a quarter moon, still visible in a sky that was starting to cloud over. She didn't stop until she reached an arroyo, where she paused beneath a mesquite bush to catch her breath.

She looked up at the moon. It was a quarter full, but bright in the clear desert air. As a little girl, she'd been fond of stripping off her frock and dancing naked by the light of a full moon. Now the light was her enemy. Her own body heat was her enemy—wasn't that how snakes located their prey? She prayed for the clouds to gather above her, an ancient prayer for rain that her grandmother had taught her, but she could only remember the first part of it. Perhaps that was enough.

She took a drink from one of the water bottles in her bag. She had two more. If she had to, she could make that last for a day or two. Yet when she pushed again at the implant beneath the skin of her right forearm, she feared she didn't have another day or two—unless she could get it out, her time left on this earth could be only a matter of minutes. It was crazy thinking, but sometimes crazy thinking made sense. That had to be how they'd found her. Getting the implant had been his idea. She'd trusted him then. She didn't trust him now. That had to be it.

She was angry with herself for not being better prepared—she needed a knife, but she didn't have one. She unbuttoned the top two buttons of her blouse and leaned forward to take the dog tags from around her neck, hoping the edge would be sharp enough to slice into her skin. It wasn't. She tried sharpening the edge of one of the tags on a rock, then pressed it one more time into her skin, scraping as hard as she could until she drew blood, but it just wasn't sharp enough. She should have done this sooner, at her uncle's trailer, where one of the old fashioned single-edged razor blades he kept to shave with would have done the job quickly and neatly.

Fortunately, the desert was full of things sharp enough to pierce her skin. She climbed out of the arroyo and moved to a large saguaro cactus, a twenty-foot-tall specimen, its taproot reaching down perhaps a hundred feet to find water, probably a five-thousand-dollar plant, she guessed, to the illegal cactus-rustlers who'd come with their four-wheel-drive vehicles and their lassos to pull the saguaros down and sell them to landscapers in Tucson and Phoenix. The rustlers weren't necessarily outsiders. Often they were tribal people who should have known better than to disturb the spirits of a plant that had stood in the same place for a thousand years. They'd lost their connection to the earth, but who was she to judge? So had she, she feared. It was why she was in the trouble she was in. It was how the evil ones had gotten to her. Her uncle had warned her, even though he was as modern as they came.

She prayed briefly to the spirit of the cactus, trying to remember the words her grandmother had taught her long ago, then positioned her arm against a long needle and leaned into the cactus until the needle pierced her to the depth of perhaps half an inch. She cried out in pain, once, then gritted her teeth and dug, dragging her arm against the needle until she'd made a cut that was perhaps an inch and a half long. She tried to get at the implant with her teeth, but it was too far down toward her elbow, and she couldn't reach. She dug again with the needle, and the pain was unbearable, but she endured it, digging with her fingernail until she was finally able to extract the device. She wiped the blood off it and then held it up to examine it, a small plastic tube, about an inch and a half long.

"Goddamn you," she spat, using the Cocopah name her grandmother used to call her, which meant "foolish girl." Foolish for all she'd done. Foolish for thinking she was better than anybody else, smarter. Foolish for losing her humility.

She flung the device as far as she could into the desert. Maybe they would think she was dead, now that it no longer moved. Maybe they would leave her alone.

She used some of her precious water supply to wash the wound, then tied her bandana around it, using her teeth to pull it tight. It would have to do. She had to keep running.

But where were her dog tags? What had she done with them?

There was no time to look for them.

She returned to the arroyo and moved up the wash, keeping to the side when it widened, hoping it would afford some minimal cover as she climbed through the creosote bushes and the palo verde. If she was reading the map right, her car had died a few miles short of the arroyo she was to take to bring her to the trail head. Perhaps this one joined the other. She had to keep moving. She tore her pants on a rock, and then a spike from an ocotillo nearly ripped her hair out, but she kept going. She'd gone a few hundred yards when she heard a snapping sound in the air behind her, a crackling, like cellophane crinkling.

She turned. There was nothing there, but she felt a presence, a shimmering quality to the darkness, zigzagging lines, like glass snakes, crawling across her field of vision, just below the visible spectrum.

They were coming for her.

She ran, the red rock walls of a shallow canyon rising to either side of her now. There was a chance that the canyon would protect her, long enough to find somewhere to hide, a ledge, a cave, a javelina den, anything.

They were coming. How had they found her?

Then, on a distant hill, perhaps a mile off, she saw a light.

It looked like a fire. A fire meant people. Out here, in the desert, at three in the morning, it probably meant people she didn't want to know, people who might do her harm, smugglers or thieves, but she didn't care—perhaps there was strength in numbers. Perhaps the presence of witnesses would be enough to make the evil ones leave her alone. Unless the evil ones wanted to kill them all, but if that was what they wanted to do, there was nothing to stop them.

She headed for the light.

Around the fire, the dancers moved, chanting as they circled, their faces painted in the reds and yellows of the earth. There was a Hopi warrior. There was a Navaho medicine man, and a Mescalero shaman, his back covered by the skins of a coyote, the image of Kokopelli tattooed across his bare chest. Two women danced naked from the waist up, their eyes closed as they swayed, enraptured by the chanting and the drumming, at one with the pulse of the universe, the orange-blossom turquoise necklaces clattering against the sacred crystals strung with leather lanyards that hung from their necks. There was a Mandan holy man, dressed in buffalo hides, and another warrior whose leathers were like those of the Cree or the Blackfoot, adorned with Sioux beads he'd purchased at a Cherokee trading post in Enid, Oklahoma. Next to him was a man dressed as a *Star Trek* captain, accompanied by his Klingon wife, and her best friend, who'd come dressed as Counselor Troy, even though at five-foot-three and a hefty two hundred twenty pounds, the resemblance stopped at the costume, the cleavage, and the curly black wig. A shy man in Vulcan ears stood back from the circle, reluctant to partake of the hallucinogenic mushrooms the leader of the group had provided but doing his best to be a good sport, a believer.

At the edge of the fire, a young woman named Rainbow stood with her back to the light, gazing up at the stars, visible to the east, the moon overhead gone now behind a bank of clouds. She'd never felt this good, ever, never known just how one-with-the-universe it was possible to become—it was everything she'd read about in her studies of Eastern mysticism and Zen philosophy, but it was better, because this, this night, this ceremony, this special group of people, had somehow managed to tie it all together, the ancient and authentic past (as represented by the Native Americans) and the realizable future, as represented by the crew from the *Enterprise*. They were at the cosmic tipping point between universal epochs, the leader said, and she knew it was true. She loved how for the first time in her life, she felt like she could be whoever she wanted to be. She wasn't sure what that was, exactly, but it didn't matter—it was the freedom itself that she felt, more than how that freedom manifested itself. So what if the Hopi warrior was really a Jewish librarian from Denver, and the Navaho medicine man owned a science-fiction bookstore in Flagstaff, and the Mescalero shaman was currently living off Social Security in Bisbee—tonight, anything was possible.

"I love you," she said to the sky, watching for movement. The ship was coming. Brother Antonionus had promised it would come. The idea made her so happy. Perhaps it would beam them up and take them with them, or perhaps it would simply study them tonight, in order to better prepare for the final ascension. It was an auspicious night. "I love you so much. I'm so grateful. I really am. I love you so much," she told the universe, letting the tears come. It was the way she'd been meant to feel. It was everything she'd lacked in Seattle, working in a cubicle for a running shoe company, dehumanized and joyless, in a town where the permanently overcast sky hung like a fat gray mattress about a hundred feet above the ground—that's what it felt like.

That was wrong. This was right.

She wondered, vaguely, what had happened to her daughter Ruby, but knew she had to be around somewhere. The universe was too benevolent to let anything happen to Ruby—Rainbow couldn't afford to worry about it. The earth would take care of Ruby. Rainbow tried to remember the lesson: Stress created negative vibrations, and negative vibrations interrupted the frequency upon which the universe resonated, whereas positive vibrations harmonized with it. That's what Brother Antonionus told them, and he'd gotten that straight from the Rigelians themselves.

"Brothers and sisters," the man in the white robes with the beatific smile on his face said, his blue eyes glazed and sparkling with an inner radiance, "People of the Light—move to the rhythm of the universe and feel the pulse of the planets. They are watching you, my brethren. They see what you do and they feel what you feel. They are waiting for their children to come home. They are coming to take us home, once we show them we are ready . . ."

Ruby was bored. She'd spent the day helping the grown-ups make a gigantic mandala in the sand that was supposed to serve as a landing pad, but she was frankly (and secretly) hoping that the UFOs didn't come tonight, even though she knew her mother would be disappointed. Ruby didn't care—her friends were having a slumber party next weekend, and she wanted to go. All in all, she was pretty excited about the possibility of traveling to another planet and hanging out with super-intelligent aliens, or at least she was at first, but the more she thought about it, the more she felt like maybe she needed to spend a little more time on this planet, and besides, when she hung out with the super-intelligent kids at school, she didn't have any fun at all.

She'd taken a flashlight and wandered off to look for javelinas, the wild pigs that sometimes followed each other around with their noses in each other's butts because they were so nearsighted they couldn't see ten feet in front of themselves. She checked over her shoulder occasionally to keep the watch fire in view, but she wasn't worried about getting lost.

She was surprised when she felt something hard rap against the top of her skull, as if a squirrel had thrown an acorn from a tree, and then another, and a third, until she realized they were raindrops, not acorns. Storms could blow up fast in the desert, she knew. She knew also that it could be dangerous to be caught in a wash, where flash floods could sweep you away in an instant.

She turned and headed back to the fire, but then she heard something and stopped.

Something in the desert.

Crying out.

She turned her flashlight toward the sound.

In the distance, she saw something move.

It was a woman, a Native American woman—a real one, not one of the fakes who liked to dance around watch fires and take their tops off.

The woman stopped when she saw Ruby's flashlight. Ruby was about to call out to her, and say something like, "Over here—come this way—you can wait with us until the storm passes," but then something happened.

She wasn't sure exactly what it was, but it was like a flash of light, without the light. Like somebody was taking her picture with a flashbulb, but she'd blinked at the last minute, except that she hadn't blinked, and now there was a bright blue streak on the back of her retina, but she couldn't say why, except that she was looking at a woman, and then the woman sort of . . . melted, and now the woman was gone.

Ruby couldn't breathe.

Ruby couldn't move.

For a second, she thought she'd dreamed what she'd just experienced. As she collected her wits about her, Ruby then thought what she'd seen was a woman being struck by some sort of invisible lightning. And lightning brought with it thunder, which, at so short a distance, should have been deafening—Ruby had heard only a soft crackling, and then a snap.

And then the woman was gone.

Maybe it was a dream, Ruby thought. Or maybe the image had been sent to her by somebody, the way some people saw the image of the Virgin Mary in the frost on a windowpane—maybe it meant Ruby had been singled out to be a witness to something special, except that she could still see the look of fear on the woman's face, and the pain she felt as she burned. Ruby could definitely smell something had burned, like the time she was trying to fry ants with a magnifying glass with her friend Cody and accidentally lit her own hair on fire. The picture of the woman melting was not an image Ruby cared to carry with her—it frightened her—but how was she going to get rid of it? Maybe if someone explained it to her.

Perhaps Brother Antonionus would know. He seemed knowledgeable about such matters.

* * *

Far away, in a darkened control room, lit only by the light of a liquid crystal display, a conversation:

"Collateral target acquired."
"Positive lock?"
"Affirmative."
"Biometrics?"
"Calibrating. One twenty-nine point five-four centimeters. Twenty-eight point two-six kilograms."
"Human?"
"Probable orthodontia."
"A child?"
"Female. Recommendations? Awaiting instructions."
"Abort."

Three weeks later, a Mexican girl named Rosario Flores, from the town of Hermosillo, in the state of Sonora, was arrested in the kitchen of a Mexican restaurant in Tucson by agents from the INS who'd received a tip that the owner employed illegal immigrants. She'd been taken into custody and searched, whereupon it was discovered that she was wearing a set of dog tags she said she'd found in the desert, hanging from a branch of a palo verde tree in an arroyo. The dog tags belonged to a woman named Cheryl Escavedo, a sergeant first class in the Arizona Army National Guard. A call to her unit by INS revealed that she'd been recently reported missing from her job at an entry-processing center in Albuquerque, New Mexico. INS was asked to hold Rosario Flores in custody.

Flores was cooperative and told INS that she'd been taken to the border in a windowless step-van, along with twenty-five or so other people, all willing to pay the coyote three hundred dollars apiece to get them into the United States. They'd been let out of the van in the dead of night, somewhere in the desert, to relieve themselves, got back in the van and drove north in the darkness and transferred to a windowless tractor-trailer, to be let out again in a warehouse in Tucson. For all she knew, she could have crossed the border anywhere from Yuma to El Paso. She was sorry she'd taken the dog tags. She found them when she was looking for a place to go to the bathroom. She hadn't known what they were. She didn't want to go back to Hermosillo. Couldn't she please stay?

When Escavedo's Jeep was found abandoned near Spirit Mountain, on the Tohono O'Odham reservation, at the side of a road called Camino del Diablo, not far from the Organ Pipe Cactus National Monument and the Barry M. Goldwater Air Force Testing Range, the Pentagon was informed. The Jeep appeared to have been hit by lightning, the local authorities said, probably after it had been abandoned. The tribal police asked the Pentagon what they wanted them to do.

The Pentagon said they'd send somebody out to investigate, and to sit tight until he arrived.

Chapter Two

TWENTY YEARS AGO, WHEN COUNTERINTELligence agent David DeLuca was a rookie cop with the Yuma police department, his first thought, looking into a missing person and an abandoned vehicle on or near the reservation, would have been that the disappearance was alcohol related. It was simply, unfortunately, a fact of life. The girl he'd been sent to find had lost both parents to alcohol, had been raised by a grandmother, no longer living, and an uncle—it wasn't unusual either to see the habits of substance abuse passed down from one generation to the next. Yet the girl had been a straight-A student at Goldwater High in Somerton, a lifelong teetotaler who'd worked in a shelter for Cocopah women from homes where alcohol abuse had led to other forms of abuse. Ben Yutahay, the tribal policeman who'd met him to assist in the investigation, ruled out alcohol. His son Marvin had known Cheryl in high school and said she didn't drink, even then, when everybody did.

Ben, Marvin, and DeLuca stood in the desert, the light growing in the east and only the last few brightest stars still shining overhead.

"If that's lightning," said Ben Yutahay, squatting in the dust next to the abandoned Jeep, "it's the funniest lightning strike I've ever seen. Not that it can't do funny things. I saw a guy once who got his shoes blown off by a direct hit but other than that, he was fine. But this is strange."

"How so?" DeLuca said. He'd worked with Yutahay twenty years ago and had considered him a friend, though they'd gone separate ways and not stayed in touch, DeLuca back east to the Boston P.D., Yutahay transferring over to the tribal authority, where he headed up a unit of "Shadow Wolves," so dubbed by the media for the way they could track the immigrant-smuggling "coyotes" and *narcotraficantes* through the desert, preferring the early morning and twilight hours, when the low sun cast long shadows that made the tracks stand out against the desert floor. With F-16s from the 56th Fighter Wing in Gila Bend making practice bombing runs in the Goldwater Proving Grounds and Marines completing their desert training before heading off to the Middle East, it was a particularly dangerous place to be an illegal immigrant. DeLuca and Yutahay had left the motel at four in the morning. After a late flight to Phoenix and the puddle-jumper to Yuma, it had been after midnight when DeLuca checked in. He was exhausted, and yet the desert sunrise somehow revived him.

"Usually when lightning hits a car, it runs down the outer surface to the ground. Sometimes it melts the tires or the windshield wipers but it leaves what's inside alone. That's why people are safer in lightning storms staying in their cars. Sometimes you get a side flash where the electricity runs along the surface from the car to something more grounded, like a tree or a saguaro, maybe. These tires are fine and there's no side flash. All the damage is inside. But like I said, you can't always predict what lightning is going to do. If you could, it wouldn't be lightning."

His hair was going gray, and he'd put on about forty pounds since DeLuca had last seen him, but other than that he was the same, with the same dry sense of humor that DeLuca remembered. His son Marvin was a spitting image of his younger self, DeLuca thought. Marvin had come along because, Ben said, Marvin was finally thinking of learning a trade and making an honest living in law enforcement, instead of sneaking around digging up rocks to sell at the big gem shows in Los Angeles or Santa Fe. Marvin was crouched next to his father, who was pointing at something under the car.

"This is her uncle's car," Yutahay said over his shoulder. "I wonder how she got it."

Ben stood and crossed to where DeLuca was scrutinizing the horizon. It was beautiful rough country, and though he was happy in Massachusetts, sometimes he still missed the desert.

"The car stopped before the rain came, anyway," Yutahay said. "There aren't any splatter marks under the car. The electrical system is a mess. I can't tell you exactly but from the sloshing, I think she had plenty of gas."

"Can you tell what time of day? Or night?"

"The weather report said the rain started falling around eleven, so it had to be before that, but probably not much before. The headlights were left in the on position, but she left these in the car," he said, handing DeLuca the flashlight and the NVGs, both Army issue. "Why would she leave these in the car if it was dark out?"

The flashlight still worked. The batteries in the NVGs had drained.

"Full moon?"

Yutahay shook his head.

"Quarter moon," he said. "Partly overcast that night, too."

"Maybe she thought she didn't need them?"

Yutahay smiled.

"Indians can't see in the dark any better than you can, David," Yutahay said. "Maybe she was in a hurry and forgot them. The tracks she left were of a person in a hurry. I wonder why, though? If she had car trouble, why not stay with the car?"

"Cell phones work out here?"

Yutahay shook his head.

"Maybe she saw the lights of a house?" DeLuca said.

"Nobody's lived around here for a thousand years," Yutahay said.

"Why not?" DeLuca asked.

"Why would they want to?" Yutahay said. "There's nothing here. It's too far from anything. Sometimes the Cocopah would spend the summers up in the high country with the Pai Pai or the Kumeyaay after spring planting, near where Cheryl's uncle keeps his trailer, but not here. The other thing I'm curious about is the mud on her tires."

"What about it?"

"It's red," Yutahay said. "I don't know of any dirt like that around these parts."

Under the driver's seat, DeLuca found a book in a brown paper bag. The book was a coffee-table sized hardcover entitled *Lechugilla: Jewel of the Underground,* and it had been signed on the title page by the photographer, a man named Josh Truitt who'd written: *"Sometimes to expand your horizons, you have to dig beneath them. Happy birthday, love, Josh and Theresa."* DeLuca showed it to Yutahay. The photographs were of exotic cave chambers, crystal formations and that sort of thing.

"Does that seem like an odd thing to bring along on a trip?" DeLuca asked his old friend.

"Maybe it was in her car before she left and she didn't want to leave it behind when she switched cars?" Yutahay speculated.

"But she left it behind here," DeLuca said.

"She left here in more of a hurry," Ben Yutahay said. He showed the book to his son. "You ever hear of this place?"

Marvin Yutahay looked at the book.

"Heard of it," he said. "It's off limits to gem hunters. You gotta get a permit to get in."

"Why's that?" DeLuca asked the younger man.

"Lotta good stuff inside," Marvin said with a shrug. "That's what I've heard."

"I think I'm done here," Ben said. "The trail leads this way. You good?"

"I'm good," DeLuca said, throwing the book back in the car. "Hey—I could be home shoveling the driveway right now. This is a walk in the park."

"Actually, the park is that way," Yutahay said, pointing toward the sun.

It was only two days earlier that DeLuca had come home from the Burlington Mall with his wife, fighting the traffic on 128, to find a message on his answering machine: "Dave, Phil LeDoux. Listen, pack your duffle and get your ass down here ASAP. Sorry to break up your second honeymoon, but we've got something we want you to handle for us. Call the SATO office at Hanscom and have them book you on a flight to Washington tonight. Then call down to McNair and have them arrange a room for you at the BOQ. I'll see you in my office tomorrow morning at 0800. Say hi to Bonnie for me. Out here."

He'd been back from Iraq for less than a month, in theory recovering from the neck injury he'd sustained when he'd been thrown through the windshield of a Humvee. The truth was, his neck was fine, and he was bored. Bonnie had seen how eager he'd been to get another assignment, his first as the leader of "Team Red," a special ops counterintelligence unit that came with a hospital bed promotion from staff sergeant to chief warrant officer 2 with a presidential waiver of warrant officer school thrown in. It had been a mistake to let his enthusiasm show, because she'd taken it personally, despite his protestations to the contrary.

The Army specialist driving the car that picked him up at the Fort McNair bachelor officers' quarters was probably twenty or so but looked fifteen in his "pickle suit," the Army dress-green or "Class A" uniform. On the advice of LeDoux's aide, Captain Martin, DeLuca had worn a uniform as well, if only to avoid all the post-9/11 checkpoint hassles the Pentagon Force Protection Agency was subjecting civilians to. Inside the Pentagon, he got lost several times, looking for LeDoux's office, where every hallway looked the same to him, and he hated to ask for directions unless he absolutely had to. Outside LeDoux's office, he'd cooled his heels, thumbing through back issues of *Army Logistician, Defense Weekly, Soldiers Magazine,* and the *Army Times.* He'd allowed himself to become excited by the idea that he'd finally be doing the kind of interesting work he'd always dreamed of doing. Frankly, the Arizona desert was beautiful, and it was nice to get a little warm weather, but all the same, finding a missing person wasn't exactly the kind of work he'd anticipated.

Yutahay must have sensed something.

"You seem a little down," Yutahay said. "I'm happy to leave it alone if you'd prefer, but I just thought I'd ask, in case you wanted to talk." Yutahay led the way, followed by DeLuca, with Marvin bringing up the rear in the procession.

"I'm swell," DeLuca said. "I just thought I'd be doing something different. When I took the job, I'd been led to believe . . ."

"That you wouldn't be shuffling around in the dust with an old Indian?" Yutahay said.

"I'm not complaining," DeLuca said. "I might have thought this was something the MPs could have handled, that's all."

"Maybe the fact that they sent you makes it important," Yutahay said. "They wanted the job done right. Personally, I always give missing person cases top priority. When I was in Vietnam, before I met you, my brother was MIA. I was artillery but he was infantry. I'd rather know somebody was dead than not know what happened to them. I think that's why I became a tracker."

"I guess I just sounded like an asshole," DeLuca said. "I apologize."

"I know what you mean, though," Yutahay said. "You want a challenge."

DeLuca felt guilty for complaining. The fact was, he'd been told he'd be leading a team on special assignments, and then, his first job out of the box, he'd been loaned to a joint command, briefed in LeDoux's Deputy Commander, G-2 office by a Colonel Oswald from NRO who'd told him, in a tone of voice DeLuca found condescending, "One of our people from STRATCOM in Colorado, a 71 Lima buck sergeant in the archives section named Cheryl Escavedo, has turned up missing and the trail seems to lead to southern Arizona." He'd handed DeLuca Escavedo's Army 201 personnel file. "Before she disappeared, she apparently swiped some classified information from one of the databases at The Mountain. They'll fill you in better when you get there, but first we want you to go to Arizona and have a look-see. Folks at STRATCOM are pretty worked up. Call your team in if you see the need but check with us first—we'd like you to handle it alone if you could."

"I recommended you when Colonel Oswald came to us because I know you used to live there and you know the territory," DeLuca's friend General Phillip LeDoux had said. "Plus, we want to keep you busy. I actually thought we'd have something for you before this, but for now, this will give you a chance to do some good and work on your tan."

"So you're giving me busy work?" DeLuca had thought, though he held his tongue.

Every once in a while, Yutahay bent down to touch the earth, squinting at the dust or fingering a branch or twig.

"You went from here over to Boston P.D., right?" Ben said, breathing easily despite the rough terrain. "You do missing persons there?"

"Whenever it came up," DeLuca said. "I was with homicide for a while. I was working elder and disabled abuse cases before I reenlisted, busting the shitheads who were abusing elderly and special needs people in shelter homes. That'll throw a cloud over your sunny disposition toward your fellow man. Assuming you still have one. Lotta homes run by the low-life scums where half the caregivers were ex-cons."

"Why'd you reenlist?" Yutahay said.

"I lost my sister in 9/11," DeLuca told him. "They never found her either."

"Aw geez," Yutahay said. "I'm sorry if what I said before made you think I thought you didn't understand."

"I was the one being the asshole," DeLuca said.

Yutahay paused at a turn in the trail.

"That's interesting," he said.

"What is?"

"Look at the spine on this saguaro," Yutahay said. "Right there—this one. That's blood."

"It's in an odd location for someone to bump into," DeLuca said.

"I don't think she bumped into it," Yutahay said. "Not by accident, anyway. The blood is too deep on the needle. And the needle is bent. So's the one next to it. Like she was using it to cut herself."

"Why would she do that?"

"I don't know," Yutahay said, looking down. "There's blood on the ground, too. She stood here for a few minutes, I think. I wish it hadn't rained. Why do you think she cut herself?"

"Snake bite?" DeLuca said. "To drain the poison?"

"Plenty of 'em out here," Yutahay said. "I haven't seen any signs of them so far, but that doesn't mean they're not here. What are you looking at?" he asked his son.

"At what?" Marvin said.

"That's what I asked you," Ben said. "You keep staring at those cliffs."

"Just looking," Marvin said. "This is Spirit Mountain, right? There's supposed to be some ruins up there. Cliff dwellings. A guy told me."

"You wanna go up and look for bling bling?" Ben said.

"Bling bling means gems," Marvin said. "Ruins don't have gems. They have pots. I don't do pots. Plus, what I heard was that the place had been cleaned out."

"What was Cheryl Escavedo like in high school?" DeLuca asked the younger man.

"She was cool," Marvin said. "Too cool for me. She never even gave me the time of day."

"She was the valedictorian, right?" Ben asked. Marvin nodded. "Really pretty girl. People thought she could be Miss Arizona. But she wasn't into her own looks. She was a nice girl, right?"

"She was pretty nice," Marvin agreed. "Not stuck up at all."

"I don't know," Ben said. "In my experience, for every beautiful woman you see, somewhere, there's a guy who's sick of her shit. Your mother could be the sole exception."

DeLuca had to smile, but he noticed that Marvin didn't.

"You know what the secret is to a happy marriage, David?" Ben said. "The man makes all the big decisions, and the woman makes all the little decisions. I've been married for twenty-eight years, and so far, there hasn't been a big decision."

They'd come about a mile from the car. Suddenly, Yutahay stopped, staring at the ground and rotating in a full circle. He walked a few paces in one direction, then a few in the other, scrutinizing the surrounding vegetation.

"That's odd," he said, noting a ridge nearby.

"What is?" DeLuca asked.

"The trail stops here," Yutahay said.

"You lost it?"

"I didn't lose it," Yutahay said. "She was wearing a boot with a pretty distinct heel signature. It doesn't go past here."

"She took her boots off?"

"Then we'd see the marks of her bare feet."

"Even if it rained?"

"Especially because it rained," Yutahay said. "We passed the point, a while back, where she was standing when it started raining."

"Then the rain washed the trail away."

"No," Yutahay said. "It stops suddenly. Why would it wash it away in that direction but not in the one we came in? There's no arroyo here or anything that might explain it. It just stops."

"Maybe," DeLuca said, thinking, "a helicopter came along and lowered her a rope."

"Ya think?"

"No," he said. "I just don't know what else could explain it."

"Maybe a dirigible," Yutahay said. "Maybe she shape-shifted into an eagle and flew away." DeLuca frowned at him. "I'm not being serious," Yutahay said. "You can't throw down a good shape-shift without years of study. I'm going to climb that ridge and have a look around. I'll be right back."

DeLuca scanned the Sonora Desert sprawling before him. Marvin Yutahay was crouched in the sand, pushing through it with his fingers until he stood and held up, for DeLuca to see, a piece of what looked like ice, although the temperature was in the high seventies and sure to rise to the eighties by midafternoon.

"What's that?" he asked.

"We call it Sky Glass, in my business," he said. "Mostly annealed silicates, maybe a little lime here, a little ash. You can find it where lightning hits the desert sand and turns the surface molten, but usually it spikes into the ground. This stuff is pretty even. If we hadn't been walking all over it, we could have been able to tell the shape. It looks huge."

He handed the thin piece of glass to DeLuca, who held it up to the light where the sun was climbing above the Growler Mountains.

"You mind if I keep this and have it analyzed?" he asked.

"Be my guest," Marvin Yutahay said as his father returned to them, a white garbage bag in his hand.

"There's a fire pit up there," he said. "All kinds of footprints. I think there must have been some kind of party. And a child's prints. A girl, I'd bet. Barefoot, but she wandered off this way. They left their garbage. We ought to be able to figure out who they were from that."

"You think our missing person had come to join the party?" DeLuca said.

"I don't think that's why she came, but maybe you were right—maybe she saw a light and headed for it. If it happened the same night, it's possible. I think we need to find out who was camping on that ridge. I'll call the uncle, too, and ask him how Cheryl was driving his Jeep."

* * *

When DeLuca called Cheryl Escavedo's number in Albuquerque, her roommate answered, a woman with a thick Russian accent who said her name was Theresa Davidova. Theresa said she didn't have anything to add to what she'd already told CID, whose report DeLuca had read. Cheryl had said she was going to be gone for a few days, but she didn't say where she was going. She'd packed a suitcase. Davidova didn't know what she'd put into it. She thought Cheryl had been seeing somebody, but she didn't know who. She thought it was an older man, but she couldn't be sure. DeLuca gave her the number of his satellite phone and told her to call him if she thought of anything else. She said she would. He told her he wanted to talk to her in person when he was in Albuquerque. She said she wasn't going anywhere.

First, he had to go to Colorado to see a man about a mountain.

Chapter Three

DELUCA RECEIVED A CALL AT HIS HOTEL IN Colorado Springs at 0600 hours, telling him his 0900 hour appointment with General Thomas Koenig was being put on hold and to stand by. He waited at the hotel until noon, read the paper, went for a run (carrying his SATphone in his hand), a swim in the pool, had lunch in a restaurant his guide book said was the best in town (using his government credit card), bought a ski parka for Bonnie on sale (using his own), got a call at 1450 hours saying the general would meet him at 1600 hours, and was halfway to Peterson Air Force Base in the government-issue unmarked Ford Taurus he'd drawn from the 901st MI motor pool out of Fort Carson when his phone rang again to tell him the meeting had been rescheduled for the following morning, with the location moved to the operations center at Cheyenne Mountain.

He spent part of the night nursing a beer in the hotel bar, listening to a musician sporting a two-inch ponytail strumming an Ovation guitar with too much chorus on his amplifier singing James Taylor and Cat Stevens covers with his eyes closed, until DeLuca couldn't take it any more (and he'd been trained to withstand torture) and went to his room, where he reread Sergeant Cheryl Escavedo's 201 file.

It was a good record, superlative, really, describing able and honorable service. She'd been named Army Space and Missile Defense Command's senior NCO for 2002 in her capacity as SIIM (Supervisor, Information Integration and Management), USSTRATCOM, Systems Center, after being transferred to Peterson AFB and NORAD from the Arizona Guard. She'd been honor graduate of her PLDC class, top PT score of her BNCOC class, and she'd taken an advanced degree in information technology management from Colorado Technical University in Colorado Springs. She'd won the Joint Meritorious Service Medal, the Army Commendations Medal, the Army Achievement Medal, drilled with the joint honor guard, had been active with the Association of the United States Army as its legislative affairs representative, served on the Pike's Peak Chapter of the International Association of Administrative Professionals, and worked at the Colorado Springs Women's Center in her spare time, though DeLuca couldn't imagine her having too much spare time. She had eleven performance awards, seven time-off awards, three attached letters of commendation, and even a note included from the children at Kit Carson Elementary thanking her for coming to their class and talking about what they did at NORAD, closing with, "Thank you for keeping our country safe." She'd graduated Summa Cum Laude from the University of Tucson, where she'd been president of the Kappa Kappa Kappa sorority, a social organization that, if DeLuca remembered his undergraduate days at the U of A correctly, only accepted total babes who wouldn't piss on you if you were on fire unless you were rich and owned a hot car. Judging from her photograph, DeLuca gathered the Tri-Kaps hadn't accepted Cheryl Escavedo, a Native American, solely as a token gesture of affirmative action. She was quite attractive, with silky black hair and big doe eyes, full lips, and a chest that could have held a lot more medals. If she wasn't dating anybody, DeLuca surmised, it probably wouldn't have been due to a lack of attention.

He rose before dawn, went for a run, grabbed a continental breakfast at the buffet, and was presenting his credentials at the gatehouse to the razor-wire-girded Protect Level 1 parking lot by 0700 hours. It was his hope that word would spread throughout the command that someone from CI was asking questions about the missing woman. It wasn't all that different from driving into an Iraqi marketplace in a convoy of up-armored Humvees and Bradleys—the noise made the bad guys scatter, but it also brought the good guys out of hiding, the informants who had the information he needed.

It had been snowing when he left the hotel, the six-mile drive up a winding mountain road something of an adventure, particularly when plows coming down the mountain seemed to thunder by at ninety miles an hour with their blades missing his car by only a few inches. But the pine trees looked lovely in the snow. Twice he passed small groups of deer, one group feeding in a field, another scampering across the road in front of his car.

There was a large office building below the entrance to the underground complex labeled Building 101—Technical Support Facility. The parking lot was only half full. At the turn into it, a billboard read: "Welcome to Cheyenne Mountain Air Force Station, our motto: **'Deter, Detect,**

Defend.' Home of the North American Aerospace Defense Command (NORAD), the United States Northern Command (USNORTHCOM), United States Strategic Command (USSTRATCOM), and Air Force Space Command (AFSPC). A Bi-National Facility," the last a reference to the fact that about a quarter of the personnel were Canadian, since an attack on the United States by Russian ICBMs (the original reason for NORAD) would most likely have to come through Canadian airspace. He was finally met outside Building 100, the security building, by an African American woman who introduced herself as Sergeant First Class Gail Davies. He took his B's and C's from his coat pocket and handed them to her.

"Welcome to Colorado," she said with a salute. "Is it . . . Mr. . . . ?"

"David," he said. "Special Agent DeLuca, if you need a title. You didn't have to wait outside for me."

"I've been in The Mountain for the last twenty-four hours," she said. "You get to where you'll take any chance you get for a little fresh air."

He was wearing a herringbone sport jacket over black pants and a white shirt, his tie pulled tight to his throat but with his top button unfastened beneath it. He'd worn a uniform in Iraq, but here he was strictly plainclothes.

"Do you ski, Agent DeLuca?" she asked, glancing at his credentials before handing them back.

"Like a six-year-old," he said. "I've gone off on weekends with my wife, but nothing like what you have in Colorado. You?"

"I snowboard. My son's a knuckle dragger. If you can't beat 'em, join 'em. Have you ever been in 'The Hole' before?" she asked, guiding him into the security building.

"I lived off my credit cards for about a year after college, if that's what you mean," DeLuca said. In Security, he was led through a metal detector, though unlike at the airport, he wasn't required to remove his shoes. A sign on the wall informed him that neither smoking nor weapons were allowed inside the complex, and that he should turn his cell phone off.

"They don't work inside the complex anyway," Davies said, leading him through a turnstile and into the mouth of a tunnel, where a bus, something like an airport shuttle, waited for them.

"The entry tunnel is a little over a mile long between north and south portals and banana-shaped. The blast doors are at the midpoint on the inside curve. It's designed so that the compression force from any detonation outside the facility will pass through the mountain and out the other side." The bus began to move. They were accompanied by a pair of young Canadian officers, one reading the paper, the other with his headphones on. "You're not claustrophobic, are you?"

"Nope," he said, though he'd had enough miserable experiences in underground bunkers in Iraq to last him a while.

"You're in luck then," she said, "because today's a full combat-readiness lockdown."

"How often do you run lockdowns?" he asked. "They're scheduled in advance?"

"It depends," she said. "Wing-level exercises are more common than global. We locked down for real after 9/11 and people stayed inside for days before we were sure what we were looking at. The doors themselves are tested regularly. They're calling today's exercise Moses 2, as in 'lost in the wilderness'—what do we do if we lose our global positioning system? It involves the 527th, so it's a bit more complicated."

"The 527th?" he asked.

"Aggressor Squadron," she said. "Like the guys who learned to fly Russian MIGs for all the Top Guns to practice against during the Cold War, only now we do it with satellites. And computers."

They paused at the blast doors and watched as they sealed shut behind them, a man and a woman scurrying past the guard to get out before it was too late.

"You're standing behind twenty-five tons of steel, or actually fifty because each blast door is twenty-five tons and curved to withstand a multimegaton weapon detonating as close as half a mile away, nautical."

"Do people get searched on their way out?" DeLuca asked. "Or in, for that matter."

"Permanent party members, no," Sergeant Davies said. "Visitors, yes." She led him into the complex, explaining as she went. "The central excavation consists of three main chambers, forty-five feet wide, sixty feet high, and two football fields long, intersected by four connecting chambers thirty-two feet wide, fifty-six feet high, and slightly more than one football field long, giving us a four-and-a-half-acre grid. You have two thousand feet of solid granite over your head. All the buildings and connecting tunnels inside are constructed from continuous-weld low-carbon steel plates to attenuate any electromagnetic pulses, and each building has its own blast doors to resist overpressure and to serve as fire doors, with blast valves in reinforced concrete bulkheads to protect the air, water, and sewer lines. The buildings and tunnels are mounted on more than thirteen hundred half-ton steel springs, which make the buildings both blast-resistant and earthquake-proof, able to move twelve inches in any direction. We have a medical facility, a gym with treadmills and elliptical machines and weight machines and free weights, and a full kitchen and dining facility, right here, serving four meals a day including midnight snacks . . ."

She opened the door and showed him the cafeteria, which included a salad bar, an entree line, and a separate line for fast-food items. He noted, on the walls, large painted murals of rocky mountain landscapes, as if to create the illusion of a window view.

"We don't have living quarters, per se," she said, "except for the firefighters who work on twenty-four-hour shifts, but in an emergency, we have cots for everyone, and if we were to run out of food, we have plenty of MREs in storage. The chefs in the kitchen also have over two hundred recipes for the preparation of human flesh, should we have to resort to cannibalism. That's a joke."

"Good one," DeLuca said.

"We have seven ops centers. Air Warning, Missile Warning, Space Control, Operational Intelligence, Combat Command, Systems and Weather, all running 24/7/365. Missile and Air Warning are probably the ones you already know about, responsible for the ADIZ, or air defense intercept zone. It's still fixed antennae and phased array radars, but that's being supplemented with space-based infrared now. Space control's satellite surveillance network tracks everything in orbit around the earth down to the size of a baseball, over twenty-six thousand objects since this place was built in 1957, with about eighty-five hundred currently in orbit, and about 20 percent of those are functional payloads or satellites, and the rest of it is space junk, rocket parts and that sort of thing. We track both for threat assessment and collision avoidance—we've rerouted the Space Shuttle twelve times to keep it from running into something up there, though the main debris field orbits about five hundred kilometers farther out than the shuttle, which orbits at about three hundred kilometers. We also try to calculate the footprint that satellites are going to leave when they reenter earth's atmosphere, with lighter impacts at the heel and the heavier stuff falling at the toe, but since the earth's surface is 70 percent water and only 25 percent of the land mass is inhabited, so far we haven't had to issue any alerts."

She ran the security card that hung from her neck on a chain through a scanner that opened a set of doors.

"I'll take you to General Koenig's office at STRATCOM, though I think he's in a meeting with NORTHCOM right now. He should be finished soon."

"That's the command set up after 9/11, right?" DeLuca said, though he already knew the answer to his question. Tasked to monitor internal airspace after the Twin Towers.

"That's correct," she said. "We have about five thousand private aircraft flying at any one time and NORTHCOM watches those. You sound like you're from the East Coast. Did you know anybody in the World Trade Center?"

"My sister Elaine worked there," DeLuca said. "She didn't get out."

"I'm sorry," Sergeant Davies said. "I'll take you to the general's office."

Despite claiming immunity to claustrophobia, he couldn't help pondering the notion that there was two thousand feet of rock over his head, and how much it would hurt if it fell on him. The waiting room outside the general's office was relatively calm, while people scurried back and forth in the hallway beyond the open door, the alarm siren a pleasant pinging sound, still ringing.

The general's secretary, a brawny lieutenant named Carr, entered, examined DeLuca's badge and credentials, and told him the general would be a few more minutes. When General Koenig finally arrived, he held up a finger to tell DeLuca he needed another minute, then consulted with his secretary behind a closed office door a moment longer. When he finally opened the door, he nodded to DeLuca without saying a word.

The office was small, for a general, but given the circumstances, that made sense. The wall opposite the desk featured a large flat-screen monitor, showing a photograph of a windblown beach that DeLuca took to be the general's screen saver. The wall behind the desk held framed certificates, diplomas, awards, and photographs, one of a younger Koenig shaking hands with Ronald Reagan, one of him with President Bush (George H.), and another with President George W. DeLuca wondered if there was one with Clinton, tucked away somewhere. Koenig was a tall man, six-foot-four and lean, in his late fifties but fit enough to pass for forty, with close-cropped black hair, a square jaw, and eyes that looked a bit too tight, as if he'd had work done on them. On the wall opposite the door was a large color photograph of a sailboat. It was the only thing in the room resembling decoration.

"She's a beautiful boat, General," DeLuca said.

"She is," Koenig agreed.

"I don't sail," DeLuca said. "And I grew up on the ocean. Long Island."

"I'm from a naval family," Koenig said. The general waited. So much, DeLuca thought, for drawing him out with small talk and personal charm.

"How's Moses 2 going?" DeLuca asked. "If I may ask."

"It's going well," General Koenig replied. "The people we get here are the best at what they do. This is where the cream rises to."

"Can I ask what the nature of today's exercise is?" DeLuca said. "Just so I understand what I'm seeing. I have a TS/SCI clearance, in case you're concerned."

"I know your clearances, Agent DeLuca," Koenig said. "Today's exercise posits the catastrophic loss of global positioning capabilities."

"Loss from what? Or who?"

"Well that would be the first thing we'd want to find out, wouldn't it?" Koenig said. DeLuca sensed Koenig was struggling not to sound condescending, but DeLuca held his ground. It was rare, in the military, to meet someone in authority who possessed both high intelligence (one memo on Koenig said his IQ had tested in the high 180s at West Point) and the ability to suffer fools gladly. The psychological evaluation in Koenig's 201 noted a tendency to micromanage, which, in DeLuca's experience, was often accompanied by a lack of patience. His instincts told him he was going to get more out of Koenig if he pretended to be exactly the sort of annoying idiot Koenig shouldn't have to explain things to. Plus, he was still pissed off at being rescheduled, something for which Koenig had yet to apologize. DeLuca'd never cared for those officers who felt rank meant never having to say you're sorry. In fact, he never cared much for officers, period.

"At the moment," Koenig said, "we're getting intel from ship-based X-band in the Beaufort Sea that suggest a kill-vehicle launch, but without GPS to reconfirm, sea-based data gets a little fuzzy. In about five minutes, those guys are going to be digging for charts and sextants."

"Who's launching kill vehicles?" DeLuca asked.

"Nobody," Koenig said. "That's a decoy. In about ten minutes, someone is going to walk through that door and tell me we have SBL ASATs. And if all goes well, about five minutes after that, somebody else is going to tell me that's wrong, too, and that the lasers that hosed us are ground-based and not space-based. All of which should have happened in about a third the time, and will, the next time we run this scenario. Am I to understand that I'm here to brief you on STRATCOM def-cons, Agent DeLuca?"

"No, sir," DeLuca said. "I just need enough to know how to put things in context when I write up my report. ASAT means antisatellite?"

Koenig nodded.

"Just so I understand, our GPS system has been hit by ground-based lasers—is that right? So that would be Soviet? Are you guys still using the word 'Soviet'?"

"Russian," Koenig said. DeLuca waited. Finally Koenig tapped at his computer keyboard. The beachscape on Koenig's plasma screen dissolved into a Mercatur-projection map of the world. DeLuca swiveled in his chair. There were lights on the map that the key identified as dedicated, collateral, and contributing sensors, marking locations at Kaena Point and Maui (Hawaii), Clear and Cobra Dane (Shemya Island, Alaska), Beale AFB (California), Socorro (New Mexico), Eglin AFB (Florida),

Cape Cod (Massachusetts), Millstone/Haystack (Halifax, Nova Scotia), Thule (Greenland), Ascension Island in the South Atlantic, Fylingdales (England), Diego Garcia in the Indian Ocean, and Altair/Alcor in the South Pacific. A caption at the bottom of the screen identified the display as the SSN or Satellite Surveillance Network.

"This is what we have on the ground, looking up," Koenig said, "radar and electro-optical." He clicked on an icon labeled MSX. "This is what we've been using to look down from space. Mid-course Space Experiment, mostly UV and very long-wave infrared. These systems track about eighty-five hundred man-made objects ten centimeters or larger, of which 7 percent are operational satellites and the rest is shit. The Russians have about one hundred military satellites active and an unknown number of sleepers, but we think for every one they light up, they put up another that they don't, and until they turn 'em on, we can't figure out what they're for. Yet. We know they have space-based lasers, but so far, power demands limit miniaturization, so anything powerful enough to knock one of our birds down would have to be big enough for us to find, even without lighting it up. On the other hand, it takes much less energy to simply blind our sensors, from space, and only slightly more from the ground. We've hosed satellites with as low as thirty watts from ground, using chemical lasers. To blow something out of the sky from the ground, regardless of spin or shielding, you need at least four hundred megawatts, or enough electricity to run a medium-sized city, because only a tenth of the energy is going to reach the target. That's still a thousand times more powerful than existing lasers. Hydrogen-fluoride-powered lasers that size in space would need about two thousand tons of fuel, so they'd be enormous. Single-use X-ray lasers powered by nuclear explosions would be smaller, but obviously you're not going to conceal your deployment. So, when we lose a satellite, we look for hosings first, kill vehicles or kinetics second, and full-power directed-energy last. And different satellites are shielded in different ways, so to defend, you have to figure out what hit you, how powerful, from what direction, and exactly when, and then you can start to know what you're up against and which offensive capabilities to deploy in retaliation. Is that enough for your report?"

"More than enough," DeLuca said. "I wasn't aware that the Russians have lasers they could use from the ground to blind our satellites. Is this recent?" This was a lie. His son Scott had e-mailed him all the material he needed to read to get up to speed, though nothing that would qualify him as an expert.

"They've had them since at least 1976," Koenig said. He clicked into archives and called up a new overlay, with four new icons superimposed over the former Soviet Union. "We got a code ten-ten on a keyhole-eleven that got painted after we sent it to watch a launch at their missile base at Tyuratam. The first Soviet GBL was at Sary Shagan. Even after the Gorbachev collapse, they kept funding laser projects in Nurek, Tajikistan, and another in the Caucasus Mountains in Kazakhstan, and one in Dushanbe. And of course, whenever they sent a bird to watch what the DOD was boosting from Vandenberg, we hosed them out of Maui and Oahu and a facility in Capistrano, though that one's been moved to Cloud Croft, New Mexico. It's one reason we sometimes smile when the liberal elite starts making a fuss about weaponizing space—

they might as well protest nuclear missiles on submarines. That cow left the barn a long time ago. The question, since the beginning of SDI in the first Reagan administration, hasn't been whether. It's been how to do it right and where to allocate the resources."

"Most people think the Space Defense Initiative is over. I think I read somebody saying Reagan only proposed Star Wars to make the Soviet economy go bust trying to keep up with us."

"Most people don't know anything," Koenig said. "Reagan proposed Star Wars because he knew that if all you really want to do is build a small town in Kansas, you have to tell Congress you want to put a million people on the moon, so that Congress can step in and say, 'No, you can't do that, but we'll let you build a small town in Kansas.' And the space program is one of the few things the Russians ever did right. In my opinion."

"Your opinion is something I highly respect, sir," DeLuca said. "So this is still going on? 'Hosing satellites,' as you put it?"

"Not as much," Koenig said. "Partly because both sides put it on the table at SALT and largely because by then, 1991 or so, it was easier to jam a satellite's communications and make it deaf than it was to paint it and make it blind. The battle for the ultimate high ground, as the media puts it, is still going on. I just got a report recently that said the Russian space defense budget for next year is going to be 50 percent higher than it's ever been before. And they're hardly the only country up there."

"I read about Rumsfeld warning against a Pearl Harbor in space," DeLuca said. "I'm assuming that means you guys are getting the funding you need, black budget or otherwise . . ."

Koenig didn't say anything. Apparently the tutorial part of the interview was over.

"Okay. Very helpful. Moving on. Cheryl Escavedo," DeLuca said. "Reason I'm here. Did you get a chance to look at the report?"

"I read it last night," Koenig said, which DeLuca found interesting, because they were supposed to have met yesterday. "How can I help you?"

"Well," DeLuca said, "whatever occurs to you, I suppose. I'm still trying to get to know her. She worked in the Systems Center?"

"Major Huston can help you there," Koenig said. "I've briefed him and told him you'll be visiting."

"And her duties were . . . ?"

"She was in archives," Koenig said. "Again, Major Huston is the one you'll want to talk to."

"What does archives do?"

"What do you think they do?" Koenig said. "We've been keeping track of everything in the sky for the last forty-five years, Agent DeLuca. It's one thing to have the information and another to be able to use it efficiently. Plus, because of our security, Cheyenne is a repository for other government files beyond our purview."

"And she had access to all of it?"

"I don't believe she had access to all of it," Koenig said. "At least not authorized access, but she definitely handled sensitive material. Major Huston can help you there."

"I'll ask him about that, then," DeLuca said. "What was your impression of her? Any sense of why she'd be taking documents?"

"My impression of her?" Koenig said.

"Yeah," DeLuca said. "Did you know her personally?"

"Did I know her personally?" Koenig said. DeLuca noted that this was twice in a row that Koenig had repeated what DeLuca had just said to him. Such repetitions were usually followed by lies. He waited. Koenig said nothing.

"I guess I was thinking that with only 230 people in such close proximity, eventually everybody would get to know everybody else, sooner or later. And a girl like her would be pretty hard to miss."

"I didn't know Sergeant Escavedo personally," Koenig said. "You're right about the proximity. You see people on the bus if you work the same shift, but people are also transferred or rotated in and out on a fairly regular basis. My impression, without meeting her and solely from reading her file and looking at her records and awards, would be that she was a good person and a conscientious soldier who was probably just trying to do her job better by taking work home on her laptop that wasn't supposed to leave The Mountain. But that's just an impression and not a fact."

"She couldn't send it to herself?" DeLuca said. "She had to carry it physically?"

"The firewalls protecting our data systems make the two thousand feet of granite over our heads right now look like eggshells," Koenig said. "But again . . ."

"Major Huston," DeLuca said. "I will definitely ask him about that. I'm just trying to figure out how she got the disks or the CDs or whatever it was out. I guess since you don't search people, she just took them with her in her briefcase. That doesn't seem terribly secure, though."

"That is under review," Koenig said. "That should not have happened. We take the idea of missing files very seriously around here, Agent."

"This one is more than just missing files," DeLuca said. "This one's a missing person. We found her car in the desert, about ten miles north of the Mexican border."

At that moment, just as the general had predicted, an officer in Navy whites knocked on the door to inform Koenig that (if DeLuca was decoding the mil-speak correctly) preliminary telemetry triangulating from the early warning sensors on two of the GPS sats indicated space-based lasers, and that a suspect Russian satellite that had turned active a few minutes before the attack was already being targeted.

"Ensign Stern will take you to systems," Koenig told DeLuca. "Will you keep my office informed if you learn anything?"

"I will," DeLuca said. "Thank you for your time."

In the corridor connecting STRATCOM to the other commands and centers, DeLuca asked Stern to pause while he examined a row of framed color photographs depicting the officers, noncommissioned officers, enlisted persons, and civilians of the year. When he came to the year 2002, DeLuca saw a photograph of Cheryl Escavedo, smiling, proud of herself, posed receiving the award and shaking the hand of General Thomas Koenig, who had just said he didn't know her personally.

Perhaps he'd forgotten.

He hadn't asked Koenig, because he didn't think he'd get a straight answer, why someone with as superlative a service record as Cheryl Escavedo would be transferred from Cheyenne Mountain to an administrative position filling out forms for new recruits at the Military Entrance Processing Station in Albuquerque. "This is where the cream rises to," Koenig had said. There was something fishy about that, beyond ending a sentence with a preposition.

Major Huston reminded DeLuca of the Ken dolls his sister Elaine had played with as a child, stiff and plastic and a bit effeminate. His smile reminded DeLuca of the televangelists he'd seen on TV, the Pat Robertsons and the Jerry Falwells, so transparently unctuous and treacly, accompanied by that pseudo-compassionate tilt of the head that always made DeLuca check to make sure no one was lifting his wallet. Huston was young, midthirties, and fit, DeLuca allowed, though his handshake was soft and clammy.

"Come in, come in," Huston said. "Sorry you caught us at such a busy moment. Can I get you a coffee or tea?"

DeLuca asked for a coffee, two creams, no sugar, after noticing there wasn't a coffee pot in the room. When Major Huston stepped out, DeLuca had a quick look around. The pictures on Major Huston's desk were of his children, a boy and a girl, both in white confirmation robes, and another of the whole family in front of a Christmas tree, Huston with his arm around his wife, a buxom overweight blonde in a white turtleneck sweater, the tree topped by a large crystal angel. On a bookshelf opposite the door, DeLuca saw three photographs framed and hinged together in a triptych, the center photograph showing Huston in full deer-hunting forest camo, with his son on the left side of the triptych and his daughter on the right, both also dressed in camo, and in each picture, a recently slain deer, the slayer lifting the head of the dead animal by the antlers to display the kill. The daughter looked like she couldn't have been more than nine or ten.

A mountain with a peak resembling a snow-capped pyramid rose in the background.

"Do you hunt, Agent DeLuca?" Huston said when he returned, handing DeLuca a Styrofoam cup of coffee. "Rebecca was so proud when she got that buck. You should have seen her face."

"I don't," DeLuca said. He somehow doubted, by the way he smirked, that Major Huston had ever fired a weapon in combat. "But I enjoy being invited over for a nice venison dinner by friends who do."

"My wife makes a tremendous venison sausage," Huston said. "Tremendous. But she's from Kentucky, where they have a long history of preparing game."

"Where did you grow up?" DeLuca asked.

"Muncie, Indiana," Huston said. "My parents were missionaries, so I was actually born in Madagascar, but we moved back home when I was two."

"What can you tell me about Cheryl Escavedo?" DeLuca said. "Or maybe you should backtrack just a bit and tell me what you do here in the systems center."

"Well, what I usually tell people is that we don't run the place, but we make sure the place runs," Huston said. "All the physical systems and environmental-mechanical systems, but all the electronics, too. Communications, computers, IT, finance. We're tech support but we're software design, too. We're a server farm, and we do network hubbing for other agencies. I don't know if you're aware, but the Internet was basically invented here as a way of routing data and communications in a nuclear war. These days, we have to monitor it for threat assessment. A big part of our job is keeping up with the tech environment, and that changes on a daily basis. We throw stuff out every month that would be an upgrade almost everywhere else. And I have to tell you, Cheryl was a big part of the team. We loved Cheryl. I was completely shocked when I learned she'd been taking home documents."

"When did you learn? Or how?"

"We run an automated surveillance program," Huston said. "One component of it is that we twin people's keystrokes, at random, so you never know if what you're doing is being duplicated and sent out for review. It's not a secret. Everyone who works here knows it's part of the deal. Cheryl Escavedo certainly knew."

"Reviewed where?"

"That's automated, too, initially, but the program is rather sophisticated. The program is designed to filter for a variety of keywords and triggers. If, for example, you were writing a letter to the Russian embassy, not that anyone here would be so stupid, but if you were, that would trigger full surveillance and oversight by the security office."

"E-mail goes in and out?" DeLuca asked.

"It does, but nothing gets in or out without being fully scrutinized and analyzed first."

"By human beings or computers?"

"Both," Huston said. "The computers suggest what to look at. We have the most secure communications in the world, Mr. DeLuca."

"And this is all done on your computers in-house?" DeLuca asked. "No exceptions?"

"Command heads can override it," Huston said. "But that's only four people."

"General Koenig?" Huston nodded.

"It was General Koenig's team that designed the system," Huston added.

"Does he look over your shoulder much?" DeLuca asked. "How much of his time does he spend in The Mountain and how much in building A?"

Huston had to think.

"I'd guess maybe 50 percent in each," Huston said. "But I'm not all that familiar with the general's schedule. And no, he does not look over my shoulder. The general is an excellent manager and part of that is being an able delegater. He expects a great deal from his people and he gets it."

DeLuca wondered what made Huston so protective of Koenig. Such protective loyalty wasn't so unusual in the Army, particularly among ass suckers and sycophants.

"So this system flagged Cheryl Escavedo's keystrokes . . . ?"

"Not precisely," Huston said. "In fact, we were running a system challenge, not unlike the exercise going on right now. Operation Holdfast, it was called, testing for structural failure and the back-up protocols that kick in when the firewall is either down or breached."

"When was this?" DeLuca asked.

"November 9, between 0436 and 0445 hours."

"Testing the night shift?"

"There's no such thing as a night shift in The Mountain," Huston said. "After you're inside for more than forty-eight hours, you lose track of time. We have to force people to take downtime or to sleep because the body's sidereal mechanisms need photoperiodicity to operate normally. At any rate, what I was beginning to say was that for a brief period of time, between when the system was down and before the back-up protocols kicked in, we were vulnerable."

"For how long?"

"I'd say no more than a minute," Huston said. "And even then, we looked pretty close at everything that happened during that minute."

"This was when she copied the files?"

"It was the most likely opportunity," Huston said. "Maybe the only one. We didn't catch it until months later, when analysts at NSA were reviewing the data from Holdfast and noticed that the clock on one of the computers had reset itself. Nobody made much of it until someone looking for anomalies noticed the clock had reset itself by months rather than minutes. What we think happened was that Sergeant Escavedo changed the clock on her computer, during that sixty-second window of opportunity, copied the files to either diskettes or CDs, probably CDs, but backdated that information so that the surveillance program wouldn't search for it when it came back on line—why look where you think you've already looked?"

"Backdated to when?"

"To 0437 hours, May 9," Huston said. "Six months to the day, hour, and one minute more, which is how long the system archives information before making the decision what to keep and what to delete, and this would have been something the program would have deleted."

"Isn't deleted material recoverable?" DeLuca asked.

"On your PC back home, yes, but the way we delete things, no."

"Just so that I understand," DeLuca said, "what you're saying is that you have no idea what was taken, or how much of it is missing. And that it couldn't have been accidental or inadvertent—it was planned. Do I have that right?"

"You do, unfortunately," Huston said. "But it had to physically leave The Mountain. It didn't go out electronically. So she could only take as much as she could copy in sixty seconds. We think two CDs at the most, or one diskette. And people aren't supposed to be able to do that, take anything out, but apparently portal security can be compromised."

"Or charmed," DeLuca said. "Like that episode of *Seinfeld,* where he was dating the blonde who was so attractive she could talk her way out of any traffic violation. Which I have to say, from all my years as a policeman, is truer than I'd care to admit."

Major Huston's face was a blank.

"You never watched *Seinfeld*?"

"That would be a television program?" Huston inquired.

"Uh huh," DeLuca said, wondering if Huston was putting him on, though he was too humorless to put him on. "Used to be. It's in reruns now."

"We don't own a television," Huston said. "We home school."

"Well," DeLuca said. "I'm not trying to be sexist here, but I'd imagine a woman as attractive as Cheryl Escavedo could get over on a lot of guys, including security guards."

"God certainly favored her with great physical beauty," Huston said. "Matched by her native intelligence. We thought her a person of all-around good character. Everyone did."

DeLuca was fishing around to see if he could pick up any sense that Huston might have had the hots for Cheryl

Escavedo, but it didn't appear that Major Huston knew what the hots were.

"Was she dating anybody, that you knew of?" he asked. "Any personal problems? Alcohol? Drug habits? Credit card debt?" Huston shook his head at each question. "And she was transferred to MEPS a week later? November 16, right?"

"That's right," Huston said.

"Did she have advance warning that Holdfast was coming? Change her schedule to make sure she was here when it happened? Anything like that?"

"I don't think so," Huston said. "I knew, and of course the command officers knew. I don't know how she could have known, other than by intuition."

"Maybe she had something in mind and was just waiting for the right moment," DeLuca said. "What sort of things did she have access to, through her job?"

"Pretty much everything," Huston said. "Just because something is archived doesn't mean it's declassified. It could have been anything from SATOP codes to intel to DARPA stuff to budget reports."

"And you keep non-CMAFS files, too?"

"We have secure NSA servers," Huston said. "But not even I know what's in them. All we do there is dust and polish."

"So Escavedo didn't have access either?"

"No way," Huston said.

"May I ask why she was transferred? With all her awards and the NCO of the Year thing, I'd think she'd be the kind of person you'd want to keep around."

"She was," Huston said. "She asked to be transferred. The first time she asked, she was denied, but when she asked again, we tried to accommodate her. Working inside The Mountain gets to some people. We want to keep qualified personnel, but we also like to keep a supply of fresh faces flowing through, just to avoid stagnation."

"Why MEPS? That seems like a step down."

"She wanted to be in Albuquerque, as I recall," Huston said. "She had friends there, or family. I'm not sure."

"What did you do when you suspected files had been copied? You reported the missing files—then what happened?"

"I believe CID in Albuquerque asked her to come in," Huston said. "It wasn't handled properly. I'm not saying she was spying or stealing anything, but if someone is doing that, you don't set up an appointment for them to come in and confess, do you? When they went to get her, she was gone. Her laptop was missing, but she forgot to clear her printer buffer, so we were able to print a copy of the last document she'd written."

He reached behind him and handed DeLuca a piece of paper from a manila folder, a letter printed on plain white paper. It was addressed to a Dr. Burgess, at the Union of Concerned Scientists. It said:

Dear Dr. Burgess,
I was hoping that we could meet in person. I've been working for several years at the Cheyenne Mountain facility in Colorado Springs, and I have information I think you might be interested in. I will try calling you again, but I'll be hard to reach so I'll have to call you. I look forward to speaking with you.

"Who's Dr. Burgess?" DeLuca asked.

"Dr. Penelope Burgess," Major Huston said. "She's a microbiologist at the University of New Mexico in Albuquerque. A frequent speaker on the dangers of weaponizing space. She says she never heard of Cheryl Escavedo or received any letters. That's all I know. Apparently the military police have talked to her. And as far as I know, the next thing they did was call you. Is that right? And that's really about all I know."

"Can I keep this?" DeLuca asked.

"It's yours," Huston said.

"Can you show me where she worked?"

Huston led him to a corner cubicle in a large room full of cubicles, computers, servers, and storage units. There were two desks in the cubicle, one empty, the other occupied by a lieutenant named Joyce Reznick, who Huston said had worked with Cheryl Escavedo for the last few months that she'd been stationed at Cheyenne Mountain. Huston introduced DeLuca as being from CI and told Reznick to answer any questions he asked. At the same time, instead of leaving them alone, Huston stood looking over DeLuca's shoulder. DeLuca considered asking him to leave but changed his mind.

"Would you say you knew her fairly well?" DeLuca asked the lieutenant. "Did you socialize in your off hours?"

"We'd meet up at birthday parties and that sort of thing," Reznick said. "I'm not sure I'd say we were close, but I guess I knew her. A little bit."

"And she had friends in Albuquerque?" DeLuca said. "That was why she transferred?"

"I guess," Reznick said.

"Do you know where the rest of her family is?"

"Her parents died in a car accident when she was young," Reznick said. "She was raised by her uncle. He lives in Las Vegas, I think."

"Did she have any money problems, that you knew of?"

"CID already asked me that," Reznick said. "I didn't know about anything. I know she hated gambling. And she didn't drink or do anything like that. She was a really good person."

"How about boyfriends?" DeLuca asked. "Was she ever engaged? Seeing anybody?"

"I don't know about that," Reznick said. "She worked all the time. I think she was seeing an older man for a while but it didn't work out."

"What makes you say that? Did she say anything specific?"

Reznick shook her head.

"She was very private about that sort of thing," Reznick said.

"What makes you think it was an older man?"

"I don't know. That's just the impression I had. I think one weekend she said she and her friend went skiing and that he had a house. I guess I just assumed anybody who had a house had to be older."

"Do you remember where they might have gone skiing?"

Reznick shook her head.

"Thanks for your help," DeLuca said, handing her his card and writing the number of his SATphone on the back of it. "Will you be sure to call me if you think of anything? Major Huston—would that be all right?"

"Certainly," Huston said. "Not a problem."

Not a problem, unless you knew all your keystrokes were being twinned and scanned by a surveillance program, and your phone was probably tapped, and your activities were being watched as well.

DeLuca had been met again by Sergeant Davies, who asked him if he was finding his way around and if he wanted to grab a bite to eat in the cafeteria. He declined. She left him with a group of impatient people waiting for the bus to the parking lot and checking their watches. It was still snowing outside, the sky an opaque gray. He'd gone about halfway to his car when he heard footsteps behind him and turned to see Lieutenant Joyce Reznick, hurrying to catch up with him.

"Will you walk with me?" she said.

"Sure," he said.

"I shouldn't be telling you this," she said. "I could get in big trouble if anybody knew I was talking to you."

"Not from me, you can't," DeLuca said. "I can protect you if you need protection. I have close friends in very high places."

"Not high enough," she said. "Cheryl didn't want to be transferred. They made her leave. Do you really think she'd prefer processing new recruits in Albuquerque to working here? And don't let Major Huston tell you how much he loved Cheryl—he thought she'd only gotten to where she was because the Army needed to have a Native American on the program. He called her a pagan once, to her face."

"I appreciate you telling me this," DeLuca said.

"I think they wanted to shut her up," Reznick said. "I think she'd found out about something they didn't want her to know."

"Who's 'they'?"

"I don't know," Reznick said. "And I don't know about the boyfriend stuff. I couldn't tell you this inside, but she told me she was gay. At least she let on that way to other people because there were so many men trying to ask her out that she had to do something to make them leave her alone. Though in the military, you can't come right out and say you're gay—don't ask and don't tell. Don't ask for your rights and don't tell anybody when they've been abridged."

"Why did she tell you, then?" DeLuca asked. "It's all right, I promise you. Any conversation you have with me is completely protected."

"So you think," she said. Her paranoia was palpable. "She told me because I'm gay. And now that I've told you, I could be court-martialed. I'll just have to trust you."

"What men?" DeLuca asked. "Who was interested in her?"

"Who wasn't?" Reznick said. "The Mountain is a pretty catty place, though the official term for it is 'close-knit community.' You hear rumors all the time."

"Rumors?" DeLuca said. "About what? Or who?"

"That she was having an affair, with a married officer," Reznick said. "But you hear things like that about everybody. I heard that about me. And frankly, when I did, I let it spread because it meant people were more likely to believe my partner was just my roommate."

"So you think Cheryl talking about a boyfriend was just a cover story?" DeLuca said.

"I don't know," Reznick said. "Either that or pretending she was gay was a cover story. I can usually tell, and if you ask me, I don't think she was. Gay."

"Why do you think she took the files?" he asked. "Assuming she took them."

"I don't know," Reznick said, "but knowing Cheryl, I'm sure she had to have had a very good reason. She loved this country . . . Colonel . . ."

"Agent DeLuca," he told her.

"She loved it more than anybody I've ever known. And she considered herself one of the original owners. But she loved what the military had done for her, too. It had given her everything. She would never betray it. I know that. That's all I can say. I have to go now."

He considered her words as he started his car. He wondered if he wanted to drive to Albuquerque tonight or wait for the storm to pass—he'd wait to see what the conditions were like, once he got down the mountain.

In the Shijingshan district of Beijing, Wu Xiake leaned out the window of the men's toilet and took one last drag on his cigarette before flicking the butt into the river below. Some day, he half-expected to flick a cigarette butt into the Yongding and watch the entire river catch fire, such was the level of pollutants and chemicals in the water. He'd gone to an illegal Website one night and read a story about how the massive levels of pollution resulting from the recent Chinese economic revolution were destroying the earth's environment at a dramatic rate, and how Chinese pesticides entering the river traveled from there to Bo Hai Bay and the Gulf of China and then the Yellow Sea and the Pacific Ocean and ended up in the Arctic Circle and ultimately in the fatty tissues of polar bears, where they acted like artificial estrogens that were making the polar bears gay. Wu Xiake had other things to worry about, besides gay polar bears.

He cursed, then returned to his cubicle. In the next cubicle, his friend Cui Chen was working on his desktop computer, moving frame by frame through the first half of the new movie that had streamed in that afternoon over the Internet from their friends in America, an action thriller starring Bruce Willis and Uma Thurman. At least this time, whoever had sneaked the digital camera into the theater to copy the film had held the camera steady. The last film that Wu had worked on, the bootlegger had coughed loudly every few minutes. Cui's job was to translate the first half of the new film into Mandarin for subtitles. Wu's job was the translate the second half, but the Boss wanted it done overnight, and Wu had had very little sleep the night before. If there was another job available to him, he'd take it, but at sixty-six years of age, who would take him? He'd once been one of the top English-to-Mandarin dubbers in the business, the voice of actors ranging from Paul Newman to Curly of The Three Stooges, with the best "nyuk nyuk nyuk" that anybody had ever heard, but now with DVDs, speed was of the essence, and nobody wanted dubbers anymore. It was much faster to go with subtitles. Everything was so hurried. His knowledge of English had gotten him this job, but he felt it was only a matter of time before the Boss got rid of him.

"Did you solve the problem?" Cui asked him in Mandarin without looking up from his computer screen.

"I can't do it. It is too idiomatic. I was thinking about it, but it makes no sense to me," Wu admitted.

"Tell me again what the lines are," Cui offered. *"Maybe I can help."*

"Bruce Willis says to Uma Thurman, 'You wouldn't be the one waiting for Mr. Right, would you, because Mister

Right left.' *And she says,* 'You look like Mister Wrong to me. Your mama must have done a number on you.' *And he says,* "If that's what you want, I don't want to be right,' *and she says,* 'You know what they say about two wrongs.' *And then he says,* 'You have the right to remain silent, but I haven't met a woman yet who I couldn't make scream.'"

"Scream?"

"Yes. Scream."

"This makes no sense at all, Wu," Cui said. *"Who is screaming, and what is she screaming about? Is she in pain?"*

"I don't know."

"What do they say about two wrongs?"

"Two wrongs are better than three but worse than one?"

"Possibly."

"Just do the best you can," Cui said. *"Much of this is not knowable. If the Boss questions you, I will tell him you are right and he is wrong."*

Wu appreciated Cui's offer of support, but he knew that if it came to where the Boss was going to be hard on them, Cui would capitulate instantly. He sat down at his computer screen and typed in the best translation he could come up with in the time given him.

"You are not the person who I thought was once here pending the arrival of the white man. And anyway, he is gone," Bruce Willis said.

"And yet you very much resemble he who isn't that person or any other," Uma Thurman replied, **"and he is not white. Surely your mother was forced to write a number upon you."**

"If it were up to me, I would rather go away now," Willis said.

"They say when you are wrong twice, that is bad, and this you know," the actress replied.

"Even if you choose to say nothing, the thing you do not say will be loud. You may yell now."

"Did you finish?" Cui asked. Wu sighed.

"I did my best. If I'm lucky, everyone will be too busy looking at Uma Thurman to read the subtitles," Wu Xiake said, adding, in English, "Why soitenly—nyuk nyuk nyuk . . ."

"I wish my wife had breasts like hers," Cui said. *"They were like that when my wife was nursing our daughter, but she wouldn't let me touch them. Like Hong Kong. Very appealing, but what difference does it make if you're not allowed to go there?"*

Wu Xiake had just moved on to the next scene when he heard a noise, a low rumbling that sounded like a locomotive was crashing through the building. The noise grew louder and the building shook, until he was certain that an earthquake had struck. He crawled under his desk, where Cui joined him as the power went out in the building and they were engulfed in darkness and dust. He coughed. It was hard to breathe. "Cui?" he called out. He was fortunate in that he still had the headlamp his wife had bought him for his birthday, to wear when he had to ride his bicycle home in the darkness, and the light was strong and the batteries were fresh. He turned it on, but the room was full of dust and smoke. Cui was crying, so Wu did what he could to comfort his friend. The noise lasted for perhaps twenty or thirty seconds, and then the building was still again. Cui was shaking. Wu held his friend.

"We must get out," Wu said. *"There could be after-shocks. Are you hurt?"*

"No, I think I'm okay."

"Follow me, Cui."

Wu put his headlamp on his head and made his way through the darkness, crawling over fallen file cabinets and shelves. In the hall, they found Ji Jiabao, the cleaning lady, trapped under her cart, so they lifted it off her and helped her to her feet. She seemed to be okay. As far as they knew, they were the only ones in their part of the building. A night watchman was supposed to make the rounds, but he was usually in the warehouse, watching movies.

When they got to the end of the corridor, Wu Xiake opened the double doors and stopped, because that was where the building stopped. He saw only flame and smoke and the stars in the open sky above, and below, a pile of rubble where the warehouse had once been, a part of the old converted factory once the size of several soccer fields now simply gone, and with it, millions of yuan worth of copied DVDs waiting for shipment. The earthquake had destroyed Shijingshan Entertainment, and yet, when Wu looked across the river, he saw that the old two-hundred-foot-tall brick chimney from the coal-burning power plant was still belching smoke—how could the earthquake demolish the warehouse but not knock down the chimney?

By the time Wu reached his bicycle, the building was surrounded by fire trucks and policemen and people manning manual pumps to bring water from the river to pour onto the smoldering rubble. He probably should have stayed to help, Wu thought, but he was just tired and wanted to go home. Yet looking back at the building, he couldn't help noting how odd it was—it was as if somebody had taken a large knife and sliced the building neatly in half in a straight line. Perhaps that was where the fault line of the earthquake lay, and yet, none of the other buildings in the neighborhood had been touched or damaged in any way. The night watchman was the only casualty.

"You don't think the Boss is going to blame us for this, do you, Wu?" Cui asked.

"I don't know," Wu said, worried. *"He might."*

"You have to tell him that I was working at my desk when it happened," Cui said. *"You have to tell him we are innocent."*

"Don't worry," Wu said, *"I'll tell him,"* though he didn't plan on going back to work any time soon.

Chapter Four

IT WAS 370 MILES FROM COLORADO SPRINGS TO Albuquerque, but DeLuca didn't like to fly, and the point was moot because a snowstorm dumping twelve to eighteen inches in Colorado along the eastern slope of the Rockies had closed the airport anyway, so he drove, sometimes in near white-out conditions, following Interstate 25 south through towns like Pueblo and Walsenburg and Trinidad, the Burlington Northern & Santa Fe freight trains on the tracks parallel to the freeway reminding him of the Polar Express from the classic children's book. The way he saw it, if he could drive thousands of miles across the back country of Iraq, getting shot at by Hadjis wielding Kalishnikovs and RPGs, and come through safely on the other side, then a little snow wasn't going to deter him. He checked in with the other members of Team Red as he drove, calling Sgts. Colleen MacKenzie, Dan Sykes, and Julio Vasquez on his mobile but getting through to none of them, so he left messages, telling them to enjoy their vacations and to check their voice mail—it was possible, he said, that he was going to need them. He called Walter Ford and Sami Jambazian as well, both former partners of his on the Boston P.D. and both working for him in their retirements, and left similar messages, noting again how, now that everyone had cell phones and voice mail, you never actually talked to people anymore. He called his wife from the road and learned his son Scott would be coming home from Iraq on extended leave, which was good news. DeLuca told Bonnie he'd check in with her when he found a motel. She said it was late (he'd forgotten he was in the Mountain time zone) and to call in the morning.

He told her he missed her.

She said she missed him, too.

He was having dinner in a truck stop in Las Vegas, New Mexico, when his telephone rang. He'd just watched an obese four-hundred-pound trucker polish off four pancakes, each the equivalent of a loaf of bread, in a room full of giant truckers eating giant pancakes, and he idly wondered how much extra diesel fuel was consumed, hauling their fat asses up and over the Rockies—it was a thought he kept to himself.

"Mr. David?" the voice said, the accent thick but not impenetrable.

"Theresa, how are you?" he asked.

"You said I would call you if I thought anything," she said.

"What's happened? Are you okay?"

"I am fine," she said. "I wanted to tell you a man called, for Cheryl. I don't know what."

"What man?"

"I will play it for you if you will wait," Theresa Davidova said. He heard some fumbling with buttons, and then a man's voice, saying: *"This is Brother Antonionus calling for Cheryl Escavedo, returning your call. I'm sorry I missed you, but feel free to call me back at the same number you called before, and I look forward to speaking with you."*

"Is that good?" she asked. "You heard?"

"Thank you, I did," he told her. "I'm heading for Albuquerque now, so maybe tomorrow I can stop by and listen to it in person—are you going to be around?"

"Yes, I will be here," she said. "I also found a note. Just two words. Sometimes Cheryl would make notes to write down telephone numbers on whatever she finds near the telephone. I found this on one of my notebooks this way, in her handwriting."

"What did she write?" DeLuca asked.

"Tom never," Theresa said.

"Tom never what? Who's Tom? And what didn't he do?"

"I don't know this," Theresa said. "This is all it says."

"I'll have a look tomorrow," DeLuca said. "I don't know what time, but I'll call first. So just sit tight until I see you tomorrow, how's that?"

"I will sit tight and hang loose," she said.

He found a motel near the airport in Albuquerque around midnight. The next morning, he went online at www.UNM.edu and learned that Dr. Penelope Burgess would be holding office hours between ten and noon.

Burgess looked up when he knocked on her door, glancing over the wire-rimmed reading glasses that rested on the end of her upturned nose. She was around forty, attractive, petite, brunette, her hair in a kind of Martha Stewart cut, though the glasses gave her a sort of Mother Hubbardish look, which was also a thought he kept to himself. She was marking the paper she was reading with a red pen. She asked if she could help him.

"Dr. Burgess?" DeLuca said. "I hope I'm not interrupting—I know these are office hours."

"I haven't had a student visit me during office hours in five years," she said. "I think they think if they do, I'm going to give them extra work. How can I help you?"

"David DeLuca," he said, extending his hand, "U.S. Army counterintelligence. I was hoping I could have about fifteen minutes of your time."

She shook his hand, exhibiting palpably less enthusiasm when she heard the words "U.S. Army."

"Sit down, Mr. DeLuca," she said coolly. "Do you have a rank or do I just call you 'Mr. DeLuca'?"

"Chief warrant officer. You can call me David, or Mr. DeLuca, or Agent if you'd prefer," he said.

"You don't wear uniforms?" she asked.

"Counterintelligence is the one part of the Army where we're allowed to go pretty much outside the box. Probably the best way to explain it is that what the FBI is to your local police, counterintelligence is to the military police. Who, I gather, have already questioned you."

"About that girl," Dr. Burgess said. "The one who said she had information for me."

"Cheryl Escavedo," DeLuca said. "We found her Jeep abandoned about ten miles north of the Mexican border, in Arizona, but we still haven't found her."

"I told the CID people I'd call them if I heard from her," Dr. Burgess said. "And I haven't. I don't know what else I can tell you. I'm being honest with you and I'm trying to cooperate, but I'm not sure I appreciate all this attention. All I know is that someone I never met supposedly wrote me a letter I never received, and now everyone is acting like that's enough to send me to Guantanamo with a bag over my head."

DeLuca took her to be a sensible woman, in which case he needed only to wait for her to realize what an extreme statement that was. She didn't disappoint him.

"I'm sorry," she said. "That was out of line. I've been up since five o'clock grading papers and each one is worse than the next. Maybe if you told me what sort of information she was going to give me, we could make some sense out of this. But I suppose that's going to be classified, right?"

"I'm supposing that, too," he said, "once we figure out what it was she took. I can tell you that she worked in the archives at Cheyenne Mountain, so she had access to pretty much everything that went through there. It could have been brand new or it could have been forty years old. We just don't know."

"And she smuggled it out of Fort CMAFS?" she said, pronouncing it "sea-maffs." "She must have been a very clever girl."

"You're familiar with the facility?"

"I used to know someone who worked there," she said.

"You work underground, too, do you not?" DeLuca asked. He'd had MacKenzie pull out what she could find on Dr. Penelope Burgess and e-mail it to him, but he'd only had time to skim the report.

"Primarily," she said. "That and other extreme environments. And in the lab."

"And this is for the Mars program? I'm asking because maybe she had something she thought you could use."

"It is for the Mars program," she said. "My work is primarily designing toward a Mars mission in 2008."

"In what way?"

"We go into places like the caves at Lechugilla or Carlsbad or the thermal vents at the bottom of the ocean and look at the life forms we find there. Non–carbon based. Chemosynthetic. Things that don't fit the usual definitions, so if they don't fit our definition of life, then what definitions do they fit? How do we distinguish between life and nonlife, and how do you build a machine that can do that? We know that at one time, Mars had water, so if some of that water was trapped underground, in aquifers and in caves, where ultraviolet radiation can't reach, then that's where we might find life."

"I wonder if Cheryl Escavedo was interested in that," DeLuca said. "Is there any overlap between what you're working on and what they might be doing at Space Command?"

"Overlap?" she asked. "Well, I'm sure there are people at Cheyenne or Kirtland who would love it if we did find life on Mars and they could turn it into a weapon of some kind. I just saw that little bow-tied White House Nazi, Carter Bowen, on *Meet the Press* the other day talking about plans to triple the defense budget. They spend money just to find other things to spend money on. But other than sharing the same launch platforms, we don't have much to do with Defense. I've been thinking, since I last spoke with the military police, that your Miss Escavedo might have been trying to reach me in my capacity as a member of UCS."

"Union of Concerned Scientists," DeLuca said.

"I've given some talks and added my name to some petitions against the weaponization of space," she said. "And since that's all they do at Space Command, maybe she had something she thought we needed to know. All she would have had to do was Google and my name would have come up. Or my husband's."

"What does he do?"

"I don't know," she said. "I was going to say I know what he used to do, but that wouldn't be true either. My husband was a physicist with the Directed Energy Lab at Kirtland. Dr. Gary Burgess. Ph.D. at sixteen. I haven't seen or heard from him in over three years. And he couldn't talk about his work when we were together, which was part of what . . ."

"Part of what what?" DeLuca asked.

"I was going to say part of what drove him crazy, but I was afraid you'd think of John Forbes Nash, and that wouldn't be right."

"The guy from *A Beautiful Mind*?"

She nodded.

"There are no analogies to be drawn," she said. "Beyond that they were equally brilliant. And lacking in certain social skills."

"The letter is addressed to simply 'Dr. Burgess,'" DeLuca said. "Is it possible that Cheryl Escavedo was trying to contact your husband?"

"It's possible," Penelope Burgess said.

"Would I be able to find him at Kirtland then?" DeLuca asked. "At the Directed Energy Lab?"

She shook her head.

"My husband disappeared, Mr. DeLuca," she said. "Quite intentionally—I didn't mean to imply foul play. He disappeared himself."

It was evident that she didn't want to talk about it, but the reasons why were less apparent.

"I don't want to press," DeLuca said, "but the problem is that I never know exactly what's relevant to my investigation and what isn't until I fill my head with more than I need and let it all sift down. I realize this may be personally difficult for you . . ."

"It's not as difficult as you might think," she said. "Our marriage had been over, or all over but the shouting, for a long time before he left. And the reasons he left had little to do with me, I think. Do you know who Arthur Bartok was?"

"I'm afraid I don't," DeLuca said.

"Arthur Bartok was the boy genius of the Manhattan Project, sort of Oppenheimer's protégé, until they had a falling out. At first, Bartok was completely caught up in the purely scientific quest and all jazzed up when he considered the huge amounts of energy he was controlling. Or releasing. It is apparently a thoroughly seductive experience, in many ways. Bartok's work involved making the hydrogen bombs he was working with smaller and smaller. People are afraid of suitcase nukes these days, but Bartok essentially built one in 1960. Then in the mid-sixties, he had a conversion experience, when he realized that proliferation was unavoidable, and that his work making bombs smaller and simpler and easier to build had contributed to that. He was one of the founding fathers of the UCS. I think Gary's circumstances were similar. At first he was caught up in the challenge and the romance, if you could call it that, just a twenty-year-old kid, walking around inside Cheyenne Mountain with all the bells and whistles and a security badge on his chest that let him go where other people weren't allowed. It was a pretty heady experience."

"What was his area of expertise, specifically?" DeLuca wanted to know.

"Electromagnetism," she said. "Field generation. But that's a general answer, not a specific one. We had an understanding, early on, that the work he was doing was top secret and that he couldn't talk about it. I knew it was important, and that he had a huge budget and a lot of people working for him, and I started to sense, oh, God, six years ago, that something was bothering him. I mean, really worrying him. I knew the Clinton people were defunding space defense so I thought it might have had something to do with that. I could see the stress of keeping so many secrets start to destroy him. And us, probably. At any rate, something changed, after 9/11. I don't know if he had a conversion experience, too, but he said after that, the handwriting was on the wall. He said 9/11 was going to do for space defense what Sputnik did for the space program in the fifties and sixties. We were ramping up, he said, and the only thing he could do, personally, to stop it, was to take himself out of it. So that's what he did."

"Ramping up?" DeLuca said.

"He was a student of World War I. And II. He said the thing about world wars was that everybody could see them coming, for years, and nobody could stop them."

"So he saw one coming, and the only way to stop it was to disappear?" DeLuca said. "That sounds pretty self-dramatizing, if you ask me."

She nodded.

"If you want my opinion, I think he'd been working for years on a particular problem, his team was, and then he solved it. But I don't think he told anybody. I think he saw where it was going to lead and then he kept the solution to himself."

"Maybe those were the files Cheryl Escavedo had," DeLuca said. "Do you think that's possible?"

Penelope Burgess shrugged.

"He didn't keep the important stuff in his computer," she said. "He would have kept it all in his head. He had a tendency to internalize things. I know after he left, some of the people who'd worked for him tried to carry on without him, and they couldn't, and they probably could have if there had been anything in his files they could use. He knew the Army wasn't going to let him delete anything, so I'm guessing he never wrote down whatever it was he learned. That's not to say other people wouldn't have figured it out. I think he just thought that if he left, he could set his program back a few years, probably not that he could kill it altogether."

"So you have no idea where he is?"

She reached behind her and took down a postcard that had been held to her bulletin board with a thumbtack. On one side was a picture of a twelve-foot-tall fiberglass kachina doll outside a convenience store, with the words WELCOME TO CHLORIDE, NEW MEXICO in yellow. On the reverse side, handwritten, were the words: *"There's only 10 kinds of people in this world, and I'm not going to be either. Be good. Gary."* It was postmarked from Chloride, New Mexico, October 12, 2001.

"That's all I've gotten from him," she said, "about a week after he left. He could be anywhere, really. Though it's hard to picture him sitting on a beach in the Caribbean, sipping piña coladas."

"I don't get it," DeLuca said, reading the card.

"It's an old math joke. There are only 10 kinds of people in this world, those who understand base two and those who don't. A one and a zero is how the number two is described in base two."

"Good one," DeLuca said. "Do you think Space Command would have let him walk away from his job like that?"

"You tell me," she said. "Do you think they would have?"

"Not unless he had something to use for leverage," DeLuca said. "He's the friend you said you knew who'd worked at Cheyenne?"

She nodded.

"Do you think he might have met Cheryl Escavedo there?"

Again she shrugged.

"It's possible," she said. "Though if you're thinking they might have been having an affair, I suppose that's also possible, but Gary was never a very sexual person. At least not with me. Are you married, Mr. DeLuca?"

"I am," he said.

"Then I imagine in your line of work, you probably understand the sort of toll it takes when you can't talk to your spouse about what you do."

"More than I wish I did," DeLuca said. "I suspect your reasons for speaking out against space defense are more than just the personal."

"Don't get me started," she said.

"I am interested," he said. "But if you don't want to go there, that's all right, too."

"Where do I begin?" she said. "I've heard somebody say if we took a mere 1 percent of the DOD space budget and put it into teaching history, we'd eventually be smart enough to avoid war and not have to spend the other 99 percent on weapons. I do understand the strategic advantages of weapons in space, but it seems like the people at Space Command find them so appealing that they ignore the disadvantages. Suppose you blind an enemy by taking out all his satellites and communication—do you think he's going to sit back and wait for what comes next, or is he going to come at you with everything he has while he still can? Not to mention that if we take war into space, we could so easily make space unusable—they told you at Cheyenne they're tracking seventy-five hundred objects, didn't they? Bigger than a baseball. There's another hundred thousand smaller than a baseball but big enough to take out the space shuttle. These things are traveling at twenty-seven thousand miles an hour, ten times faster than a high-powered rifle bullet. A marble at that speed has the impact of a one-ton safe dropped off a three-story building. A BB has the impact of a bowling ball hitting you at one hundred miles an hour. My friend Sally Ride told me after her last Space Shuttle mission, they found one of the windows was pitted by a paint fleck—a paint fleck was almost enough to knock them out of the sky. You watch all these science-fiction movies where they blow something up in space and poof, there's a ball of fire and the whole thing disappears and leaves a big empty void behind—that's not the way it actually works, if you think about it. Blow up one satellite and you have another 100,000 fragments. One of those hits another satellite or one of the 3,000 discarded rocket boosters out there, and you have another 100,000 fragments. And don't think space is so big that it couldn't happen, because we tend to orbit our satellites in altitude bands. Some are out there at 25,000 kilometers, some are at 7,000, some at 700, most are at 900 to 1,000 and the 1,500- to 1,700-kilometer range, and there are more going up all the time, ever since we abrogated the 1972 ABM Treaty in June 2002—the chances of initiating a cascading chain reaction billiard ball sort of effect have gone up. If that happens, no more Hubble Telescope, no more International Space Station, no Cosmic Background Explorer . . ."

"And no Mars program?"

"If you think I'm only thinking of my own self-interest, you couldn't be more wrong," she said.

"I'm sorry," he said. "I know you're not—I regret the implication."

"And then someday it starts to fall back to earth, hardened uranium, plutonium for satellites powered by nuclear reactors—it boggles the mind."

"It boggled Gary's, I gather," DeLuca said.

"I told you not to get me started," she said. "The hardest part is that nobody can see what's going on out there, so Space Command and STRATCOM and everybody else is free to do as they please, with unlimited black budgets and all the best intentions, I suppose, and it's all kicked into overdrive since 9/11. That's what Gary meant by 'the handwriting's on the wall.' Sometimes I get angry because he didn't take me with him."

"Would you have wanted to go with him?" DeLuca asked.

"No," she said, giving it some thought. "I don't think so. I've never been able to put my head in the sand. What do you think? Do you think I'm a pessimist? Do you think the glass is half full or half empty?"

"I think the glass is twice as big as it used to be," DeLuca said. "I appreciate your talking to me, but I know you have papers to grade." He rose to his feet. "Do you know a guy named Josh Truitt, by any chance? Photographer?"

"I've seen his pictures, but I don't think I've ever caved with him," she said. "Why?"

"Just curious," DeLuca said. "When I talk to people, sometimes the most useful question I can ask is if they know each other. How about somebody named Brother Antonionus?"

"The *Star Trek* guy?" she said. "Brethren of the Light?"

"I don't know anything about him," DeLuca said. "His voice was on Cheryl Escavedo's answering machine. What are the 'Brethren of the Light'?"

"They're waiting for somebody in a space ship to come pick them up and carry them away," she said. "And no, I've never met him, but they're in the local newspaper every once in a while because their headquarters are in Albuquerque."

"I hope I get there before the space ship comes," DeLuca said.

"Be careful," she told him, walking him to the door. "I hear he's mighty darn persuasive at getting people to join his cult."

"I'm already a Red Sox fan," DeLuca said. "That's enough of a cult for one person."

The walled compound occupied by the Brethren of the Light was in the foothills east of town, in an exclusive neighborhood of gated compounds and long driveways.

He'd been told, by whoever had answered the phone when he called, that he wouldn't need an appointment but that no one could guarantee when Brother Antonionus was going to be receptive. "Well if he's not, I guess I could come back," he'd replied, to which the woman on the phone answered, "Oh, no—he only sees people when he's not receptive."

A long circular driveway, made of two-toned stone pavers, led to the house, a mansion in the Spanish mission style, with decorative wrought-iron bars over the windows and red tiles on the roof, the grounds landscaped in junipers and potted grasses, aloe and century plants, groomed to perfection and currently being attended to by a crew of people wearing red jumpsuits, clipping and raking and weeding and sweeping, though DeLuca didn't see any landscapers' trucks in the driveway. He parked behind a Toyota Prius with a decal on the rear window that said "Starfleet Academy." The only other car was a white Rolls-Royce, polished and detailed to perfection. The snow that had fallen the night before, leaving eighteen inches in Colorado but only a dusting in Albuquerque, had already melted, the sun bright overhead in a cloudless sky.

There was a large open-air porch and a set of carved wooden doors, the knocker a brass angel. After a moment, DeLuca was met by a young woman, also in a red jumpsuit but with an apron over it, her smile beaming, if that was the word, and from what he'd read about the Brethren of the Light, it was.

"I'm David DeLuca," he said. "Here to see Brother Antonionus."

"I'm God's Miracle," she said. "Welcome welcome welcome. I'm pretty sure he's unavailable right now but you're welcome to wait. Do you like cinnamon rolls? There should be some hot out of the oven in a few minutes. With pecans or without?"

"With," he said. "When you say unavailable . . ."

"I mean he's receptive," she said. DeLuca must have had a puzzled expression on his face. "He's receiving instructions. The downloads usually don't take all that long." He suspected she didn't mean that Brother Antonionus was online. "Would you like a cup of coffee or tea? Or would you like to focus for a few minutes while you wait?"

"Focus?" he said.

"Good Attentions," she said (though it was possible he hadn't heard her correctly), pointing to what probably would have been a large dining room, in a normal house, converted here into a computer room where he saw two people, in red jumpsuits, wearing what looked like bicycle helmets with wires coming out the back, staring at computer screens. "There's a pod open if you want it."

"I'm good," he said. "Thank you."

He took a seat in a leather chair, one of two facing a large fireplace where a small warming fire burned. God's Miracle took a sprig of sage from a large basket and tossed it on the fire before returning to her kitchen duties. On the coffee table between the chairs were a few magazines, including *UFOlogy Today, Extra-Terrestrial Journal, Maxi-Brain,* and *Redbook.* He picked up a copy of *Maxi-Brain* where, just inside the cover, he found a full-page advertisement for AlphaWare, with a picture of its president and spokesperson, Brother Antonionus, wearing a beatific smile, his eyes twinkling behind his round wire-rimmed glasses. The products being offered included serenity-inducing audiotapes of ocean waves and loons oodling in the twilight; a Good Attentions software kit *("The road to heaven is indeed paved with Good Attentions . . .")* with a bicycle helmet wired to a black box that could interface with a Mac or PC, technology proven to help children and adults with attention deficit disorder; an Optico-Aural Stimulator that looked something like a jet pilot's helmet with flashing/blinking lights inside and multiphasing white noise lavations guaranteed to deliver deep-relaxing alpha-wave brain activity; and finally a room Ionic Aromatizer that could project a variety of therapeutic fragrances, with a set of free refills if you ordered now. There was a Website with a full catalogue of other products as well.

DeLuca reviewed what he knew of Brother Antonionus, based on what Dan Sykes had managed to dig up and e-mail him the night before. He'd been born Malcolm Percy, in Milwaukee, in 1944, ordained as an Episcopal minister in 1968 but asked to leave the ministry after falling under the influence of Dr. John C. Lilly, whose early work studying dolphin intelligence had led him down a path that ended with his taking hallucinogens and sitting in sensory deprivation tanks for days at a time, a practice Reverend Malcolm Percy had recommended to his congregation. After being homeless for the better part of the seventies, with a few arrests up and down the West Coast for disorderly conduct, credit card fraud, and shoplifting here and there, Malcolm Percy had resurfaced as Brother Antonionus, founder of a company called Maxi-Brain that sold home sensory deprivation tanks and other bliss-generating mechanical devices, all intended to deliver "natural" highs by artificially inducing the autonomic release of pleasure-producing organic chemicals such as endorphins, adrenaline, and dopamine, though according to Dan Sykes, most people who used Maxi-Brain devices were usually stoned or tripping on something else first. Brother Antonionus had opened a chain of Maxi-Brain Spas across the country where people who couldn't afford to own his equipment could stop in for a brain tune-up, selling franchises to true believers at a time when the New Age movement was at its peak. As far as Dan Sykes could learn, Antonionus still owned a controlling share in the spa business, though most of them had shifted away from the brain-machine business and into massages and acupuncture, and he owned a business called AlphaWare that produced the devices, software, and educational tapes and DVDs DeLuca had seen advertised in the magazine, but somewhere in the 1990s, Antonionus's focus had shifted to leading a group of people who believed UFOs were going to come and carry them away, to heaven or outer space or another planet, Sykes couldn't be certain, "The Next Condition," they called it. Dan's e-mail had said:

In a nutshell, Percy has managed to convince his followers (100+?) that he's from another planet and that the body he now occupies is just a shell he has to wear, like a deep-sea diver's dive suit, and that if his followers do what he says (which includes giving him all their worldly possessions), they can shed their own bodies and transcend this ol' world. He says all the ideas he gets for brain machines and whatever were sent to him by his home planet, Rigel, I believe. Funny—he doesn't look Rigelian.

It's mostly old technology that he repackages, but he's got some tech connections somewhere, to be sure. Now they go out into the desert and hold "Ascensions" and wait for UFOs with signal fires/drums/chanting, etc., based on Revelations 11:12, "Then they heard a loud voice from heaven saying to them, 'Come up hither.' And in the sight of their foes, they went up to heaven in a cloud."

One report I read, written by someone who dropped out of the program, said he's been spiking the punch at his "Ascensions" with Viagra and Ecstasy, then the Maxi-Brain goggles produce maxiboners and the party turns into an orgy (theologically speaking, a kind of Adamism, meaning an effort to return to the innocence of a pre-lapsarian Garden of Eden when sex was guilt-free and plentiful—or so they say). This might explain why no one is disappointed when the UFOs don't show up. But this is unconfirmed. Good luck. Keep your nose clean. Dan.

After about ten minutes, a young man in a red jumpsuit asked DeLuca to follow him. Brother Antonionus was seated at a glass-topped table with a Macintosh G5 on one corner and a cordless telephone at the other. Six crystals were arranged in an arc on the table directly in front of him, the largest the size of a banana. The walls of the room were painted white and empty of all adornment, with a matched pair of floor lamps in the far corners, bracketing the table. The man seated at the table was also dressed in a red jumpsuit, though his had quilted padding sewn into it that made him resemble a racetrack pit-crew member in fire-retardant coveralls, minus the sponsor decals. He also wore a white turtleneck that, with his bald head, made him look something like a light bulb in a socket, lacking only the lampshade to complete the image.

"You're David DeLuca," the man said. "I'm Brother Antonionus. How can I help you? You're with the Air Force, is that right?"

"Army," DeLuca said, showing Malcolm Percy his badge and credentials. "Counterintelligence. Thank you for giving me a few minutes of your time—I gather you have a pretty full schedule."

"I'm due to receive my midmorning reports in a few minutes, but I think I can squeeze you in," he said.

"Reports from whom?"

"From all my waiters and waitresses," he said. "That's a bit of an in-joke, but that's what we call ourselves because we're all waiting. You must be busy, too."

"I'm looking for a girl who seems to be missing," he said. "My information says she apparently called you, because you called back and left a message on her machine."

"And her name is?"

"Cheryl Escavedo," DeLuca said. "Sergeant Cheryl Escavedo. Arizona Army National Guard."

Brother Antonionus tapped a few keys on his keyboard, reading from his monitor.

"She called here . . . February seventeenth. Would that make sense?"

She'd disappeared on the nineteenth.

"Does it say there what she might have called about?" DeLuca asked.

"Nnnnnnope," Antonionus said, manipulating his mouse until he was satisfied with his answer.

"And you called her back when?"

"Well," he said, clicking again, "it's on my to-do list for four days ago, but I'm not sure when I got around to it. What's today? Saturday? I think I called her back Thursday. I could check my phone records."

"That's all right," he said. "We could check them, too, if we needed to. I'm just mainly interested in why she might have been calling you."

"Is she in some sort of trouble?" Antonionus asked. "You have a very disturbed aura right now."

"We're not sure," DeLuca said. "We'd like to talk to her before we reach any conclusions. And I apologize for my aura."

"We get a lot of calls, Detective. Is it Detective? We get calls from people all over the world, every day, inquiring about either our products or the Metamorphosis System. I'd say at least once a week someone shows up on our doorstep, seeking one thing or another."

"What do you do with them," DeLuca asked. "The people who show up?"

"Well, we try to accommodate them, if we can," Antonionus said. "We don't want anyone going away disappointed. Some seekers are ready and others need more preparation, so we give them a program kit to take home, and sometimes we refer them to one of our satellite campuses. That probably sounds like a pun, doesn't it? I wish I'd thought of it. How is your marriage, Detective? My sense is that your wife wishes you'd change something. Your line of work, I think. Forgive me for intruding but when I hear things whispering in my ear, it's hard to ignore them."

"I appreciate your concern," DeLuca said. "Can you think of any reason why Sergeant Escavedo might have called you on the seventeenth? Anything going on, on or around that date?"

"Not around here," Antonionus said. "We had an Ascension ceremony on the nineteenth, but that was in Arizona."

"Whereabouts?" DeLuca asked.

"A place called Spirit Mountain," Antonionus said. "I'd received instructions that a ship would be using a meteor shower that night to conceal a landing. Unfortunately, in my current condition, I'm a bit aphasic at times. I think I understand things, but I don't."

"Did a ship in fact come that night?" DeLuca asked. He wasn't really interested in the answer, except that Antonionus had been in proximity to the disappearance, and that meant he might have seen something. It was also more than a coincidence, and that meant something, too. Somewhere in the bullshit, there could be information DeLuca could use.

"One did, but it wasn't Rigelian," Antonionus said, rather matter-of-factly, as if ships arrived all the time.

"What was it?"

"I'm not sure," Antonionus said. "They signed a trade alliance with a collective from the Sega quadrant but I wasn't aware that it had gone into effect yet. My understanding was that they'd be stopping for hydrogen only. Do you want me to find out what kind of ship it was?"

"That won't be necessary," DeLuca said. "I'm sure my friends at CMAF can tell me that."

Antonionus snickered.

"Oh, yes, I'm sure they can," he said. "They'll be very helpful."

"How did you know where the Ascension was going to take place?" DeLuca asked.

"How?" Antonionus said. "How do monarch butterflies know which way is Mexico? Or more to the point, how do they know they know? I'm not trying to be deliberately elusive, Detective. There are simply things I know, but I have a harder time saying how I know them. The body you see is a shell I've been forced to wear. The angel inside of me is my true self, from somewhere quite different from this world. Yet the shell is what I have to work with here, to speak and to understand. A big part of its job is to interpret the wisdom of its truer self. We all have angels inside of us, Detective, yourself included. In which sense, describing freeing our angels as the next condition is a bit of a misnomer, because they are already with us. The next expression might be a better term, but, you know, too late now."

"I guess what I'm really wondering is, how would Cheryl Escavedo have known about your Ascension?" DeLuca said. "We found her Jeep at the base of Spirit Mountain, so it makes me wonder if she was coming to join you, for whatever reason."

"Some people are drawn to them," Antonionus said. "People wander in all the time simply because they've been called. Other people might have seen our ads in the popular magazines. Ascensions are also posted on our Website. Whenever possible. I usually know months in advance, but not always. One time I recall I was given about fifteen minutes' notice, but fortunately, we were nearby. You say you found her Jeep—I take it then that you're unable to account for Sergeant Escavedo's whereabouts?"

"That's right," DeLuca said.

"Have you taken into account the possibility that she was taken?" Antonionus asked. "I suppose for someone like you, this is still beyond the realm of possibility, but there was a ship that night. They all have the technology. Probably a third of the people here today have been abducted and most of the others know someone who was. It's all been well documented and supported by authorities as well respected as Harvard psychology professor Hilton Jaynes. I don't expect to change your mind here and now, Detective, but if you're looking for someone who went missing at Spirit Mountain that night, it is the most logical explanation. Don't they say the explanation requiring the fewest assumptions is the one most likely to be true?"

"That is what they say," DeLuca said. "But it's really more a question of quality than quantity. I'd rather have an explanation with ten small reasonable assumptions than one big dubious one."

"Dubious is one of the nicer things I've been called," Antonionus said, smiling again. What was with all the smiling? "Do you really think, with over a hundred thousand other planets in the cosmos, just like earth, just as inhabitable, that we're alone in the universe?"

"Do you really think I'm going to believe a grown man who's dressed like a cross between Santa's helper and Pee-wee Herman didn't just pull that number out of his ass?" DeLuca wanted to say, but he held his tongue.

"I guess what I'm trying to say is that I've found a lot of missing people over the years, and of all the reasons that they've been missing, that's never been one of them," he said instead. "I try to be open to new ideas, but I can't help but base my decisions and hunches on past experience. But if you could get the name of the ship, we'll throw it into the system and see what happens."

"I'd love to see how you'd do with a Good Attention program," Antonionus said, clasping his hands together over his heart. DeLuca was still waiting for the charisma he'd heard of to kick in, but so far, all he was seeing was the same sort of bemused confidence he'd seen in a hundred other deluded morons, with a random meting out of benevolence that probably made his followers feel good about themselves. "The technology allows the player to control the images on the screen with his mind. You might think that's dubious, too, but they're using it in schools to help children with attention deficit disorder learn to focus. I think you'd be absolutely off the charts. I don't think I've ever met anyone with such a perfect blend of convergent and divergent thinking."

"Where do you get your crystals, by the way?" DeLuca said. "I think I'd like to get one for my wife."

"My advisers," Antonionus said. "A variety of places, really. Some were gifts. This one spoke to me in the desert and asked me to pick it up. Her up—she doesn't like it when I call her an 'it.'" He put his finger on it. DeLuca half-expected it to light up.

"Do you ever buy crystals from a kid named Marvin Yutahay?" DeLuca asked. "Native American kid. Gem hunter."

"Not to my knowledge, but then I never buy crystals, period. Others here may know about him. Would you like me to ask?"

"That's all right," DeLuca said.

They were interrupted by a knock on the door. God's Miracle entered and said they were ready with their midmorning reports. DeLuca rose to leave, laying his card down on Brother Antonionus's table.

"Thanks for the help," he said, "and for the kind words. Time I took my divergent thinking elsewhere."

"Miracle will see you to your car," Antonionus said.

"Thanks, but I can find it. Do call me if you hear from Sergeant Escavedo."

"I will," Antonionus said. "I promise I will."

When he got to his car, he discovered it had been washed and waxed by a young woman in the requisite red jumpsuit who was putting a few finishing strokes to polishing the hood. She looked at him, then glanced nervously over his shoulder to see if someone was behind him.

"Are you a police officer?" she asked him.

"Not exactly, but something like that," he replied.

"Can you help me find my daughter?" the woman said, panic rising in her voice. "My name is Rainbow. My daughter's name is Ruby. I think they have her, but I don't know where she is. They won't let me talk to her."

"Who has her?" DeLuca said. "Who won't let you talk to her?" But the woman calling herself Rainbow rushed off, fearful that her pleas had been overheard, and disappeared into the house to make her midmorning report.

Because of Posse Comitatus laws, there were strict limitations preventing military interference in matters of civilian justice—nobody wanted America resembling some South American banana republic where the army and the police were the same thing. At the same time, the Patriot Act gave law enforcement and intelligence agencies more leeway these days. DeLuca had two options, regarding the woman named Rainbow's request. He could (and probably should) relay her plea to the local authorities and let them handle it. They were no doubt accustomed to a whole slew of wacky statements and claims coming out of the Brethren of the Light compound. He certainly didn't have time to look into it personally, but he could assign someone to it if it took on any greater significance. If two girls had disappeared at the same time, on or around the same time and place, that was certainly significant.

He had two more stops to make, first at the Military Entry Processing Station where Escavedo had worked. It was a dead end, a nondescript beige federal building where no one had anything really helpful to contribute. Cheryl had seemed disgruntled and unhappy in her work, DeLuca learned, but then again, everybody there seemed disgruntled and unhappy in their work. She hadn't made any close friends, and in fact seemed aloof and distant, as if she didn't want to make any close friends. She didn't talk to anybody, and kept to herself, mostly, did her job and went home, no overtime, no self-initiated projects—it didn't sound like the Cheryl Escavedo DeLuca had read about in her 201 file. One coworker recalled Escavedo receiving a bouquet of flowers on Valentine's Day, but she didn't tell anybody whom they were from. When DeLuca called all the local florists in the Yellow Pages, none of them had any record of delivering flowers to the MEPS building on Valentine's Day.

His last stop of the day was the apartment Cheryl Escavedo shared with Theresa Davidova, the ground floor of a two-story house with a large porch in the front and a smaller one in the back. He'd hoped to listen to the message on her answering machine and read the note Cheryl had left, the words "Tom never . . ." When he got there, he knocked on the front door and rang the bell, but no one was home. When he called the number Theresa had given him, it rang and rang. He wondered why the machine didn't pick up. When he walked around the house, he saw that the back door was open a crack. When he opened it, he was suddenly startled when a cat darted past him. According to the writing on the litterbox, the cat's name was "Boo." There was a half-empty bowl of cereal on the table (Boo had drunk all the milk) and a box of Honey Nut Cheerios in front of it, the top open, next to a glass of orange juice, untouched. The answering machine was gone from the kitchen counter, the telephone wire and power source unplugged. The case of power bars on the kitchen counter was overturned and empty. A search of the rest of the house turned up little, though there were clothes strewn on the bed as if someone had packed very quickly.

He was in the kitchen again when a red International Harvester pickup with a black camper on the back pulled into the driveway. A young man got out, late twenties, fit-looking in jeans and work boots and an unzipped gray hooded sweatshirt over a black T-shirt, his longish black hair swept back but unruly, his beard closely trimmed. DeLuca stepped out on the porch to meet him.

"Who are you?" the young man asked, stopping in his tracks.

"David DeLuca, Army counterintelligence," he replied, flashing his B's and C's. "Who are you?"

"Josh Truitt," the young man said. "My girlfriend lives here. What are you doing here?"

"I'm looking for Cheryl," DeLuca said. "She your girlfriend?"

"Theresa," Josh Truitt said. "Is she here?"

"She's not," DeLuca said. "Were you expecting her?"

"We were supposed to have dinner," Truitt said. "I called all day but she didn't answer and the machine didn't pick up."

"Were you here earlier?" DeLuca asked.

"Just got here," Truitt said.

"It looks either like she left in a hurry or she was expecting to be right back," DeLuca said. "Her answering machine is missing. I'm guessing she usually doesn't take her answering machine with her when she leaves the house."

"We were supposed to go camping," Truitt said. "Tomorrow morning."

"Where were you going?"

"A canyon I know in the Gila Wilderness," Truitt said. "Near Silver City. I was going to surprise her."

"Does she have any friends she might have contacted?"

"I just spoke to both of them and they haven't heard from her," Truitt said. "Her boss from the bar and a woman from church."

"Did she have any enemies I should know about?" DeLuca asked.

"Why?" the other man asked. "Why do you want to know?"

"I'm investigating her roommate's disappearance," DeLuca said. "I spoke to Theresa on the phone once, and then she called me back. We were supposed to get together. She said she was going to be around. You gave Cheryl a copy of your book."

"For her birthday," Truitt said.

"How long had you known Cheryl?"

"Just for a few months. Maybe six months. Since she got transferred to Albuquerque."

"How did she meet Theresa?"

"She saw a sign at the laundromat that Theresa put up, looking for a roommate," Truitt said. "But they really hit it off."

"Did she have a boyfriend?" DeLuca asked.

"She had friends," Truitt said. "I don't know if they were boyfriends. She'd go away for weekends. Either back to Colorado Springs or to Arizona. She didn't seem like she wanted to talk about it."

"About boyfriends?"

"Yeah."

"Any idea why not?" DeLuca asked.

"Not really," Truitt said. "When someone asks you to respect their privacy, you don't say, 'And why exactly is it that you want me to respect your privacy?' You just back off."

"How about Theresa?" DeLuca said. "In my business, coincidence is something you learn not to believe in. Was there somebody she might have been running from? I need to know, Josh."

The younger man hesitated.

"Yeah, there was," he said at last. "A guy named Leon Lev. He'd been saying she owed him money."

"How much?"

"Twelve thousand dollars," Josh Truitt said.

"And that would be because . . . ?" DeLuca suspected he knew the answer.

"Lev was her pimp," Truitt said. "The guy is . . . I was going to say evil, but I don't want to sound like George Bush. She moved here from El Paso to get away from him. I guess she thought if she came here, he'd leave her alone."

"Where does he live?"

"Juarez," DeLuca said. "You don't want to go there, and you don't want to meet him, trust me."

"If I only met the people I wanted to meet," DeLuca said, "I wouldn't have anything to do. Hang tight and call me if you hear from her. She'll probably turn up on her own. There's safety in numbers. It's how we work. I'm sure she'll call you. Nobody stays underground for long." DeLuca laughed. "I forgot who I'm talking to. You probably know people who stay underground for months."

"Beware 'The Mole,'" Truitt said.

"What does that mean?"

"It's sort of an urban legend, except that it's not," Truitt said. "Cavers are notoriously secretive. Finding a new cave that hasn't been disturbed for ten or fifteen million years is like finding a new planet in the solar system. And the more beautiful it is, the sooner it's going to be turned into a tourist show cave with a McDonald's in the entry chamber, so when we find something, we keep it to ourselves, as long as we can, and we shun the guy who lets the word out. But if you do find a cave, you get to tag it. Mark it, with your personal tag . . ."

"That's not despoiling it? Leaving graffiti, after fifteen million years?"

"You don't spray paint 'Class of 2004' in six-foot letters," Truitt said. "You do it in a way that honors the cave, somewhere inconspicuous, like signing a painting in the lower-right-hand corner. So The Mole is a guy who tags caves that nobody else has ever heard of before, so people get all excited and rope to the bottom of a thousand-foot tube, and there's his tag. People say he lives underground. Or that he was born without eyes. He's an albino who can't expose himself to sunlight. It's more than just a story. I've seen the tags myself."

DeLuca looked at him. Josh Truitt was babbling because he was scared.

"All I'm saying is that some people stay underground," he said. "Theresa was afraid of Lev. She said she paid him the money she owed him, but he kept claiming there was interest due. He's a complete pig. And a true psychopath. If your bombs are as smart as people say they are, one of them would have found Leon Lev a long time ago."

DeLuca headed back to his hotel. He felt like he knew less now than he had when he woke up, but that wasn't quite true. The day had raised a thousand new questions, and he wasn't going to have time to answer all of them by himself. He had a number of calls to make, to Colleen MacKenzie and Dan Sykes and Julio Vasquez and Walter Ford and to Sami Jambazian, and maybe a couple of other people he wanted to add to his team. Before he did that, he needed to talk to Colonel Oswald, and Phil LeDoux too. Friend or not, DeLuca was angry. He was angry because it was becoming apparent to him that he'd been lied to. He wasn't going to do anything more until somebody told him what he was really looking for.

As he approached Noshaq Pass, in the Hindu Kush mountain range, on the border of Afghanistan and Pakistan, Army counterintelligence agent Sergeant Frank Pickett was growing frustrated. They were at sixteen thousand feet, working their way northeast across the Qadzi Deh glacier, and he needed to make a phone call. He'd given the battery to his SATphone to Amal, Ali Abu-Muhammed's chief lieutenant, for safekeeping, but Amal didn't know that the phone, developed by DARPA, had a second battery and was still usable. Pickett had been feigning altitude sickness as an excuse to lag behind, but Amal had stayed with him. Posing as a Russian arms dealer, Pickett had been working in the FATA along the Durand line for six months, selling SAM-7s and SAM-7As to Pashtun *maliks* in Khost and Bajorr and Miran Shah, each weapon he sold encoded with a concealed DARPA-installed GPS transponder, but the missiles were armed—he would have lost credibility had the test firings been less than effective. As a result, he'd gained access to a Talibani named Abdul Sahibzada who offered to introduce him to a Waziri chieftain who might be interested in buying antiaircraft weapons. That offer proved to have been a ruse. Instead, Pickett had been taken to meet Abu-Muhammed, currently considered second or third in command of Al Qaeda forces in the Federally Administered Tribal Areas and someone believed to meet regularly with Osama Bin Laden. Pickett had worked for a month to win Abu-Muhammed's trust, brokering minor arms deals elsewhere, and it now looked like his hard work had paid off. He had reason to believe, based on what he'd learned at the campfire the night before, eavesdropping on people who were unaware that he was as fluent in Arabic as he was in Russian, that he was being taken to Razmak to meet with Al Qaeda leaders, including Bin Laden himself. It was information he wanted to pass along to U.S. Central Command in Kabul, but unless he could shake Amal somehow, he wouldn't be able to.

"You catch up with the others," he told Amal in Russian. Amal had been a student in Moscow. His Russian was poor, but he was the only one who spoke it, which was why he'd been assigned to accompany the man he believed to be a Russian arms dealer.

"I will wait," Amal said. "It is good."

There were a dozen Talibani and Al Qaeda soldiers traveling in the group, accompanied by eight regular Pakistani army troops from the Balochistan regiment with Pashtun loyalities, the group's supplies carried by mules also bearing perhaps half a ton of raw opium in burlap saddlebags flung across their backs. Pickett had little doubt that IMINT was following the caravan's progress via satellite, the images from their body heat registering clearly to any infrared camera against the cold backdrop of the glacier, but knowing where they were wouldn't matter unless CENTCOM also knew what they were doing.

Pickett was considering how the presence of Pakistani troops precluded calling in an airstrike when he saw, up ahead, a flash of light, and then a second, joined by the sound of men firing their rifles, but at what? He looked up, as did Amal, listening for the drone of airplanes overhead. He heard nothing. He understood that Predators and G-Hawks could fly in virtual silence, but they fired missiles, and he hadn't seen or heard any explosions. Ahead, he saw a third flash of light, then a fourth, and with each flash, the sound of rifles firing abated. Amal sent tracer rounds into the sky, firing blindly and running ahead to join the others. Pickett saw a lone mule racing across the glacier, and then it, too, disappeared in a flash of light. A hundred yards in front of him, Amal stopped and fired his weapon into the sky two more times. Then he was gone.

When he reached the spot where Amal had stood, Frank Pickett saw only a perfectly round hole in the ice, burned down into the glacier as far as the beam from his flashlight could reach.

He ran ahead until he arrived at the place where the caravan had been. There, he found a single backpack, a *kaffiyeh,* and the hindquarters of a mule that appeared to have been sawed in half, as well as a half dozen deep holes in the ice identical to the one where Amal had disappeared, each hole perfectly round and perhaps twenty feet across. Pickett had seen similarly round potholes worn into solid rock by eons of erosion, but nothing he understood could explain how such holes could appear instantaneously.

It took him a minute to gather his wits, and then he turned on his satellite phone and called in to CENTCOM, giving his name and identification code.

"How can I help you, Agent Pickett?" the lieutenant he spoke with asked.

"What do you mean, how can you help me? You can start by telling me what just happened," Pickett said.

"What just happened where, exactly?" the lieutenant asked.

"Right here," Pickett said. "36° 26.03' north and 71° 53.84' east. Just now."

"One minute," the lieutenant said, coming back a few moments later.

"Not quite sure what you're referring to, Pickett," the lieutenant said. "We've got nothing on our screens. Agent Pickett? Are you still with me? Pickett?"

But Pickett was gone, and where he stood, a final hole. By the time Central Command in Kabul was able to scramble a pair of Warthogs the next morning to overfly and surveil the site at 36° 26.03'N and 71° 53.84'E, the previously symmetrical round holes had been carved and blended into the glacial landscape and there was nothing to be seen, save for a lone mule, six miles away and still shaking. When the SOCOM was able to put men on the ground, flying in a Pavehawk HH-60 stripped of all excess weight to allow it to fly at that altitude, they found evidence that suggested a party of men had fallen into a bergschrund that had evidently been concealed by a snow bridge that collapsed—such was the danger of traveling on glaciers. The body of Sergeant Frank Pickett of Army counterintelligence was written in the report as unrecoverable, along with a recommendation that he be given a Bronze Star for valor, posthumous.

Chapter Five

IT ONLY SOURED DELUCA'S MOOD FURTHER when Colonel Oswald told him he couldn't answer his questions because he was asking about a Special Access Program and he wasn't read on. DeLuca had called on his encrypted satellite phone. "There's a reason why we compartmentalize, Agent DeLuca," Oswald said. "Your job is to find the girl, and find the disks, period. I know you CI guys think there isn't a door in the world you can't walk through, and if LeDoux tells me I'm out of line here, then I'll be first in line for a crow sandwich, but right now, that's how it's going to be."

DeLuca had to wonder how far a crow would fit up a colonel's ass. Why was it that so often, joint commands meant so many majors and colonels and generals seeing who could be a bigger prick?

He bought a ticket on the next commercial flight to Washington and was at the Pentagon by 0800 hours the following morning. He'd left a message on Phillip LeDoux's voice mail because he didn't want to disturb his private hours with his new wife, but apparently LeDoux had taken a break from his connubial bliss long enough to collect his messages. DeLuca had said he was flying in for a briefing at the general's earliest convenience, with or without Oswald in attendance. It was evident by the look on Oswald's face that LeDoux had chewed him out.

"Agent DeLuca," Oswald said, returning DeLuca's less-than-snappy salute. "The general will be with us in a minute. He's meeting us in briefing room six. Let's take a walk, during which I'll try to describe for you how delicious the crow omelet I had for breakfast was, chased with a slice of humble pie. There is apparently much about CI I don't understand, nor did I appreciate that Team Red is itself Special Access. General LeDoux explained to me how you were formed as CI special ops. This whole intelligence shake-up has got me a bit confused, and I don't think I'm the only one. At any rate, I hadn't been briefed, and that's no excuse, but I apologize. I'm not just a full bird—I'm an old bird, too."

"No apology necessary, sir," DeLuca said, impressed by the colonel's contrition. The halls of the Pentagon were full of people, scurrying to and fro, including an admiral in a wheelchair who had to be ninety years old. They passed a barbershop, a gift shop, a copy center, and a post office. "I'm sure I probably struck something of an inappropriately strident tone myself."

"General LeDoux warned me," Oswald said. "And I do like people to speak frankly."

"Just because I'm curious, what did he say about me?" DeLuca asked.

"He said you could be an asshole," Oswald said. "A stubborn asshole, but that there wasn't anybody he'd rather share a foxhole or a dive bar with."

"The general is evidently going soft," DeLuca said. "He used to call me a dickhead."

LeDoux explained that he had a funeral he had to go to later that morning for a former member of the Joint Chiefs of Staff who'd passed away at Bethesda. The conference room was a long narrow windowless room with wood panels up to the chair rail and tan walls decorated with framed pictures of various vintage airplanes. There were glasses of water on the table and notepads with pencils next to them for whoever wanted to take notes.

"Got your message, David," LeDoux said. "I hope you weren't too hard on the colonel here. I had to get permission to read you on to this mission separately, because that's how sensitive this is. I also have to warn you—I had to put the PowerPoint together myself because nobody in tech support has the clearance to do it for me. It should be glitch-free, but you never know. Apologies in advance."

He lowered the lights, as a cue on the flat screen monitor mounted on the wall asked for a password.

"Why don't you tell us your concerns first?" LeDoux said as he typed in his ID code. "What exactly brings you back to Washington?"

"It just doesn't take that much intuition to know when I'm being bullshitted," DeLuca said. "When people start contradicting each other or offering me answers to questions I haven't asked yet, to lead me in a certain direction, or they know I'm coming before I get there—I start to get a sense I'm being given a cover story. They give me this elaborate explanation for why they don't know what information Cheryl Escavedo took, which sounds plausible, I suppose, but they don't offer me a thing about what she was working on the day or the week it happened, when I know they've got that in the duty logs. My gut tells me this is a whistleblower event and not espionage. Whistleblowers who are conscientious—and I have every indication that Escavedo was a conscientious soldier—usually go through channels first before they take things into their own hands. I get nothing on that. Everyone is acting like this happened out of the blue for no reason. That's not how things happen. There's a lid on. And then, in a matter of a few days, I find out two other people are missing, and I can't even start to tell you why—maybe it's nothing, but how often do three people, connected to the same event, go missing in the same week?"

"What other two?" LeDoux asked.

"Escavedo's roommate," DeLuca said, "and apparently a girl, in a cult that Escavedo was trying to contact."

"A cult?"

"Don't ask," DeLuca said. "It's probably unrelated, but it's something I have to look at to make sure. Apparently Escavedo tried to contact them. The bottom line is, I'm going to need more people."

"You're calling in your team?" LeDoux asked.

"We're meeting tonight in Albuquerque," DeLuca said. "I'm trying not to be a pain in the ass, Phil, but when I took the mission with Team Red, I had the impression I was going to be given what I need. I can't do my work with my hands tied and a blindfold over my eyes. That's good enough for magician's assistants, but it doesn't work for CI."

"Okay then," LeDoux said. "Fair enough. Colonel Oswald, why don't you give us a little background."

"I'm going to walk you through some basic history," Oswald said. "I want this to be understood in context. I'm sure you know a lot of this already, but bear with me."

Words came up on the screen:

1981 SDI
1982 Russian test ASAT
1985 Congressional test ban/COIL
1988 MHV canceled
1989 KE-ASAT
1997 MIRACL/LPCL
1998 KE-ASAT minus $37mil/SBLRD
2000 $7mil
2001 $3mil
WTC
2002 SBL-IFX
2004 THEL/BRILLIANT PEBBLES

"I'll try to be brief," Oswald said. "I'm not going to talk about strictly surveillance birds, because that's National Reconnaissance Office and not STRATCOM. You know about President Reagan's Space Defense Initiative, SDI, the so-called 'Star Wars' program. In 1982, in response, the Russians tested a high explosive shrapnel-based antisatellite weapon, an SS-9 booster that detonated at fourteen hundred miles. Sort of a warning shot, I guess. Most of our milsats were higher than that, and only nine out of twenty Russian tests were successful, but that said, it was an operational system."

He clicked his mouse, and a new screen appeared.

"In 1985, a Democratic Congress bans testing anti-satellite weapons for fear of sparking a new arms race. That doesn't mean we can't test antiballistic missile weapons, and that includes the Chemical Oxygen-Iodine Laser, from TRW and Lockheed-Martin, with a wavelength that can penetrate atmosphere, but it needs a 6.6-second dwell at ten kilojoules to produce enough energy to pierce a missile casing, and of course there are other problems with target acquisition and tracking—basically missile tails and nose cones are already hardened against heat, so the only way to take out a missile with a laser, to this point, is to hit the fuel tanks. The point is, antisatellite research continues, disguised as antimissile work."

He clicked again.

"Nineteen eighty-eight. MHV stands for Miniature Homing Vehicle, which is a two-stage missile fired from an F-15, a $1.6-billion Air Force program that gets killed, at which time the Army pushes forward with a KE-ASAT program, a rocket-launched kinetic energy satellite, which is basically an orbiting bomb that we could fly up next to a Russian satellite and blow it up. Funding for KE-ASAT peaks in 1991 at $91 million and declines under Clinton. Secretary of Defense Cohen says he wants capabilities that are temporary and reversible, meaning he wants to blind or jam instead of destroy, pursuant to the argument that a fully blinded nuclear foe is more dangerous than a sighted one."

He clicked. DeLuca saw the image of a large white building, in a desert setting, with the word MIRACL beneath it.

"October 1997, the Army tests a Mid-Infra-Red Advanced Chemical Laser from a test bed in White Sands, challenging the vulnerability of our own satellites, supposedly, but the offensive capabilities of a ground-based laser are obvious, as are the limitations. The technology is hydrogen-fluoride, which is an improvement over oxygen-iodine, but the thing is huge and requires tons of fuel. There's talk of mounting them on river barges. We also test an LPCL, a Low-Powered Chemical Laser, thirty watts, but it's enough to blind. Meanwhile the kinetic stuff is getting hammered in Congress. Clinton uses a line-item veto to wipe $37.5 million from the KE-ASAT budget in 1998. At the same time, Boeing/TRW wins a contract to build a Space-Based Laser Readiness Demonstrator, the SBLRD, to use laser technology to destroy missiles in booster phase from space. The schedule is for a 2008 launch or 2005 accelerated, depending on funding. Kinetics continues to be defunded, with only seven and a half mil in 2000 and three million in 2001. Then comes 9/11."

The colonel clicked again. On the screen, the image of a large satellite.

"SBL-IFX is what SBLRD turns into, Space-Based Laser Integrated Flight Experiment. Funding isn't a problem after 9/11. Also hydrogen-fluoride, which is nice in space because it reabsorbs waste heat, but the bird is still something of a battleship, 42,000 pounds with a 2.8-meter beam that kills down to 40,000 feet, with a 5,000-kilometer range. But cruise missiles fly considerably lower than 40,000 feet, and there are 7,500 of them already deployed with nuclear warheads, and we have no confidence that we're going to keep these out of the hands of terrorists and rogue governments forever."

Colonel Oswald took a drink of water, then clicked again. DeLuca saw a picture of what appeared to be a truck-mounted antiaircraft cannon, except that the cannon didn't look like anything he'd ever seen before.

"Some think, at this point, that THEL is the answer. Tactical High-Energy Laser, developed as part of the Nautilus program with the Israelis, who didn't much care for defending themselves with plastic sheeting and duct tape while SCUDS were falling on their heads during Gulf One. The original THEL is megawatt class continuous wave deuterium-fluoride, like MIRACL, but it has to be made compact and mobile enough to be deployed in theater. Hughes Aircraft builds the tracking system and the rest is Lockheed-Martin/Boeing/TRW. We get a beam out of a five-inch gun turret with 350 degrees of motion, capable of acquiring targets as close as 450 meters. We're getting $170 million U.S. annually, mostly going to Northrop-Grumman and Ball Aerospace for miniaturization, and $80 million from the Israelis, paid to Rehovot Air and Yehud Industrial. In the year 2000, the MTHEL, a mobile THEL, tests and takes down twenty-three out of twenty-four Katyusha rockets—this is again at White Sands. Last summer the thing was knocking mortar rounds out of the sky with a 97 percent batting average. Artillery shells, SAM-7s—it's unbelievable, really. Fantastic fire control. We're not far at all from having a fully effective tactical defensive shield. I can't tell you how happy that makes the Israelis. We have three Humvee-mounted THELs in Iraq at present, hunting IEDs. We're probably looking at V-22 tilt-rotor and CH-47 Chinook and Bradley-mounted battlefield THELs by 2006, deployed out of C-130s, and possibly shoulder-fired by 2008. At which point the limitations become more human than technological."

"Meaning?" DeLuca asked, though he knew the answer.

"Meaning, how much discretionary power do you really want to give to any one individual?" Phil LeDoux said. "It's not just a defensive weapon. If you think we were worried about Stingers getting into the wrong hands, THEL makes the Stinger look like a popgun. There wouldn't be a commercial flight in the world that would be safe. We're not even sure we want our own soldiers in the field to have that much power, because all it would take would be to have one guy have a very bad day and you'd probably kill the whole program."

"And Cheryl Escavedo was working with the THEL program?"

LeDoux shook his head.

"This is just the background," LeDoux said. "What's sensitive here is what was black-budgeted. Nobody really stopped researching antisatellite weapons in 1985—some pretended to be ABM programs and the rest went from white to black. Without getting into specifics, what you need to keep in focus is the degree to which technology has increased its capacity while reducing its size. I had a Kaypro 10 portable computer in 1985 that weighed almost one hundred pounds and had enough memory to store thirty pages of text, and I think I paid three thousand dollars for it. Today there's more technology in the little pieces of plastic crap they give away in McDonald's Happy Meals. So, smaller and smaller, and more and more powerful."

"Nuclear-powered satellites?"

"Oh, yeah," LeDoux said. "But the problem with satellites is how vulnerable they are—they get wiped out by solar flares, let alone by ASAT systems. Thermal management is critical to their design—internal temperatures have to be maintained within a very narrow range, and they're not designed to redistribute heat. Most have a lethal radiance of ten watts per square centimeter, plus they don't maneuver, so ASAT-SBLs could take their time knocking them out. We've been armoring our own birds in a variety of ways ever since DOD directive TS.3100a, but we're still vulnerable. So, what's the best way to hide a satellite?"

"Make it invisible?" DeLuca guessed.

"You got it," LeDoux said, clicking on his mouse. The word at the top of the screen read "DARKSTAR," and beneath it, a photograph of a man standing next to what looked like a large black flashlight, a canister about five feet long and two feet in diameter. LeDoux allowed DeLuca a few moments to absorb the image.

"The nickname is 'Deathstar,'" Oswald said. "It's a good thing George Lucas doesn't sue us for copyright infringement. This is an early prototype, by the way, about ten years old. The new ones are smaller. Darkstar is a fully cloaked satellite, using the same Stealth technology we use to hide our Stealth fighters and our Stealth bombers, more effectively, actually, since in space you don't have to allow for aerodynamics. NRO was working with the CIA on Stealth birds at a clip of about $9 billion a year, classified as 'Misty,' mostly Lockheed-Martin, and Darkstar was piggybacked on a black program. It's a tunable microwave infrared laser with a two-thousand-megawatt capacity. Minneapolis–St. Paul draws about two thousand megawatts. The problem with atmospherics has been something Space Command has been working on for years. The longer the wavelength, the more atmosphere you can penetrate but the more power you need to push it through. Darkstar was designed as both an ASAT and an ABM weapon, and finally, to perform all the same functions as THEL. It puts it all together. Fully maneuverable, and small enough that you can launch it to geosynchronous with as little as a Delta II platform, though that far out, you start to lose range even at two thousand megawatts. At geotransfer orbit, the dwell is in microseconds for even hardened targets like cruise missiles flying at twenty or thirty meters above the ground. Radar exposure increases only .07 percent when it reconfigures and essentially decloaks to fire, and it's coated in heat-and light-absorbent materials. In other words, no one is going to see this thing unless we want them to see it. The only way would be to be looking in exactly the right place at exactly the right time, but without being able to track it, it can't really be done."

"Wait a minute," DeLuca said. "This thing can shoot down cruise missiles?"

"That's right," Colonel Oswald said.

"Thirty meters above the ground?" DeLuca said. "What's to stop it from taking out ground targets? They don't even move."

Colonel Oswald and Phil LeDoux exchanged glances.

"Where space defense is concerned," Oswald said, "there's what we can do, and there's what the enemy thinks we can do. And it's always been a delicate balance. It's game theory, but it's played for real. We don't want our enemies knowing what we can do, any more than we want them knowing what we can't. We want them to think we're stronger than we really are, because that creates deterrence, but we don't want them to think we're so strong that they have to act to defend themselves, because that generates aggression. That's why this is sensitive—if word of Darkstar were to get out, the first thing the media would start talking about is death rays. Is it a death ray? Yes, actually, it is. It's a tunable beam, so it can do anything from start a campfire to obliterate a building or an underground bunker to, perhaps, destroy a city."

"Or a person," DeLuca said.

"Do you think we wouldn't take Osama Bin Laden out that way if we could find him?" Oswald said. "Biometrics acquisition is a whole different question. The task range is extremely broad. One of the original applications of Darkstar was to develop a laser that could be used to destroy asteroids headed for earth, and with sufficient dwell time, it could probably actually do that. MIRACL was a cover operation. That is, MIRACL is a fully operational ground-based laser, but it was a Darkstar prototype, firing at the same time, that took out the target. MIRACL was just a big public show to explain what happened."

"When is Darkstar scheduled for deployment?" DeLuca asked. Oswald and LeDoux again exchanged glances.

"We've launched two," Oswald said. "Prototypes, but operational. Darkstar1 went up dark and Darkstar2 went up lit, but D2 malfunctioned and eventually broke into pieces over the Indian Ocean."

"What about the other one? D1?" DeLuca said.

"We can't find it," LeDoux said. "Maybe the same thing happened to both of them, though they were on opposite sides of the earth when number two went black. No sunspots or solar flares. We can't seem to light D1 up, and the backup systems to turn it on and decloak it have also failed. The likelihood is that it was damaged and is inoperative."

"Unless it's not, and it's up there, fully operative, and we just don't know where it is," DeLuca said.

"I'm afraid that's about the size of it," Oswald said. "It's not going to do anything it's not told to do—there are semiautonomous systems on it, but it still has to be activated and programmed from ground. Again, we have every reason to believe it's nonoperational."

"But?"

"But, two months ago, we had a malfunction on a launch pad at Fort Greely, Alaska. A Titan IV was boosting an NFIRE/KE-ASAT vehicle as part of Brilliant Pebbles when it blew apart on launch."

LeDoux clicked his mouse to post a map and then a photograph on the monitor, a picture of a burned rocket casing.

"They're still putting up kinetic energy vehicles?" DeLuca asked. "Why, if we've got Darkstar?"

"The official explanation was that Brilliant Pebbles is ongoing and necessary to knock down Russian or Iranian or North Korean ICBMs in their booster phases and/or midcourse, which is what it was designed for," LeDoux said. "The real reason it was being sent up was to find and destroy the unlit Darkstar before it could be captured and reverse-engineered. Near-Field Infrared is the best space-based infrared system we have."

"So you think D1 took out the Titan?"

"We don't know," Oswald said. "The sci-fi people are going to see that as Darkstar defending itself, even though it has no AI capabilities whatsoever. But a study of the debris suggests a possible laser hosing."

"Then a week later," LeDoux added, "in a place called Pine Gap, Australia, a mobile PAVE-PAWS radar truck was struck by lightning, or that's what it looked like, even though there wasn't a cloud in the sky. Since then, we've lost a Dutch weather satellite, a British telecom bird, and a twenty-year-old Russian milsat, which they said was due to solar flares, but it was in low earth orbit and shadow when it happened. You'll get full reports on all these events."

"And you think the missing Darkstar is doing this?"

"Not necessarily," LeDoux said. "It's entirely possible that someone else has managed to launch a similar satellite. The idea that someone else could take control of one of our satellites is beyond comprehension, but it wouldn't be the first supposedly secured system we've seen compromised. We just don't know."

"Russians?" DeLuca asked. "Ex-Soviet assets?"

"Possibly," LeDoux said. "Destroying one of their own birds to throw off suspicion. Our best intelligence says there are at least nine countries technologically capable of orbiting space-based lasers, though nobody was supposed to be able to do it for another ten years. How many of them could take it to the level of Darkstar is hard to say, but theoretically, some could. Darkstar was supposed to be the final deterrent and the balance holding THEL in check—the one weapon that would never fall into the wrong hands. We're not saying that it has. We're just saying that it's possible. There may be other explanations for what happened at Greely and at Pine Gap. We have other people looking into those."

"And how is Cheryl Escavedo connected to any of this?"

"STRATCOM is in charge of Darkstar, run out of Cheyenne Mountain," LeDoux said. "Apparently some Darkstar data was misfiled and archived by mistake. Sergeant Escavedo was tasked to correct that mistake, even though she wasn't supposed to know or understand the nature of the files she was pulling. We're concerned that she did understand them."

"And/or copy them?" DeLuca asked.

"And/or copy them," LeDoux confirmed. "I've already talked to General Koenig about this briefing, and I've told him Team Red is completely read on—he's fully prepared to help you in any way he can, but he's also told you most of what he knows about Cheryl Escavedo. I'm also not sure how necessary it's going to be for you to tell your team about Darkstar. I understand why you felt like you were being given the run-around, because you were. I'll leave it to your discretion as to what you tell your team and what constitutes need-to-know, but as I'm sure you've gathered, the fewer people read on about this, the better. Just as the fewer people who know we're having problems, the better."

"I'm flying back to Albuquerque tonight to brief the team," DeLuca said. "I'll give it some thought. I'm not going to put anybody in danger just to keep them ignorant."

"I understand," LeDoux said. "I wouldn't expect you to. FYI, Darkstar is held up until this gets resolved. We're talking over $100 billion. That's going to come right out of your paycheck if you fuck up."

"Speaking of funds . . ."

"Tell Captain Martin what you need."

He met with his team that evening in his room at the Red Roof Inn, on Mulberry Street, near Kirtland AFB. Walter Ford couldn't get away from the criminology classes he taught at Northeastern University's College of Criminal Justice, still one class in Research and Evaluation Methods and another in Statistical Analysis, but this year a third course in Computer Crimes had been added to his course load. Ford said he'd do what he could from home. Ex-cop and Army reservist Sami Jambazian had done as much work on his charter boat as he could and was twiddling his thumbs until the weather improved—he was glad for the chance to fly south into a warmer climate. DeLuca's flight arrived half an hour before Sami's, so he waited for him and met him at the gate. Jambazian was in one of his usual sour moods, complaining of how he was never able to strike up a good conversation on an airplane—what was wrong with people?

"Has it ever occurred to you that maybe it's you and not them?" DeLuca said.

"I'm the world's friendliest guy," he said. "If you're not friendly to me back, then the hell with you."

"I rest my case."

Colleen MacKenzie had flown in earlier from California, where Mack had spent Thanksgiving and Christmas with her family after leaving Balad and the Sunni triangle behind, which was more than enough time to drive her crazy. She'd escaped by signing up for a Russian-language refresher course at the Defense Language Institute in Monterey, a program she'd cut short when DeLuca called. Dan Sykes had opted to stay in Washington at his father's D.C. residence, rather than at the family home in San Francisco, and arrived on the flight behind DeLuca, who wondered if there was anything to be read into the fact that Sykes and MacKenzie had been romantically involved during their time in Iraq, but they'd elected to be apart once they were stateside again. "What happens on deployment stays on deployment" was a slogan in the military long before Las Vegas coopted the concept, and it was usually a good idea, a really good idea, to let go of such emotional attachments, which rarely survived divorced from the "Temporary Duty" context in which they were generated. DeLuca just hoped there weren't any hard feelings between them. Hoolie—Julio Vasquez—was the last to arrive, driving the 750 miles from Los Angeles to Albuquerque in his personal car, an immaculately restored candy-apple-red 1974 Cadillac Eldorado convertible, with an in-dash eight-track cassette player and a box full of Mexican conjunto/Tejano tapes on the floor beside him. It was late by the time the whole team was able to assemble, and everyone was hungry, so Sykes took orders and made a run to the Burger King up the street.

When he got back, DeLuca briefed the team, stopping short of mentioning, at least for now, anything about Darkstar itself. He said only that a United States military satellite program had been compromised and that files concerning it had possibly been stolen, by a girl who was currently missing, as was her roommate, and that the only potential witnesses he'd found so far were an odd group of UFO cultists. He told Sami it would be his job to infiltrate the Brethren of the Light, but he didn't tell the others why. Years ago, Sami had been following a Mafia-owned tanker truck across the state line when he saw a UFO. He'd made the mistake of telling his story to the poker group, which had not stopped giving him shit about it ever since, which was why DeLuca didn't mention it to Team Red. Sami would find out if the little girl was truly missing. Hoolie and Mack would concentrate on Leon Lev, who, at the moment, was the only human bad guy DeLuca could point his finger at. Dan Sykes would look for Theresa. Walter Ford could dig into the history and the personality of General Thomas Koenig, as well as that of

Major Brent Huston. DeLuca had a hunch about them and just didn't trust them, even after he understood the reasons for their prior deceptiveness.

"I'll stay on Cheryl Escavedo," he said, opening his suitcase on the bed and distributing the contents. "Now for the party favors. In each Ziploc bag, you will find, compliments of Captain Martin, a fully encrypted SAT-phone for each of you with built-in GPS, with all your call numbers already added to the contact list, as well as encrypted PDAs for sending files. These are for secure communications, but keep your cell phones in case we want to make calls we might want others to listen in on. Spend some time playing with your new toys so we're all up to speed on how they work."

As he spoke, the telephone in his kit rang. Hoolie was punching buttons on his own phone through the plastic.

"Phones work," he said, hanging up.

"You'll also find some walking-around money and your new government credit cards," DeLuca continued. "Don't go crazy, but get what you need and don't worry about it. You each have the information we've compiled so far in your packets, so read 'em tonight, and tomorrow, I'll tell you how to proceed."

He didn't tell them about Darkstar because—was he being paranoid? Overcautious? A mobile radar truck in Australia had been hit by lightning, and Cheryl Escavedo's Jeep had been hit by lightning. What were the odds of that? Cheryl Escavedo knew about Darkstar, and she was missing. Theresa knew Cheryl, and now she was missing. Again, what were the odds? Somebody wanted to keep Darkstar a secret, he suspected, just as he suspected somebody was using satellite technology for his own purposes—somebody who'd figured out how to access satellite intel. This meant that people who knew about Darkstar were in greater danger than people who didn't know. Communications could be intercepted, even from encrypted phones.

After everyone had gone back to their rooms, he stood on the balcony and looked up at the night sky. A refrain from an old song played in his head: *"Are the stars out tonight? I don't care if they're cloudy or bright, 'cause I only have eyes . . . for you . . ."* He wondered what eyes were up there, and who was watching from above. Satellites had saved his life, more than once, in Iraq. He'd never thought of them as a threat before.

He didn't like it, now that he did.

Chapter Six

DELUCA WAS IN THE PARKING LOT BEHIND THE motel the next morning, stretching after his run, when a middle-aged woman stepped out of her shiny stainless-steel Jet Stream motor home to yawn and squint at the rising sun. The name on the back of the motor home, painted in an elaborate pink scroll outlined in gold, was "Ms. Kitty." The woman was dressed in a gray hooded sweatshirt, shorts that fell well below her knees, flip-flops, and a red plaid flannel bathrobe over it all, untied at the waist. She was about five-foot-two, with short salt-and-pepper curly hair tumbling in disarray above her ears, square black-rimmed glasses, and freckles across the bridge of her nose. She had a stainless-steel travel mug in her hand, which she raised in greeting as she smiled broadly.

"Hello," she said. "Do they have coffee in the lobby? Or sweet rolls?"

She had an East Coast accent.

"I believe they do, but I think it's for guests only," DeLuca said.

"Oh, that's okay—I always pay slippage for using the parking lot," she said. "I'll be right back."

DeLuca didn't feel obliged to wait for her, but he was nevertheless still there when she returned.

"Good run?" she asked cheerfully, sipping her coffee, a baked good in her other hand and a copy of *USA Today* tucked under her arm. She had a slow and deliberate walk, almost a shuffle, barely lifting her feet as she moved.

"Pretty good," he said. "I don't know what the altitude is here, but it feels like I'm not quite acclimated."

"It's 5,314 feet," she said. "Hold on—I've got something for you."

She disappeared into her RV, then returned with a paper bag in her hand, and in the bag, a bottle of beer. DeLuca thanked her but said it was a little early for drinking beer.

"Look at the label," she said. "I'm told there are only twelve bottles of this stuff in existence."

DeLuca did a brief double take. The label read "Herr Totenbrau," with a crude line drawing of a skeleton passed out in an alley with a beer in his hand. "Herr Totenbrau" translated as "Mr. Death-Beer," and it was a homebrew that DeLuca and Phil LeDoux had made in their off-duty hours, years ago when the two of them were stationed in Germany, manning listening posts along the East German frontier. Phil still had one sixpack, and DeLuca had the other, with the understanding that some day when they'd both retired and the world was at peace, they'd get together and have a drink.

"With General LeDoux's compliments," the woman said. "I would have knocked on your door when I got in at *four o'clock* this morning, but I was driving all night and I was just *wiped*. Peggy Romano." She extended her hand.

"David DeLuca," he said, shaking her hand, which she then wiped on her bathrobe.

"I know," she said. "You wanna step into the RV? Tell you what—why don't you take a shower first, and *then* you can see my RV."

He was back in fifteen minutes, a Styrofoam cup of coffee from the lobby in his hand. Peggy Romano was at the dining table, reading the sports pages. There was a signed photograph of WNBA player Sue Bird, framed and hung on the wall by the sink, and a Diana Taurasi bobble-head propped on the dashboard, next to a small stuffed teddy bear wearing a red Christmas scarf.

"You follow women's basketball?" DeLuca asked.

"Do I *follow* it?" the woman said. "I'm obsessed. I dream about it. I get all the games on dish. I'm obsessed. My entire goal in life is to sleep with one WNBA player. I think it's because I'm short. You want a tour?"

"Sure," he said. "Why 'Ms. Kitty'?"

"Mobile Secure Combined Intelligence Tactical Telecommunications and Yada-yada-yada. But I couldn't use a C for 'combined' or people would call it 'Ms. City.' Come on. It won't take long," she said. In addition to a kitchen/dining area, shower, and sleeping compartment in the rear, the motor home was packed floor to ceiling with enough technology to give the operations center at Cheyenne Mountain a run for its money. There were four computer stations in the central section, each with its own flat-screen monitor, a plasma screen that folded down from the ceiling above the dining area for briefings, and the tabletop, which appeared to be smoked glass, converted to a full-color touch-screen LED display as well, with a virtual keyboard embedded but repositionable and a graphics support that let the user draw on the screen in color.

"I don't know why, but I like looking at maps when they're flat and not on the wall," she said. "It's up to you. Don't worry about what's in the closets, because I'll take care of that stuff, but it's mostly servers and processors and communications stuff. All you really need to know is that we're fully firewalled, shielded, encrypted, scrambled, armored, and the glass is bulletproof to withstand an RPG. All your calls and your wireless goes through here, uplinked to a satellite not even NSA knows about—they know about it, but they think it's something else."

"I assumed you were NSA," DeLuca said.

"Not anymore, I'm not," Peggy Romano said. "I'm a private contractor now—I'm the guy they call when they don't want anybody to know they're calling the guy. Like in those old movies, where the blonde takes off and says, 'I'll send someone for my things.' Send who? I could never figure out who that would be, but that's who I am, in a way—I'm the techno-fixer they use when they can't call the super."

"Who's they?"

She laughed.

"Like I'm going to tell you?" she said. "If you want to check my credentials, you can talk to LeDoux, and I'm fully read on to Darkstar, so you tell me how you want to play it."

"I haven't told my people about that part," he said.

"Probably wise. Just keep me posted. I just want to reassure you that nothing comes in here that you don't want, and nothing goes out that you don't want. I'll do all your tech support, and I imagine your people are trying to figure out the PDAs we gave you, right about now, so please tell them I'll be happy to walk them through the setup protocols. The rest of this is just like what you're used to using, but call if you need me. I've got printers and graphics to cook up any IDs you need—all I ask is that this is a $35-million vehicle, so please use coasters and restock what you use from the minibar. Which is gratis. And no cats because I'm allergic to them. I'll write down the code for you to get in and out. I'm going to get a room at the Red Roof so that you people can have some privacy in here, and if I'm not there, I'll be at the pool. One last thing . . ." She handed him a paper bag full of keys on assorted keychains. "These are for all the cars in the back row." She pointed out the window to a row of vehicles of various makes and models, ranging from a new Mercedes to a beat-up fifteen-year-old Toyota pickup. "You tell me how you want these things registered and I'll take care of it. I can also fix parking tickets. I'll check back in an hour."

"Okay," DeLuca said. "Peggy?"

"Yeah?"

"That's not your real name, is it? Peggy Romano?"

"Not even close," she said. "By the way, I read the report you sent LeDoux, so you might be interested to know—Hilton Jaynes is speaking tomorrow night at the university. Room 103, Regener Hall, North Campus. Toodles."

When she was gone, he logged on and sent Walter Ford an e-mail:

Walter,

Get on SIPERNET and tell me what you can find out about girls disappearing in the desert along the

U.S./Mexican border, let's say Yuma to El Paso, going back 25 years. Don't ask me what I'm looking for because I don't know. Patterns, anomalies, etc. I recall things from when I was with Yuma PD but I'm not up to date, beyond what I read in the papers. Also, tell me what you learn about Koenig/Huston ASAP. I want to talk to them again but I need more info first. Personal stuff, to push their buttons a little. Thanks.
David

MacKenzie and Vasquez drove south to meet in El Paso with an old friend of DeLuca's, a man named Wes Vogel who'd been an instructor at Fort Huachuca before joining Immigration and Customs Enforcement. Vogel would take them across the border and introduce them to Colonel Martine Guzman, head of the Chihuahuan State Anti-Drug Joint Task Force. Sami took the Mercedes for the short drive to the Brethren of the Light compound, with the intention of giving them the car and all his other worldly possessions if they'd let him join. He'd spent five years undercover in Boston playing the part of a Mafia-connected drug dealer, taking down various Colombian and Jamaican gang members venturing north out of Brooklyn and Central Falls, Rhode Island, to peddle their wares. It had been a while since he'd had to get over on anybody, "But hey, what are they gonna do to me if I fuck it up—shoot me with their phasers?" He spent the morning in preparation, Googling the Brethren and chatting on the phone with a reporter from the local paper who covered the UFO beat, pretending he was writing a book on UFO cults.

DeLuca managed to reach Cheryl Escavedo's uncle on the phone and asked if he could see him. When the uncle, a man named Henry Soto, said he'd be flying to Atlantic City that evening and would be out of town for the next two weeks, DeLuca grabbed a flight out of Albuquerque International on Southwest and was in Las Vegas by lunch.

Soto's office was in a downtown building on the corner of Fremont and Fourth, across the street from the Golden Gate Hotel and Casino. A Native American receptionist, a woman about fifty in a floral dress with gray hair pulled back in a ponytail, asked him to wait a moment, picked up the phone, and called to make sure her boss was free, then showed DeLuca in. Soto stood to greet his visitor, offering him his hand and nodding as he shook.

"Please sit down," he said. "Can I tell Louise to get you anything? Coffee or tea?"

"I'm fine," DeLuca said. Soto was in his midsixties, DeLuca guessed, heavy, his hair black with a touch of gray, brushed straight back and worn long over his collar. He was dressed in a black suit, a white shirt, a red tie held in place with a tie clasp that featured a tasteful sampling of the kind of beadwork DeLuca associated with the Cocopah. The horn-rimmed reading glasses on the end of his nose added a professorial note to his appearance. On the walls of the office were large framed color photographs of various Indian casinos around the country, Mystic Lake in Minnesota, Foxwoods in Connecticut, sometimes with an inset of Soto shaking hands with officials DeLuca presumed were the owners. Soto's job involved recruiting, training, and supervising Native American employees for positions within the gaming industry, with the goal of making Indian casinos 100 percent Indian-operated, even at the highest executive levels where currently non-Indian industry professionals drew salaries. "We do everything except the entertainment," Soto had explained on the phone. DeLuca saw photographs of Soto shaking hands with Wayne Newton, Siegfried and Roy, Celine Dion, Sinbad, even one of him standing between George Burns and Bob Hope. DeLuca made sure not to admire anything he saw too much or let his gaze linger, because the Cocopah were such a generous people that they often gave you something if you were careless enough to comment that you liked it. A plaque on Soto's desk read "Xawitt Kunyavaei—Sovereign Nation of the Cocopahs."

"You flew Southwest?" Soto said. DeLuca nodded. "You must be hungry—they're so cheap they don't even give you peanuts. Come on—I'll buy you lunch. Louise? Mr. DeLuca and I are going to be across the street. I'm leaving my cell here but if there's an emergency, you know where to find me." He turned to DeLuca. "I always leave my cell phone when I'm having lunch with somebody. Do you know there are people who will take a cell phone call in the middle of talking to you? My people had a way of dealing with such rude sorts."

"What was that?"

"Usually we crossed the river to get away from them," Soto said, grabbing DeLuca gently by the arm. "Come on."

Traffic on Fremont at midday was light, the neon struggling to hold on until nightfall. The floor of the Golden Gate was surprisingly crowded, Soto explaining that at this hour, the older casinos downtown did better business, per square foot, than the giant ones out on the strip, "mostly old people who came here years ago when this was ground zero. You win one time in a place and you get sentimentally attached to it, even though none of these places bears much resemblance to what they used to be. The steak is okay but stay away from the Mexican food—it's not as good as one might hope."

The waitress who took their order wore a skimpy uniform, spilling out of her low-cut top when she bent over to clean the table. Soto noticed that DeLuca noticed. He smiled.

"Just so you know, she used to be a man," Soto said. "I told her I thought she overdid it with the implants but I guess she was trying to make up for lost time. Anyway, you said you wanted to talk about Cheryl. I've already spoken to Ben Yutahay, but I wondered if you had anything more to tell me."

"Not much," DeLuca said. "I found some people who may have been in the area, but I haven't found anyone who saw anything. Yet. And I talked to her roommate, who said she left a note—I shouldn't say she left a note, but the roommate found a piece of paper, a scrap, with the words 'Tom never . . .' on it. Do you know if she knew anybody named Tom?"

Soto shook his head.

"I don't think so, but she was never much into sharing her personal life with me. I'm just the old fuddy-duddy, to her. We talked, but not so much about that sort of thing."

"You raised her, right?" DeLuca asked. "I'm a little unclear on how that was."

"Her father was driving drunk with her mother, my sister," Soto said. "I was raised for the first part of my life by my grandparents after I lost my folks when I was six, so it wasn't so unusual for us."

"In Somerton?" DeLuca asked. "I used to be a policeman in Yuma, so I know U.S. 95 pretty good."

"I know," Soto said. "Your name rang a bell when I heard it so I made a phone call. You testified against my cousin's boy at one of my first trials. I was a property lawyer but they asked me to speak for him anyway. It was for vandalism. He was guilty, but what I remembered was that you told the truth. There were other cops in Yuma who would have lied on the stand. Testi-lying, they call it. Especially against an Indian."

"I know," DeLuca said. "Where did you study law?"

"Billy Mitchell in Minnesota," Henry Soto said. "After my grandmother died, I became an orphan, and the BIA had a program to place Native American orphans in the homes of white people, to help us assimilate. I was raised by a Lutheran family in South Minneapolis. A minister and his wife. They were very nice. Some people tell me I still have a Minnesota accent."

DeLuca had noticed something odd about the way Henry Soto spoke but hadn't been able to place it.

"It must have been difficult to go from a place as hot as Yuma to a place as cold as Minnesota," he said.

"Actually I loved it," Soto said. "I learned how to skate and went to the U of M on a hockey scholarship. I was small but fast, and I think the white boys were scared of me. We didn't have goons or enforcers, back then, but we wouldn't back down from anybody. I came back after I got my degree and studied for the Arizona bar, and I think maybe that inspired Cheryl a little bit, because I was the first person in our family, one of the first in our whole band, to go to college. I told her she could do anything she set her mind to."

"Ben said you kept the Jeep at your trailer, " DeLuca said. "Is that a family place she might have gone to for comfort?"

"I think so," Soto said. "Though it might not be the kind of comfort you're thinking of. It's up in Pai Pai country. It's just a trailer, but I used to take her there, just to get away from things. I kept the Jeep there for hauling things and doing chores."

"Have you been there lately?" DeLuca asked. Soto shook his head. "Would you mind if I went and had a look around?"

"I wouldn't mind," Soto said. "It's not locked. I'll have to draw you a map. It's not easy to find."

"Do you know of any reason why she might have headed from there for Spirit Mountain?" DeLuca asked.

"Why Cheryl would have?" Soto said. "I don't really know. She didn't care much for the traditional things. Religion and so on. I know sometimes Cocopahs go to Spirit Mountain when they're on a vision quest. There are Hohokum places there that are very old, but few know about them. I don't think Cheryl did. Maybe she did. Sometimes the younger people become disillusioned and come home to get religion. Maybe she was headed for Mexico?"

"Maybe, but the road she was on dead-ended a few miles from where we found the car. She wouldn't have made it."

"Well, it's easy to get lost," Henry Soto said.

"Did she say anything was bothering her?" DeLuca said. "Anything that made you think she was in trouble of any kind?"

"I don't think so," Soto said. "I've been racking my brain. She didn't like being transferred, but she knew the Army did that sort of thing."

Huston had told DeLuca she'd asked to be transferred.

"Can I ask you one last question?" DeLuca said. "This might be a bit difficult for you. One of her coworkers said she thought Cheryl was gay. Do you have any reason to think that might be true?"

Soto thought.

"Hmmm. I don't think so, but how would I know?" he said. "Was her roommate . . . ?"

"No. She had a boyfriend," DeLuca said.

"Maybe she'd be a better person to ask," Soto said.

"She might be," DeLuca said, "but we don't know where she is."

DeLuca rented a Hummer2 at the Yuma airport, a beefy yellow and black model that looked like a Checker cab that had lost its temper and turned into the Hulk. The hole in the roof where the SAW gunner sat, in the military version, had been replaced with a sliding glass moon roof, and without the extra two thousand pounds of armoring, the vehicle was much more responsive, but it was still a beast. He liked the air-conditioning, the power windows, and the CD player. Ben Yutahay said, when DeLuca picked him up, that he knew families of four that lived in smaller quarters. DeLuca handed him the map Henry Soto had drawn and asked Yutahay if he knew the area.

"I've been up there hunting," Yutahay said. "It's pretty rough country, and it's going to be dark by the time we get there. If Cheryl Escavedo went there to hide, it would have been pretty hard to find her."

"That depends on what you've got looking," DeLuca said. "My son works with satellite image intelligence and he tells me they've got cameras that could measure Fidel Castro's bald spot. And Sergeant Escavedo certainly knew that."

"They can't watch everywhere, can they?" Yutahay asked. "They would have to know what to look for, I would guess."

"I think you're right," DeLuca said.

The road took them east, then south toward a place called Sheep Mountain, in the Sierra Juarez range, the blacktop rolling in roller-coaster fashion for several miles until it turned to gravel, the desert flora of jumping cholla and creosote bushes and prickly pear. He'd brought along a pair of five-gallon gas cans, just in case the H2 ran low, and it seemed to be consuming a gallon every thirty or forty feet. They stopped at one point at a fork in the road that Henry Soto had failed to include on the map, but a brief consultation with Peggy Romano and a check of his GPS receiver put them back on course. While they were stopped, Yutahay scrutinized the tire tracks in the road, but it had rained enough in the interval to wash out any useful information. They drove for another hour, never making better than fifteen or twenty miles per, stopping occasionally for Ben to get out and examine the road, squatting to touch the ruts and grooves with his fingertips. He said he couldn't be certain of the timing, as it was hard to determine the rate of sign decay without knowing exactly what the weather had done, but he recognized the tire prints left by the Jeep, heading out, and he thought he saw the narrower tracks of a smaller car, headed in, something with fifteen-inch tires with about thirty-five thousand miles on them.

"I think she was going pretty fast, and then she slowed down," Yutahay said. "Her right front tire went out of alignment since the last time we stopped. That happens sometimes when you hit a pothole at fifty or sixty miles an hour."

They found the trailer another five miles down the road, parked in a hollow with a grove of cottonwoods for shade and a small mountain stream trickling behind it for drinking water. Escavedo's Honda Civic was parked in the trees beside the trailer. The sun had set, an early star twinkling on the horizon that Yutahay identified as Venus, but there was still enough light to have a look around. They examined the car first. Yutahay took the backseat, where he found an article of clothing on the floor.

"What's this?" he said, holding it up to the light.

"Thong underwear," DeLuca said. "Something that fell out of a suitcase?"

"Maybe," Yutahay said. "My wife used to wear these but they gave her a rash so she got rid of them, but she still has the rash. I guess you could say the thong is gone but the malady lingers on."

"*You* could say that," DeLuca replied.

He'd hoped to pop open the glove compartment and find a stack of diskettes held together with a rubber band, but no such luck. The keys were in the ignition. A quick turn revealed that the car was nearly out of gas. She'd gone past the point of no return. The radio was tuned to 1190 AM. In the trunk, he found a receipt from a supermarket in Yuma. DeLuca showed it to Yutahay.

"What do you think?" he said. "Two weeks' worth of food?"

"Maybe three," Yutahay said, looking at the list. "Nothing perishable. That means she knew when she bought the food that she was coming here, since there's no refrigerator, without electricity."

"Let's have a look inside," DeLuca said. "I'll grab the flashlights."

A canopy of corrugated green fiberglass extended from the side of the trailer, propped on a frame of two-by-fours, and beneath it, two lawn chairs and a table. Yutahay said that judging from the footprints in the dust, there was only one person occupying the trailer, wearing size eight Army-issue desert combat boots.

"Are those dog prints?" DeLuca asked.

"Coyote," Yutahay said. "Cleaning up the table scraps. I think she ate a meal out here."

DeLuca found a kerosene lantern on the table inside the trailer and lit it. Yutahay searched the bedroom end of the trailer while DeLuca searched the kitchen. There was a pair of binoculars on the table, focused at infinity, beside an ashtray with three cigarette butts in it. He examined what was in the trash, compared that to what was in the cupboards, using the grocery list as a guide, and determined she'd been in the trailer no more than two days. There were no cigarette butts in the trash—who smoked three cigarettes in two days? Someone trying to quit, or someone trying not to start again. The only other thing of interest in the trash was a rubber band she'd used to pull back her hair, with a few hairs entangled in the knot. He put the rubber band in a plastic Ziploc evidence bag, to have the hair tested—it would tell him if she'd done any drugs in the last six months, but he doubted he was going to find any such indicators. Ben showed him where she'd laid two uniforms out on the bed, her dress blues and her forest green camos, as if she were choosing between them to decide what to wear.

"Guess she couldn't make up her mind," Ben said.

"No," DeLuca said. "It means she's wearing her DCUs. She probably picked the desert camo because she knew when she left that she was headed south."

"Do you think it means she was hoping to come back?"

DeLuca shrugged.

"Would you wear thong underwear with a camo uniform?" Yutahay said.

"I'm sure it's more common than anybody knows," DeLuca said.

The Winchester rifle mounted above the door was unloaded and hadn't been fired. There were no diskettes or CDs anywhere. DeLuca stood in the doorway, gazing out at the darkening landscape.

"It's probably not going to be worth it, but do you think you could come back with some men and really go over the grounds here and make sure she didn't hide anything under a rock?" he asked. "Maybe she walked out and dug a hole somewhere."

"I could do that," Yutahay said, opening the door to the wood stove. "Though it looks to me like she pretty much kept to the trailer. This might be of interest to you."

He'd fished three scraps of paper from the wood stove, computer printouts, partially burned but with enough text on them to discern the subjects. Yutahay spread the scraps out on the table while DeLuca shone his flashlight on them.

Escavedo had evidently Googled for the words "Shijingshan," "Qadzi Deh," and "Congressman Bob Fowler."

"They didn't burn completely because she forgot to open the flue," Yutahay said.

"Destroying evidence?"

"Maybe she was just trying to start a fire," Yutahay said. "It gets pretty cold up here. There was kindling on top of the paper, but that didn't burn either."

On their way back to Yuma, DeLuca tuned the Hummer's radio to 1190 AM, where he found an all-night phone-in show, hosted by a man with a very calm and soothing voice named Ed Clark. The in-studio guest had an interesting theory about the Kennedy assassination, one he'd recently published in a book called *Angry Are the Gods.*

". . . there was no invasion being planned, per se. And in fact, a review of some of the best telescopic imagery we had of the moon at the time will show you that the base the Travelers were building in the Sea of Tranquility was at a rudimentary level, we think for a simple lack of funding, but of course we can't know that. What we do know is that shortly after President Kennedy promised we were going to put a man on the moon, activity at the aliens' lunar base increased tenfold. But as the last caller correctly pointed out, the Travelers' own way of experiencing the uni-mind ultimately misled them because they projected that paradigm onto a terrestrial governmental system that was anything but. It was quite reasonable, from their point of view, to believe that killing President Kennedy would have been an effective way of stopping the space program to protect their base on the moon, because the command to go there originated with him."

The author spoke very deliberately, authoritatively, as if the things he was saying were things anybody in their right mind would of course know and/or agree with.

"Now, as to the caller's second question, why, if the Travelers were able to effect a soul-transference with Lee Harvey Oswald, which by the way is a one-way street, sort of like a kamikaze suicide mission, because once you cross, you can't cross back, so why, if they could occupy Oswald's body, why couldn't they just occupy President Kennedy's body and then have him call off the space program? That question is somewhat simpler to answer, because we know that perhaps the most reliable way to identify the Travelers living among us, intuitively, is by their charisma. Though few of us trust our intuition. That's the one thing they can't hide, and in fact it often becomes amplified, depending on the type of individual they possess and occupy. But what they can't do is occupy someone who already has charisma, and I think most Democrats over the age of fifty or sixty will recall that perhaps no human being in modern American recollection had more charisma than John Kennedy. Human charisma is toxic to them. In other words, it wouldn't have worked. And you can see, watch the old videotapes, and compare the aura that Kennedy projected to the one that exited from Lee Harvey Oswald's body when Jack Ruby shot him, Sunday morning, 11:21 A.M., November 24, 1963, at police headquarters, and they are measurably different. Measurably different."

"Is he trying to say aliens from outer space killed Kennedy?" Ben Yutahay asked. He'd been riding with his eyes closed. DeLuca had assumed he was asleep.

"You don't buy it?" DeLuca said.

"I always thought it was the wife," Yutahay said. "It usually is in domestic cases. It sounds kind of Hopi to me. They believe in star-people."

"You're listening to the Ed Clark show, Sea to Shining Sea, *1190 AM, WROZ, out of Roswell, New Mexico,"* the host sang out. *"Back to the show after this. Did you know that interest rates for home equity loans . . ."*

"I listen to this guy sometimes when I'm on patrol at night," Yutahay said. "It can be quite amusing, I have to say. Some of the people who call in are out of their minds. One night a woman called and said the aliens had replaced her husband with someone who was much better, but sleeping with him would have meant she was being unfaithful—what should she do?"

"What'd Ed say?"

"His advice was to go ahead because when they brought her husband back, they'd wipe his memory. She said it wasn't his memory she was worried about, it was hers. People that night thought that was a fairly interesting moral dilemma."

"What was the conclusion?"

"I think people said it wasn't cheating if your lover was in another dimension. Then they started talking about cross-dimensional marriage and polygamy. They were against that."

DeLuca checked his watch. It was too late to give Bonnie a call. They passed a curve in the road where three white crosses staked into the ground, decorated with plastic flowers, marked the spot as dangerous. Yutahay closed his eyes again. DeLuca nudged the volume on the radio down a notch.

"We've got Bartleby in Chloride, New Mexico. You're on the air."

"Hi, Ed—how you doing tonight? Love your show," Bartleby said.

"I'm quite well, quite well indeed," Ed Clark said placidly.

"Listen, I'm just calling to correct the caller before last, Warren from Illinois."

"Yes," Ed Clark said. *"Go ahead."*

"He was saying that the Helstaff site at White Sands was an anti-UFO battery . . ."

"For our listeners," Clark interrupted, *"Helstaff is no relation to Flagstaff. Helstaff is . . ."*

"H-E-L-S-T-F," Bartleby said. *"High-Energy Laser System Test Facility. And calling it 'The Miracle Program' sounds like your caller was missing the acronym there, too. It's not 'M-i-r-a-c-l-e,' as in virgin births or gas for under a dollar fifty a gallon. It's 'M-I-R-A-C-L.' Mid-Infra-Red Advanced Chemical Laser. The Russians were building one in Tajikistan, their version of Helstaff, at a place called Dushanbe, before they ran out of money. At any rate, I doubt that MIRACL or anything ground-based that the Russians have would pose much of a threat to an alien vessel. They can give a sitting unshielded bird in close-earth orbit a pretty good sunburn, but they're not going to do much to the kind of ships you're talking about, assuming they could acquire the target in the first place."*

"I would think any aggression on our part would also invite retaliation," Ed Clark said.

"Well," Bartleby said, *"you might be right, though that's a pretty terrestrial mindset you're talking about. Even supposing that were true, we'd have to pose a much*

more significant threat than we do, at least at present. MIRACL just can't generate enough power to be much more than annoying. Though maybe that posits a terrestrial mindset too."

"How does it work?" Ed Clark asked. *"The MIRACL laser?"*

"Well," the caller said, *"it's basically a megawatt laser with a continuous wavelength between 3.8 and 4.2 microns. You burn* C_2H_4 *ethylene and NF nitrogen fluoride in something like a rocket engine and then catch the excited fluorine atoms and mix them with deuterium in the exhaust cavity to make deuterium-fluoride, stabilized and cooled with helium. The resounder mirrors extract energy in the exhaust cavity and reroute it into a fourteen-square-centimeter beam, which is a nice little bit of directed energy, but the drawbacks are multiple. It takes tons and tons of fuel, it's slow to power, hard to retarget, and it's a sitting duck on the ground. It's just not the weapon of the future that some people say it is."*

"Would that future weapon involve antimatter technologies, then?" Ed Clark asked.

"It would," the caller said. DeLuca felt a bit disappointed. Up to that point, the caller had sounded rather reasonable and informed, but now he was venturing into pure woo-woo land. Antimatter? He thought of the episode of the old *Star Trek*, where the good Captain Kirk somehow slipped into the parallel universe where everyone including Spock was immoral and scheming—was that a sly dig at the Nixon White House at the time?

"Do you know the history of antimatter research?" Ed Clark asked.

"I do," Bartleby said. *"We probably can't really limn it here, but you go back to a colleague of Einstein's named Paul Dirac, who theorized in 1929 that electrons and protons had mirrored counterparts with reversed charges, which he called antielectrons, or positrons, and antiprotons. Those theories were confirmed in 1936 when a Caltech scientist named Carl Anderson saw a positron fly through his lab, and then antiprotons were detected at Berkeley in the fifties, the point being that this is stuff that has been with us and studied for a long time."*

"And the energy potential of antimatter is phenomenal, as I understand it," Clark said.

"Oh yeah," Bartleby said. *"It's maybe ten billion times the power of dynamite. One gram, which is about a fifth of a teaspoon, would equal twenty-three space shuttle fuel tanks as a propellant. As an explosive, fifty millionths of a gram would have been enough to take down the Alfred P. Murrah Federal Building in Oklahoma City—colliding positrons and antielectrons is probably the ultimate energy source in the universe. It's kind of hard to imagine another, but then our imaginations have always limited us, so who knows."*

"And this is a fairly rare substance?" Ed Clark said.

"Antimatter?" Bartleby said. *"Well, it is in this universe, by definition, but in the larger cosmos, there's just as much antimatter as matter, so I guess I'd have to say no, it's not rare. One of the concerns scientists working with this stuff have had has been that a man-made collision of significant size might create a cataclysmic chain reaction in which all the matter in this universe would collide with all the antimatter in the mirrored universe,*

which would mean the largest energy release since the original big bang."

"And me with only four more payments to go on my dinning-room table set," DeLuca said, but now Yutahay really was asleep, snoring softly with his head against the window.

"But that's what they said about splitting the atom," Ed Clark said.

"That's true," Bartleby agreed. *"And thank goodness we didn't listen, or we wouldn't be blessed with the ten-thousand-plus nuclear bombs we have today. They're talking about suitcase nukes today, but tomorrow, we could have antimatter superbombs a thousand times more powerful, the size of maybe a small transistor radio. And the scientists are big on the idea of antimatter bombs because after the initial burst of gamma radiation, there wouldn't be any residual contaminants, so they're thinking of them as 'clean' bombs. It's sort of insane."*

"And what exactly is stopping this technology, at present?" Ed Clark asked. *"I'm assuming, because all indications suggest an alien invasion by the Lizaurian Second Wave some time before 2011, that DARPA and some of the other agencies are proceeding apace . . . ?"*

"Well," Bartleby said, *"DARPA is certainly involved, but most of the research, the black-budget stuff, is going on at the DEL at Kirtland, the Directed Energy Lab, and at the Munitions Directorate at Eglin Air Force Base in Florida, and the NASA Institute for Advanced Concepts in Virginia, and various programs at places like the Institute of Advanced Study at Princeton, and Livermore, MIT, Cornell, Nellis, Wright-Patterson . . ."*

"Area 51?" Clark interrupted.

"Except that Area 51 is like cyberspace," Bartleby said. *"I had a friend that somebody years ago wanted to hire to be their Los Angeles presence on the Internet, and he had to explain to them, there is no Los Angeles in cyberspace. There's no California and no United States either—it's one world now. As for your question as to what's stopping it, the technology always stopped before at creating a perfect penning field, because you obviously can't grab a bit of antimatter and stick it in a glass jar like catching a ladybug. You have to store it in something it can't collide with, which means you have to trap and pen it in an electromagnetic field, but that field has to be perfect or the particles escape, and once you generate it, you have to maintain 100 percent integrity or you lose containment, which means at least a nuclear power source, and maybe something else."*

"And this is being developed to power warp-drives, munitions?" Ed Clark asked. *"Where's the priority right now?"*

"Right now, I couldn't tell you," Bartleby said. *"There was a guy working on an antimatter drive for a trip to Alpha Centauri, a few years ago anyway, but he's a complete idiot. And weapons, yeah, but I think the most attractive application is as a power source for a space-based laser system. And that actually just might work as a weapon to use against alien craft, but as we said earlier, once we become an actual threat, we invite retaliation or more likely preemptive strikes. The Israelis blew up an Iraqi nuclear reactor in 1984 to stop Saddam from developing his nuclear weapons program. My point is that power invites power. Power begets power. Power assimilates and corrupts and coopts the people who de-*

ploy it. Power protects itself. Where it ends is anybody's guess, but the handwriting is on the wall."

"So what you're saying is that the invasion of the Lizaurian Second Wave could come much earlier than 2011 as a preemptive strike?" Ed Clark asked.

"I'm saying the handwriting is on the wall," Bartleby replied. *"I'd personally be more worried about us accidentally shooting ourselves in the foot than any sort of external threat. I'm sure the government encourages people to focus on things like alien invasions instead of what's really going on. When a program reaches a certain size, the only way to conceal it is with disinformation. No offense to your listeners. The problem is that with this kind of power, you can't just shoot yourself in the foot. You'll blow your whole leg off. Metaphorically speaking."*

"Interesting interesting stuff," the host said mellifluously. *"This is Ed Clark,* Sea to Shining Sea, *WROZ 1190 AM from Roswell, New Mexico. When we come back, was Frank Sinatra a Traveler? With that kind of charisma, it's hard to deny, but what does your intuition tell you? But first, is your mattress too firm? Too soft . . . ?"*

DeLuca turned the radio off.

It was crazy, of course, to pay any attention whatsoever to such nonsense. Yet there was something about the way the caller identifying himself as Bartleby spoke that was undeniably credible. He was obviously educated, or at least well read. He wasn't defensive, he didn't name the people who were doubting or persecuting him for his ideas, and he hadn't felt the need to reinforce his statements by naming authorities who believed him or friends who supported him, either, which was how DeLuca usually knew somebody was bullshitting or lying to him.

He made a mental note to have somebody get Ed Clark's call list for him. As strange as it was going to sound, he kept coming back to a single question—where was Cheryl Escavedo going when she vanished, and why was she going there—what did she want? He knew enough now to know she was running from somebody, frightened, smoking cigarettes and watching with binoculars focused at infinity, but at the same time, as far as he could tell, she hadn't left a note for anybody, either in the trailer or in the Jeep. People who thought they were going to die left notes. She believed she was going to be all right. Did she believe in UFOs? If she did, did she believe she was going to meet one? In which case, it didn't matter what DeLuca believed. It only mattered what Cheryl Escavedo might have been thinking. So far, he couldn't tell if she was running away from something or toward something. Or both. Why Shijingshan? Why Qadzi Deh, whatever that was? And why Bob Fowler?

Chapter Seven

DELUCA SENT THE RUBBER BAND WITH THE hair on it and the piece of lightning glass that Marvin Yutahay had found at the site where Cheryl Escavedo disappeared to a pathologist in Boston he knew, a man named Mitchell Pasternak who'd been an assistant to DeLuca's old friend Gillian O'Doherty, who'd served Suffolk County, Boston, as chief coroner and medical examiner for years. Pasternak had taken her place. He was young and cocky, but he could usually back up the claims he made. Gillian had taught him well before she died, killing herself in her lab late one night after discovering she'd accidentally infected herself with weaponized smallpox and realizing that without Biosafety Level 4 protocols and apparatus in place, self-annihilation was the only way to stop the plague that was sure to follow. It was a heroic act of self-sacrifice, though she would have argued that it was just common sense. Pasternak was the one who discovered the body, or what was left of it, a pile of brittle bones inside the alkaline-bath tissue digester her lab used to dispose of animal carcasses. She never liked to leave a mess, even at the weekly poker games she'd been part of, always clearing the bread crumbs from her chip tray and tidying up after everybody else when the game was over. The Army had pathologists and forensic labs at Fort Gillem in Georgia, but they were too slow and tended to get bogged down in paperwork. DeLuca asked Pasternak for a full workup on both pieces of evidence. Before she died, Gillian had left instructions for her assistant telling him that he was to cooperate fully with any requests from her old friend David. She was a thorough woman. DeLuca missed her.

He e-mailed Walter Ford and asked him to find out what he could about Shijingshan, Qadzi Deh, and Bob Fowler—what they might have in common.

Dan Sykes showed up in the Ms. Kitty the next morning with a bruise on his cheek. DeLuca took one look at him and said, "I hope the other guy looks worse."

"Unfortunately, the other guy is a bar stool," Sykes reported. He'd spent the night asking questions at the bar where Theresa Davidova worked, a strip club called Foxies on Central Ave that was a popular hangout for military personnel from Kirtland. A fight had broken out between a group of intoxicated Air Force PJs and a group of Army Rangers who'd made a bet about who could do more pushups with a naked girl on his back. A volunteer from each group had taken the stage, where, each with an accommodating dancer mounted on his shoulders, the competition commenced. The rescue jumper was up to thirty and still going strong when the Ranger collapsed, which didn't surprise Sykes, because the PJs were the guys who trained to fly in and rescue the Navy SEALs and Army Rangers and Green Berets who were too exhausted to rescue themselves. PJs were arguably the fittest people in the military and perhaps the craziest. When the Rangers insisted on weighing the girls to arrive at a figure for most-total-pounds-lifted before paying up, even though the girl riding the PJ was clearly larger, the fight broke out, starting in the bar and spilling into the parking lot.

"I thought you were a black belt in karate," DeLuca said.

"I am," Sykes said. "Opponents, I can take. Bar stools flying through the air that I don't see coming, I'm less effective against."

"Did you learn anything useful?" DeLuca asked.

"I'm not sure," Sykes said. "A couple of the girls who worked there were Russian and none of them had heard anything. There's kind of a sex workers' pipeline running from Russia through Juarez and then El Paso and then here. They knew who Leon Lev is, either personally or by reputation, and they all said he's a nasty piece of shit, but nobody had seen him or any of the goons who work for him in the bar any time lately. I also went over the apartment again and found this," he said, laying a medicine bottle on the table.

"Which is?"

"Prescription allergy medicine," Sykes said. "Theresa's. She didn't take it with her, wherever she went."

"What was she allergic to?" DeLuca asked. "She lived with cats."

"The boyfriend said cats didn't bother her, but most tree and flower pollens did, which was why I thought this was a little odd."

He tossed a Ziploc bag on the table, and in it, a single rose petal, dried out to a deep maroon.

"That's full-sized, probably long-stemmed, maybe two or three weeks old. I found it inside the vacuum cleaner bag, but it was the only one. It wasn't crumpled or broken, and it was one of those Mighty Mite canister vacuums with a lot of power, so it was probably sucked up before it was completely dried out, or it would have crumbled."

"So three or four weeks ago, allowing for the time it was in water, Theresa got one or more long-stemmed red roses, put them in a vase, they dried up, she threw them out but missed a petal and that ended up in the vacuum. Was it her birthday?"

"I don't think they were for her," Sykes said. "That's what's odd—she was allergic to flowers. Truitt didn't give her any. She had admirers at the bar . . ."

"She was just a bartender, right? Did she ever dance?" DeLuca asked. Sykes shook his head.

"Maybe it was a secret admirer, but nobody who knew her would have sent her flowers. So maybe they weren't for her. Maybe they were for Cheryl Escavedo. She got some at work, right? Maybe it was the same bouquet. She would have kept them in her room. So I looked under her bed and behind the end table and guess what I found?"

He produced a second glassine bag with a matching rose petal.

"We'd need a lab test to prove they come from the same plant, but they certainly look like they do," Sykes said. "None of the local florists have any record of making any deliveries to that address in the time frame given."

"I know. I already checked," DeLuca said. "So somebody sent Sergeant Escavedo roses."

"Unless she bought them for herself," Sykes said. "Maybe to cheer herself up."

"But do you buy roses to cheer yourself up?" DeLuca asked. "You buy tulips, or daisies, or carnations. Roses are too loaded with meaning. Maybe."

"Maybe," Sykes said. "I'm talking with the boyfriend later today to ask about it to see what he remembers."

"Good work," DeLuca said.

"We might go back to the strip club to see what we can scare up," Sykes said. "I figured I'd bring the boyfriend in and troll him around to see what happens, but I gotta get a cash advance on the credit card for garter-belt money first."

"Our tax dollars at work," DeLuca said.

Mack and Vasquez were disappointed when Colonel Martine Guzman, of the Chihuahua State Anti-Drug Joint Task Force, asked to reschedule their meeting so that he could fly to Mexico City to meet with the leader of the national antidrug task force and members of the armed forces. Wes Vogel, DeLuca's friend at the ICE, had given them the name of a club across the border that Leon Lev owned but warned them against traveling in Juarez alone, and to stay on Avenida de Juarez if they went and avoid the side streets where *los pandillas* controlled the neighborhoods. They'd posed as newlyweds, but apparently no one believed that young newlyweds would come to Juarez on a honeymoon—that wasn't the kind of tourism the town once called Paso del Norte was known for.

They paid the twenty-five-cent toll and walked across the Rio Grande Bridge on foot. Immediately cab drivers asked them if they wanted to see the *zona roja,* a trip to "Boys Town," perhaps—were they interested in women, or maybe a "donkey show"? The cabbies said they knew of safe bars where the whores specialized in couples and threesomes. *"Te quiero, bonito chocho,"* men hissed to MacKenzie in the one bar where they stopped, a place called The Persian Slipper. *"Eres casi demasiado bonito—cuanto cuestas? Te parece bien por la boca? Hace sexo al estilo Griego?"* She was waiting alone while Vasquez talked to a Nana, the old woman who inspected the men for venereal diseases before they accompanied the girls upstairs to one of the various rooms. Mack pretended she didn't speak Spanish, but when a pair of American sailors approached her in English, she switched to Russian.

"You'd better make an arrangement with the bartender if you want to keep your tits," a girl next to her said in Russian. *"The rest of us tip him five dollars a customer."*

"I told her I was told to talk to Leon, and she said he didn't come in that often but the bartender could help me," Mack reported to DeLuca upon her return to Albuquerque. "I said my friend Theresa Davidova recommended this place and did she know her? She said she didn't. She said Leon didn't like to put too many white girls in one place. It might be our way in. Hoolie could be my pimp."

"Colleen . . ."

"I just got a 5-5 rating at DLI—my Russian is almost native," she said. "And don't tell me it's dangerous. I just spent eleven months in Iraq. I think we know how to take care of ourselves."

"I paid the Nana a hundred dollars and she gave me the whole story," Vasquez said. "I told her I was writing a book on sex tourism. Lev owns two upscale restaurants and a resort in the fancy Condesa District—he lives at the resort, which is more like a private club and spa, but he made his nut running whorehouses, and he still owns something like twenty of them—I wrote down the names. Tia Maria's on Begonias Street. Club Hombre on Martinez. Zoom Zoom on Otumba. Diablo's on Mariscal. Casa Bambinas on Degollado. The Nana didn't know how many girls total, but what she did say was that for the last ten years, he's made more money pushing porn on the Internet than he does in the clubs, and five years ago he got into the film business, and I don't mean adapting Chekhov classics for *Masterpiece Theatre*. Really hardcore stuff, much harder than what used to come out of Mexico. The guy's becoming one of the biggest porn suppliers to Latin America."

"By himself or with somebody?"

"Lev is backed by the Cabrera family, which took over the Mexican cartel after the untimely demise of Amado Carillo Fuentes in Sinaloa-Chihuahua and Jaime Nevares in Durango and the Arellano Felixes in Tijuana. Cipriano Cabrera has God only knows how many politicians in his pocket, and part of what he does for them, in addition to cash, is supply them with girls, which he gets from Lev. Lev was basically a white slave trader for years, right after the Soviet Union fell apart—he'd bring poor Russian and Romanian and Bulgarian girls over, telling them he'd find them work as domestics or temps, and peddle them on the streets."

"The Nana said she made a living looking at dicks but she'd never seen a bigger prick," Mack added. "We figured we'd put out the word that there's a girl from his hometown working the *zona roja*—if that doesn't get his attention, we'll think of something else. The other thing we heard is that Cipriano Cabrera's bodyguards have flooded town and started listening to police scanners and spreading extra threats and bribes around, which is what Cabrera does before he visits in person—he lives in Hermosillo. So something is going down."

"It's some kind of summit meeting, according to what I could pick up," Vasquez said. "Vogel said he'd heard one had been planned. He's got some SIGINT, but they're pretty cagey about what they say on their cell phones. The chatter's been about a wedding, a big party, but nobody knows anybody who's getting married."

"Connect that to Theresa Davidova," DeLuca said.

"I'm not sure it connects," MacKenzie said. "I'm thinking, what if he's put her back to work to pay off the money she owes him? Lev gets the girls for the parties—maybe Theresa is going to be there. I was thinking of saying I used to dance at the bar where she worked in El Paso."

"Just be careful," DeLuca said. "Talk to Dan if you want to know anything about Theresa. And brief me before you do anything, and make sure you get backup from Vogel. He'll know the ropes down there—don't forget what happened to Kiki Camarena," he said, referring to the DEA agent who was tortured and killed by Mexican cartel members in 1985.

He couldn't reach Walter Ford for an update, and there was nothing in his e-mail. Ben Yutahay called to say they'd found a receipt suggesting the trash they'd found near where Cheryl Escavedo had vanished was purchased at a CostCo supermarket in Albuquerque. Brother Antonionus called to say the name of the space ship hovering over Arizona that night was the *Zak-4*. He hoped that was helpful. DeLuca showered and changed before the lecture. He asked Peggy Romano if she wanted to go with him, but she only laughed.

"Sorry, but there's a game between UConn and Duke tonight," she said. "I hate Duke. They're the New York Yankees of college basketball."

He arrived early and found a seat at the back of the auditorium in room 103, Regener Hall, north campus, University of New Mexico, and watched the room fill with college kids, boys in goatees and girls in shirts that exposed their bellies even though it was below freezing outside. Already seated, down front, was a contingent from the Brethren of the Light in full crimson regalia, and seated among them he saw Sami, next to Rainbow, who was talking animatedly, her hands moving in the air above her. DeLuca was pleased when a familiar face appeared in the seat next to him.

"Do you mind," Penelope Burgess said. "I might need to hold your hand if I get too scared." A part of him wouldn't have minded her touch. It wasn't hard to figure out which part of him.

"I didn't think you'd be up for this kind of thing," DeLuca said.

"Unfortunately, it fits loosely under the rubric of what I teach—alien life forms. I don't want my students accusing me of being closed-minded tomorrow."

When the lights came down, the dean of students introduced the speaker, listing his accomplishments. Hilton Jaynes was professor emeritus and holder of the Adler chair in the psychology department at Harvard. He'd won the Pulitzer Prize in 1988 for a book he'd written on early cognition, and numerous other prizes, grants, and awards.

He'd turned his attention to UFOs in the mid-nineties, when he began to interview and study over a hundred subjects who'd reported having one or more abduction experiences. He'd written up his results in a book entitled *Chosen by the Gods,* which became a commercial bestseller and the cause of great controversy in the academic community. The methodology of his work had been gone over with a fine-toothed comb, both by academics at large who disagreed with his conclusions and by his own faculty review board at Harvard, where there was some concern that the old professor had gone off his rocker. After careful review, their conclusion was that he had not, that his methodology and his research were sound, and that his conclusions were drawn from solid scholarship and scientific practice. They were, however, conclusions the psych department found difficult to embrace: that UFOs were real, they'd been visiting earth for a long time, and they would be with us in the future.

"I give you Dr. Hilton Jaynes," the dean concluded.

Jaynes was in his sixties but young-looking and vigorous, dressed in a black turtleneck sweater, gray pants, and black shoes, his white hair combed back and falling over his collar. He seemed like the kind of guy who would be equally comfortable at an academic seminar or at a party at the Playboy mansion. He spoke from memory, with a gentlemanly southern accent.

"At 4:00 A.M. on January the fifth, 2001," he began, "in the town of Millstadt, Illinois, four police officers and a bartender on his way home from a one-night stand with a cocktail waitress all found an arrowhead. The arrowhead was black, triangular, two stories tall and about the size of a football field, and it was floating in the air above the cornfields, moving slowly on a southwesterly course at perhaps fifteen or twenty miles an hour, maybe a thousand feet above the ground. There were three bright lights on it, one at each corner. One of the police officers was a man named Curtis Marshall, and he had a camera on him and tried to take a picture, but it didn't come out very well. The vessel hung in the air for about twenty minutes, then rose and flew off in a northerly direction. Twenty minutes. Five reliable witnesses, four of them officers of the law trained to observe and give testimony. So they filed their reports, the police officers did, sworn to tell the truth, saying just what they saw with their own eyes and experienced with their senses, and I should say two officers were together but the other two were in separated locations. The bartender had stopped by a tree to take a leak. Independent of each other, they all saw the same thing. Described it the same way. Later, one of the officers said it must have been a blimp. Man-made. Recanted his story, but the other four gentlemen stuck to what they'd said originally. Today, the only officer who kept his job is the one who recanted. Two of the police officers were fired and the third was so harassed that he quit. The bartender left town after a series of events, including kids making crop circles in his lawn with an herbicide."

Jaynes took a drink of water. He was a mesmerizing speaker, DeLuca had to admit, with a deep plangent tone to his voice, full of emphasis and dramatic pauses. DeLuca glanced at Penelope Burgess, who seemed bemused.

"What is it in our natures that makes us resist the inexplicable? Where did we lose our capacity for ambiguity? How did this black and white either/or mentality arise, where we make room for that which is literal and visible but have no room in our hearts and, more to the point, in our minds for the unseen and the spiritual? There was a time, early in human evolution, when the gods spoke to us all the time. You study cognitive evolution and you find that way back when, the two halves of the human brain were less integrated, physically less connected, the cerebral cortex much smaller, without half the ganglions we have today, when the right brain, the controlling superego brain, tried to speak to the left brain, the emotional brain, it sounded to us like God talking, a big voice of unimpeachable authority saying, do this, do that, that's right, that's wrong. Nobody knew it wasn't God. And sometimes, the lizard brain back here, the cerebellum, just got scared and started stomping around like Godzilla, crushing every new thought upon arrival—that's what the Godzilla brain is good for, but it's not good for much else. For the most part, we accepted spiritual experiences beyond our ken. Took 'em at face value. A burning bush was God pointing the way. Ezekiel lifted bodily into heaven was just that, a rare occurrence and awe inspiring, no doubt, but we didn't ostracize the folks who were there to witness. Nobody lost their job. Nobody got their lawn trashed. Things from the unseen realm could show up all of a sudden in our physical literal world and it was all right. It was okay.

"Nine years ago, I started interviewing people who said they were abducted by aliens, taken aboard space ships, studied, probed, specimens taken, sperm from the men and eggs from the women, frozen by light and lifted bodily from their beds and cars and homes. I listened to hundred of stories. Young, old, men, women, kids, doctors, farmers, children two and three years old. You can imagine what the Godzilla brains at Harvard thought about that when I began my work . . ."

He stomped around the lectern, imitating Godzilla, to much laughter and applause.

"You gotta admit he's fun," DeLuca said.

"There's a reception afterward if you'd care to be further amused," Burgess whispered back.

Hilton Jaynes spoke for another half hour, offering the proofs to his conclusion, that alien spacecraft had, for a number of years, beginning about the time man first started bouncing radio signals off the stratosphere, been visiting earth, taking human beings bodily into their ships and using them for what appeared to be a breeding program to create a hybrid race, not motivated by any sort of Mars-needs-women mentality but to save the planet Earth, a place that was rapidly and irreversibly despoiling itself. DeLuca couldn't tell how many people in the audience (not dressed in red overalls) were buying it, but the man at the podium had a convincing way about him, and enough charisma to warrant suspicion as a "Traveler," along with Frank Sinatra and Elvis. Jaynes cited five factors that argued against abduction as an endogenous phenomenon produced purely in the psyche: the extreme consistencies from story to story and person to person; the lack of experiential basis for such stories, nothing in the lives of the Chosen to give rise to what they said happened to them; the physical proofs, cuts, lesions, scars, and so forth, following their abductions; the independent observations of spacecraft in the areas where abductions occurred by members of the media and impartial witnesses; and the fact that the phenomenon had been observed by children too young to be aware of the cultural references from which such reported experiences might be falsely drawn.

When he was done, he opened the floor up to questions.

"Dr. Jaynes," a young woman in the third row said, standing as she spoke. "Have you been to the Groom Lake facility at Area 51, and how do you explain the fact that several of the people who worked there later showed up in doctors' offices with evidence of genetic cross-pollination with aliens?"

She sat down.

Jaynes sipped from his water bottle.

"You're talking about the 'Fish People,' I gather?" he said, looking at her and then nodding. "To answer the first part, no, I have not been to Groom Lake. I've driven the length of Alien Alley, Nevada Route 375, and I was brought in the darkness illegally one night to Freedom Ridge by a group of interceptors, after the government closed it off, and we looked through binoculars and night vision goggles, but I didn't see anything remarkable. Saw a delta-winged craft that we now know as the Stealth bomber, but that's old news. As for the so-called 'Fish People,' I believe the scaly skin you're talking about, that's it, is it not? That's what you're referring to? My understanding is, that's been proven to be a kind of epidermal eczema caused by the burning of toxic materials upwind of the facility. I'm good with that explanation. You see, dear, when there is a scientific explanation, I'll take it. It's when science is misapplied or applied unevenly to serve the Godzilla brains that I take umbrage. Yes, sir—you in the back row."

"I'd like to read you some statistics . . ." the young man began.

"Oh-oh," Hilton Jaynes said, to laughter. "There's one in every crowd. Yes, sir. I apologize for interrupting you."

"I'd like to address a comment you made about the lack of common experiential basis," the questioner said, "because you very frequently talk about the lack of any psychological consistencies between the selectees—that their stories have consistency, but there's no one type of person who consistently gets abducted . . ."

"Son, we've gotten identical stories from aboriginal tribesmen in Australia and Inuit people in Canada and a village in Ghana," Jaynes said, "people with widely disparate cultural and experiential circumstances. I've interrupted you again—what is your question?"

"My question is this. I'm referring to the study you're probably aware of done by Bascomb and Halvorsen . . ."

"Yes, yes."

"Where the majority of your test subjects were reinterviewed. Bascomb and Halvorsen compared the statistical probabilities of abductee personality types against the general population. So let me give you and the audience the statistics. Sixty-six percent of the abductees had imaginary friends as children, against 12 percent in the general population. Nearly 100 percent were susceptible to hypnosis, which you used during your own interviews, though only about 30 percent of the general population is thought to be susceptible. Seventy-six percent said that at some time in their lives, they'd heard voices or things talking to them, against 7 percent general. Eighty-three percent claimed to have had psychic experiences, premonitions, telepathic experiences, and so on. Eighty-eight percent had what they described as 'out-of-body' experiences, either floating sensations or full astral projections.

Ninety-two percent said they'd sleepwalked or had waking dreams, night terrors, hallucinations. Half said they been communicated with by some kind of spirit or higher intelligence, and about three-quarters said they'd seen ghosts. In all of these aspects, the rate for the general population is between 10 and 15 percent. So my question is, how can you claim there is no consistent psychological type of abductee, when statistically it seems pretty clear they are all quite prone to fantasy, as it's been historically regarded by the psychological community?"

Jaynes paused, smiling at his accuser.

"I'll bet you were up all night working on that one," Jaynes said, drawing more laughter. "No, no, people, don't laugh. This young man has a very good point. A very good point. I would take issue with some of his numbers, but let's assume that in general he's right. He has a valid point, but he's nevertheless missing mine. Let me give you one more statistic, sir. You wanna know what's going on in the sky, maybe we should talk to the people who live in the sky, who work there. Four years ago, there was a survey of airplane pilots. Done at Columbia University by a man named Jacobs, if you want to check his work. He asked over a thousand pilots whether or not they'd ever seen any unidentified flying objects, but he gave them two ways to answer. One was anonymously, the other wasn't. In the one that wasn't anonymous, 2 percent said they'd seen UFOs. In the one that was, 54 percent said they had. I've been standing up here talking about the difference between the people who are open to the unseen and people who aren't. We know what happened to those police officers in Millstadt, Illinois, and I think you know what would happen to an airplane pilot who said he saw a flying saucer, don't you, son? The selectees who came forward to speak with me were the selectees who had indeed already exhibited receptivity to the unexplained and were comfortable with a higher level of ambiguity. It can be statistically proven that I have only spoken with a very small percentage, just the tip of the iceberg, because the vast majority of the Chosen aren't going to come forward now, are they? Years ago we thought child abuse was rare, until people started coming forward and we find out that sadly, it's not so rare at all. There is much we do not speak of. Just as there is much we do not know. My message is that we must be open to the mystery if we are ever to penetrate it."

He fielded a few more softball questions and then thanked his hosts. Penelope Burgess said his speaking fee was seventy-five hundred dollars—she hoped the students got something out of it. DeLuca caught sight again of Sami. Apparently Brother Antonionus had stayed home.

"So what'd you think?" DeLuca asked her.

"I think it's significant that the funds to pay for this are coming out of the student entertainment budget," Burgess said. "Some people were upset that they gave him a room in the science building, but he's still a Harvard psychologist."

"So what'd you think?" DeLuca repeated.

"I think I want to flatten Tokyo," she said. "Wanna go down and meet him? I'm skipping the reception."

They made their way to the stage, where Jaynes was surrounded by people asking him to sign their copies of his book. Three were dressed as *Star Trek* characters, and another wore an alien Halloween mask. It seemed fairly clear, by the way Jaynes hugged two of the Brethren of the Light members, that they knew each other already. When Penelope Burgess introduced herself, his eyes lit up and he told her he'd read the last three papers she'd published and was interested in reading more—the idea of measuring extraterrestrial life fascinated him—would she be interested in having lunch? She politely begged off, but he seemed sincere and earnest in his praise. She introduced DeLuca as her date, though it was DeLuca's impression she'd used the word *date* to let Hilton Jaynes know she wasn't interested in him the way the three flirty coeds standing next to her evidently were. Judging by the way Jaynes smiled at them, it seemed equally evident that despite his advanced age, he probably didn't have much trouble scoring groupies.

"How are you, sir?" Jaynes said, shaking his hand. "Thank you for coming."

"What do you make of the Brethren of the Light?" DeLuca asked him in his friendliest voice. "I'm guessing it's not unusual for such groups to attend your lectures."

"Not unusual at all, Mr. DeLuca," Jaynes said. "All are welcome. What do I think of my more eccentric fans? Sir, I grew up in a little town called Falling Waters, West Virginia, right on the Potomac—the Winchester and Western Railroad ran through my backyard, and later my father moved us about forty miles northeast, to the town of Gettysburg, Pennsylvania. And you know what happened there. My whole life, I saw crazy men dressing up in costumes to reenact all the various battles from the War of Northern Aggression. I recall a friend of my father's who cut up a wool bath mat to make a vest and splashed battery acid on a pair of gray work pants from Sears to affect the tattered and scruffy look of a true Johnny Reb, and he used to stand in his backyard, practicing his rebel yell, prior to the reenactments he attended. Ended up shooting his own hand off with a cannon he tried to build from a section of sewer pipe. Thought he was channeling the spirit of his great-grandfather. Believed that with all his heart. I have seen men inspired to the point where they behave quite foolishly, but that doesn't mean the Civil War didn't happen now, does it? That answer your question?"

"That pretends to answer the question, but actually it evades it," DeLuca said. "I was asking something quite specific."

"Well, in that case," Jaynes said, "I shall have to recuse myself, because Malcolm Percy was a classmate of mine at Yale, and a fellow Bonesman. A few years behind me, so I cannot say that I knew him. He was recently voted the second most embarrassing Bonesman in the history of the organization. I'll leave it to your imagination to guess who the most embarrassing one might be. Goodnight, Mr. DeLuca."

Jaynes was swallowed up by groupies as he made his way toward the door. Penelope Burgess said she had papers to grade but would love a drink first and wouldn't mind company. DeLuca wasn't sure what kind of hint that was, but he scratched his nose, just in case, long enough for her to see his wedding ring, just in case she was interested, and then said he needed to get back to his motel.

"No luck finding Ms. Escavedo?" Burgess asked.

"Nothing so far," he said. "Oh, yeah—does the name 'Bartleby' mean anything to you?"

"Bartleby?" she said. "Wasn't that a wine cooler?"

"You're thinking of Bartles and Jaymes," DeLuca said.

"Bartleby," she repeated. "I can't think of anything. I remember a short story I read in college called that, but don't ask me to remember any more than that. Why?"

"Just a name that came up earlier," he said. "Probably not important."

He excused himself and made his way across the room, to where the woman who'd washed his car the day before was standing, her back to him.

"Hello, Rainbow," DeLuca said. "How are you? David DeLuca—we spoke at the mansion."

"Oh, yes," she said, as if she suddenly remembered. "How are you?"

"David DeLuca," he said, extending his hand to Sami.

"This is Sami," Rainbow said. "He's an initiate and that means he has to observe seventy-two hours of silence, but I'm sure he's pleased to meet you."

DeLuca shot Sami a look, then turned to Rainbow.

"I was worried about your daughter," he said. "Ruby?"

"Oh, that," she said, "oh, no, don't worry, Ruby's fine. She was just with a friend but she's great. We're not allowed to use cell phones or she would have called. Anyway, thank you. Have a great evening."

Brief eye contact with Sami told him the things Rainbow had just said were not true.

An hour later, he was back at the motel. He'd pounded down a Whopper and fries (wondering why on an unlimited expense account he wasn't able to eat better), showered, and was standing on the balcony when the phone rang. It was Dan Sykes, wondering how the lecture had gone. DeLuca did his best to summarize. Sykes hadn't learned much at Foxies, other than that there was an awful lot of what he thought was illegal contact during the lap dances, with the owners and bouncers looking the other way.

"Going from there to prostitution doesn't seem like that big a leap," Sykes said. "Or vice versa, I suppose."

"You were an English major at Stanford, right?" DeLuca asked. "Do you remember a short story called 'Bartleby'?"

"'Bartleby the Scrivener,'" Sykes said. "Herman Melville. Why?"

"What's it about?"

"Dammit," Sykes said. "I knew there was going to be a test someday."

"Just in general," DeLuca said.

"As I recall, it's about a guy who hates his job," Sykes said. "I think he works for an insurance agency, or maybe it's accounting, doing something really mindless, anyway, and his boss is a dick, so one day when the guy tells him what to do, Bartleby says, 'I would prefer not to,' and then when they ask him to explain, he says it again, 'I would prefer not to.' That's all he says to anybody about anything, like the raven in the Edgar Allan Poe poem that says 'Nevermore.'"

"And what happens to Bartleby?" DeLuca asked.

"I think he starves to death or something," Dan Sykes said. "They ask him if he wants to eat and he says, 'I would prefer not to.'"

"Why?"

"I don't know," Sykes said. "It was symbolic for the Industrial Revolution or something. I could have that all wrong. It wasn't one of my better classes."

"See you in the morning."

He needed sleep, but he wasn't tired yet. He knew he would be soon. He looked at his watch. Again, it was too late to call his wife. He picked up a pair of binoculars he'd packed for the trip, cheap 10 x 25 Bushnells he'd bought years ago to watch Patriots games at Foxboro from the nosebleed section, and stared at the horizon. He watched an airplane lift off from Kirtland, then turned his glasses skyward. Even in the wash of city lights, the magnification afforded by a simple pair of binoculars filled the night with stars. With his naked eye, he found Orion's belt, vaguely recalling that one of them was the star Rigel. He stared at Orion's belt. Just below the buckle, he saw a smaller star, more reddish in color than the others. He watched it for a few seconds.

Then it blinked out and disappeared.

He checked with his naked eye, then again with his binoculars, but it was gone.

He was no expert, but he was pretty sure that wasn't supposed to happen.

Chapter Eight

"DELUCA RESIDENCE, SCOTT SPEAKING," THE voice on the phone said.

"You're back," DeLuca said. "How was your flight? How's Kirkuk? How's IMINT?"

"Hey, Dad," Scott said. "The flight was good. Nine-hour layover in Germany. Kirkuk still sucks. Image intelligence is still up in the air."

"Ha ha. How long are you home for?"

"I have a month. Me and some buddies were going up to Stratton for a week, but other than that, no plans. How's Arizona?"

"I'm in Albuquerque right now," DeLuca said. "We're making progress."

"You want me to get Mom?"

"In a minute," DeLuca said. "I had a favor to ask—can you access your files from home? I mean, from our house?"

"I could, but I didn't even bring a laptop . . ."

"You could use the computer in my study."

"Dial-up or DSL?"

"DSL. But you're going to need my password. BonnieBunny. One word, capital B's."

"BonnieBunny?" Scott said. "Your password is *BonnieBunny*?"

"Just do it."

"Hang on—I'm walking to your study. What am I looking for?"

"I need to know what satellites were flying over Albuquerque last night around midnight. I can tell you exactly where I was looking. I think I saw something."

"You saw something?" Scott said. "What did you see? Flying saucers?"

DeLuca explained what he'd seen, a star, or so he thought, that suddenly blinked off, maybe at about five o'clock on the dial, if the center of the clock was the middle star in Orion's belt, at a distance of about a thumb's width, if you held your hand at arm's length.

"It went black?" Scottie said. "You're sure it wasn't an airplane? Maybe it was just testing its landing lights."

"I'm sure it was something like that," DeLuca said. "I just want to know what I saw. Satellites, airplanes, UAVs, whatever. Can you do it?"

"I'm going to have to go to a couple of different places, but yeah, I probably can," Scott said. "I'm more used to looking down than looking up. Knowing where to look is going to help narrow things down. You're sure of the time and location?"

"Zero zero zero three hundred hours, a thumb from Orion's buckle toward five o'clock."

"Gotcha. I'll have to call you back."

"Let me give you a new number to call . . ."

He talked to his wife, though all he'd been allowed to tell her was that it was a missing person mission, and all he could tell her now was that the person was still missing. He didn't know how much longer he'd be. She told him what was going on in her life, and they talked about domestic things, how the guy who plowed the driveway had broken the curb and didn't want to pay for it, and how she thought the guy who delivered the fuel oil was pissed at them because they'd been so late paying the bill. His friend Doc had called, she said. She asked about Sami, whose ex-wife, Carolyn, was Bonnie's friend. Between feeling distracted and all the things he couldn't say for security reasons, the conversations they had when he was away on a mission were rarely satisfying. When she said it was currently snowing in Boston, he suggested that when his mission was over, maybe she'd like to fly down to Tucson for some warm weather. She said that might be nice.

When he called Walter, Walter's wife Martha answered. Walter was out fetching an armload of firewood. He told DeLuca, when he came to the phone, that he had some files to e-mail him.

"Maybe you could give me a summary," DeLuca said. "I'll read the reports later."

"I could do that," Ford said in his usual methodical manner. "Where would you like to start?"

"How about the partially burned printouts we found in the wood stove?" DeLuca said.

"Okay," Ford said. "Shijingshan, first, is an industrial district in the western suburbs of Beijing. Mostly light manufacturing. Some high tech."

"Military or defense industry?"

"Not to any great extent. It's also the center of China's entertainment industry. Or trying to be."

"Anything significant happen there in the last week or so?"

"I have a Chinese student who was online reading the Shijingshan papers," Ford said. "She said other than a small earthquake, things have been pretty quiet."

"An earthquake?"

"Yeah," Ford said. "Took out a bootleg DVD factory. Minimal damage."

"How about Qadzi Deh?"

"That's the name of a glacier in the Hindu Kush mountain range, on the border between Afghanistan and Pakistan. Near Noshaq peak, the second-highest mountain in Afghanistan. Over twenty-four thousand feet. Not much turned up when I Googled, but I found something interesting on SIPERNET. Did you know a CI agent named Frank Pickett?"

"I met him once," DeLuca said. "I couldn't say I know him."

"The glacier is in the FATA or Federally Administered Tribal Areas. That's the lawless part on the border where they think Bin Laden is hiding. Pickett was working with a group of Talibani and Al Qaeda guys, posing as a Russian arms merchant. They were crossing the glacier, for whatever reason, when they had an accident and fell into a ravine or something. I guess there were these big cracks in the ice that got bridged over with snow, but when they put their weight on it, it collapsed. They weren't roped together or anything. Apparently it's fairly common."

"These were guys who were used to living in the mountains and walking around on glaciers, though, wouldn't you say?" DeLuca said. "Seems a little odd that they'd step in a hole."

"Beats me," Ford said. "I guess. All that was left was a mule. They had guys on the ground looking around, and they said it was an accident. I'll forward you the report. How any of this connects to Bob Fowler, I have no idea."

"From New Jersey, right?"

"Yup," Ford said. "One of the leading liberals on the House Armed Services Committee. Big opponent of Space Defense. Which is what this is about, right?"

"It is. I'll call his office," DeLuca said. "Moving on. How about 'girls disappearing in the desert,' for a hundred, Alex?"

"Yuma to El Paso," Ford said. "I could extend to Tijuana if you want. It's not a nice picture. It's also not possible to get hard numbers, on either side of the border. Before 1986, the numbers weren't good but they were steady. You had six a year in the Yuma area, about the same in Douglas and Nogales, and about twenty a year in the Juarez area. The numbers jump in '86 . . ."

"The year Congress banned antisatellite testing," DeLuca interjected.

"Okay," Ford said. "That didn't turn up in the research we were doing. Nineteen eighty-six was when the Cali cartel started moving drugs across the border. Hang on—I just found my notes. A Colombian named Miguel Rodriguez Orejuela, and he started dealing with the big Mexican guy, Amado Carillo Fuentes, who coordinated the Meraz and Quintero and Felix families. Anyway, the Mexicans had been mostly laundering money for the Colombians, but I guess starting in 1986, the Colombians trusted the Mexicans enough to let them move product, in a number of ways, but one was using mules, meaning women with condoms full of cocaine hidden in their body cavities. The Mexicans knew how to move marijuana, prior to this. So anyway, the numbers jump, across the board, by an average of maybe 15 percent. Some of the mules died when the condoms broke and some were shot and robbed. The numbers jump again after 1994, when the North American Free Trade Agreement was ratified and American companies started building *maquilas* just across the border, mostly around Tijuana and Juarez, meaning more potential victims. A lot of naïve country girls coming up from the south to put televisions together and what have you."

"I read about that," DeLuca said.

"It's hard to talk about women who disappear because there are so many illegal immigrants who cross the border and immediately hide from the authorities, so the fact that nobody hears from them doesn't mean they've been murdered. It's a lot of guessing, based on the number of bodies found and estimated numbers of victims not found. And there aren't any good numbers south of the border, where the police activity is considerably less than it is north of the border, which may not be a bad thing—the Mexican police are probably responsible for a certain percentage of the *desaparecides,* either because they've been paid off by the cartels to do their dirty work or because they're still technically fighting on the right side of the drug wars but using the same methods to fight fire with fire—there are all kinds of stories of people, men and women both, taken into custody by the Mexican police and turning up in the desert dead a month later. I wouldn't trust a Mexican cop with a nickel unless I had to."

"So what's the best guess?" DeLuca asked.

"Both sides of the border, Yuma to El Paso, in 1994, about two hundred women a year, and ten years later, about 850 a year. And the numbers cluster around Juarez, partly because there's a serial killer working there, killing hookers and factory girls—they arrested a bus driver, but he's not the guy. Maybe 370 women, they think, since 1997. I talked to a guy at Interpol who said there isn't a more corrupt city on earth than Juarez, and that includes places like Lagos, Nigeria, and all the other banana republics. I'm giving you just the low estimates. You can double those numbers to get the high estimates."

"What about the Spirit Mountain area?" DeLuca asked.

"That's actually one of the safer areas," Ford said. "Maybe because there's nothing there."

"What about General Thomas Koenig?" DeLuca asked. "Or Major Brent Huston? What did you find out?"

"Both of 'em are a piece of work, I can tell you that much," Ford said.

"Start with Koenig."

"Family seafaring credentials go back to the whaling days. Great-grandfather admiral George Koenig captained an American submarine in World War I and later an aircraft carrier and eventually headed the Naval Academy at Annapolis. His son, Thomas Koenig's grandfather, was Admiral Edwin G. Koenig, who was chief of naval operations during World War II. I thought this was interesting—the guy commanded more men than Eisenhower and MacArthur combined and nobody remembers him, probably because he was such an asshole. A mean drunk, off duty, liked to punish innocent subordinate officers to set an example for the others, used to grope the thighs of officers' wives under the table at dinner parties, court-martialed the captain of the USS *Indianapolis* after it sank and nobody came to the rescue because the Navy needed a scapegoat, let his friend Kimmel hang for Pearl Harbor, worked a member of his staff to death, literally, guy had a stress-related heart attack, but instead of lightening the load or increasing his staff, he posted a doctor to stand by for the next heart attack. I remember hearing stories about the guy. Usually in the Navy, if they like you, they name ships and bases after you. This guy never got a thing named after him, and he commanded two million men, the biggest naval fleet in the history of the world."

"Sounds like the guy Koenig inherited his personality from," DeLuca said.

"Could be," Walter Ford said. "Though I'm not so sure it skipped a generation. Koenig's old man was Rear Admiral Edwin Koenig, Jr., but that was a tombstone promotion. I stand corrected—Grandpa did have something named after him. Ed Junior commanded the USS *Hollander* during the Vietnam War, aircraft carrier, and wore the medal proudly when his ship won a unit citation, except that he was no longer captain when they won it, so somebody caught him wearing a medal he didn't deserve. Turned out he was wearing three others he didn't deserve, including a Purple Heart he awarded himself when his ship hit a mine that made him spill his coffee in his lap."

"If an old lady can sue McDonald's for six million dollars over spilled coffee, why can't a guy get a Purple Heart?" DeLuca said.

"Stella Liebeck," Ford said. DeLuca was always surprised by his friend's memory. "Anyway, when they caught him at it, he denied it, and when they proved it, he ate his gun. Little Tommy had been accepted at Annapolis. He'd gone to a military prep school called Decatur Academy, where they pretend they're in the Navy instead of those schools where they pretend they're in the Army . . ."

"Like VMI."

"I guess," Ford said. "Anyway, that's where he was when he heard his old man had killed himself. After the way the Navy treated his old man, which was actually a lot fairer than his grandfather ever treated anybody, he switched to West Point and graduated first in his class. Supposedly he's got a wicked high IQ. Anyway, from there on, his record gets a bit murky. He was ordered to get counseling at West Point but there's no record of who he saw or why. His official 201 doesn't mention it. One of his classmates I spoke to said he probably had an anger management problem because of a couple of fights he was in. He said the chip on the guy's shoulder wouldn't fit under his uniform. My kids sifted through a whole bunch of stuff and found his name on a few documents and so on. We're trying to piece together a time line. He made major at the Pentagon, 1979, working at the DIA, mostly in Iran, and colonel when they posted him to be the military attaché to the U.S. embassy in Berlin, 1980–82, then Moscow, 1982–88, where his job was to debug the building and make the computer system there 100 percent secure. You can probably imagine what that involved, with encryption codes and protocols and whatnot, but what they tell me is that he didn't just lead the team—he made himself into a first-class software engineer. Microsoft offered him a job as vice president and a pile of dough but he turned them down. He went from Moscow to NATO and tried to get a combat command during Gulf One, but I gather by then they had him labeled a techie, so he didn't get it. I talked to a woman who worked in the secretarial pool for him who said he was not at all happy about that. Then Space Command and then STRATCOM, first in Nebraska at Offutt and then at Cheyenne. The details are in the report."

"What's your gut say about him?" DeLuca asked.

"My gut says he's still got a chip on his shoulder bigger than the mountain he works in," Ford replied. "Over the years, there've been four campaigns, letter writing and lobbying the secretary of the Navy and so on, to get a ship named after his grandfather, and two to have the charges against his father reversed. The general himself isn't connected to any of them, because that would be unseemly—you're supposed to grab your ankles and take it like a man—but if you dig a little deeper, you find they were all started by guys Koenig went to prep school with. What are the odds of that? You know he put 'em up to it."

"Could you get me a list of all his classmates?" DeLuca said.

"Can do," Ford said. "Want to know about your Major Brent Huston?"

"Sure," DeLuca said. "I've already got the ultraconservative Baptist part, if you want to skip that."

"I don't know if you've got it in full," Ford said. "Like for instance, when he was eleven years old, he was the victim of an exorcism. Or not the victim—the beneficiary, I guess. His parents thought he had demons. Turned out he was having epileptic seizures, but they insisted it was demons."

"Did they stop?"

"I don't know," Ford said. "They stopped talking about it. The Army put him on antiseizure meds. He originally wanted to go Air Force but the seizures disqualified him from ever flying in anything. He met Koenig in Moscow, and followed him to NATO and then STRATCOM. The other weird thing was that when he was in Nebraska, he asked a junior officer if he'd care to come to church with him to worship, and the guy was Jewish, from New York, but he figured he'd score a few points and humor the boss, so he went, and Huston started speaking in tongues. I guess he was trying to convert the Jew or something, make a big impression on him, but the Jewish guy wrote up a report that Huston had lost his mind, and there were other officers who didn't care for Huston's holier-than-thou attitude who tried to get him chaptered out on a psych charge, until Koenig himself stepped in and went to bat for him."

"And he was doing the same work as Koenig?" DeLuca said.

"Computer security," Ford said. "Cracking the God Paradox, aptly enough."

"Which is?"

"Can God create a problem bigger than He Himself can solve?" Ford said. "In human terms, the question is, is the mind capable of creating a code that it can't itself crack, because until it does, you're never going to get complete security. I read a report that said Koenig's team solved it, with random number generators and things like that. Of course, you still have the Brink's problem."

"Which is?"

"Most armored cars get robbed from the inside," Ford said. "A security code is only as good as the people who write it. Somebody could always put in a trap door or a Trojan horse or a time bomb or an event portal of some kind, same way a locksmith can always make himself an extra set of keys. The way around that is to use more than one locksmith. Divide it up, get three or four teams to each write a discrete part of the code, and no one team knows what the other teams are doing. Your General Koenig didn't do that because he wanted it all under one roof. His."

"And?"

"Maybe it's nothing. It's just that most security codes set up firewalls to stop people from outside getting in. There are internal surveillance programs, but, you know, there are ways around everything. You can disable the surveillance once you're in, but if you start out already inside the firewall, you can work behind the wall. Or you set it up to keep sending false positives while you go about your business. A lot of things can happen once the barbarians are inside the gates. You can run a doubler program that says you're in one place when you're in another, cyberspace-wise. Any number of things. There's a printout I put together for my computer fraud class that I included in what I sent you."

"I appreciate it," DeLuca said. "Did you turn this into another class assignment?"

"Naw, but I asked a couple of graduate students to check into it," Ford said. "I came up with another connection you might be interested in."

"Which is?"

"I ran the name Leon Lev through the system, but all SIPERNET gave me was ties to some Albanian hoods running a bunch of Italian restaurants in New York City, so I called our friend Mike O'Leary at the Bureau. He said there was a KGB goon named Leon Lev who worked out of the Moscow directorate in the eighties. Remember that Marine guard at the U.S. embassy who got caught bonking a Russian woman who turned out to be a spy, back in 1984? Lev was the guy who hooked them up. They used to call that a 'honey trap.' I don't know if that's what they still call it, but apparently that was his job, and his boss was Vitaly Sergelin."

"The Russian oil bazillionaire?"

"Now, but then, he was one of the top guys in the KGB. A colonel. He and Putin were like Hope and Crosby, and his whole deal was trying to crack the U.S. embassy."

"So he and Koenig would have known each other," DeLuca said.

"I don't know if they *knew* each other, but they would have known *of* each other," Ford said. "After perestroika and all that, when the Soviet Union fell apart and there was a big scramble to privatize what used to be industries controlled by the state, there was a major power grab for the oil business, and Sergelin came out on top, but not without a number of horseheads in the beds and various people not-so-mysteriously disappearing, and O'Leary said Lev was Sergelin's main boy, until he had to more or less split town when he started leaving too many bodies around. O'Leary said they lost track of Lev after 1996 or so. Do you know what he's doing now?"

"Apparently he owns a number of whorehouses in Juarez," DeLuca said.

"Well," Ford said, "you know what they say about the cream rising to the top."

"Or the scum sinking to the bottom," DeLuca said.

"Scum would actually be on the top, too," Ford said. "Sludge would sink to the bottom."

"That must be why it's so hard to tell the cream and the scum apart," DeLuca conceded.

* * *

DeLuca wondered if it was purely a coincidence when, half an hour later, his phone rang.

"Lieutenant Carr calling for General Koenig—will you hold?" the voice on the phone said. Nothing about, "Are you in the middle of something right now?" But then, generals rarely asked if they were interrupting anything. Something about Carr had rubbed him the wrong way from the first time he'd met him at Cheyenne Mountain. He'd struck Dan Sykes the wrong way, too, literally, defeating him at an intraservice full-contact karate tournament a year earlier when Dan had failed to wipe the sanctimonious smirk off Carr's face, too eager, Sykes admitted, for the opportunity to hit an officer. DeLuca waited. When Koenig came on the line, his tone was oddly solicitous.

"Agent DeLuca," he said. "Glad I caught you. I had a briefing with General LeDoux. *Er sagt daß Sie pflegten in Deutschland als Übersetzer zu arbeiten.*"

"Not exactly as a translator," DeLuca said. "We worked at a listening station on the border. Near Mannheim. You were in Berlin, as I understand."

"Es war alles soviel einfachere, als wir wußten, wem der Feind war und wo er lebte, nicht war?" "It was all so much simpler when we knew who the enemy was and where he lived, wasn't it?" the general had asked. "Listen, I wanted to hear where you are with this. As you now understand, there were things I wasn't permitted to speak to you about when we met at The Mountain. Now that you're read on, I wanted to follow up and see if there was anything else you needed to ask me."

"I appreciate that, sir," DeLuca said. The question was, did Koenig want to give DeLuca information, or was he trying to get information from DeLuca? Counterintelligence agents were the only members of the military permitted by the Army's own justice code to mislead or lie to a superior officer as part of an investigation, which was part of why officers hated talking to CI agents. It was DeLuca's understanding that he was under no obligation to keep Koenig informed, no matter how much interest Koenig showed. His reports went to LeDoux, who was free to disseminate them however he chose. It was possible that Koenig's offer was to be taken at face value. It was also possible that a game of chess had begun, and it was DeLuca's move.

"I do have some questions," DeLuca said. "My first would be what information you think Sergeant Escavedo might have copied. You said before that she might have been taking work home. I gather you don't think that now. Colonel Oswald said there was Darkstar data that was accidentally archived. Who was responsible for that?"

"Unfortunately," Koenig said, "no one was responsible, unless you want to blame the people who wrote the program that automatically sorted the data for storage, in which case, since I headed the unit that wrote the codes, I'm responsible. I'm not going to make a scapegoat out of anybody who worked for me, Agent DeLuca. If you need to put that in your report, please feel free to do so."

"I don't see where that's going to be necessary," DeLuca said. "So it was an automated data dump that she caught—did she catch it *because* it was in error?"

"We think so," Koenig said. "Major Huston tells me she probably found the file and thought, 'What's this doing here?' And then looked in it, like any good soldier would. The mistake was where it was sent, because apparently it hadn't been encoded properly. She shouldn't have been able to open the file."

"And what was in it?"

"Well," Koenig said, "we're not entirely sure, other than that it had been sealed in October of 1990, so it wouldn't have been anything terribly current. We think it might have been the specs on a prototype we were test-bedding that actually never worked, so the danger of that leaking could be described as minimal. That specific data. But the fact of the program itself is one we're still shutting down. My fear, and Major Huston's, is that Sergeant Escavedo may have had some contact with former Soviet assets."

Again, DeLuca wanted to take the general's statement at face value. At the same time, one of the most obvious tells, interrogating a suspect, was when the suspect tried to cast suspicion on someone else. People who were truly innocent rarely had any idea who might be guilty, whereas people who were guilty always had a reason to divert suspicion.

"Were you aware that Sergeant Escavedo had a Russian roommate?" Koenig said. "A woman of questionable virtue, as they were once described."

"I was aware of that," DeLuca said, wondering if he should be admitting as much. "They met through a sign posted on a laundromat wall, apparently."

"And you believe that?" Koenig said.

"I'm looking into it," DeLuca said. "Why was Escavedo transferred to the MEPS center in Albuquerque? Up to that point her service record appeared to be outstanding."

"Two reasons," Koenig said. "According to Major Huston, he was afraid Sergeant Escavedo was developing a drinking problem. He'd found an empty bottle of vodka in her desk. We have zero tolerance for substance abuse at CMAF. The other reason was the rumors surrounding her about her sexuality. My personal opinions about don't-ask/don't-tell are irrelevant here, by the way. As you've seen from the photographs, Sergeant Escavedo was an attractive human being. When some of the men in The Mountain learned that she was gay, they expressed a great degree of discomfort, working with her. You can sit there and tell me that they weren't mature or politically correct or whatever you want, but things inside The Mountain are different from things outside The Mountain. If it was Lackland or Kirtland or Peterson or anywhere else where people didn't work in such close quarters, it might not have made a bit of difference. The mentality inside The Mountain is more like a submarine than anything else. Discomfort means people can't do their jobs. We just lost a lieutenant named Reznick who decided to make an issue of it—what people do with their private lives is their business and none of mine, but when it compromises the security of this nation by causing problems at STRATCOM, we put a stop to it. They can resolve these things however they want, in the courts or in the media, that's up to them, but inside The Mountain, anything that compromises efficiency has to be dealt with promptly."

DeLuca recalled that Major Huston had specifically said Escavedo didn't have a drinking problem. Perhaps he'd chosen not to reveal that, the first time DeLuca had asked, but if so, why not?

"To me, it's a matter of family values," DeLuca said. "If those people wanted to all go live on an island somewhere, I'd be the first to buy them a ticket, and if they want to serve their country, that's fine, too, but if they want to flaunt their lifestyle in front of my children, that's a whole different issue." This was, in fact, entirely the opposite of DeLuca's actual personal view, but he wanted to see what Koenig said.

"I'm looking at a picture of my kids right now," Koenig said, "and I couldn't agree with you more."

DeLuca didn't have to check his notes—he recalled, quite clearly, that General Koenig's office inside The Mountain did not contain any family photographs, something he'd found odd at the time. Koenig's screen saver was a picture of a windswept beach, and it hadn't scrolled through a gallery of photographs, the way some computers did. Every computer screen DeLuca had seen in Iraq had pictures of kids as screen savers. DeLuca had thought it odd that Koenig didn't have any pictures of his family in his office. But perhaps Koenig was calling from his office at Peterson.

"How's the weather there, by the way?" DeLuca asked.

"It was snowing, last I checked, but I've been at CMAF since this morning, so I don't really know," Koenig said. That answered that.

"Do you ski, General?" DeLuca asked. Joyce Reznick (who was probably cleaning latrines at a post somewhere in the Aleutians right now) had said Escavedo had gone skiing with an older man who owned a house. DeLuca was fishing, but the more lines you had in the water, the more likely you were to catch something.

"Haven't the time," Koenig said, clearly growing irritated at the small talk and struggling to remain cordial. Evidently DeLuca's good opinion mattered to him, now.

It hadn't before. "We have a house in Aspen, but we never get there."

"So what do you think happened to Darkstar1?" DeLuca asked. "Or Darkstar2, for that matter?"

"I think it's dead," Koenig said. "For the same reason that Darkstar2 went black. Right now we're looking back at launches from former Soviet assets. That was where I was going when I told you Escavedo had Russian contacts. Personally it's my belief that both D1 and D2 were taken out by Russian ASATs, before they became operational. I don't know how they knew what to target, but they had more ASAT capabilities than anyone else, second to us, and plenty of reasons to not want Darkstar to become operational. You can take all the conspiracy theories I've been hearing and shove 'em all—the simplest explanation is usually the correct one. It's a fight for the high ground."

"Are you thinking it was a tactical laser?" DeLuca asked. "'When we lose a satellite, we look for hosings first, kill vehicles or kinetics second, and full power directed-energy last.' Your own words, sir."

"Probably," Koenig said.

"We recovered three scraps of paper from a wood stove that Escavedo apparently tried to burn," DeLuca said. "Three different subjects. Shijingshan, Qadzi Deh, and Congressman Bob Fowler. Mean anything to you?"

"Fowler is on the House Armed Services Committee," Koenig said. "What were the other two?"

"Shijingshan is a suburb of Beijing. Qadzi Deh is a glacier on the Afghanistan-Pakistan border," DeLuca said.

"Nothing rings a bell," Koenig said. "Would you like me to look into it?"

"That's all right," DeLuca said. "I just wondered if you had any projects regarding any of the above."

"Negative," Koenig said.

"What about Vitaly Sergelin?" DeLuca asked. "You think it's the Russians. Is it possible that he's connected? Or is he too busy running his oil company?"

"Vitaly Sergelin is running a lot more than just an oil company," Koenig said. "It amazes me when people think the KGB somehow magically disappeared after perestroika. Just how is that supposed to work? You're the most powerful secret institution in the Soviet Union, and then after a few sham elections, you're reduced to nothing? As far as I can tell, all they did was print new stationery. Sergelin is exactly who I would suspect. He was directing the Soviet ASAT program at the time that everything fell apart over there. I'm sure any investigations into his recent activities would bear fruit."

Koenig was again trying to direct DeLuca's investigation. Why? DeLuca was surer now than he'd been before. Koenig was involved in some way. The question was, in what, and how?

"I'd appreciate it if you kept me informed," Koenig said. "Lieutenant Carr will put you through if you call—I'll leave standing orders with him to that effect."

"Will do," DeLuca said. "By the way, just for your own records, Cheryl Escavedo was not gay. I'm pretty sure of that. Right now we're trying to track down who sent her flowers, but we have a number of witnesses who saw her with an older man. I'll keep you in the loop, though."

"Thank you," General Koenig said. "That would be fine."

He hung up without saying good-bye.

If this was a chess game, DeLuca wanted Koenig to feel like he was under attack. In a real chess game, DeLuca might have offered a poisoned pawn, hoping his opponent would take the bait. At the moment, DeLuca understood that he himself was, in this case, the bait, but he needed to make the threat real and offer something of value if he was going to press his opponent into making a mistake. Maybe Koenig wasn't his adversary after all.

But he was certainly acting like one.

DeLuca called the office of Congressman Robert Fowler. He expected to talk to an aide, but when he explained who he was, he was put on hold for a minute, and then the congressman himself came on the line. DeLuca expressed his surprise.

"I always have a minute for a member of the armed services," Fowler said in a cheerful hail-fellow-well-met-and-don't-forget-to-vote-for-me-in-November sort of way. "If you're calling with information about the investigation, however, I'd rather you come in in person, if you can."

"I wasn't aware of any investigation," DeLuca said.

"This isn't about prisoner abuse, then?" Fowler asked.

"No, it's not," DeLuca said, vaguely aware now that Fowler was part of a committee looking into the subject. "Let me cut to the chase because I know you're busy. I'm in the middle of an investigation myself and your name came up. Something I thought you should be aware of, though I'm not at liberty to disclose in full what it's about. Have you, by any chance, been contacted by a person named Cheryl Escavedo?"

"Cheryl Escavedo?" Fowler said.

"Sergeant Cheryl Escavedo."

"Not to my knowledge, but I could ask my staff. Why would you like to know?"

"We found a printout she'd left behind with your name on it, and thought maybe she was going to try to contact you," DeLuca said.

"Perhaps she was, but if she was, I'm not sure I'd tell you, without knowing more about why you want to know," Fowler said. "Military personnel are free to contact me and to know with certainty that what passes between us will be protected by complete confidentiality."

"Well," DeLuca said, "again, I'm limited as to what I can say, but I'm pretty sure she wouldn't have been contacting you about your investigation. Just to put it in context, your name was mentioned along with two other things, places, actually. One was a suburb of Beijing and the other was a mountain pass in Pakistan. And bad things happened recently in both places. I'm not saying you necessarily need to take any extra precautions, and we're way too early along in the investigation to reach any conclusions, but I just thought, you know, you have a list of three, and bad things happen to two of them, you should tell the third."

"Just what are these 'bad things' you're referring to?" Fowler said. "I take it this is my own personal orange alert call, so I think I need to know what we're talking about."

"Well," DeLuca said, realizing how foolish he was going to sound. "In one, in China, there was apparently an earthquake. The Pakistan incident was similar."

There was a pause on the other end of the line.

"You're calling to warn me about an earthquake?" Fowler said. "Well, Agent DeLuca, I'm planning on taking my family sailing this weekend. We keep a boat in Cape May, so where we're going, I don't think earthquakes are going to be much of a problem. But thank you for your call."

"Congressman," DeLuca said quickly, before Fowler could hang up on him, "I realize how idiotic this sounds, all right? I wish I could tell you more—if I could, I might not sound quite so much like a man with his head up his ass."

"I work in Washington, D.C.," Fowler said. "I'm used to that. To tell you the truth, Agent, I was afraid you were calling to threaten me, but if you were, you probably wouldn't have threatened me with earthquakes, because not even the Army can cause those. The only person I ever knew who could make the earth move was Jerry Garcia, and he's dead."

"If I gave you my private number, would you call me if anything unusual happens?" DeLuca said. "I can tell you this much—I'm on a missing person investigation, and Sergeant Escavedo is the one who's missing. We're just trying to figure out what she might have been thinking before she disappeared."

"Good enough," Fowler said. DeLuca gave him the number for his encrypted SATphone and thanked him for his time.

In Juarez, MacKenzie and Vasquez set up shop, starting in the afternoon, in a bar called Club Zorro, Leon Lev's most recent acquisition. Nobody there seemed to recognize the name Theresa Davidova. Vasquez made a deal with the bartender and didn't dicker the price down when the bartender told him the house wanted fifteen dollars off the top from each transaction. MacKenzie, under the name Mila Zukova, was dressed as a "sexual service provider," in black leather pants and a black lace halter top, accented with a blonde wig and enough makeup to paint a small barn. The customers, who paid Hoolie a hundred dollars up front, were all DEA agents Wes Vogel sent across the Rio Grande Bridge dressed as sailors and soldiers and sex tourists. MacKenzie spent an hour with each of them, talking about sports or the military or who their favorites were on *American Idol,* which put them at ease when it was time to make the requisite moans and screams for authenticity's sake, in case anyone was listening through the walls (Vasquez had already checked the room for bugs). She helped one man with his daughter's algebra homework. Three, she took out into the hall and kissed goodbye, to make it look good in view of the Nana, a round mustachioed woman who sat in a folding chair at the end of the hall, reading a wrestling magazine. Mack's "satisfied" customers were asked only to talk her up on their way out the door. By late afternoon, once word had gotten around that there was a white girl getting one hundred dollars a throw (twice what the best Mexican whores could command), men other than DEA agents began to arrive, though Vasquez told them Mila had had a very busy day and was finished for the evening. His attention was piqued when a hard-looking mono-browed gringo who spoke broken Spanish with a heavy Slavic accent said he wanted to speak to the white girl. When Hoolie tried to intercede, the man said he wasn't a customer and pushed his way past, the bartender shooting Hoolie a look to say, "Don't fuck with this guy."

Vasquez caught the man at the top of the stairs, tugging on his coat. The man turned and pointed a finger in Hoolie's face.

"Touch me again, pimp, and I'll cut your heart out and feed it to my dog," he said. "What room is she in?"

"That one," Hoolie said, pointing with his eyes.

MacKenzie was sitting on the edge of the bed when the man entered, Hoolie right behind him. She looked at the stranger.

"I will do anything except Greek," she said in Russian. *"You pay him first."*

"My name is Dushko Lorkovic," the man said in Russian, but with a Serbian accent. *"You're the girl from Suma?"*

Mack nodded.

"My boss asked me to invite you to a party, if you were good-looking enough," the Serb said. *"Tonight. He'll pay you a thousand dollars. You'd better go if you want to work in this town."*

"I don't go anywhere without my boyfriend," Mack said. *"Who's your boss?"*

"You know who he is. He owns this place. Why are you here?"

"I want to make adult films. I was told your Leon Lev could help me."

"Does this idiot know that?"

"He thinks he's my manager, but once I pay him back, I'm done with him. He's harmless."

"Tell him to get lost."

"Please," Mack said. *"He has friends in Los Angeles who know my sister. I just have to pay him back."*

The Serb looked Hoolie over again.

"You can bring him," Lorkovic said, *"but wear something nice. And tell him to take a bath."*

He gave her a card from his pocket and wrote her name on the back of it, plus one.

"Give this to the men at the gate and they'll let you in. I heard you were a dancer. Do you still dance?"

"I can dance," she said.

"Then bring your dancing shoes, Mila," Lorkovic said.

"What'd he say?" Hoolie said once the Serb had gone. "You were talking about me, weren't you?"

"We've been invited to a party," Mack said. "And we both speak very highly of you."

A phone call from DeLuca got Captain Martin, General LeDoux's aide, to scramble a Predator out of Nellis to overfly Lev's ranch for a falcon view. MacKenzie and Vasquez studied the photographs thoroughly to get a sense of the layout of the property. The UAV would stay in the air, armed with a Hellfire missile, in case firepower was needed on short notice, with a pair of A-10 "Warthog" gunships circling beyond the horizon to support them. Wes Vogel said he had an INS man who'd been undercover in Juarez for almost a year who he thought he could get into the party, though it was rather short notice—if he could, the man would identify himself by using the name of Hoolie's childhood pet, a black dog named Oso.

As they expected, they were thoroughly searched at the front gate, asked to walk through a metal detector, and scanned with a hand-held scanner on the other side, as well as patted down, two men in black suits doing the patting while three more with MAC-10 machine pistols stood watch nearby. Hoolie paid the cab driver fifty dollars to wait outside the gate, where he got in line with a number of other cabbies and chauffeurs leaning against their limousines. MacKenzie thought the man who patted her down spent more time than he needed to searching her. She'd found a black silk dress with a slit up the side at a shop on Avenida Juarez. Hoolie was dressed in a charcoal gray suit and black shirt, his hair gelled to perfection.

"Éste no tendrá el culo tan apretado cuando Leon se acaba con él," the man who frisked MacKenzie said.

"Espero que él ahorre algo para nosotros," his friend replied.

"What'd they say?" MacKenzie asked as they walked down the long driveway toward the music, the path lit by a string of Chinese paper lanterns.

"The first one said he couldn't understand what a hot chick like you was doing with a loser like me, and the second one agreed with him," Hoolie lied.

The grounds were illuminated by colored lights and torches, including a large ring of lights in the middle of the west lawn that served as a helicopter landing pad. A white Sikorsky S-92 was parked at the far end of the lawn, while a Cobra gunship patrolled overhead. Hoolie told MacKenzie the band was playing conjunto/Tejano music, a musical form indigenous to the Rio Grande Valley developed by and for migrant farm workers and as authentic an American art form as the blues.

"My old man is old school—all he likes is mariachi," Vasquez told MacKenzie. "He thinks conjunto is for the lower classes. This song they're playing right now is by a group called Las Panteras. They're maybe the biggest group in the borderland. They sing about the *narcotrafi-*

cantes like they were Robin Hoods, just because guys who make billions of dollars selling drugs occasionally build a soccer field or a library for their communities, like that makes them heroes."

When they rounded the corner of the house where the band was set up by the pool, Hoolie's mouth dropped.

"What is it?" MacKenzie asked.

"Remember when I said the band was playing a Las Panteras song?" he said. "That's them. They're the band. That's Las Panteras."

"Voy a hacer que usted me ame esta noche," they sang, *"abra su corazón . . ."*

Perhaps as many as three hundred people circled the dance floor or milled about the pool with drinks in their hands. There were a dozen food stations forming a semicircle beyond the pool, with ice sculptures and large floral arrangements on the tables, where massive amounts of food were elegantly displayed, and a half dozen well-stocked open bars, one with a fountain pumping margaritas from the mouth of a large ice dolphin. A tin horse-watering trough the size of a small boat was filled with ice and cold beer, with stainless steel pans full of lime wedges pressed into the ice at either end. Platoons of waiters in white shirts, black pants, and brocaded Mexican vests circled bearing trays of canapés and grilled shrimp and Thai chicken skewers and other hors d'oeuvres or to freshen drinks. A phalanx of bodyguards stood watch as well, young men in Hawaiian shirts and earpieces or walkie-talkies, some of them openly bearing machine guns or wearing shoulder holsters. The male guests at the party were dressed in expensive suits and shirts but no ties, save the occasional string tie or bolo, gold chains still the favored bling accessory, topped by white or black cowboy hats. The women wore chandelier earrings and cocktail dresses of minimal coverage if they wore anything at all—in the pool, a dozen young women cavorted topless. Half of the women at the party were Latina, the other half Anglo, the men about 90 percent Mexican. Vasquez and MacKenzie circulated but didn't see Theresa Davidova anywhere in the crowd. Josh Truitt had supplied them with a photograph.

"Let's check in the house," Vasquez shouted over the music.

Another hundred people filled the mansion. Guests milled about the kitchen or smoked by the fireplace, where the head of an enormous black bull was stuffed and mounted on a plaque above the mantel. Original paintings by Frida Kahlo and Diego Rivera hung on the walls, the furniture Spanish mission style, the couches rich coffee-colored leather, the floor made of Valencia tile and terra cotta. A large rec room three steps down had been converted into a small strip club, where dancers writhed to loud hip-hop music beneath colored lights and strobes and fog machines, some girls giving lap dances that went well beyond any lap dances Vasquez had ever seen before. The bar doubled as a cocaine station where guests could either snort the drug in powdered form or smoke it as crack. A number of other drugs were evidently available as well, an old man serving as a kind of bartender/pharmacist in attendance to assist people with their selections.

Again, Theresa Davidova was nowhere to be found. Hoolie suggested searching upstairs, though a trio of bodyguards at the bottom of the sweeping staircase were stopping anyone from going up. Mack took Hoolie's arm in hers, moving to the patio, overlooking the pool scene below, Hoolie turning to eye the house for any kind of fire escape or other means of accessing the upper floors.

"A dónde usted piensa ir?" a man in an embroidered red silk shirt asked them. "You look like maybe you're lost, amigo." He was young, good-looking, with a mustache and sideburns, his hair combed straight back.

"We're looking for a friend of ours," Vasquez said. "A woman named Theresa Davidova. We were supposed to meet her here."

"I'm looking for a friend, too," the man said. "My dog, Oso. He's a Chihuahua but he's old. He wanders off sometimes."

"I had a dog named Oso, too," Vasquez said. "This is my friend Mila."

"Galiano Diega," the man in the red shirt said. "How do you like the party? Wes said you've never been to one of these before."

"I was at a frat party in college that made this look like a three-year-old's Chuck E Cheese party," Vasquez said.

"The hardcore stuff is happening down by the spa. I think maybe you need a party favor," Diega said, slipping something heavy into Vasquez's coat pocket. When he reached in, he felt a small automatic pistol, a .30-caliber Beretta, he guessed, though he didn't take it out to examine it. "I was here two days ago and managed to stash these," Diega said. "Would you like some gum? Compliments of Peggy Romano."

He held out a small box, which he slid open to reveal two pieces of gum, which didn't look all that appetizing considering that they'd already been chewed. Vasquez took one and MacKenzie the other, recognizing them as suboral nanotransmitters developed by DARPA, each resembling a wad of gum concealing a two-way radio, made entirely of plastics that wouldn't trigger metal detectors or show up on X-rays. To transmit, you simply spoke normally, and with a little practice, using a minimal ventriloquist technique, agents could speak to each other or to their controllers without moving their lips. To listen, you clenched the device between your teeth, the vibrations transferring sound to the ear along the jawbone. If you got caught, all you had to do was swallow your gum.

"How's our girl doing?" Vasquez heard DeLuca's voice ask, as soon as he activated his transmitter.

"Your girl is right here, so don't talk about me in the third person," MacKenzie said.

"Nice dress," DeLuca said. "We've got you on UAV cam."

"It's the Kevlar push-up bra that creates the effect," MacKenzie said. "Don't look down my dress. No sign of Theresa yet, but there are other places to look. What's going on?"

"Just sitting around the motor home," DeLuca said. "Vogel's man will fill you in there."

"This is big," Diega told Vasquez and MacKenzie. "Bigger than anybody knew, and we don't have the numbers to do anything but watch. The big Sikorsky at the end of the lawn belongs to Cipriano Cabrera. The Cobra overhead is flying cover for him."

"That looked like Mexican Air Force to me," Vasquez said.

"It is," Diega said. "I couldn't believe the people he brought with him. He had the heads of the Fuentes family, Oscar Quintero, Pedro Meraz, Henry Zaragosa, the new head of the Felix family, I don't know his name—it's like the who's who of the Mexican drug lords. Diega Murillo from Colombia. Plus the mayor, a man from the president's office, a bishop—I never saw anything like it. And they all came here to meet somebody."

"Who?" Vasquez asked.

"I don't know, but I heard it's some new business partner," Diega said.

"A G5 landed on Lev's private airstrip about ten minutes ago," DeLuca said. "Whoever was in it is choppering in now."

MacKenzie, Vasquez, and Diega watched from the patio as a large black Eurocopter Twinstar landed in the circle of lights on the lawn. As the rotors spun down, a door in the side of the luxury helicopter lowered to the ground. Two bodyguards exited first, followed by a man in a black turtleneck, his hair thinning on top. He had a blonde girl on one arm and a black girl on the other, and he was followed by two more bodyguards, one carrying a pair of briefcases, the other carrying an AK-47. Diega identified the two men walking out to greet the visitor as Cipriano Cabrera and Leon Lev.

"Peggy's got a face recognition program running right now," DeLuca said. "We'll let you know who the new guy is as soon as we learn anything."

"What's going on at the spa?" Vasquez asked Diega.

"Spa," Diega said, "movie studio—take your pick. That's where Lev makes his films. There's more money in Internet porn than there is in drugs these days, so the cartels are diversifying."

"They're shooting a movie?"

"Something like that," Diega said. "Just a party flick. Sometimes they get distributed but sometimes he just gives them to his guests as souvenirs. Probably nothing too extreme tonight, considering. No barnyard animals. But you can never tell."

"Wait here," Vasquez said to MacKenzie. "I'll go look for Theresa. You keep an eye on the visitor. Where are they meeting?"

"Upstairs," Diega said. "In the conference room. I tried to get a bug in there but I couldn't."

"If you want me to come with you . . ." MacKenzie said.

"Wait here," Vasquez said. "I'll be right back."

He made his way around the dance floor and headed for the spa, a collection of single-story buildings roofed in red tile, the walkway lit by flaming torches.

"What am I going to be looking at?" he asked into his transmitter.

"It's a little hard to tell from bird's eye, but it looks like about fifty men and maybe twenty or thirty women, out in the open. I can't say how many more indoors. Be careful. It's pretty raw."

"And watch out for the Serb you met earlier," Peggy Romano added. "Dushko Lorkovic. We pulled his file—he was one of Mladic's top thugs in Srebrenica, probably killed a couple hundred Croats either on his own or using the death squad he commanded. And two of the previous owners of the bars that Leon Lev bought who refused to sell."

"This is confirmed or spec?" Vasquez asked.

"One hundred percent confidence," Romano said. "There's an open warrant out on him from the International War Crimes Tribunal at The Hague."

The spa area was surrounded by an adobe wall, where two men stood guard at a wrought-iron gate. Vasquez walked past them as if he knew what he was doing, and they let him pass, convinced by the authority of his gait. He heard a rustling in the bushes to his left, and a low moaning. Beyond that he came to a hot tub, where a young Latina was having sex with three men, while a fourth man filmed the action. There was a gas-fired pit in the central of the courtyard, and beyond that a large padded mat, something like the wrestling mats Vasquez had competed on in college, where a circle of people had gathered. When Vasquez pushed his way toward the center, he saw a young man engaging with what appeared to be identical triplets, a cameraman circling them. Vasquez realized he probably didn't have to worry about calling too much attention to himself. Two-thirds of the men and women were naked, but others were clothed and simply observing. Couples groped each other in the darkened corners, on couches and in large easy chairs. There was a lap pool and a large pool house where a full-blown orgy was in progress, perhaps twenty men and fifteen women in various assemblages and combinations, with two cameramen maneuvering through the bodies. Vasquez looked into various rooms and places and stayed only long enough to satisfy himself that Theresa Davidova was not among the participants.

When he returned to the patio, Diega was alone.

"Where's my partner?" Vasquez asked.

"Lev's man took her," Diega said. "I couldn't stop him. He said he'd be right back."

"What man?" Vasquez asked. "The Serb?"

Diega nodded.

"He said Leon wanted to meet her."

"DeLuca—where is she?" Vasquez said. "Can you patch me through to her?"

"She's not transmitting," DeLuca replied. "The last message we got said she was going toward the back bedroom, down the hall."

Vasquez moved with as much speed as he could without drawing attention. Toward the back of the house, the music muted now in the distance, he opened a bedroom door, Diega right behind him, drawing his weapon as he entered, though he knew that if he fired it, the others would be on him in seconds.

Nothing.

They backed out, trying another door, but the room was again empty. A light shone from under the door at the end of the hall. They approached silently. Vasquez heard somebody inside speaking a Slavic language, his speech a drunken slur. He opened the door to see the Serb with his shirt off, unbuckling his belt, while MacKenzie sat on the edge of the bed. Lorkovic held his arm out to show Vasquez the hunting knife he held in his hand.

"Here comes the brave pimp to protect his whore," the Serb managed to say.

Vasquez decided not to wait for him to finish his sentence. He crossed quickly and feinted to the right to make the Serb lunge awkwardly at him with the knife, dancing left to catch the man by the wrist, which he cracked into splinters behind the man's back, wrapping his arm around Lorkovic's throat and dropping with all his weight to snap the man's neck, sparing the International War Crimes Tribunal at The Hague the trouble.

He rose from the body as it twitched, moved to MacKenzie, and asked her if she was all right. She had a heavy clay ashtray in her right hand, which she'd hidden behind her back, and appeared to be angry.

"I'm fine," she said. "I can take care of myself." She tossed the ashtray on the bed, now that she no longer needed to hit the Serb on the side of the head with it. "He was about to tell me what happened to Theresa. If you could have waited two more minutes, we might have known."

"Good work, Hoolie," DeLuca said. "We'll find Theresa."

"I don't think she's here," Vasquez said, turning to Mack. "What did Lorkovic say to you?"

"I said I wasn't working tonight and that I only came to find my friend Theresa," MacKenzie said. "He said, 'You want Theresa Davidova, I'll show you Theresa Davidova.' That's all I could get him to say."

"*Show* you?" DeLuca said. "Like, 'show you the body'?"

"Or show you the video," MacKenzie said.

"Do they make snuff films here?" Vasquez asked Diega.

"I don't know," he said. "They make everything here. But I haven't heard of that."

"I'm pulling you out," DeLuca said. "That's an order. The man in the Twinstar is Vitaly Sergelin. You two are done for the night."

They put the body in the shower after stripping it and hanging the clothes on a hook behind the door—perhaps someone would think he'd slipped on a bar of soap.

Outside, the music had changed from conjunto/Tejano to hip-hop as a hardcore Latino rap group took the stage, the scene by the pool starting to resemble the scene in the spa. There was a commotion on the stairs behind them. They turned to see Cipriano Cabrera leaving the meeting, arm in arm with Vitaly Sergelin. Leon Lev was right behind them, followed by the other members of the cartel and their aides and bodyguards. From the looks on everybody's faces, the meeting had gone well, with much laughter and conviviality in evidence. Leon Lev gestured with his arm and suggested that Cabrera and the others join the party, but they only shook their heads and headed for their respective helicopters, Lev wearing the disappointed look of a man who'd gone to an awful lot of trouble and expense for nothing. MacKenzie heard him bark an order to one of his aides, saying, "Get me Dushko!"

They watched as first the black helicopter and then the white one rose from the ground, the ferocious backwash kicking up a cloud of dust. Hoolie looked at his watch. It was eighteen minutes after midnight. They were standing by the cab when they saw the explosions in the sky, a relatively small one followed by a much larger one, then balls of fire as the fuel ignited, burning debris blowing out and falling from the sky in slow motion. There was a numb silence, and then the ranch filled with shouting and screaming as panicked people began to stream out the gates of the resort, men and women piling into limousines and cars and peeling out as fast as they could, while inside the gates, men with machine guns and rifles held their weapons at the ready, looking confusedly into the sky and talking into their walkie-talkies and trying to figure out what had just happened.

"The Rio Grande Bridge," Vasquez told the cab driver. "Quickly. Can we drop you off somewhere?" he asked Diega, who said the bridge would be fine.

When they were clear of the chaotic scene, Vasquez bit down twice on his transmitter.

"What happened?" he asked. The cab driver eyed him in his rear-view mirror.

"Two choppers down," DeLuca told him. "No apparent survivors."

"Cabrera and the Russian?"

"Negative," DeLuca said. "Cabrera and the Cobra that came with him. The Russian got away."

"Stingers or SAMs? Or triple-A?"

"Negative," DeLuca said. "Nothing lit up."

"RPGs?"

"Negative," DeLuca said. "Too high to hit."

"C4? Maybe someone put an IED on the chopper during the meeting."

"Maybe," DeLuca said, "but who put one on the Cobra? It never landed."

"Did we shoot 'em down?" MacKenzie asked. "What'd we have in the air?"

"Nothing," DeLuca said. "We had the UAV but both Hellfires are intact. The A-10s weren't in the area."

"So how, then?" Vasquez said. "And who, if it wasn't us? Colombians? Rivals? The Mexican government?"

"Hang on," DeLuca said. "We're processing the intel now. We'll let you know."

They went over it again and again. When both helicopters took off at once, in opposite directions, DeLuca had had to make a quick decision, which one to follow. He let the Russian go, knowing it was probably going to take him to the private airstrip where his Gulf 5 jet was waiting, and instead sent the UAV after the white Sikorsky carrying Cipriano Cabrera and friends. The Predator kept the aircraft securely in view of its variable aperture infrared camera. Peggy Romano reran the pre-explosion sequence several times, the camera clearly showing the heat from the engine and the body heat from the passengers. The data stream refreshed twenty times a second. Slowing the stream to virtual stop-time, it appeared that at 0022 hours, eighteen and fourteen-twentieths of a second, everything was normal with the Cobra gunship, the first to explode. By 0022 hours eighteen and fifteen-twentieths of a second, the external temperature of the aircraft had reached fifty thousand degrees Fahrenheit, a near-instantaneous ignition, imparting so much energy to the aircraft that according to Peggy Romano's best estimate, the largest piece of debris to survive the explosion was a three-inch-long piece of rotor. The same thing happened a mere 1.7 seconds later with the second helicopter. The best thermobaric shells the military had only reached sixteen hundred degrees at midplasma, and detonations radiated out from the center, an entirely different signature from what DeLuca had just witnessed.

In other words, it wasn't a bomb on board, and it wasn't a missile. Nor, Romano said, was it a signature similar to anything a MIRACL or THEL laser would leave. If it was Darkstar, DeLuca concluded, then Darkstar was armed with a weapon unlike anything LeDoux had briefed him about, and LeDoux would have told him what he knew.

"Send your data and your report to Captain Martin," DeLuca told Romano. "Tell me something—who else knew we were flying a Predator tonight? Who else could know?"

"The operator at Nellis," she said. "And his team, I suppose."

"Our downlink here is secure, right?"

"Right," Romano said.

"How about between Nellis and the bird controlling the UAV?"

She shook her head and shrugged.

"So somebody could have intercepted the feed?" he said.

"Conceivably," he said. "It's encrypted, but that can be defeated."

"The God problem," DeLuca said.

"Pardon me?"

"Just an expression," DeLuca said. "And the Predator was flying good? No mechanical problems?"

"None."

"Clear from being damaged by any flying debris?"

"Clear."

"Any reason you can think of, then," he asked her, "why we lost contact with the Predator two seconds after the second chopper went down?"

Chapter Nine

DELUCA'S PHONE RANG THE FOLLOWING MORNING. He'd risen early to read through the scientific papers Dr. Penelope Burgess had given him. The morning news programs were reporting the crash of a helicopter believed to have been carrying Mexican drug lord Cipriano Cabrera, an attack believed to have been led by rival *narcotraficantes* hoping to take over the cartel. Mitch Pasternak sounded like he had a cold. DeLuca told him maybe he should see a doctor.

"For a cold?" he said. "With the doctors around here, I'll end up on my own table. Don't worry about it—I wear a mask half the day anyway, so when I need to, I can blow my nose without using my hands. I got the results back on the items you sent me. What do you want first?"

"Maybe the hair sample," DeLuca said.

"Not much there," Pasternak said. "Female, young, used conditioner. What else do you want to know? No sign of drug use of any kind. Clean as a whistle. Was this person from some sort of ethnic group?"

"Isn't everyone?" DeLuca asked. "She was Native American."

"I thought she might be," Pasternak said. "The piece of beach glass you sent me is a bit more interesting."

"Because?"

"My first thought was that you were wasting my time. It was a rock, and it was clean, no blood, no hair, not used as a weapon. But it was a strange sort of rock—I had a rock collection as a child. I won first place in my second-grade science fair with it, as a matter of fact. I had a piece of obsidian I used to carry in my pocket that the sample you sent reminded me of. At any rate, I chipped off a piece and ground it into powder to run a spectrographic analysis."

DeLuca wasn't sure he liked the way Pasternak teased him along. Gillian just gave it to you straight. On the other hand, Pasternak was much droller, his sense of humor even darker than Gillian's, if that were possible.

"Can we skip the 'I'm-so-clever-you-have-to-guess-what-I-know' part?" DeLuca asked. "I'm kind of on a schedule here."

"What fun is that?" Pasternak said. "Well okay. My second thought was that you'd sent me a bouillon cube from the primordial soup. It was full of DNA."

"Can we say whose?"

"We can't," Pasternak said. "There's no point in sending it along to the FBI because it's not in any sequence. You need intact strands to identify someone. This stuff was scrambled to where an ordinary pathologist might say, 'Well, it's organic, but beyond that, we can't tell.' You think this was a lightning strike?"

"Something like that," DeLuca said.

"Well, your lightning bolt or something like that definitely hit something," Pasternak said. "Using what I have in my lab, it would be hard for an ordinary pathologist to say if the DNA we've got came from a cactus or a coyote. Fortunately . . ."

"You're not an ordinary pathologist?" DeLuca guessed.

"Exactly," Pasternak said. "I took another sample and sent it to a friend of mine at Helixa who said he'd run it through one of his amplifiers . . ."

"That's the genome project lab in Cambridge?" DeLuca said.

"One of two in the race," Pasternak said. "NIH was the other, but NIH had a much slower approach, taking the thing in order and moving from one end to the other. The thing Carl Schiffler at Helixa came up with was a way of breaking the chromosome down into its one hundred thousand separate parts, much like the scrambled DNA in the sample you sent me, and then they'd amplify each gene a million times or whatever and then put the whole sequence back together. Anyway, my friend was able to narrow it down a bit. This came from the Sonora Desert, correct, and not from the jungles of Borneo or the Congo?"

"Correct," DeLuca said. "Near the Mexican border."

"Well then it's probably not an orangutan or great ape of some sort," Pasternak said, "which means it's human."

"And this Carl Schiffler guy is certain?" DeLuca asked.

"Carl Schiffler is 100 percent certain of everything he thinks he knows, but he's not the person I asked," Pasternak said. "He owns Helixa, but he's not who I talked to. Carl Schiffler wouldn't give me the time of day. Or he would, but he'd lie. But yes, my friend is certain."

"Male or female?"

"Absolutely."

"So how did it get in the glass?" DeLuca asked. "Could lightning do that?"

"Lightning can do anything," Pasternak said. "I don't know if you're going to remember this, but a couple years ago in South Africa, there was a soccer game, and one of the teams hired a witch doctor to put a hex on the other team, so during the game, the sky clouded over and there was a lightning strike, and all the players on one team got hit. And it's not like they were all standing in a group—they were spread out all across the field, mixed in with the other players. That's an absolutely true story. You can look it up."

"I imagine the witch doctor didn't have much trouble finding work after that," DeLuca said.

"He's probably got his own infomercial," Pasternak said. "So could lightning fuse sand into glass? Sure. Could that fusion incorporate genetic material? I suppose, though it doesn't seem likely. I did some research on lightning strikes. We don't get a lot of those in Boston, so I have no personal experience with lightning victims. Only 10 percent or so are fatal. There's a guy in Italy who's been hit six times and he's still an atheist."

"You'd think he'd learn to stay indoors anyway," DeLuca said.

"You would," Pasternak said. "Maybe he likes it. Maybe he works for the railroads and he's never had any money."

"Meaning what?"

"Meaning he's a poor conductor," Pasternak said. "Anyway, you get a huge range of variables, depending upon the strength of the strike and the proximity, if it's a direct hit or a side flash, lots of things. There've been cases where the victim suffers first- or second- or even third-degree burns, and others where the victim himself is relatively untouched, but his clothes are burned right off of him. Or her. If I'd have known that was possible in junior high school, I could not have stopped praying for lightning to strike Stephanie Goldbaum. As a rule, burning is minimal, or maybe not minimal, but it's not like the janitors at the power plants who get fried when their keys get caught in the transformers. Lightning is a current and currents travel on the outer surfaces of things. Burns tend to be associated with the things people are wearing, jewelry, belts, piercings, hats, wet clothing. The air surrounding the bolt heats up to around fifty thousand degrees, which then expands and causes the thunder you hear, but an average stroke of say a million volts, or just under a thousand times what comes out of your sockets at home, and maybe thirty thousand amperes, only lasts .0002 second. They think some bolts get as high as three hundred thousand amps and ten or fifteen million volts, which is probably going to sting, but that's more the exception than the rule. That's on the ground. There are discharges of megalightning above the clouds in the form of sprites and blue jets that reach fifty miles into space and carry billions of volts. Somebody who's hit on the ground, you get heart failure, respiratory paralysis, hearing loss, vision problems, EKG abnormalities, and a whole lot of psychological sequela including memory loss, confusion, inattentiveness, and irritability, which may all come from thinking God hates you, but burns are, well, they're a part of it, but they're not the biggest part."

"So you couldn't, for example, vaporize a person with a lightning bolt?"

"Vaporize somebody?" Pasternak said, laughing. "My God, who are we worried about—Zeus? I guess my best answer is, I don't know, but I really don't think so. You could maybe vaporize a mouse or a rat. I don't think anybody's gone out in a lightning storm with a kite and tied the other end to a rat to find out."

"You don't know DOD," DeLuca said. "I can almost guarantee you, someone has."

He'd just called the radio station WROZ and left a message to ask to speak to Ed Clark, of *Sea to Shining Sea,* when a chartreuse Neon pulled into the motel parking lot and Sami Jambazian got out, dressed in his own clothes again. DeLuca greeted him warmly and invited him in, handing him a cup of coffee, black with two sugars, the way he knew Sami liked it.

"Thanks, but we're not allowed to drink caffeine," Sami said. DeLuca shot him a questioning look. "I've been trying to decaffeinate myself for a long time anyway, so I figured I'd go with it. I had a headache for a day but it went away. It's the not eating meat part that's hard—I'm so constipated I think I'm gonna blow up. Don't worry—I'm taking something for it."

"Welcome back to Earth," DeLuca said. "You traded the Mercedes for a Neon?"

"It's the group car," Sami said. He looked around at all the technology inside the Jet Stream. "Jesus. Nice place you got."

"We also have Playstation 2 and TiVo. So what do you think? What's up with the Brethren?"

"It's interesting," Sami said. "They're not stupid. They look like they are, but they're not. They just really want somebody to lead them. They're tired, and probably a little naïve. I think for a lot of them, the best part is being told what to wear and eat and drink and think and say, and then they get jobs trimming the rose bushes and it's like the best vacation they ever had. Something like that. They all really support each other, which maybe looks weird from the outside, but from the inside, it's all they want. They hug a lot."

"Don't forget we love you, too. You have any trouble getting over?"

Sami shrugged and changed his mind about the coffee, filling a cup from the thermos on the table.

"I just told them the story I told you and the guys at poker," Sami said. "It's easy when you don't have to make anything up."

"How about Rainbow?" DeLuca asked. "What's the line on her daughter?"

"Rainbow's a sweet woman," Sami said. "I like her. What you see is exactly what you get. It's kind of refreshing, after all the bullshit Carolyn put me through. Whatever. Rainbow literally couldn't hurt a fly. She stepped on a ladybug yesterday and I thought she was going to commit suicide over it. Her ex-husband treated her pretty bad, and the way she grew up, this is like the first place where she's really felt loved and accepted. Other than by her daughter."

"You were trying to tell me something at the lecture," DeLuca said. "Rainbow was trying to convince me everything was all right. Why was that?"

"I think she was trying to convince herself," Sami said, pausing as if he was considering what he would say next carefully, or as if he felt uncomfortable continuing. "The best I can tell, Ruby may have been abducted."

"Did the kidnappers ask for ransom?" DeLuca said. "Whatever it is, I'm sure we have enough in the discretionary fund to pay it, and if we don't, I can call Captain Martin. What? What's with the look on your face?"

"I don't mean that kind of abduction," Sami said. "I mean she was taken. In a ship. And then they brought her back, but she was so shook up about it that they have her somewhere to debrief her. They told Rain she could see her daughter soon, but they didn't say when."

"Just so we're clear here," DeLuca said, "when you say taken by a ship, are you talking about a UFO?"

Sami looked at him. DeLuca was surprised. Sami was one of the gruffest, most cynical people he'd ever met—DeLuca knew his friend would not become so emotional unless something serious was on his mind.

"It's really not easy to talk about some of this shit, you know," Sami said. "I'm here to help you in any way that I can, David, but it would be nice to think you could be here for me a little bit. I don't think that's asking for too much."

"Jesus, Sami, that goes without saying," DeLuca said. "Just take your time. I'll listen to whatever you have to say."

"It was hard enough, telling you guys at the poker table what I saw that night," Sami said. "I mean, I knew you were going to give me shit about it, but I thought somebody was going to be maybe the least bit curious. Something really phenomenal happens to you, that's never happened before, you expect a little more from your friends."

"It's not a very sensitive group," DeLuca said of his weekly poker game. "I think everybody felt maybe a little threatened by what you were saying. Like maybe we were losing you, so giving you shit was everybody's way of pulling you back toward us."

DeLuca saw Peggy Romano out the window, walking toward the pool in her bathrobe with a towel over her arm. She waved to them. Sami sipped his coffee.

"What you told us was that the . . . thing you saw . . . hung above the road for about a minute and then took off," DeLuca said. "Was there more to it than that?"

"Yeah, there was," Sami said. "These guys with the Anguilo crew were driving around in tanker trucks, dumping toxic waste on the dirt roads up south of Monadnock. I had to hang pretty far back because of how empty the roads were, but I had some NVGs to drive with my lights off if I had to. So I see him hit his brakes, and I come up in the dark, and I see him pulled over, he opens his valves, he gets back in and drives away, so I gotta stop and get a sample from the ditch first, and then I can pop him. And if he gets away, it's okay because I got the license for the truck. So I'm alone in the woods, with my engine off, and it's really quiet, until I hear this humming sound, and then all of a sudden, I see this bright light, and I look up and there's a ship right over my head. And . . . they take me up . . ."

His voice was shaking, and he had to struggle to slow his breathing.

"It's all right, Sami," DeLuca said. "You take your time."

Sami wiped the corners of his eyes with the folded paper towel DeLuca had given him to use as a coaster.

"This whole deal has been a bit overwhelming for me, I gotta tell ya, David. For the longest time, I thought I was just crazy, and then I thought maybe I wasn't, but either way, nobody would ever understand. I never heard of this Hilton Jaynes guy until the other night, and I never met anybody else who went through what I did until I met Rainbow and the others. Not all of 'em but a lot of 'em. I can't really tell you why, but it was a big part of what drove Carolyn and me apart, me knowing something I couldn't talk to her about. I tried once and she wouldn't hear it."

"It must be quite a relief, knowing you're not alone," DeLuca said.

"Oh, God," Sami said, looking as if he was going to cry again. "Yeah. It's quite a relief." He took a deep breath and sat up straight in his chair.

"So what happened?" DeLuca asked. "In the ship?"

"Just the usual stuff you hear about," Sami said. "I know you're going to think this is nuts, but what they told me was that they were breeding a better race to take over, once we fuck our planet up to where nobody can live here anymore, which they said was about a hundred years off, on the outside, and maybe twenty years on the inside. The way we're polluting everything."

"And you'd know," DeLuca said, "given how you just saw a guy dumping by the side of the road."

"Yeah," Sami said. "Exactly."

"Was that how they put it?" DeLuca asked. "Did they use the phrase, 'fuck up our planet'? I'm not doubting you, I'm just curious."

"That's how they put it," Sami said. "It seemed kind of funny, at the time. You don't expect extraterrestrials to curse. I didn't see anybody because it was too bright, but I heard the voices. Like, inside my head, I heard them. So they did the probes and they took some sperm and then they sent me back. And my memory was like, wow, was that real or did I fall asleep and dream it? Because it was sort of halfway between something you know for real and something you only think you know for real. So I wrote everything down in the car, before I started to lose it. I mean, it was so real, but it was also so strange that you think it can't be real."

"So you think Ruby was taken, you said? But she's back?"

"I was able to star-six-nine Malcolm Percy's personal phone after Rainbow talked to him and he told her everything was all right, and he'd called his sister in San Antonio, Alexandra, so I had your brother-in-law Tom at Homeland Security pull her recent purchases and whatever—all of a sudden, three days after Ruby disappears, she's buying American Girl dolls and Lucky Charm cereal and renting Hilary Duff videos. Antonionus won't tell Rain anything, but I got the address, so we're driving there tomorrow. I gotta ask you, David—do you believe me? Be honest."

"I don't know what I believe," DeLuca said, though that wasn't quite true. "I know we all have a things-that-can't-be-explained category. I thought what Hilton Jaynes said was really interesting, and I know you wouldn't lie to me, so yeah, I believe you."

"Okay," Sami said. "I should get back. If you're gone too long, they send a tractor beam after you. I'm kidding."

"I know," DeLuca said.

"Just so you know," Sami said, "I can deal with this on my own. I only told you because it's relevant to the investigation. Otherwise, I'm fine, keeping it to myself."

DeLuca knew what Sami was trying to tell him.

"Just so you know," DeLuca said, "this whole conversation is classified, so nobody is going to know except you and me."

"Walter knows," Sami said. "You can talk about it with him if you need to. I told him back when it happened. He never said anything, did he?"

"Not a word," DeLuca said.

"I didn't think he would," Sami said. "Do you think maybe Cheryl Escavedo was abducted?"

"Right now I'm thinking she was killed," DeLuca said. "That's the way I'm going with this."

"You said the tracks stopped in the middle of nowhere," Sami said. "That's consistent with an abduction."

"I know," DeLuca said. "I'm not rejecting the idea of abduction out of hand. I just think there were more reasons why somebody would want to kill her than there were reasons why somebody would want to abduct her. All the usual crap we had to deal with when we worked homicide."

"Maybe they wanted it to look like an abduction?"

"Or maybe they wanted to lead us toward a conclusion that no one else would believe, as a way of dead-ending us," DeLuca said.

"Anyway," Sami said, "I'll let you know what we find out when we're in San Antonio."

When DeLuca opened his e-mail, two messages were of interest. The first was from his son, Scott.

Hey Pops. Hope you're using sunscreen. It snowed again here today.

By the way, I cleaned up your disk and defragmented your hard drive for you—this thing was running dog slow.

Anyway, to answer your question, sorry, but we had nothing in the sky at three minutes after midnight, a thumb from Orion's buckle towards five o'clock, or a fist, or an arm, or anywhere close to that. We had a KH-11 in that area about an hour later—are you sure of the time? Maybe you forgot to reset your watch. But even then, there's no reason why you'd see it and then not see it. My best guess is that you saw some sort of commercial airplane, but I don't have that data. Maybe Albuquerque air traffic control or Kirtland would have records. Or maybe it was somebody else's bird, though I tracked all the satellites we know about and came up with zilch there also. Sorry I can't be of more help.

Coincidentally, I got some news that we lost a Predator over El Paso (approx) just after the drug lord's helicopter went down, though, of course, that part wasn't in the papers. I was curious so I logged into IMINT and saw that there was a third helicopter, so I asked about it and a buddy over at SIGINT said one of our milsats picked up a ping from a transponder on the third helicopter, definitely government issue but not coded to any particular carrier, ten seconds before the other two choppers were targeted. Is that interesting? FYI.

Mom says hello. She says to tell you the desert getaway vacation is sounding better and better but

she needs a few days' notice if you still want to do that. A week. She just yelled that to me from the living room. Let me know what else I can do.
Scott

He immediately called Wes Vogel and asked him if he'd managed to get any agents aboard Sergelin's helicopter, or if perhaps Galiano Diega had somehow managed to attach a GPS transponder to the aircraft. Vogel said no, not to his knowledge, anyway. DeLuca thanked him, then sent Captain Martin an e-mail asking him to poll all the other relevant intelligence agencies ASAP and find out if the CIA or anybody else had an agent on the Russian's Twinstar.

The other message he'd received was from Walter Ford, an e-mail containing a list of General Koenig's classmates from prep school. DeLuca recognized three names. One was a famous movie actor. Another was a congressman from California, a representative from the San Diego district named Richard Benson. The third name was that of Malcolm S. Percy. In a postscript, Ford added that the building lost in the earthquake in Beijing was the home of Shijingshan Entertainment, a business that was in the middle of an international intellectual properties lawsuit.

DeLuca wrote a quick e-mail to Dan Sykes, who was due to return some time that afternoon:

Dan,
Here's a quick one for you, when you have time. Koenig, Brother Antonionus (aka Malcolm Percy) and Rep. Richard Benson (R. Cal.) all went to prep

school together. I'm guessing your dad and Benson must be tight. Do you know him? Would you call Benson and chat him up about Koenig/Percy/Decatur Academy? Was there a relationship, etc. Also, what's the relationship between Benson and Fowler? Just connecting the dots. No picture yet. It would help if the dots were numbered, wouldn't it?
David

He drove to the University of New Mexico campus after being told by the department secretary who'd answered the phone that Dr. Burgess would be finished teaching at two o'clock. He walked discreetly behind her as a student, an earnest young fellow with a crewcut, followed her from class, pestering her with questions all the way to her office door. When DeLuca knocked, she opened it quickly and said, exasperatedly, "What? Oh. It's you."

"Your student left," DeLuca said. "The coast is clear. I thought you said students avoided you during office hours."

"Come on in," Burgess said, smiling and rolling her eyes. "These aren't my office hours. It's the goddamn GI Bill. These guys get out of the service and come to school for free, and they're the best students I have because they're so disciplined and motivated, but they won't leave me alone. I had one follow me all the way to my car."

"Isn't that what the GI Bill was supposed to be for?" DeLuca said.

"It is," she agreed. "I just need time to catch my breath once in a while. What can I do for you?"

She was dressed in a white turtleneck sweater and a denim skirt that fell just to the top of the knee-high suede boots she was wearing. She had, DeLuca thought, an interesting way of getting more attractive each time he saw her, not that it meant anything to him—just an observation.

"I read the papers you gave me," he said. "I was hoping we could talk about them a little bit."

"All right," she said, "but I didn't get a chance to eat before class and I'm starving. Do you eat pizza?"

"I'm Italian," DeLuca said. "I eat pizza."

She walked him to a place called Dinardo's, off-campus but full of students eating slices and pecking away on their laptops or reading books while they ate. DeLuca and Burgess got a booth by the window. Outside, across the street, a group of protesters marched carrying signs saying, US TROOPS OUT OF IRAQ and STOP THE OCCUPATION. After they ordered, Burgess asked him what he thought of the protesters.

"They remind me of myself," he said. "I marched against Vietnam. I was really young and the war was practically over, but I guess I felt a small sense of accomplishment when it ended. Actually, not when it ended—when Nixon resigned. Which was sort of the same thing, in my mind."

"You marched against the war but you enlisted anyway?"

"Later," he said. "It's a long story."

"What about now?" she said. "What about the signs?"

"Do I think the Army should get out?" he said. "Yeah. Don't get me wrong, Doctor . . ."

"Penny," she said.

"Penny," he agreed. "And I'm David. I was saying, don't get me wrong about one thing—I have a lot of good friends in the Army and they're good men who do the toughest job on earth extremely well. My only problem is that the Army is really good at one thing, and that's blowing stuff up, but after you conquer a country, you don't want the Army anymore. War's a mess and it's a bitch to straighten everything out afterward, and I know because that's exactly what I was doing over there, but it just seems to me that once we kicked Saddam out, we didn't know what to do next. It seemed like every time I helped rebuild a school or get a hospital's generator restarted, some insurgent would blow up a car and then the Army would come in and level the building. And how else do you respond? Maybe I don't know how you win hearts and minds, but I don't think you do it by blowing stuff up. The Army fights fire with fire. I think you fight fire with water. I think maybe if we had a civil reconstruction corps that was as well trained and equipped as the Fourth Army and maybe with as many numbers to do the job, we could avoid what we've got now. But what do I know."

"You were there," she said. "You know more than I do." She gestured out the window. "And more than they do. I have wondered if farming out the reconstruction jobs to the lowest bidders was such a good idea."

"Halliburton was the *lowest* bidder?" DeLuca said. "That's news to me."

"You wanted to talk about my work?" she said.

"Mostly I want to ask a whole lot of stupid questions," he said. "Just to clear some things up in my head." He'd meant to talk with her even before his conversation with Sami, but the talk with Sami had added a few new dimensions to his line of inquiry. "I promise I won't follow you to your car."

"You, I'd welcome," she said. "Ask away."

"Well," he said, "from what I understand, this probe you're developing to detect life on Mars is sort of like an electronic sniffer. Is that a fair categorization? I say that because when I was in Iraq, actually, we had recon teams with sniffers to look for biologicals and chemical agents—my understanding of how they worked was that they collect the chemical elements in the air, all the spores and bacteria and viral particles, and then they break them down into their molecular parts and give each molecular building block an electrical charge so that it can be read, and then they compare that signature against the ones stored in the onboard computer. And from reading your paper, it sounded to me like the probe you're building is something more sophisticated but similar. Is that right?"

She smiled.

"You're very perceptive," she said. "My husband told me ten years ago that I should have patented the work I did on that. Yes, the sniffers you used in Iraq were more or less developed from work a number of us started as graduate students, actually. I never expected my work would ever have a defense application . . ."

"Given that it could save millions of lives some day," DeLuca said, "I think you should be pleased. But that's essentially what you're sending to Mars?"

"Essentially," she said. "Although after we compare the particles we find to what we already know, we're going to have to compare them to what we don't already know, because life there may not fit the definitions we have of life here. The program is going to have to be adaptable."

He noticed that the girl at the booth next to them was crying while the boy she was with held her hands. She was getting dumped, apparently. The girl looked like a sorority sweetheart. The boy had Elvis sideburns, pierced eyebrows, and a tattoo on the back of his neck of some Chinese character. DeLuca suspected she'd land on her feet.

"And you use lasers to read the molecular particles," he said.

"That's right," Burgess said.

"I'm interested in what lasers can do," he said. "Just sort of generally speaking. How they can measure things and affect things."

"Okay," she said. "I suppose I know a little bit about that."

"Your husband was working with lasers, too, right?" DeLuca said.

"Rather different kinds of lasers, but yes," she said. "He was."

"So let me just ask you," he said. "So I can get a picture in my head. Generally speaking. Energy is energy, and it takes different forms at different wavelengths, but it's all the same thing, right? Microwaves, infrared, X-rays, radio signals, they can all be lased, right?"

"Right," she said.

"And at low power levels, like what you're talking about, you can read the feedback you get from a molecular building block and tell what it is, right?"

"You can measure certain properties of the electrical field surrounding it," she said.

"And everybody generates an electrical field, right?" he said. "That's what sharks have in their noses to detect prey in the water. They can read the electrical field of an injured fish, or something like that, right?"

"You probably know more about sharks than I do," she said. "All I know is what I see on the Discovery channel. But yes to your question about electrical fields."

"And CAT scans and PET scans measure the electrical activity of various tissues and parts of the body," he said. "Isn't that how they work?"

"I believe it is," she said. "If you want to drastically simplify it."

"Drastically simple is the best I can do," DeLuca said. "And to read something, lasers send a pulse and then they measure how that pulse is modified by the return. That's how the scanners at the supermarket work, reading the bar code."

"Again, to drastically simplify, I suppose the answer is yes. You can also phase the signals from one or more lasers to watch what happens at the interface."

"That's good," DeLuca said. "And the lasers in your Mars probe can adjust the wavelength to send different pulses to measure different things, right?"

"Right," she said.

"So in theory, just in theory," he said, "could you use a laser to identify a person by his electrical field?"

"In theory, you could," she said, "though he'd have to be isolated from surrounding fields. That's why we've been doing the work we've been doing in caves, and at Sinkhole. Past tense. Sinkhole was a government neutrino lab deep underground, connected to the Carlsbad system. Shut down now. You need to work in places like that.

Though I suppose the bigger the computers get, the more easily we'll be able to pull discrete data from a larger field of conflicting information. It's kind of like hearing one voice in a roaring crowd."

"But in theory, you could do it," he said. "Say, with a person standing all alone in the desert, as opposed to us sitting here in this restaurant?"

"In theory, yes."

"You know, the Army is working with a tactical microwave beam for crowd control," he said, "part of the nonlethal initiative, where they can use a dish mounted on top of a truck to zap a crowd with microwaves to get it to disperse. Apparently people feel like their skin is burning and it's quite uncomfortable, so they run away. Have you heard of this?"

"I think I read about it in the paper," she said. "I remember wondering, if they had such a thing to deliver energy at nonlethal doses to disperse crowds, what was stopping them from increasing the power until they were working with lethal doses?"

"I wouldn't think anything is stopping them," DeLuca said. "My understanding was that at the tested power level, it only affects the target's skin. So, in theory, you could develop a laser, or tune a laser, to only affect a particular kind of body tissue. The way they use ultrasound to break up kidney stones but leave the kidneys alone."

"I don't know," she said. "I suppose it might be possible."

"So in theory," he said, "suppose the target was a cornstalk—could you focus or tune or phase a laser to destroy or denature the cell walls in a cornstalk, without hurting the rest of the plant?"

"You mean, could you use a laser to make crop circles?"

"Yes."

"I think you could."

"Burn the lips and udders off a cow?"

"Yes."

"Could you hit a person with an energy beam that might affect only the rectal or vaginal tissues, to give him a warm feeling that makes him feel like he's been probed?" he asked her. She looked him in the eye for a moment.

"I guess you could," she said. "You could probably even project the image of the Virgin Mary onto the side of a building."

"But why would you want to do that?" he said. "Why would you want to use technology to mislead people?"

"Maybe just because you can," she said.

"Could a laser cause an earthquake?"

"No," she said. "At least I don't think so. Earthquakes are caused by the release of subterranean pressures. Lasers can't cause subterranean pressures. Or release them. I don't see how.

"One last question," he said. "The lasers in your probe work at very close range. What limits the range?"

"There are a number of variables," she said. "One is the amount of power you need to generate and sustain. And the sensitivity of the measuring instruments. The dosages of the X-rays you get at the dentist or in a hospital are vastly smaller than what they were twenty years ago. "

"That's interesting," DeLuca said. "You've been very helpful."

"I don't see how," she said. "The last I knew, you were looking for a missing girl. What does any of this have to do with that?"

He couldn't tell her what he was really thinking—he was really thinking that Cheryl Escavedo had been zapped, vaporized, erased from the planet by a powerful weapon that no one knew was up there, one that could, at any instant, zap and/or vaporize anybody Darkstar deemed a threat.

"I don't know," he lied. "Like I said, I just ask a lot of stupid questions and then wait for the answers to become less stupid in my head. Sometimes they do and sometimes they don't."

"I think you could have been a good scientist," she told him. "Do you mind if I take the leftover pizza home? I can always zap it in the microwave for a midnight snack. Unless you think using the microwave is too dangerous."

"It's all yours," he said. "Thanks for your time."

When he checked his messages, he learned that Ed Clark had called him back, saying only that he'd be on the air tonight and could possibly talk tomorrow. DeLuca decided that tomorrow would be too late. It was two hundred miles to Roswell, but it was only four in the afternoon—he could be there by seven, he estimated, or earlier if the roads were as straight and as bleak and empty as he expected they'd be.

They were. He made Roswell by seven-fifteen, delayed by a speeding ticket he picked up along the way. He passed a number of UFO-related tourist traps on his way into town, including a place claiming to have an exact replica of the alien body taken from the UFO crash in

1947, as well as a motel called the Ali-Inn and, of course, the International UFO Museum and Research Center. There was a fantasy bookstore and a place selling telescopes and related material to help you spot the visitors from other planets before they spotted you. He picked up a sandwich at an Albertsons and headed for the radio station, a small single-story white building in the middle of nowhere, at a crossroads in the desert that was technically in the town of Dexter. The radio tower reached high into the starlit sky, its red warning light blinking a thousand feet above the ground, which explained how WROZ was able to broadcast from "sea to shining sea." An awning protruded from the side of the building to form a carport, and beneath it, two lawn chairs. No one answered when DeLuca knocked on the front door of the radio station. When he went around the side, he found a second door that was open. He knocked again and didn't get an answer, so he let himself in.

The hallway was lined with metal shelving overflowing with books and tapes and paperwork, with a light coming from a room at the end of the hall. There, he saw an empty office, one wall to the office a large glass window, and beyond that, the broadcast booth, where a sixty-ish gentleman in a white cowboy hat was talking into a vintage microphone, earphones covering his ears, which was why he hadn't heard when DeLuca knocked. When DeLuca waved to him, the man held up a single finger and continued talking into the microphone. The radio feed was playing over a loudspeaker, a commercial Clark was reading for an Indian art gallery in downtown Roswell. When he was finished, he plugged a tape cartridge into the player. DeLuca heard a conversation going on between Clark and a caller. The man in the cowboy hat rose from his chair and opened the door to the office. He was wearing a khaki safari jacket over a denim shirt, jeans, and cowboy boots.

"Ed Clark," he said. "What can I do for you?"

DeLuca noticed that the man had a small pistol in a holster that snapped onto his belt, the weapon worn at the hip. He could understand why someone might want protection, working all alone in the middle of nowhere.

"I thought your show was live," DeLuca said. "I don't know why, but I guess I'm surprised."

"If Garrison Keillor can do reruns, why can't I?" Clark said.

"I'm David DeLuca," DeLuca said. "I left you a message."

"Ah yes," Clark said gruffly. "Mr. DeLuca. I know who you are, and I know who you work for."

DeLuca had worked with deluded people before, particularly in his capacity investigating crimes in eldercare homes when he was attached to the state police in Massachusetts. Sometimes you could get more useful information from them if you just played along. Antagonism, on the other hand, rarely got you anywhere.

"Well in that case, you know why I'm here," he said.

"I think I do, but why don't you tell me?" Clark said.

"Why don't you tell me?" DeLuca said. "I told them if anybody was going to know about this, it would be Ed Clark. They said you're just guessing."

"And what'd you say to that?" Clark asked.

"I said if he's guessing, then I wanted to know who was doing the math because the odds of being right so many times had to be astronomical."

Ed Clark eyed him suspiciously for a moment, then took a briar pipe from one of his jacket pockets and a plastic pouch of tobacco from the other, filling the pipe with coarsely cut tobacco and tamping it in with his finger.

"This is about the robots, isn't it?" he said. DeLuca nodded solemnly. "Let's talk outside."

DeLuca followed him. Under the carport, Clark struck a kitchen match against the cinderblock wall of the station and lit his pipe, exhaling several large clouds of smoke before drawing one he could savor. He gazed at the sky.

"See anything interesting up there?" DeLuca asked him.

"If I did, I wouldn't have to tell you, now would I?" Clark said.

"I suppose not," DeLuca said.

"Is it what I think it is?" Clark said. "One got loose, didn't it?"

"I think you know why I can neither confirm nor deny that," DeLuca said.

"And you're the animal catcher," Clark said. "Is that it?"

"I can't confirm that either," DeLuca said, "but if I was, and you were in a position to help me, would you?"

"Hypothetically?" Clark said.

"Hypothetically," DeLuca said.

"And why would I help you?" Clark asked.

"I think you know why," DeLuca said. "There's always a quid pro quo, isn't there? And it's not like it's the first time, is it?"

"No, it isn't," Clark said. "What can I do for you?"

DeLuca stared up into the sky.

"Just supposing I was the 'animal catcher'?"

"Just supposing," Clark said, drawing thoughtfully on his pipe.

"We were monitoring your show the other night," he said. "As we always do."

Clark nodded, saying nothing.

"We think he called you. He identified himself as 'Bartleby.' By now you must have developed a sixth sense about whether your callers are human or not."

"I'm pretty good," Clark said. "Though I suppose every now and then somebody slips past me. Mostly it's in the diction and the word choice. Some people still think androids can't use contractions."

DeLuca laughed.

"I thought he sounded pretty darn smart for a human," Clark said. "Not that aliens aren't free to call my show. Or robots. I just like them to identify themselves. I don't like getting jacked around."

"Of course. No one does," DeLuca said. "The problem is that he rerouted the matrix so that we couldn't trace the call."

"As you programmed him to do," Clark said. "And now the chickens are coming home to roost."

"Go ahead and tell me you told me so," DeLuca said. "But when you're done, I need your call logs from the show. Or was that a tape, too?"

"That was live," Clark said. "I'll get you the logs. Just answer me one question."

"What is it?"

"How'd he get loose?"

"If we knew that, I probably wouldn't be here," DeLuca said. "Right now he's fighting his homing program. We think he learned the budget was being cut, so he acted out of pure self-preservation and ran off. If he manages to recode his homing program, there's no telling where he'll go."

"I'll tell you where he'll go," Clark said.

"Where?" DeLuca said.

"Where else? Washington, D.C. To blend in with all the other robots. And maybe to take down the president. Or whoever is cutting his budget."

"If you're right," DeLuca said, "then that's a chance we can't afford to take."

Clark ambled back into the station, limping slightly, favoring his right side. When he returned, he handed DeLuca a pink phone message memo with the name Bartleby written on it and a number. DeLuca looked at it.

"That number's from Chloride, New Mexico," Ed Clark said, pointing with his pipe stem. "'Bout two hundred miles due west. But you gotta go around White Sands."

"I know where Chloride is," DeLuca said. "And I think I know where Bartleby is. Thanks for all your help."

The old man looked at him expectantly. DeLuca wondered what he could possibly be expecting.

"Well?" the old man said at last.

"Well what?" DeLuca said.

"Aren't you going to wipe my memory?"

"Oh, that," DeLuca said. "Not until the mission is over. Until then, this conversation never took place. There's a chance he'll call back or even . . . pay you a visit, in which case that pea gun on your hip isn't going to do a damn thing. If he calls again or if you see anything, I want you to be fully aware, and I want you to call me." He gave

Clark his phone number, but for his personal satellite phone and not for the encrypted one. It was just a hunch.

"What do you mean, if I see anything?" Clark said. "You don't think he'd come here, do you?"

"Hey—this is just a hypothetical conversation, Ed," DeLuca said. "There's nothing to worry about."

"But as long as I carry the memory of it," Clark said, "I'm not safe, am I? Because now I'm a threat. And you guys are just going to leave me here for bait, aren't you?"

"Oh, come on, Ed," DeLuca said with an exaggerated wink as he headed for his car. "You know we don't work that way."

At the intersection of Routes 380 and 70, DeLuca stopped to look at the map. It was too late to head back to Albuquerque, and he was tired, and Chloride wasn't exactly on the way but it wasn't entirely out of the way either, so he headed west on 70. As he drove, he called Peggy Romano and had her reverse-search the phone number Ed Clark had given him. She told him it was for a Circle K convenience store on Route 52, at the edge of the Gila Wilderness. He also asked her to set up another appointment for him with General Koenig—it was time for another visit, but this time, he had enough information to make the conversation interesting. "What am I—your receptionist, now?" Romano asked him. "By the way, Ben Yutahay called. He didn't say what it was about but I gave him your direct number, so check your voice mail."

When he checked, Yutahay sounded hoarse.

"Hello, David," he said. "Listen, I was wondering if you could do me a favor. My son, Marvin, was supposed to come to dinner two days ago, but he never showed up and he didn't call and I can't seem to reach him on his phone. He usually checks in, but not always. I know you can find out if he's used his phone and things like that, so I was hoping you could look into it, if you have time. It's probably nothing, but he's all I've got, so I guess I get a little more worried than I probably should. Thanks."

DeLuca called Peggy Romano back and asked her to run an electronic search for Marvin Yutahay. If he'd used his phone or a credit card or an ATM card in the last forty-eight hours, she'd know.

He drove into the darkness of the high desert, the sky above him an enormous canopy of stars, and no moon anywhere to wash them out. The night was beautiful, and yet after a few minutes, driving into utter nowhere, the landscape a big blank as far as the eye could see, he started to feel just a bit paranoid—maybe it was the coffee he'd drunk, but he caught himself wishing he had more than just his police .38 and his Army-issue Beretta. He wished he had somebody in the car with him, or somebody to talk to on the phone. He kept thinking that he was being watched, followed, tracked, measured, analyzed, and that at any moment or second, in a flash of light so sudden he'd never even see it, he could vanish without a trace, like the sailor who gets knocked overboard and sinks into the middle of the wine-dark sea.

Marvin Yutahay was probably camped out somewhere beyond the reach of cell phones and satellite dishes, but he was a big boy who could take care of himself. Maybe he'd had car trouble, or maybe he'd met a girl who'd taken him back to her place and wasn't finished with him yet.

DeLuca turned on the radio, just for company, and found 1190 on the dial.

"I had an interesting visitor tonight," Ed Clark was saying calmly. "Of course I can't tell you who it was or what planet he was from, but in case anything should happen to me, I've written . . ."

He turned the radio off—he'd given Ed Clark all the time and attention he intended to give him for one night.

The weather turned as he headed into the high country, the sky clouding over, which made him feel no more secure—the best surveillance satellites had been able to image through clouds for some time. When it started to snow, he turned on his wipers and let up on the gas, slowing down when the road began to slip beneath his wheels. He was dog-tired. He wondered if a town the size of Chloride even had a motel. He considered calling Peggy Romano and asking her to find out, but he knew she'd probably chew his head off for using her as a travel agent. He hoped he was close, because a quick check of the gas gauge told him he was down to a quarter of a tank. He'd just stifled his third prolonged yawn in a row when something suddenly loomed in his headlights.

He slammed on his brakes, but his tires failed to bite, the car fishtailing, the shape directly ahead of him motionless, an image caught in his headlights for a split second, two large eyes reflecting back the light from his headlights, before he struck it with his right front fender just as it appeared to leap, the thing flying over the hood of the car and bouncing off the windshield to land somewhere behind him.

He stopped.

He got out, leaving the car idling by the side of the road.

About twenty feet behind the car, illuminated in the red of the Taurus's taillights, he found a large female mule deer lying on its side, breathing heavily, its big brown eyes full of fear as it lifted its head. It tried to move but couldn't. DeLuca knelt next to it. It was a doe, her antlers having molted, in their place only soft fuzzy stubs. He felt her legs for broken bones, but she didn't seem to feel pain when he touched her. He felt her ribs and noticed something else—she was pregnant, her belly distended, with something kicking inside.

"Shhh," he said in a soothing voice, trying to quiet the animal. "You're going to be all right. I don't know any first aid for deer, but I'm going to call somebody who does."

His words seemed to have an effect. For a moment, all seemed calm. He heard only the car running, and the delicate sibilance of snowflakes falling on pine needles.

Using his personal SATphone, he was dialing directory assistance with the intention of calling the state police when he noticed something odd, a disturbance in the air overhead, as if he were looking at the northern lights shimmering, but closer—and how was it that the aurora borealis might penetrate the cloud cover?

He heard a buzzing sound, and then a disk of brilliant white light descended from the clouds, the ship (for there was really no other way to describe it) perhaps fifty feet across, hovering above the road, maybe two hundred yards in front of the car. In brief bursts, beams of light shot from the saucer to the ground, scanned a moment, then stopped, as if the ship were searching for something with a spotlight. It was moving away, at first, then reversed direction, moving toward him, just as the deer struggled to its feet. DeLuca held it tight, his arms around the animal's neck.

The ship continued its search. DeLuca had no time to think of a better plan, so he took the chain bearing his dog tags from around his neck, used the strap attached to his cell phone to tie the phone to the chain, dialed the first number from his contact list and looped the chain around the deer's neck. As the ship drew closer, he dived under his car, concealing as much of his body as possible beneath the still-running engine, even though it was a tight fit and the exhaust manifold burned his leg. The heat from the engine would mask his infrared signature, and the electrical field would mask his own. The deer stood fixed in the roadway.

"Go!" DeLuca shouted.

The animal didn't move.

He grabbed a handful of snow and gravel and threw it at the animal. This time it took off, running into the woods, limping heavily on its right front leg. It had gotten perhaps thirty or forty yards from the road when a beam of light caught it, and then, in a flash, the animal was gone, leaving behind only a cloud of steam that quickly dissipated. DeLuca was reminded of the old magician acts where the guy would throw down a smoke bomb and vanish into thin air.

He watched from beneath the car. He dared not move, holding his ground. The saucer scanned the area where the deer had been, drawing closer. When it was directly overhead, a circle of light surrounded the car, melting the snow that had fallen on the road. The ship lingered a moment longer, then, apparently satisfied, moved on, continuing to scan the road in brief bursts of light.

Another hundred yards down the road, the saucer turned off its lights and lifted suddenly into the sky.

DeLuca waited a long time beneath the car. The temptation was to get into the car and drive away as quickly as possible, but it was a temptation he couldn't afford to give in to. Two hours was the approximate dwell window of the milsats that overflew Iraq, but he couldn't wait that long. His other problem was that if the car ran out of gas, he could find himself in trouble of a different sort. He still had his encrypted phone, but he didn't dare use it until he'd talked with Peggy Romano to make sure it was still safe to do so. Finally, after perhaps thirty minutes, he crawled out.

He dusted himself off and stood motionless beside the car, sniffing the air, listening, watching the sky, the light snow still falling. He grabbed a flashlight from the car and went to where he'd last seen the deer, but there was nothing, no deer, no phone, and only the faintest smell of burned hair in the air. If the ground had been scorched, the falling snow had already covered it up.

He shut off his flashlight and walked back to the car. He wasn't sure what he'd seen. He knew what he was supposed to believe he'd seen, but that and what had actually transpired were often two very different things.

Chapter Ten

DAN SYKES CALLED JOSH TRUITT AFTER THE Navaho Tribal Police office in Shiprock issued a report that a vehicle registered to Theresa Davidova, a white 1984 Toyota pickup, had been found on the reservation, at the end of Rural Road 2634a in a place called Sudano Canyon. When Sykes called Shiprock, an officer named Jim Chee told him the truck had been covered with a camouflage tarp.

"Sometimes people do that when they don't want anybody messing with their stuff," Chee said. "Then snow covered the tarp." The truck had been found by a Navaho rancher who'd been tracking a mountain lion that had been killing his sheep. "We can't tell you how long the truck's been there or where the driver might have gone," Chee said. "We left things the way we found them, for now. There's a cabin farther up the canyon where people stay. If you want, I could come with you to check it out."

"Just impound the vehicle until we can process it," Sykes said. He thanked the officer and said he'd call him if it turned out he needed assistance. DeLuca had asked him to take a different approach and see how far it went—he was to suppose that General Koenig's suspicions were correct. Davidova hadn't met Escavedo via the bulletin board at a laundromat—assume it was more intentional than that. Assume Cheryl Escavedo was gay, and that Davidova had used that to draw her in somehow. According to several of the strippers Dan interviewed who'd danced with Theresa Davidova, she'd swung both ways upon occasion, something Josh Truitt seemed unaware of. Suppose the circle connected in the other direction—Sergelin had told Leon Lev to find somebody who worked at Cheyenne Mountain, somebody with access to Darkstar data. He'd found Escavedo and sent Davidova to make contact, perhaps as a way of paying off the debt she owed him.

"Any idea why Theresa might have gone to Shiprock?" Sykes asked Truitt after he told them they'd found her car.

"A pretty good idea, actually," Truitt said. "We were there together, last summer. I brought her along as an assistant on a shoot."

Truitt drove. They stopped at a general store called Eli's Trading Post at the intersection of Sudano Canyon Road and 2634a, a wooden structure in serious disrepair, with a gas pump out front and a handwritten note on the door that read MEKING A DELIVRY—BACK LATER, MARY but no indication when the note had been written. It was two o'clock in the afternoon.

They found Theresa's truck half an hour later, parked well off the dirt road in an oak grove at the bottom of a hill where the road narrowed and became impassable, though occasionally, Truitt said, 4WD off-road clubs went in farther with their H2s and knob-tired winch-equipped Jeeps. Sykes examined the Toyota, but there was little information to be gained. She'd taken the flashlight from the glove compartment, where Sykes found a deck of cards and a black lace bra, but Truitt said he'd seen her take the bra off beneath her sweater and store it in the glove box after they'd come home from a party. There was a cell phone recharger plugged into the cigarette lighter socket, and a felt tip pen with its cap off on the passenger seat. The floors were clean, almost as if they'd been vacuumed, and the dashboard was free of dust, as if it had been wiped. Sykes had a pretty good idea that whoever had cleaned the car had taken care not to leave fingerprints or DNA. They'd know more once they ran the vehicle through the FBI lab in Denver.

"The cabin is a couple miles in," Truitt said, opening the tailgate of his truck and handing Sykes a pair of snowshoes. He donned a pair as well, throwing a large backpack over his shoulders.

"You want me to carry anything?" Sykes asked as Truitt handed him a pair of ski poles to assist the hike.

"I carry my own stuff," Truitt said. "For the record, I hate bellboys, too."

"What's in the bag?" Sykes asked as Truitt headed off.

"Things we might need," Truitt replied over his shoulder.

Sykes had a hard time seeing how any Jeeps or 4WD vehicles would ever make it up some of the steep declivities they traversed. They hiked in silence for about half an hour, traveling perhaps three kilometers until Josh Truitt pointed to a cabin backed up against a limestone cliff. There was no smoke coming from the smokestack, a bad sign, Dan guessed.

The cabin was empty, but someone had been there. A jar of blue Berry Blast–flavored Gatorade sat on the table, frozen solid. The bed had been slept in, and under it, Truitt found a paperback copy of the latest Harry Potter book, which he said Theresa had been reading. A kerosene lamp sat on the table, half full of fuel. Sykes found three power bar wrappers in the wastebasket.

"There was a deck of cards in the glove compartment," he said. "Were they Theresa's?"

"She was teaching herself to play Texas Hold 'Em," Truitt said. "She wanted me to take her to Las Vegas. Apparently Cheryl's uncle lived there."

"If you were going to spend some time in a cabin in the mountains," Sykes asked, "wouldn't you bring a deck of cards? Why leave it behind? It's not like it takes up that much room."

"Maybe she forgot."

"Maybe."

Sykes moved to the door and peered at the sky. There was no point trying to look for tracks. He saw prints in the snow where a chipmunk or possibly a squirrel had scrambled across the porch, but beyond the overhang, the new-fallen snow would have covered over any signs indicating what direction Theresa might have taken.

"You said you were here on a shoot?" Dan asked Truitt.

"That's the next place I was going to suggest we look," Truitt replied.

Dan Sykes strapped on his snowshoes and followed the photographer up the canyon, struggling to keep pace, and Sykes was in excellent physical condition, a triple black belt in karate and something of a workout fanatic. He figured Truitt had to be one of those guys they simply called "genetic" back at CI school at Fort Huachuca, physical freaks with mutations that gave them oversized lungs or massive hearts or extra red blood cells. The path was simpler to find as the canyon walls began to converge, the trail climbing through drifts that were ten feet deep, giving way to windblown areas of bare rock.

"This is New Mexico karst," Truitt explained. "If we had time, I'd chip you off a piece of wall and show you the seashells and marine fossils in it. Two hundred fifty million years ago this area was the bottom of the sea. The whole Chihuahuan Desert, actually. It's basically a limestone uplift, and whenever you get that, you get a lot of caves, where the eons of rain percolate through the rock and form underground rivers and aquifers."

"Like Carlsbad?"

"Carlsbad is a little different. And Lechugilla, which is a whole lot different."

"What's Lechugilla?"

"It's a cave near Carlsbad," Truitt said. "But unlike precipitate caves formed by ground water percolating down, Lechugilla was formed over millions of years by sulfuric acids bubbling up from below. It's probably the most fantastic cave in the world. Not to mention the most complex."

"You shot the coffee table book for that one, right? The book you gave to Sergeant Escavedo."

"I shot it, but somewhat reluctantly," Truitt said. "Half the time I photograph a cave, I come back a few years later and it's been ruined by amateur cavers leaving their footprints all over the place or breaking off crystals for souvenirs, and all because I gave the place a little publicity. Fortunately they put a sealed vault door on the only entrance to Lechugilla and a permit system and they actually police the place to make sure nobody's been in there without a license. It's probably the most beautiful place on the planet. Also one of the most dangerous. Do you like caves, Agent Sykes?"

"Not particularly," he said.

"Well then you're really going to hate this one," Truitt said.

After a steep rise, they came to a clearing where the ground leveled off. The canyon wall opposite rose vertically for five hundred feet, but at the base of it, there appeared to be an area where the snow hadn't fallen. Closer examination revealed that the snow had in fact fallen but it had melted, the air as they approached getting warmer and mustier smelling. Surmounting a small ridge, Sykes glanced down at what appeared to be a dark grimace in the earth, a crescent-shaped gash at the base of the wall from which, he saw, a small bat flew out, and then another.

"Probably another hour before the emergence," Truitt said, looking at the sky and taking his snowshoes off where the ground was free of snow. Sykes did the same as Truitt dug into his backpack, extracting a pair of LED headlamps. He handed one to Sykes, then handed him a pair of gauntlet-style rubber gloves and a roll of silver duct tape.

"Tape your pants to your boots and your sleeve cuffs to your wrists. Don't tape the gloves on because you might need to take them off. Take off your coat and your fleece but wear this on your head, college boy style," he said, passing Sykes an Arizona Diamondbacks cap, then a pair of paper surgical masks. "One of these should last you half an hour, maybe an hour. When it gets too wet to breathe through, you can switch to the new one. It's not that big a cave, but it's damn nasty. It goes down three chambers and there are no major drops or constrictions, but it gets slippery, so that's why I've brought these," he explained, taking a pair of climbing ropes from his pack and strapping on a belt of climbing gear. "We're not belaying or anything—all I'm doing is setting guylines, pretty much. The first chamber, not counting the entry corridor, is approximately star-shaped. The one after that is sort of like a hot dog and the final one is like a hamburger bun. The snakes are active year round inside but they're Mexican boas so they're not going to hurt you." Finally he handed Sykes a pair of goggles, something like a diving mask. "This is just because I got a wicked eye infection once. I don't know if it was from the cave or what, but I'd prefer that it not happen again. There's all sorts of microscopic stuff in the air. You ready?"

Bats were emerging from the mouth of the cave at a rate of two or three a second, the sun still above the horizon but below the canyon walls.

"Leave my coat here?" Sykes said.

"You're not going to need it," Truitt said, testing his large hand-held flashlight and handing a second one to Sykes. "The thing about cave environments is that unless they're challenged, they're incredibly stable. This one hasn't changed much inside for maybe a million years, so unless something happened that I don't know about, the temperature in the star chamber is going to be ninety-three or ninety-four degrees, and hot dog is about a hundred and hamburger is a hundred and ten, hundred percent humidity and not a breeze, so it's basically like a pitch-black sauna, full of shit. And snakes. And bugs. The Indian name for it translates as 'Home of the Dark Spirit.' The Spanish name was *'Lugar de las Matanzas.'*"

"'Place of the Killings,'" Sykes translated.

"'Slaughters.' I've got dry clothes to change into when we come out. Ready?"

"Can't wait," Sykes said.

Truitt led the way. The gash in the earth sloped down about thirty feet while the ceiling rose to where the two men could stand as they descended the portal slope, Sykes placing his feet as precisely as he could in the footholds Truitt chose. The heat and humidity struck him immediately, an overwhelming wall of oppressive dankness, though the smell was tolerable, something like mushrooms, perhaps. The floor here was a mixture of mud and guano, perhaps eight inches thick. Truitt said it would get thicker the farther in they went. There were blurry footprints in the muck. Sykes asked Truitt to stop while he examined one.

"The thing is," Truitt said, "because of how stable it is in here, those could be from yesterday or a year ago or ten years ago. You could probably measure the amount of bat shit that's fallen into them and get an approximation, but it's hard to tell. See that over there?" He shone his flashlight on a set of pictographs on the wall, two human figures fighting what appeared to be a bear. "That's Anasazi. Maybe eight thousand years old, and it looks like somebody painted it yesterday. This place is still relatively unknown. I only heard about it from a caver I met who was part Navaho. The Indians were generally not big on caves. They considered them places where evil dwells."

"Why would Theresa come here?" Sykes asked.

"I'm not sure," Truitt said. "The bats' collective body heat is what keeps it this warm, so sometimes people use bat caves to weather snowstorms, but she could have stayed in the cabin if that was the problem."

He called out, "Theresa!" but there was no reply.

"You think she's still in here?" Sykes said, a steady stream of bats fluttering past him now.

"Maybe," Truitt said. "Nobody can stay in here for more than a few hours. By the way, you hear those crickets?" He shone his flashlight on a pair of monstrous crickets the size of tarantulas fixed to the place on the sidewall. "Those are the caver's best friend. Cave crickets live by the entries, so if you ever get lost and can't find your way out, head for the sound. They're also the bat's alarm clocks. They're photoperiodic so they read the light dying outside the cave and start chirping at sundown, and that lets the bats know it's time to emerge. The next room is the vortex room."

Where the slope bottomed out, Truitt shone his light in the air, where thousands, perhaps millions of bats swirled in a frantic circle. The sound they made was something like fat raindrops falling on a canvas awning, the air stirred by a million pairs of wings.

"I'm guessing this is maybe a tenth of what's here," he said. "They do this to get the juices flowing before they emerge. I heard one estimate that there were probably eight million bats in this colony, but it fluctuates depending on the bug populations outside—you can study the guano layers and extrapolate climate changes from what kinds of bugs the bats were eating over a given period. These are all insectivorous Mexican brown shorttails. They have a slightly better sonar than fruit bats where the prey doesn't move, so that's why nothing is hitting you." He shone his light on the cave floor, a series of mounds and swells. Sykes saw one, then two, then three pale white snakes, about the size and thickness of baseball bats, as well as cockroaches two and three inches long, some in motion and others collected in mats. "The snakes mostly wait for something to die and hit the cave floor, but they can also snatch a bat out of midair if the bat gets careless and flies too close. Needless to say, anything that dies and hits the floor, like baby bats that can't fly yet, either gets swallowed or taken apart pretty quickly."

He shone his flashlight on one of the mounds, a rock covered by a thick coating of guano, and then he struck a gash in the coating with the spike of his climbing axe. The coating was alive and moving, filled with cockroaches and coprophagic beetles, worms, millipedes, and assorted larvae.

"This is why this stuff makes such unbelievable fertilizer," Truitt said, shining his light 360 degrees, though there was nothing unusual to be found. "As I said, it just gets better and better farther in."

They passed through the narrowest part of the cave, an aperture the width of a garage door with a ceiling low enough that Sykes had to stoop, a heavier stream of bats streaking past him, and occasionally he'd feel a feathery wing brush against him. They'd been in the cave for ten minutes and Sykes was already soaked in sweat.

The hot dog room was perhaps fifty yards long, forty feet wide, and thirty feet high. To the side, Truitt shone his light on a small skeleton, a set of ribs arching from the muck.

"Coyote," he said. "Maybe came in here looking for a snack and got lost, I'm guessing."

At the far end, he drove a piton into the wall, tied a rope to it, and threw the coil into the final chamber, explaining that the descent was steep and slippery. Sykes stood at the crest of the precipice, shining his light below, then at the ceiling, where millions of bats covered every square inch of the surface. The temperature was unbearable, the humidity even higher. His face mask was too soaked with sweat to breathe through anymore, so he held his breath and replaced it with his second mask. He noticed that Truitt had lowered his and asked him why.

"The mask is mainly to prevent histoplasmosis, which is a fungus that gets in your blood, but I've already got it. Chicken farmers and people who keep pigeons get it, too. It's sort of like mononucleosis, but you can carry it in your blood your whole life and never become symptomatic. When you do, it's mostly just fatigue and listlessness you feel. They call it 'cave-sickness' in South Africa."

"This place makes me understand why we bury ourselves in solid wood coffins," Sykes said. "Everything in here is what lives underground and gives people the creeps—this is exactly what most people don't want touching them."

"I disagree," Truitt said. "I've actually told people that when I die, I'd like my body left in a bat cave. It's pretty much a complete recycling. Sort of suits my Buddhist leanings."

"Did you ever talk to Theresa about that?"

"She had the idea before I did," Truitt said. "When we did the shoot here, she thought it was the most remarkable place she'd ever been. She came along as my assistant, mostly to hold my strobes. Veteran cavers don't like bat caves, for obvious reasons. She thought it was cool. Figuratively speaking."

"Do night vision goggles work in caves?" Sykes said, momentarily sorry he had forgotten his.

"Turn your headlamp off for a second," Truitt said. Sykes did, and then Josh Truitt did, too. Immediately the sussurant sound of bats' wings flapping increased, their prior efforts and energies suppressed by the photons produced by the flashlights and headlamps. The utter darkness was very nearly disorienting. "This is a complete lack of light," Truitt said. "NVGs amplify minute amounts of available light, but in here you don't even have minute amounts. So no, they don't work."

He lowered himself down the rope, hand over hand, more sliding than walking with his feet. Sykes followed him into the final, hamburger bun chamber. At the bottom of the descent, he swept the cave floor with his flashlight and saw something white with black lettering on it, the plastic sleeve from a Cyalume chemlite. He picked it up and placed it in one of the Ziploc bags he'd brought to collect evidence.

"Light stick," Truitt said, joining his flashlight beam to Sykes's beam. "Some cavers use them to mark the way, like leaving breadcrumbs on a path through the woods, because the way out of a cave never looks like the way in did. Though I don't know what kind of idiot could get lost in a cave this simple."

"That's not what this one was for," Sykes said. "This one is military issue. It glows in the infrared range, so that it's invisible to anybody who's not supposed to see it."

"But you can see them with night vision goggles, right?" Truitt said.

"Yup," Sykes said. "NVGs and one of these would have lit this place up like a ballroom." He shone his flashlight back toward the top of the slope they'd just descended. "I'm going to guess that whoever brought this here either dropped it accidentally and didn't know it or dropped the wrapper and knew it but didn't have a rope to climb down to get it. Is there any way to climb out of here without the rope?"

"One person?" Truitt said. "It wouldn't be easy. Maybe not even possible. I'd hate to be forced to find out."

"So suppose someone is running from somebody. Being chased . . ."

"Theresa?"

"Yeah," Sykes said, working through the scenario as he spoke. "I'm just thinking out loud. She's in the cabin but she sees a car coming, or maybe someone on foot, so she runs. And there's nowhere else to go but here, really. She comes in the first chamber, the entry corridor, and waits, thinking maybe whoever it is isn't going to follow, but he does. So she runs to the star room. He follows. She moves to the hot dog room and hides. She sees his lights. Is she using lights? She has to turn hers off or he'll see her, but she can see him coming closer. Finally, she slides down the slope and comes here, desperate. He stands up there, at the top. He puts his NVGs on and cracks an infrared chemlight. Now he can see the whole room, and he can see her, but she can't see him. He doesn't come down because he doesn't have a rope and he knows he can't get up without one."

"But he knows she can't get out either, so he leaves her here," Truitt said.

"He doesn't know that for certain," Sykes said. "For all he knows, she can get out. He's probably armed. I don't know. I'm just thinking."

After ten minutes, the two men splitting up to search both sides of the cave's final and lowest chamber, Sykes heard Truitt call out and crossed over to him. Truitt shone his light on the sole of a hiking boot, a women's size eight or nine, Sykes guessed, sticking out of the muck.

"That looks like hers," Truitt said.

"You might not want to see this," Sykes said.

"I want to see it," Truitt said.

Sykes moved closer and lifted the boot, until the skeletal remains of a foot fell out. The bones had been picked clean. Brushing away the guano lightly with his fingers, he found the femur, the tibia, the hips, the rib cage, the spine, the bones cleaned of flesh and integuments. He saw, draped over the vertebrae at the clavicle, a gold chain and pulled it free, a small diamond crucifix, set in silver. He handed it to Josh Truitt.

"This was hers," Truitt said.

Sykes dug a bit further until he found the skull and lifted it from the muck, brushing it clean with his fingers. Quite unintentionally, he held it so that the light from his flashlight shone inside the skull and then out again, illuminating both the entry hole and the exit hole where some sort of projectile had pierced the skull.

"Oh, God," Truitt said.

"I'm sorry," Sykes said. "Are you all right?"

"Uh-uh," Truitt said, his voice shaking. "Not even a little."

"Any idea how long she might have been here?" Sykes asked. "How long it would take the . . . cave life to do this?"

"In a cave this active, I've read where the cryptozoa can strip a cow carcass clear in twenty-four hours," Truitt said. "Some labs still use a similar technique to clear skeletons."

"I'm going to have to bring this in and send it to the lab," Sykes said. "We can send someone later for the rest of the remains . . ."

"No," Truitt said, handing Sykes his backpack. "Just give me the skull when you're done and I'll bring it back here and put it with the rest. This is where she'd want her bones to stay."

Once outside the cave, they changed into the dry clothes Truitt had brought and donned their winter gear again, showshoeing back to the cabin in the darkness, using the headlamps to show the way. The night sky was clear and full of stars.

They stopped at Eli's Trading Post for gas, coffee, and sandwiches. Eli had died years ago, and the place was now run by his wife, Mary, a pleasant Navaho woman with a long gray braided ponytail and weathered skin, dressed in jeans and a denim shirt. Sykes asked her if she'd mind answering a few questions concerning the truck the tribal police had found up canyon.

"I'll tell you what I told them," she said. "I heard it pass by, four days ago, in the afternoon. But I didn't see who was driving it. They said it was a girl. If it was, she didn't stop to buy anything."

"How about afterward?" Sykes said. "Did anyone come by afterward? Somebody who might have been following her?"

"I told Jim Chee there was a man," she said. "But I had never seen him before."

"Do you mind if I show you some pictures?" Sykes asked. When she said she didn't mind, he called Peggy Romano and asked her to download the photographs to his SATphone. The first picture he showed the old woman was of Leon Lev. She shook her head. She shook her head again when he showed her the picture of Dushko Lorkovic. He asked Peggy to run any other photographs she had in the Escavedo file past the old woman, who shook her head each time, no to Brother Antonionus, no to Hilton Jaynes, no to Cipriano Cabrera, until she suddenly put her finger on the phone and said, "That one—that one was here."

She'd put her finger on a picture of Major Brent Huston.

"You're certain?" Sykes asked.

She nodded slowly.

"Do you remember what he said, or what he bought?"

"He didn't say very much," Mary said. "I usually try to have a conversation with whoever comes through here. Sometimes I get so lonely I think maybe I'm imagining them. But I remember what he bought."

"What?" Sykes asked.

The old woman moved from around the counter and went to where the shelves held cleaning supplies, turning and holding up a bottle of Windex antibacterial glass cleaner.

"And a roll of paper towels."

Chapter Eleven

PEGGY ROMANO HAD NO INFORMATION ON MARvin Yutahay. He hadn't used his phone, visited an ATM machine, or charged anything on his credit cards in the last forty-eight hours.

"Anything else you want me to do?" she asked.

"Not right now," DeLuca said.

"Why are you calling me on a pay phone?" Romano asked.

"Having trouble with my mobile," he told her.

"How was your night last night?" she asked.

"Interesting," he said. "Tell you when I get back to camp."

DeLuca found the Circle K convenience store on County Road 007, the road that led from Chloride into the Gila Wilderness, next to an abandoned tourist trap that had at one time been dubiously called Pochahontas Ville, and still had a fading painting of an Indian maiden on the façade (bearing a strong but probably coincidental resemblance to Janet Jackson), with the words FEED THE BEARS in red and blue letters three feet high. He saw a series of pits, cinderblock cells sunk into the earth, with a system of chutes and pulleys that apparently visitors could use to drop or lower whatever it was they'd feed to the poor animals held in the cells. There was a shuttered-up gift shop, a teepee constructed of plywood next to it, and a circle of bleachers in the back forming a ring, maybe forty feet across, and beside that a large cage, twenty feet high and thirty feet square at the base with trees and perches inside where evidently someone had kept and displayed something large, eagles, perhaps, or apes or monkeys, though there was no tire swing.

In the store, DeLuca bought a newspaper and a cup of coffee. The headline on the *Weekly World News* said "EARTH UNDER ATTACK BY ALIENS; BUSH TO SEND NATIONAL GUARD TROOPS TO MOON." "Of course he'd send Guard units," DeLuca thought. *USA Today* was running a story about how the New England Patriots were quietly building a football dynasty. DeLuca checked the news for his home state of Massachusetts. The "Big Dig," the new freeway tunnel running beneath downtown Boston, had sprung multiple leaks and was closed for repairs. "What do you expect for twenty billion dollars—you get what you pay for," he thought.

A young girl in braids, braces, white eyeliner, and a tight belly shirt that allowed three inches of flab to form an O-ring around her middle was working at the cash register. When DeLuca asked to speak to the owner, the girl said he was in the back. When DeLuca asked her to go get the owner, the girl said he was sleeping. When DeLuca asked her what time he usually woke up, she said she didn't know. When DeLuca said he'd come back and asked her if there was a place nearby where he could get breakfast, he heard a voice call out from the back, "I'm up! I'm up! Hang on a second, goddamn it. I just have to find my pants."

A minute later, a man appeared in the doorway, looking something like a troll who lived under a bridge. He had wild hair, wild eyes, and a full beard that came down to midchest. He was wearing blue jeans held up by suspenders, a red T-shirt and a black fleece vest over that, on his feet only flip-flops. He ran his fingers through his hair to push his mane away from his face and poured himself a cup of coffee from the Bunn machine.

"Jesus, Connie—this coffee tastes like you made it yesterday," he said.

"I did," the girl said. "It's perfectly good. There's nothing wrong with it."

"She didn't charge you for that, did she?" the man said, pointing at DeLuca's cup.

"It's all right," DeLuca said. "I've drunk worse."

"So have I, but you shouldn't have to pay for it," he said, pouring the rest of the pot down the drain and handing the empty pot to the girl, then opening the till and giving DeLuca back the dollar eighty-two he'd paid for what he had to agree was not good coffee. "How can I help you, sir?"

"I was looking for the owner?" DeLuca said.

"That would be me," the man said, offering his hand. "Arthur Bartok. What can I do for you?"

"David DeLuca," DeLuca said, taking it. "I was interested in PochahontasVille so I was hoping to talk to you about it."

"Historically?" "Bartok" said.

"In part," DeLuca said. "I'm actually thinking of retiring to New Mexico, with my wife, and I'm looking for business opportunities to buy into. I was just in the UFO museum in Roswell yesterday and the place was packed.

I'm just thinking out loud, so I apologize if I sound like an idiot, but I was wondering if the property might possibly be for sale? Or lease?"

"Bartok" looked at him.

"Right now I own a bar back home, but my wife and I both want to do something that doesn't involve working nights," DeLuca continued, though he knew by the way "Bartok" looked at him that he wasn't getting across. He saw, in the man's eyes, an unmistakable intelligence. That told him he had the right man. There was tension now in the way "Bartok" carried himself, his eyes glancing momentarily down below the cash register, where DeLuca suspected he kept a gun.

"You want to restore PochahontasVille to its former luster?" "Bartok" said.

"I don't know," DeLuca said. "I just like the area and thought I'd ask."

"I was thinking maybe I'd sell it to PETA as a monument to animal cruelty," "Bartok" said. "People used to bring in black bears they'd trapped or half-shot and they'd put 'em in the pits and feed 'em dog food, and then every once in a while there'd be a special show where they'd take a bear and stake him in the middle of the ring and set dogs on him. That's the last known bear-baiting ring in the United States. After that ended, they used the place for cockfights and dog fights. Cockfights are still legal in parts of this country. Though I don't suppose that's what you had in mind."

"I was just thinking of opening a UFO museum," DeLuca said. "I thought maybe this would be far enough away from Roswell that there wouldn't be any competition. Are there other UFO attractions nearby?"

"This whole state is a UFO attraction," "Bartok" said. "Thirty-four percent of Americans believe in UFOs and only 26 percent believe in evolution. Fifty-one percent believe in ghosts. Eighty-six percent believe in the devil. What do you believe in, Mr. DeLuca?"

"I believe in the devil," DeLuca said. "I know because I was married to his sister for four years. Do you believe in UFOs?"

"But of course," "Bartok" said. "I also think professional wrestling is real. Do you believe in UFOs?"

"I'd prefer not to. Though after what I saw last night, I'm starting to wonder. I guess you could say I believe in power. I believe power invites power. Power begets power. Power assimilates and corrupts and coopts the people who deploy it because power protects itself," DeLuca said, quoting from "Bartleby's" soliloquy on the radio.

"Bartok" eyed the girl behind the cash register.

"Let's go sit in the beautiful sunshine and talk," he said. He led DeLuca outside to the ring of bleachers and climbed halfway up the nearest one, leaning back against the riser behind him. The sky was clear blue, the temperature already in the sixties and climbing.

"You're Army," "Bartok" said. "CI, I'm guessing."

"And you're Dr. Gary Burgess," DeLuca said. "Arthur Bartok would have to be in his eighties by now. Or should I say, 'Bartleby'? How'd you know I was Army CI?"

"Well, you said you'd drunk worse coffee, and the only place you could do that is the Army," Burgess said. "CI was just a guess." He pointed to the center of the arena. "That's where they'd stake the bear. Some of the bigger ones would fight for hours. Fifteen, twenty dogs. Eventually the dogs would rip it to pieces. This passed for entertainment. Are you a dog lover . . . what is it? Captain? Major?"

"Agent," DeLuca said.

"How'd you find me? Don't tell me NSA is monitoring the Ed Clark show now?"

"They're not, but I was," DeLuca said. "You used the phrase, 'handwriting is on the wall.' Your ex-wife said that's the phrase you left in your note."

"How's Penelope?" Burgess asked.

"She's okay, I guess," DeLuca said. "Maybe you should ask her yourself."

Burgess stared at the horizon.

"They know where I am," Burgess said. "They would never let someone like me just walk away. I guess when I left we had an old-fashioned Mexican standoff, but they know where to find me."

"And you're not afraid they're going to do something?" DeLuca asked.

"They can't," Burgess said. "Before I left, I wrote a night watchman program. You know those old night watchmen in the factories who had to go from station to station and turn their key at various locations, and if they failed to reach a station and turn the key, a siren or a bell of some kind would go off? That's my protection. I have to enter a password once a week, and if I don't, the data dumps to a couple different places. China. Iran. The *New York Times.*"

"The Union of Concerned Scientists?"

Burgess nodded.

"Why can't they just intercept your password and use it themselves?"

"Because it changes every week," Burgess said, pointing to his head, "and I'm the only one who knows what it's going to change to."

It was DeLuca's understanding, according to some digging he'd done, that Gary Burgess's IQ was off the charts; he was a college graduate at thirteen and a Ph.D. at sixteen who'd been able to compute long, complicated mathematical equations in his head, a "Good Will Hunting" sort of polymath who'd grown up a tough kid in New York City and ended up solving Raphael's Fourth Theorem at the age of eighteen after mathematicians had tried unsuccessfully to solve it for hundreds of years. It was the kind of mind the Defense Department took particular relish in diverting to its purposes, DeLuca had always thought.

"And you think they'll never figure out the pattern?" he asked.

"I'm sure they'll try," Burgess said, wagging his eyebrows to say he wasn't worried. "And when they do, they'll come for me. But until then, I'm safe."

"What data is there to dump?"

"Geez, DeLuca—if I told you that, it would sort of defeat the purpose of the standoff, wouldn't it?" Burgess said. "As long as I'm the only one who knows, everyone else is safe."

"That's why you left Penelope, wasn't it?" DeLuca asked. Burgess didn't answer. "All right then. Suppose I just guess. I'll tell you what I'm thinking and you just stop me when I'm wrong."

Burgess reached into his pants pocket and took out a pack of cigarettes, offering one to DeLuca, who declined.

"If the world knew how close we are to the apocalypse, everybody would be smoking," Burgess said. "Frankly,

I'm surprised R. J. Reynolds hasn't adopted that as a marketing strategy."

"Closer than even you know, I think," DeLuca said. "Darkstar is deployed."

Burgess stared at him.

"I'm all ears," he said at last.

"That's the good news," DeLuca said. "The bad news is, we don't know who's operating it. I'm guessing your part was working on the penning fields. Your wife said your specialty was magnetic fields. I Googled some of your old articles and tried to read them but they were way over my head. The problem was always that antimatter couldn't become a viable defense option until a perfect field was created to contain it. And you did that. But you quit when you realized what they were going to do with it. That's what's powering Darkstar, isn't it? Antimatter."

"You read too much science fiction," Burgess said.

"That might be," DeLuca said. "Right now though, I'm like the world's most realistic guy. And if you were as realistic as I am, you'd see that with Darkstar operational, watchman program or no watchman program, their reasons for keeping you alive are growing thinner all the time. Like the Stealth program. How many times can you fly a black delta-winged airplane over a Missouri cornfield before you have to admit, yeah, we have black delta-winged airplanes?"

"I'd heard they launched two and one was damaged and the other was black," Burgess said. "Are you saying it's not?"

"Officially?" DeLuca said. "It's not. Unofficially, strange things have been going a lot more than just bump in the night. Last night, a disk of light appeared above the road in front of me. Could Darkstar do that?"

Burgess nodded.

"They've been doing that for years. You take two beams and set one slightly out of phase with the other and intersect them," he said. "Like when two spotlight beams intersect at the circus, except that only the intersection registers in the visible spectrum. I think Darkstar could probably do just about anything they can do with laser effects at a Phish concert."

"Vaporize people?" DeLuca asked.

"That was sort of the whole idea, originally," Burgess said.

"The Hitler question?"

"You got it," Burgess said. "Why bother sending a thousand Marines into Panama if we could just beam a Noriega or a Saddam Hussein into a million particles while he's lying in his bed? Think of the lives we'd save. And the expense. Bad for Halliburton, good for TRW."

"Bin Laden?"

"If Darkstar really is deployed, like you say, then yeah, absolutely. If I were him, I'd stay in my cave. You're talking about the virtual instantaneous projection of nearly infinite power. With or without as much collateral damage as you want, depending on how the beam is focused and directed. You talk about a surgical strike—this is the same technology doctors use to operate on people's eyes without damaging the surrounding tissue."

"And power corrupts."

"No shit?"

"So who's they?"

"Who is or who was? I was working for Space Command when it was Air Force. I got out after it was reassigned to STRATCOM."

"Did you know Cheryl Escavedo?"

"Who?"

"Cheryl Escavedo," DeLuca said. "Cheyenne Mountain, archives. Native American. Good-looking."

"We may have crossed paths inside The Mountain," Burgess said. "If we did, I can't remember. I did most of my work at the DEL at Kirtland. Why?"

"She was trying to contact you, I think," DeLuca said. "Either you or your wife."

"Why?"

"We don't know," DeLuca said. "They say she stole some disks. What do you know about General Thomas Koenig? Or Major Brent Huston?"

"What do I know about them?" Burgess said. "One is insane and the other makes the insane one look sober as a judge. Koenig is a paranoid control freak with delusions of grandeur and a persecution complex. Huston thinks he can talk to God. And he's obsessive-compulsive. They both think they have enemies inside and outside the military. Koenig hates Democrats. Huston thinks homosexuals are after him. So he has delusions of cuteness, I guess. I worked for both of them at Cheyenne."

"Could Koenig take control of Darkstar?" DeLuca asked. "Best guess."

"Best guess," Burgess said. "Hmm. I was going to say I didn't think so."

"But?"

"It depends on how long he's been thinking about it. If someone started at the inception . . . Hmm. Interesting. You think it's Koenig?"

"I don't know," DeLuca said. "I know he came into STRATCOM as the security protocols guy, so he had all the keys."

"Yeah, but having the keys wouldn't be enough," Burgess said. "He'd have to have the core codes too, and those were all over the place. One person couldn't do it alone. Or two. You couldn't do it in-house without somebody posing a security risk. I mean, somebody would figure it out and blow the whistle or leak it or write a book or whatever. I don't know if you're big into conspiracy theories. I've always found it hard enough to get more than three people all on the same page at the same time right out in the open. He could parallel-engineer it out of country, but that would take a lot of money."

"Would there be enough money for that in the black budget?"

"I don't know. That's why they call it a black budget. But even that has to be accounted for. My part of the project was pretty high priority, but even I couldn't just ask for more money any time I wanted it."

"How about if you engineered it in the Soviet Union? Nongovernment. Private funding?" DeLuca had had a hunch that oil billionaire and ex–KGB section head Vitaly Sergelin was involved the first time he'd heard the name mentioned. He hadn't been sure how to connect him, until now. He'd found an evaluation Koenig had written for the CIA during his time at the U.S. embassy in Moscow expressing an odd respect for his opposite number. It wasn't that unusual for two former enemies to develop a relationship.

"They'd have the talent," Burgess said. "Or they used to. And the way things are over there, you wouldn't have to pay that much to lure away the best people from government work. I could probably make you a short list of who to look at over there."

"I'd appreciate that," DeLuca said.

"Of course, anybody using Russian resources or giving Russian scientists top-secret U.S. files would be guilty of treason, even if the Russians didn't really know what it was they were working on."

"Would Koenig be capable of that?"

Burgess thought about it, not answering at first. A red hawk circled in the sky above them. DeLuca watched it, feeling that he had some idea now of what it felt like to be a field mouse.

"Tom Koenig is paranoid, but he's bright. A lot of paranoids are bright. Seeing patterns is what you get when you have too much brain sometimes. He micromanages everything because he wants to and because he can, and when things go well, he gets all the credit. And things have gone well for him. I thought he was the most egotistical bastard I ever met, but even I had to respect what he accomplished. It seemed clear to me that he thought he could do everything. And that would include single-handedly appointing himself the world's policeman. He hated the bureaucracy, and how it took so many people so much time to make what he considered simple decisions. He admires people who take things into their own hands, unless that means they take them out of his. I could see him using Russians, if it suited his purposes. He wouldn't have thought of it as treason. He'd think of it as his personal contribution to globalization."

"What about Huston?"

"He'd do whatever Koenig told him to do. Whenever Koenig said, 'Jump,' Huston said, 'How high? And on whom?'"

"I want to bring you in," DeLuca said. "When the time comes, we're going to need your testimony. Could you do that?"

"And leave all this?" Burgess said.

"You can help us," DeLuca said.

"Help who?" Burgess said. "I just wanted out of it. I still do. I didn't want to be personally responsible for what happened. I never thought I could stop it. You can't stop an idea."

"The Mexican standoff isn't going to hold for much longer," DeLuca said. "Let me ask you something. The penning field that traps the antimatter. What powers it?"

"You need a fail-safe nuclear power source," Burgess said. "You can't afford to have a power outage. There'd be a solar backup array, but if you go to that, you lose your stealth."

"What happens if you lose power?"

"You lose containment."

"Meaning what? An explosion?"

"Possibly. If the power loss is catastrophic. The penning field is the filter. Antimatter is by definition repellent to other matter. It's not nonmatter, or reverse matter or parallel or mirror matter—it's matter that hates matter. The energy is released when you force the antiprotons and antielectrons to collide with posimatter, and the electromagnetic field is what controls how much is released, what kind, what rate. The resounder mirrors focus it into wide or narrow beams but the penning field controls the wavelength and the amperage. The thing is designed for a controlled release in full in case of system failure. An uncontrolled release would create a very large explosion."

"How large?"

Burgess shrugged.

"There's nothing to compare it to. Maybe a million times Hiroshima? Bigger than the meteor hit that killed the dinosaurs? Ten thousand Krakatoas? It gets kind of meaningless."

"But not the second big bang they're talking about?"

"One can only hope."

"So how do you stop this thing? Is that what would happen if somebody somehow manages to target a Darkstar and blow it out of the sky with a conventional kill vehicle?"

Burgess nodded.

"That was one of the better arguments against deployment," he said. "They were still discussing it when I left. The argument was that you couldn't have two countries boosting rival Darkstars without creating a catastrophic environment, but if you could assure that you were the first in orbit, you could prevent the second from launching. There wouldn't be a space race because it would be over before it started. You'd have unchallenged control of the ultimate high ground, and from there you could pretty much call the shots. I'm sure Koenig would have come down on the side that said while we sit here jawing about this in Armed Services Committee closed session hearings and policy meetings and blah blah blah, somebody else could be putting one of these in the sky. And he never did figure out how to suffer fools. I imagine the people who sent you are pretty eager to see you solve the problem."

"They expressed some urgency," DeLuca said. "I'm not sure I understood the gravity of it until now."

"I'll talk to whoever you want me to talk to," Gary Burgess said.

"I think you should talk to Penelope," DeLuca said. "Does she know any of this?"

Burgess shook his head.

"She can't," he said. "She never can."

"Sit tight," DeLuca said. "I'm going to talk to Koenig."

"And say what?"

"I'm not sure," DeLuca said. "You're under arrest, maybe. My advantage at the moment is that he thinks I'm dead. Is there a place in Chloride to rent a car? Or buy one?"

"Take my truck," Burgess said. "It looks like shit but don't worry—it runs like shit, too."

Chapter Twelve

WHEN DELUCA GOT BACK TO ALBUQUERQUE, he called a team meeting in the RV. Sami was still in San Antonio and incommunicado. Sykes had sent the remains of Theresa Davidova to Mitch Pasternak for processing. He'd calculated the shooter's position and the angle of fire and managed to find the round that killed her. He'd sent the round to Mitch Pasternak as well.

"You don't want to know what I had to dig through to find it," he said. "Somebody seriously needs to go into that cave and change the litterbox. Josh took it pretty hard."

"You think Huston was the shooter?" Vasquez asked.

"I don't know," Sykes said. "Maybe he was going there to talk her into coming back and someone else was the shooter."

"If he's the shooter, what's the reason?" DeLuca asked.

"He was having an affair with Cheryl Escavedo?" MacKenzie speculated. "Or else he met Theresa Davidova when she was a prostitute and obtained her services and then felt guilty about it. Maybe he was involved with both of them. Wasn't Jimmy Swaggart into three-ways?"

"Or maybe he's just pious and there's nothing sinister underneath," Vasquez said. "Let's not start suspecting people just because they put up an innocent front. Some people actually are innocent."

"Name one," Sykes said.

"Hoolie has a point," DeLuca said. "Putting Huston on the scene doesn't make him guilty. His being a conservative doesn't make him guilty. Everybody here knows you need more than proximity."

"We'll look for it then," MacKenzie said. "We did get some interesting intel on the helicopter downings. We ran the names through the system and one came up twice. Vitaly Sergelin. When the British communications satellite GeOx-4 went dark, shares in Global Oxford Telecom went through the floor, dropping by fifty Euros the first day and another eighty the next, until a company from Luxembourg called Eurostat came in as a white knight and stopped the slide by buying the remaining shares. You asked us to look into who profited from the lost satellites. Vitaly Sergelin owns Eurostat. And Global Oxford is trading again where it was before the slide, creating a windfall for Eurostat."

"What else?" DeLuca asked.

"Two years ago, his daughter Anna is a freshman at the University of Arizona and by all accounts a major party girl," MacKenzie said. "She picked U of A for the climate and because of its reputation as a party school. For security purposes, she's enrolled as Anna Johnson. One night, she ditches her bodyguard and goes to a frat party where she hits it a little too hard and dies of a drug overdose. The drugs she took are traced to a junior named Miguel Cabrera. Son of Cipriano. Is that reason enough to seek revenge and blow two helicopters out of the sky? Why not? Tucson police found the body of the bodyguard who was supposed to be keeping her out of trouble in seven different pieces in a dumpster behind an El Gigante. One cop I talked to said Leon Lev and Dushko Lorkovic were the two lead suspects but they couldn't get a single witness to talk about it so they couldn't make the arrest."

"What happened to Miguel?"

"Dropped out and disappeared," said Vasquez. "Presumed hiding, somewhere in Sinaloa. Wes Vogel thinks Mazatlan."

"Can somebody please explain to me how any of this connects?" Sykes said. "I'm not trying to rock the boat, but if I can speak frankly, I think we need to know a little more about this satellite program that's been compromised. I was fine with just looking for a person, but if you ask me there's a little too much darkness around here. If there's a solid reason for it, I'll respect that and back off, but I feel like I'm driving around without an X on the map to head for. Just saying, 'Go that way and tell me what you see' is a little frustrating."

"I gotta agree," Vasquez said. "We got Mexican drug dealers, we got Russians, and we have some sort of space program—I'm confused. And I'm a big enough man to admit it."

"I admitted it first," Sykes said. "That makes me bigger than you."

"It does not," Hoolie said.

"It does too," Sykes said.

"Seriously," MacKenzie said. "What are we doing here?"

DeLuca exchanged glances with Peggy Romano, who nodded.

"Fair enough," he said. "I'll try to keep it short. Let me start by saying that getting read on to this is going to increase your personal jeopardy—that's why I was trying to avoid it. I don't suppose anybody wants out?"

He paused, though he knew the question was largely rhetorical. He gave them as full a briefing as he could about Darkstar, with Peggy Romano filling in some of the background details regarding the parts of the Star Wars program that she knew from her time at NSA. He concluded by presenting some of Gary Burgess's thoughts on how whoever had seized control of Darkstar1 had run and/or financed a parallel development program, possibly in the Russian Union.

"So you're saying Darkstar took out Cabrera?" Vasquez said. "Like a bit of target practice?"

"Burgess says they've been practicing for a long time," DeLuca said. "Tuning the output and calibrating target acquisition software and whatever."

"They're using NRO intel," Romano said, "but they're inside the gates. The only way to catch them at it would be to know when they're going to need intel and then shut the whole system down to see who's the last person on the other end of the line. And they're not going to shut down the whole system."

"And Cheryl Escavedo stole information proving Koenig had seized Darkstar?"

"Possibly," DeLuca said. "Peggy has a theory."

"Stealth satellites aren't 100 percent invisible," she said. "They are when they're inactive, but when they deploy to fire, according to Burgess, they give back a radar signal. The problem is that the signal reports an object that's significantly smaller than its actual size. The reduction is maybe 90 percent, and these things are pretty small to begin with, as we understand it. So if it gives back a signal the size of a baseball, say, then that's not technically invisible. Cheyenne Mountain and Space Command have been tracking objects the size of baseballs or larger for the last forty years. Twenty-five thousand, with about eighty-five hundred currently in orbit."

"Peggy thinks Darkstar is disguising itself as something currently in orbit," DeLuca said. "Or more than one thing. If it wants to park over western Russia, it finds something already flying over western Russia, destroys it, and assumes its orbit, then moves on when it needs to go somewhere else."

"Wouldn't that leave holes when it vacates?" MacKenzie said.

"It would," Romano said. "But these guys break up or reenter all the time, and they're too small to leave footprints. They're shooting stars. Who can say what's what?"

"And Escavedo worked in archives," Sykes said. "She had all the records of which objects are where and when."

"Whoever's controlling Darkstar needs their own dish to transmit the command and control signals," Romano said. "If they were using ours, we'd know it. And I'm not talking about something the size of what's on the roof of Ms. Kitty. So we're looking for something at least thirty feet across. We're also looking for anomalous events. For example, we got a report that a group of rebels in Chechnya attacking one of Sergelin's oil pipelines was wiped out in the middle of nowhere, and a survivor who'd been lagging behind because he'd stopped to use an outhouse said he saw a flash of light. We're still trying to tie down the exact time and place, but if we get enough of that sort of thing, we might be able to predict where Darkstar is going to be. Right now, the only thing that can take out a Darkstar is another Darkstar. Anything kinetic, it's going to see coming well in advance and take out. When it reconfigures to fire, it's exposed for only a few seconds. Nothing could get to it in time except some form of directed energy. I have to correct myself—that's not the only way to take out Darkstar. We could disable it from the ground if we can find out who's running it and intercept them."

"And you think it's Koenig?" Vasquez said.

"He has means and motivation. Nobody else is on the radar," DeLuca said. "He tried to tell me Sergelin was heading up a Russian ASAT program, but I think Sergelin is his partner and he was just trying to send me on a wild goose chase. We'll know more if we can tie Huston to Davidova. Maybe they were afraid she knew what Escavedo knew, or that she had the disks. The fact that they're trying to erase their tracks, so to speak, makes me think they're getting either careless or cocky or paranoid or all three. The good news is, that increases the likelihood of their making a mistake. The bad news is, that mistake could be killing one of us."

"We don't know what their reconnaissance or biometric identification capabilities are, exactly," Romano said. "Is it strictly NRO intel or do they have something beyond that? The whole idea was to find people like Bin Laden and take them out surgically, rather than send troops or bombers or whatever, and to get 'em before they have a chance to duck back into their spider holes. The point is that there are probably a number of ways they can target you, with or without SIGINT, so what we were thinking was that rather than try to hide indoors or wear sombreros, we'd send a false positive. I wish I could say I was as confident as I was before that all communications passing through this vehicle are secure—I still believe they are with 95 percent certainty, but 95 might not be good enough, so what I've done is recoded the GPS report signals on your personal phones and SATphones and mission transponders to send a phantom image, an echo, so that anybody looking down is going to think we're all one hundred meters farther west than we actually are, meaning if Darkstar wanted to hit us, it would hit that white van at the end of the parking lot instead. Maybe we should put an orange No Parking cone there, come to think of it. Anyway, the first shot should miss. I couldn't say how long it would take them to realize they missed, or by how much. I'd say if it happens, toss your phones as far as you can and take cover, but at least it will give you a fighting chance."

"Just be careful," DeLuca said. "Dan, you're on Major Huston. Mack, Hoolie, you're still on Leon Lev—he set up Cabrera, so he's onboard. He connects Koenig and Sergelin. I've got a stop to make and then I'm going to talk to Koenig. Alone."

"I don't think . . ." MacKenzie began.

"Alone," DeLuca repeated. "Any backup that goes with me is going to be unprotected in the firing zone. It's possible that if I tell him he's blown, he'll make a deal."

"It's also possible he'll melt you like the Wicked Witch of the West," Sykes said.

"I promise I'll wear sunblock," DeLuca said.

* * *

An hour after the briefing, a green Neon pulled into the parking lot. Sami was carrying a bag of groceries in each arm as he followed Rainbow and her daughter Ruby to the motel office, where he booked them a room across the hall from his own.

DeLuca had just finished getting dressed after a shower when Sami knocked on his door. Sami filled him in on the last twenty-four hours. They'd driven to San Antonio, where they found the house where Malcolm Percy's sister Alexandra lived, in the King William District, south of downtown. She'd answered the doorbell with a smile on her face and invited them in when she recognized them as members of the Brethren. When Rainbow identified herself as Ruby's mother and said she wanted to speak to her daughter, Alexandra Percy demurred and asked Rainbow if she'd gotten permission from Brother Antonionus, to which Rainbow replied that she didn't need permission.

"Alexandra called her brother and I guess he said it was okay," Sami said. "The poor kid was terrified to go outside. Then when we get back, he tells Rain she's no longer one of the Brethren and that her transport ticket has been rescinded. Look, I know it probably sounds silly to you, but it really meant something to her. She's taking it pretty hard."

"How about the kid?" DeLuca asked. "How's she holding up? She tell you what she saw?"

"I told her I was taking her to a man who was going to explain to her what happened," Sami said. "I told her she didn't have to say anything until we met him."

"Well let's go then," DeLuca said. "Who're you taking her to?"

"You," Sami said. "They're in room 432."

The girl Ruby was sitting in a stuffed chair by the window, playing a hand-held video game, dressed in pink sweatpants and a pink zippered sweatshirt with a hood. Her mother, Rainbow, was watching a pay-per-view movie on television, *The Bridges of Madison County,* starring Clint Eastwood and Meryl Streep. Rainbow was wearing jeans and a black shirt, rather than the festive red DeLuca had seen her in before. It made him sad. Sami introduced DeLuca, saying, "Ruby, this is my friend David, and he wants to help you understand what you saw in the desert. Is it all right if he talks to you?"

"I guess," she said, not looking up from her game.

"Can I call you Ruby?" DeLuca asked, sitting opposite her at the table.

"My name is Susan," she said.

"She changed her name," Rainbow explained. "I think all nine-year-old girls change their names. I wanted to be called Stella until I was twelve."

"Can you tell me what you saw in the desert, Susan?" DeLuca said. "The night you were out there with your friends?"

"I didn't see anything," she said.

"Did you see a girl?" DeLuca asked. "A Native American girl with long black hair? Kind of pretty?"

"She was Native American?" Ruby asked.

"Yup," DeLuca said. "Cocopah, from near where I used to live, in Yuma, Arizona. I used to know a lot of Cocopahs. Her name was Cheryl Escavedo."

"What kind of Indian name is that?" Ruby/Susan asked.

"It's Spanish," DeLuca said. "There was a lot of intermarriage over the years between the Cocopah and the people who lived south of the Mexican border. And she was also a soldier. Do you remember if she was dressed like a soldier? Was she wearing sort of tan pants and blouse with little spots and lines on the fabric?"

"I don't know," she said. "It was dark. And then it wasn't."

"What do you mean?"

"I mean I only saw her in the light for a little while. Like when somebody takes a picture."

"Like the flash on a camera?"

"Yeah," she said. "Sort of."

"How far away were you?" DeLuca asked. "Like from here to the door? Here to that car? Here to that silver motor home over there?"

"Not so far, maybe," she said.

"It's great, Susan, that you can remember and tell me about what you saw, because we were hoping to find out what happened to Cheryl Escavedo."

"It was an ascension," Rainbow said. "It was probably a mistake, because we were there waiting and she wasn't even one of us."

"If you don't mind, I'd like to just hear it from Susan," DeLuca said to Rainbow, as gently as possible. "Could you tell if she was carrying anything? Did she have anything in her hands?"

"I don't think so," Ruby said.

"Was she walking or running or standing still?"

"She was running."

"Then what happened?"

"She was caught in this light."

"But only for a split second?"

"Yeah."

"Was she lifted up? Did you see her sort of floating?"

"No."

"Maybe you looked away for a second?" Rainbow offered.

"I didn't look away," Ruby said. "She was just there one second and then she wasn't."

"What did she look like? What was the expression on her face?"

"I didn't see her face. She was looking down. Sort of bent over."

"Did you hear anything? Smell anything? Feel anything?"

"It was hot. Like the wind was hot."

"Did this light come from anywhere? Like when you shine a flashlight?"

"I don't know," Ruby said. "I don't think so."

"And did this scare you?" DeLuca asked.

Ruby looked at her mother, tears welling up in the corners of her eyes.

"Were you afraid it could happen to you?" he said. "And you don't want it to happen to you, even though you know you're supposed to be happy about it. Because that's what your mom and her friends have been waiting for. But it's not what you've been waiting for, and you didn't want to disappoint your mom."

"I just want things to stay the way they are," Ruby said, her voice trembling. "I don't want to change."

"It's all right," DeLuca said, thinking. "You don't have anything to worry about, Susan. It wasn't an ascension. It sounds to me like Sergeant Escavedo shape-shifted. Her uncle told me her totem was a raven, so that's probably what happened." He turned to Sami. "Her uncle will be relieved to hear that. He was worried that she was in trouble."

"So she turned into a raven?" Ruby said. "Like in *Brother Bear*?"

"Brother Bear?" DeLuca said.

"The movie," Ruby said. "This Indian named Kenai dies and his soul goes into a bear."

"Yeah, something like that," DeLuca said. "Anyway, she's okay. Thank you, Susan. Sami—can I talk to you in the hall?"

He walked Sami toward the elevators to make sure Rainbow and her daughter wouldn't be able to hear them through the door.

"I don't have time to explain but just keep them indoors and you guys should be all right. Rent all the pay-per-view movies you want and order room service but keep them inside. Romano will get you up to speed. What name did you register them under?"

"Mary and Karen Peterson," Sami said.

"Good," DeLuca said. "Who are they?"

"That's them," Sami said. "That's their real names."

"Okay," he said. "Talk to Romano. And don't talk to anybody from the Brethren. Any of you."

Peggy Romano had called General Koenig's office and spoken to Lieutenant Carr, who informed her that the general was spending the weekend at his ranch in Arizona, outside the town of Ajo, between the Goldwater Testing Range and the Tohono O'Odham Indian Reservation. It was a ten-hour drive from Albuquerque. DeLuca had one stop to make before getting onto the freeway.

He let himself in the back door to Cheryl Escavedo and Theresa Davidova's apartment. It was probably a waste of time, but he'd been turning over in his mind where she might have hidden the disk. She would have put it somewhere where somebody could find it if something happened to her, but not somewhere obvious, like between the mattresses, and probably somewhere where she'd have access to it in case she wanted to take it with her quickly. She knew she was in danger, but she wasn't sure how much, or she would have taken greater precautions. Something Dan had said had given him an idea.

The cat wound herself through his legs, so he went to the cupboard and opened a fresh can of cat food for her. The cat purred in appreciation, devouring the contents of the dish DeLuca had set on the floor. He picked up her litterbox, which by now had a strong smell to it, dragged the wastebasket out from beneath the sink and slowly, carefully, poured the dirty cat litter and the dried cat shit into it. Nothing. When he lifted the newspaper lining the bottom of the pan, he saw a Ziploc bag containing a single writable CD. It was something like storing it with a natural two-week timer. She probably expected Theresa to find it. Had she in fact found it and put it back?

He ran the Ziploc bag under the faucet, watered the plants, then turned off all the lights and stopped back at the Red Roof Inn, where he gave Peggy Romano the CD. Romano sneezed.

"I'm allergic to something here," she told him. "Where'd you find this?"

"The cat had been . . . playing with it," DeLuca told her.

A cursory perusal revealed only a series of financial reports that didn't mean much to either of them, not the smoking gun DeLuca had hoped to find. He told Romano to forward the contents to Walter Ford.

"Call me as soon as you learn anything. By the way," he said. "We're going to need to find somebody to take care of their cat, apparently. Let me know if you can think of anything. And if you have time, we need a couple American Girl dolls for room 432."

A message from the Democratic representative from New Jersey was waiting for him when he checked his voice mail. The message said, "Agent DeLuca, Bob Fowler here. Sorry for my surliness, the last time we spoke—I had a staffer check you out and we were both impressed. No contact here, that anybody can turn up, from Sergeant Escavedo. And the sailing in Delaware Bay was delightful, but I do appreciate your concern. Please let me know if there's anything else I can do for you."

Chapter Thirteen

THE HOUSE WHERE MAJOR BRENT HUSTON lived looked pretty as a postcard, a large, newly constructed neocolonial in the foothills outside Colorado Springs, in a neighborhood of large pretty-as-a-postcard newly constructed neocolonials on cul-de-sacs with American Eagle–themed mailboxes. Huston's house was immaculately groomed, the kind that could sit for fifty years and never approach cozy, with trimmed hedges, manicured border gardens, and a line of young spruces as symmetrical as Christmas trees separating the front yard from the back, a pair of maples in the front yard with slate flowerboxes around their bases, the driveway clear of snow due to heating coils embedded in the blacktop, according to the thermal imaging camera that Sykes and Jambazian had brought along, rendering the walls of the house as transparent as glass. The house still had its Christmas decorations up, including a small crèche made from plastic figurines on the lawn beneath the French window. According to the thermal images viewable on Sykes's PDA, Huston was alone, sitting in front of the fireplace reading a book, or perhaps a magazine. Sami stayed in the car to keep the house under surveillance while Sykes rang the bell.

"Guilty," Jambazian told Sykes via his nanotransmitter, viewing the thermal image. "When he heard the doorbell, he threw whatever he was reading in the fireplace."

"I'm guessing it was either *Juggs* or *Mother Jones,*" Sykes said.

"Can I help you?" Huston said, opening the door. Sykes presented his badge and credentials.

"Agent Danforth Sykes, Army Counterintelligence," he said. "I'm with Agent DeLuca's team. I was hoping I could have a word with you. I know it's Saturday but we were told you wanted to be briefed 24/7 ASAP, and we decided against using even encrypted phones, at least for the time being. May I come in?"

"Of course, of course," Huston said. "I apologize for my manners. My wife and kids are up in Telluride skiing today so I wasn't expecting anybody. Please come in. Would your friend in the car like to come in as well?"

"My driver needs to wait in the car," Sykes said.

"Now I'm your driver?" Jambazian said.

"Make yourself at home," Huston said, leading Sykes into the living room, where the fire was still dying down. "Can I get you anything? Coffee or tea?"

"I'd love a cup of coffee," Dan Sykes said.

While Huston was in the kitchen, Sykes surveyed the room. The house was spotless. He wondered where Huston kept his mess. The book he'd read on obsessive-compulsives said many of them were phobic about other people's germs but lived quite comfortably amid their own filth. Perhaps his affliction was something Huston kept secret even from his own family. There were religious icons everywhere, a Bible on the coffee table as well as paintings on the walls of various familiar Christian images, not one hung even slightly atilt. All the books on the shelves were neatly faced and arranged in alphabetical order by title. The arms of the chairs had lace antimacassars, neatly aligned. Christmas music played softly from the next room, even though it was well past the season.

"What's keeping him?" Sykes asked sotto voce.

"He's washing his hands," Jambazian said. "And if this camera is reading correctly, he's using water that's almost scalding. Five-four-three-two-one . . ."

Sykes heard the water shut off in the kitchen.

"Three minutes exactly," Sami said. "He's either locking or unlocking the sliding glass door to the back patio. I couldn't say why."

"Do you take it black or with cream, Agent Sykes?" Huston called from the kitchen.

"With cream, thanks," Sykes said.

"Just so you know, he's using some sort of powdered coffee white," Sami said a moment later.

Huston set the cup on the table in front of Sykes and sat opposite him, rising briefly to poke the fire in the fireplace.

"So please," Huston said, seeming more composed now than he had before. "Tell me what you've learned. Have you found Sergeant Escavedo?"

"We have not," Sykes said. "But we're starting to think she might have met with foul play, as they say in the Agatha Christie books. Her roommate went missing five days ago. We found her car on a Navaho reservation in the Four Corners region near Shiprock. We tracked her to a cabin in a remote canyon and finally to a cave at the base of the canyon."

"A cave?" Huston said. "This was the roommate, you say?"

"Theresa Davidova," Sykes said. "A Russian girl. Been in this country for three years."

"Russian?" Huston said. "You think this is the Russian connection General Koenig was concerned about?"

"Possibly," Sykes said. He'd found no smoking gun, taking the tack that Davidova had sought out contact with Escavedo, no note from Leon Lev saying, "Theresa, make contact with this woman for me and I will let you go." At the same time, the odds that the sergeant had made a connection with the Russian girl purely at random seemed remotely small. If Sergelin and Koenig were partners, perhaps the former KGB colonel didn't completely trust his American counterpart. Perhaps he wanted to gain some sort of leverage over him. Suppose, DeLuca had said, that Sergeant Escavedo and General Koenig, a married man, had had an affair and Sergelin found out about it? That would have been useful information to him. Sergelin could parlay information like that into power—a say over the targets Darkstar chose.

"Davidova had been brought here by a man named Lev," Sykes told Huston, "who owns a number of strip clubs and brothels in Juarez. Her boyfriend said she stopped working for him over a year ago, but that she was still afraid of him and that she thought that Lev was looking for her because he claimed she still owed him money. We think Davidova might have given him the disks Cheryl Escavedo stole, to wipe out the debt. We're not sure if Sergeant Escavedo told Davidova about the disks or if Davidova found them on her own."

"You don't think Davidova killed Escavedo, do you?"

"It's possible," Sykes lied.

"Do you know what was on the disks?" Huston asked.

"Not yet, but we're going to take down Leon Lev and shake him until his teeth fall out. The problem is that Lev is ex-KGB. Did you ever hear the name when you were working in Moscow?"

Huston shook his head.

"Lev is a fairly common name in Russia," Huston said. "I might have heard it, but I didn't know the guy."

"His body temperature just rose," Sami told Sykes. "He's stressing. I think he's lying."

"That's probably true," Sykes said.

"What do you mean by 'probably'?" Huston said. "Are you insinuating that I'm not telling you the truth?"

"I was just referring to how common the name might be," Sykes said. "At any rate, we found the girl's body in the cave. She'd been shot. Through the head. If Lev did it, we'll know as soon as we can get a blood sample from him."

"You need a blood sample?" Huston asked.

"We want to look for mycotoxins in his blood," Sykes said. "If he was in the cave, he would have been inhaling air that contains microscopic fungal spores from the bat guano. Once that gets in his blood, he'd develop a disease called histoplasmosis, which can actually be fatal if it isn't treated, once the fungus starts reproducing in the bloodstream. The same airborne spores will be on the clothes he wore and on his boots and whatever, so we should be able to tie him to the cave, and the lab boys can run the genomes for the specific spores that would connect Lev to that exact cave. We also have the bullet, so if we can connect it to the gun and the gun is in Lev's possession, we've got him. Of course, that's if we go by the book. Thanks to the Patriot Act, we might be able to skip a few steps, plus, he's not an American citizen so we can classify him as an enemy combatant if we want to, without having to worry about all the Jewish liberal ACLU media types coming down on us."

"Interesting," Huston said.

"His temperature went up again," Jambazian told Sykes.

"Anyway, I can't stay, but that's what we know, Major, and we wanted you to know as soon as we did. We have somebody who's going to talk to General Koenig. We have to decide at what point we want to bring the Pentagon in, but my sense was that you wanted to handle this as much in-house as possible—is that right?"

"I appreciate your discretion," Major Huston said.

Back in the car, Sykes suggested they relocate and watch the house from somewhere more concealed, but Sami disagreed.

"Let's stay put for a second and see what he does," Sami said. "If we sit, he's forced. He's aware of us but he doesn't seem all that concerned." They watched the screen, an outline of the house in cool blues and greens, the radiators represented by orange lines, the fire in the fireplace a bright red.

"Where'd he go?" Sykes said, looking at the screen on the PDA.

"He went down into the basement," Sami said, pointing at the screen with his finger, then at the kitchen. "This is the stove. He filled a lobster pot with hot water and turned the heat up under it. Okay—that's him," he said, his finger following the outline of a yellow figure. "He's in the living room now," Sami said, narrating what he saw on the screen. "He's looking at us through a crack in the curtains. He's moving to the fireplace. He's throwing something in the fireplace. Probably the clothes he wore. Why wouldn't he have burned them before?"

"Maybe he's a hoarder," Sykes said. "He's back in the kitchen. What's he got in his hand?"

"His boots," Sami said, interpreting the image. "He's putting them in the pot on the stove. He's making boot soup."

"I think that was in one of the MREs they gave us in Iraq," Sykes said. "Do you think he'll flip on Koenig?"

"Eventually," Sami said. "Dave DeLuca is the best I've ever seen at getting people to turn toward their best self-interests. I saw him flip all kinds of people as a cop in Boston. Gangbangers, made guys, politicians. The guy could sell snow to an Eskimo."

"What's Major Brent Huston doing now?" Sykes said.

"He's washing his hands again," Sami said. "We have three minutes. Wanna pop him?"

"Why not?" Sykes said. "As long as we're in the neighborhood."

Sykes approached the front door to make the arrest, drawing his Beretta automatic and chambering a round as Sami circled the house to cover the back. Sami cursed when a motion detector mounted at the side of the house triggered a set of floodlights and no doubt an alarm inside. When he rushed through a foot of snow to the patio doors, he found the kitchen empty. Sykes met him there.

"He's not upstairs," Sykes said.

They were staring at the door leading to the basement when they heard an engine roar to life in the backyard. Sykes bolted down the stairs while Sami rushed to the patio, in time to see Huston racing across the backyard on a snowmobile, spraying snow behind him as he sped away. Jambazian fired once, and Sykes fired twice from the basement door, both men watching as Huston disappeared into the pine trees. There was a second smaller green and yellow John Deere snowmobile in the covered area beneath the back deck where Huston parked his snow machines, but Huston had managed to rip out the ignition before departing on the larger sled. Sykes ran a hundred yards into the woods, following the tracks Huston had left in the snow, but stopped where the tracks joined a network of snowmobile trails, with no way of telling which way Huston had turned. He listened, the far-off whine of the four-stroke engine growing fainter and fainter. When he called Peggy Romano and asked if there was any aerial surveillance available, she said there wasn't.

Huston was gone.

Hoolie and Mack managed to get an appointment with Leon Lev when they told the bartender at Club Zorro that they had information Lev might be interested in buying, a CD-ROM they'd gotten from Theresa Davidova that had formerly belonged to Cheryl Escavedo. They insisted on meeting in a public place, in neutral territory, and not in one of the clubs Lev owned.

They met at noon at a McDonald's on Avenida Juarez, a short walk from the bridge. The restaurant was crowded with families and kids and businessmen on their lunch breaks, the counter manned by a dozen young men in green striped shirts and paper hats. The boy wearing the headset and manning the drive-thru window was a double for the boxer Oscar De La Hoya, Hoolie thought as he ordered a chicken Caesar salad for himself and a Coke for MacKenzie. Leon Lev arrived in a massive black Chevy Suburban with dark tinted windows. He was dressed in a loose-fitting black tracksuit over a red T-shirt, a thick gold chain around his neck and large silver and turquoise rings on several of his fingers. He was accompanied by a younger man of perhaps forty, wearing black pants and a black shirt under a silver-gray sport coat, as well as four larger and younger bodyguards, who took up conspicuous positions by the doors. Lev smelled strongly of vodka when he sat down opposite them at a central table.

"I am Lev," he said in Russian. "This is my new friend, Martine Guzman. The colonel is here to make sure you don't hurt me." He chuckled to himself, looking at Vasquez. "Who are you? Are you the one who killed my friend Dushko?"

"Esteban Bernal," Vasquez said, combining the names of two of his favorite accordion players. "This is . . ."

"I know," Lev said. "You are Mila Zukova from Suma. Why don't I remember you?"

"Why would you remember me?" MacKenzie said in Russian. *"I was six years old when you left Suma. Unless you were hanging around school yards."*

"My friend Martine is a very important man," Lev said to Hoolie. "He works for me now, but he is very important. Just ask him. He could arrest you for killing Dushko if I wanted him to. Did you know that?"

"Your Serbian friend slipped on a bar of soap," Vasquez said.

"I will tell you the truth. I was tired of him," Lev said. "Serbs have always thought they're better than Russians. That's why we wipe our feet on them. You want to work for me, Esteban Bernal? I'll give you a job. I'll put you in charge of soap."

"I work for myself," Hoolie said. "I work with Mila."

"My God," Lev said, laughing. "You are in love with this whore." He turned to Guzman. "They're in love." He turned to Hoolie. "Maybe I'll fuck your girlfriend just to show you I can. Maybe I'll fuck her right here on the table. Mila from Suma—have you ever been fucked at a McDonald's?"

He laughed.

"Maybe we'll sell our CD to someone else," Hoolie said. "I know that there are many other people who would be interested."

Lev shoved half a cheeseburger into his mouth and washed it down with his Coke, then held his paper cup up for one of his bodyguards to refill. He picked at his French fries.

"And what's on this disk?" Lev said, shoving three in his mouth. "I've never heard of this Escavedo person. But a friend of mine says he might be interested."

"What's on it is information," MacKenzie said. "Information you wouldn't want to fall into the wrong hands."

"Information about what?" Lev said. "If you want me to buy something from you, you have to tell me what it is I'm buying?"

"Information that proves you shot down Cipriano Cabrera's helicopter, for one thing," MacKenzie said.

"I did that?" Lev said, his voice filled with mock indignity at the accusation. "How could I do that? Why would I want to kill my new business partner? That makes no sense."

"You think you can control the cartel," MacKenzie said in Russian, as if she didn't want the others to understand. *"You think you can control the consequences of what you did, because you have an illusion about how powerful you are, but deep down, I think you are afraid. I think you are afraid of the United States government. And I think you are afraid of Miguel Cabrera, because you know he'll seek revenge for his father. I think you have a great many new concerns. I don't think you want more trouble than you've got now."*

"Listen to me, you piece of shit whore," Lev said in English, grabbing MacKenzie by the wrist and pulling her toward him. "I'll tell you what I think. I think you have no idea what's on that disk, because if you did, you'd know the United States is the last place that I would be afraid of. We've been taking girls just like you out into the desert and using them for target practice for years. So you watch out who you think you can threaten." He released her, regaining his composure. He laughed again. "And as for Little Mickey, man, that's funny. I knew Miguelito since he was five years old. He used to call me Uncle Leon, and right now, I think he would rather be down in Desemboque making his Girls Gone Wild videos with drunk American college girls. I killed his father and I will kill him, too, if he even comes close to me."

"How close do you need him to be?" MacKenzie asked in unaccented English. "Because he just made that sandwich you ate. And he heard every word you said. And I'm guessing he's just dying to tell you what was in it."

From behind the counter, the Oscar De La Hoya lookalike waved to him, removing the headphones and holding them up for Lev to see. At the same time, MacKenzie produced the transmitter she'd worn on her bra strap.

"Buenas tardes, Tio Leon," Miguel Cabrera said.

If Lev had been paying attention, or had he been less drunk, or less cocky, he might have noticed how, gradually, all the children at the McDonald's had been ushered outside, their mothers given fifty dollars American to take them somewhere else for lunch. He would have noticed that the restaurant was full only of men, young men with bulges beneath their shirts. Three of the men behind the counter leveled Tec-9 machine pistols at Lev, while a fourth aimed a Striker 12-gauge "Street Sweeper" shotgun at his head from the soda station. Guzman got to his feet, then stood at attention and saluted both Vasquez and MacKenzie before moving to the bodyguards, handing each of them a stack of fifty hundred-dollar bills. He returned to Lev, reached into the pocket of his sweatshirt, grabbed the keys to the Suburban, and tossed them to one of the bodyguards.

"Good-bye, Leon," Guzman said, leaning over and speaking into the Russian's ear. "It was a pleasure working for you. Be sure to give my regards to Cipriano when you see him."

MacKenzie and Vasquez stood as well.

"Tell me what happened to Theresa Davidova and I'll ask 'Little Mickey' to be gentle with you," she told Lev.

"I don't know anything about that whore," Lev said. "She called me and asked me if I could get her a gun and I told her to go fuck herself. I don't know any more than that."

"Who in the United States government are you working with?" Vasquez asked.

"I don't know," Lev said.

"Miguel," MacKenzie said, turning to the man behind the counter. *"Would you please go easy on my friend Leon?"* She turned to Lev again. "Sorry, but it appears he doesn't speak Russian. Enjoy your Happy Meal. Don't forget the toy. Maybe the genie from *Aladdin* will grant you one last wish."

Crossing the bridge back into the United States, she and Vasquez agreed that Lev was telling the truth about Theresa Davidova, and about not knowing whom his partners in the American government were.

"What do you think they're going to do to him?" MacKenzie asked.

"I don't know," Hoolie said. "But I think I'd want to wait a couple months before I ate at that McDonald's again. You never know what's in the ground beef."

Chapter Fourteen

DELUCA STOPPED FOR GAS IN LAS CRUCES AND picked up three e-mails on his PDA while he waited for the tank to fill. The first was from Ben Yutahay.

David,
Would you give me a call when you get a minute? I know how busy you are. A friend of Marvin's told me that my son told him he was going to Ajo to see somebody about Cheryl. My son's friend admitted that Marvin and Cheryl Escavedo were seeing each other but Marvin couldn't tell me because of his wife. He was afraid I would be ashamed of him. Do you know who in Ajo he might be going to see? I'm going to go there to ask around but please give me a call if you know anything.
Ben Yutahay

The second e-mail was from Walter Ford. It read:

David,
Had some of my kids working overtime on this, though they didn't know the full import of what they

were discovering, as I kept them intentionally uninformed.

Sorry if you were looking for something sexy here. The document your friend P. Romano sent contains accounts and bookkeeping information, going back thirty years. Most of the accounts are numbered so I couldn't begin to tell you what's what, exactly, without the key, but it appears to be several subaccounts connected to a larger budget. You'd probably want a bunch of accountants to go over it in detail to really tell you what it means.

There is, however, a file containing a summary that was last opened a week before Cheryl Escavedo disappeared. Part of it's a spreadsheet listing total annual disbursements to companies like Lockheed-Martin and TRW and Boeing and Raytheon—I would assume the figures are supported in the rest of the document. We're talking about billions of dollars, David. In short, three things of note.

- *First, payments to GNA, which is Global Netherlands Atmospheric—you said a Dutch weather satellite went out shortly after D1/D2 launched. They owned it. They're owned by Kirkos Industrial, which is owned by Vitaly Sergelin. Question: Who profited from loss of satellite? Conclusion: GNA/Kirkos (satellite was insured for $250 million)—or this was a way to conceal transfer of funds.*
- *Second, this program was spending more money than it was budgeted for. That may be more the rule than the exception for*

government programs, but how were overruns met?

- *Third, one of the smallest accounts on the spreadsheet, only $23 million (only!), is described as "Home improvements / Nantucket." That's a lot of bathroom tile—doesn't Koenig have a house in Nantucket? This one is underscored with three question marks after it, the author's, not mine. Here's my guess: Escavedo was trying to document expenditures Koenig made, appropriating government money for work on his house. Question: What is the reason for this? Conclusion: It gave her leverage. Question: How was she using this leverage? Conclusion: Blackmail is a possibility, but that doesn't sound like her. Self-protection is another.*

Another point of interest. The summary lists dollar amounts, to the unrounded penny. For example, 1998, Lockheed-Martin, $12,587,905.32. Also totals, very precise. Those totals appear, digit for digit, in a speech given at last month's Union of Concerned Scientists meeting in Denver, where the costs of the space race were discussed. The person giving the speech was Dr. Penelope Burgess. Question: How did she arrive at these figures, if this information is/was classified? Conclusion: Cheryl gave her the information. We looked at Dr. Burgess's phone records and e-mail accounts (just the AOL one, not the unm.edu account) but cannot verify contact.

Walter

P.S. Your boy Dan asked me to pull Congressman Benson's voting record regarding military expenditures. He might have gone to Decatur Academy with Koenig, but I don't see any current possible connection. He's voted against every proposed Space Defense Initiative program he could, tried to kill MIRACL, tried to cut the budget for THEL to next to nothing, etc. That bill, by the way, was cosponsored by Bob Fowler. UCS loves 'em both. I agree in general with the idea that Koenig might have friends in high places, but Benson isn't one of them. Koenig had a "secret club" or society at Decatur they called the "Key Club." Young conservatives filled with conspiracy theories and love for Richard Nixon. Benson was kicked out. Looking into membership roster.

P.P.S. Did a little more looking into Shijingshan Entertainment. The intellectual properties lawsuit against them was brought by Dimension Video, a big DVD distributor in the U.S. Koenig is a major shareholder in Dimension, whose stock went up when SE went down.

The final e-mail was from General LeDoux's office, written by his aide, Captain Martin.

Agt. DeLuca,
The general said you were asking about NORAD with questions as to alternative command and control. Such capabilities exist wholly or in part at NASA in Houston, at Vandenberg/Edwards in

California, at NSA, and in the White House operations center, with a hierarchy of override and security protocols. Recall that part of the Reagan Space Defense Initiative was a recognition of the need to build greater redundancy into the system, multiple launch sites, multiple C&C centers, etc., given proliferation and/or increasing accuracy of Sov./Sino ICBM targeting capabilities. This was when the Global Positioning System was on the drawing boards, but it was coming, and both sides knew it. Space Command at that point prepared for the possibility of the catastrophic loss of the Cheyenne Mountain facility by installing a second backup site at the former Sinkhole Laboratory in Carlsbad, which is nearly a mile underground. The White House also wanted another option if executive branch relocation were required, beyond the current (then) options. Sinkhole's computers were upgraded, post-9/11, but other than a skeleton crew of maintenance personnel that visits only sporadically, it is unmanned and nonoperational. Officially, the existence of Sinkhole is denied.

Please let me know if there's anything else I can do to assist you.

Yours truly,

Captain Charles C. Martin

DeLuca called Ben Yutahay and arranged to meet him in the parking lot of a pancake house in Ajo, a desert copper mining town (the mine now closed) of four thousand people centered east of the Cabeza Prieta National Wildlife Refuge, south of the Barry M. Goldwater Air Force Testing

Range, north of Organ Pipe Cactus National Monument and west of the Tohono O'Odham Indian reservation, in the valley between the Sauceda and Growler mountain ranges. He'd put nearly seven hundred miles on the odometer of Gary Burgess's truck, driving through the night and reaching Ajo as the sun was rising. He stopped first at a local real estate office to ask for directions to the Koenig ranch. The woman he spoke with, a gravel-voiced blonde woman named Rita, said she was well aware of the Koenig ranch, which, at nearly three hundred square miles, was the largest piece of privately held land in Pima County and one of the largest in Arizona.

"One of the least friendly, too, if you ask me," she said. "Every once in a while they might send a man into town for supplies or call a local plumber if something breaks, but as a rule they fly everything in and out on their own private airstrip and act as if the town wasn't even here. That and the eight-foot fence don't add up to coming off as exactly neighborly, but that ain't changed in fifty years, so why should it now?"

"Why an eight-foot fence?" DeLuca asked.

"Keeps the game in," Rita said. "Too high to jump. Tom Koenig's been growing exotic Asian speckled deer and African antelopes and what have you so his old schoolmates and Army buddies can come in and hunt 'em. Nothing is so thrilling as murdering an endangered species. The rumor is that he's got an albino elk in there, too, which the Indians consider sacred."

"There's nothing illegal about owning a private game preserve," DeLuca said. "Even with exotics."

"Illegal, no," Rita said. "Just unfriendly. Most ranchers around here let the hunters and the hikers and the gem hunters have access, unless they have some sort of protected Anasazi or Hohokum sites on the property. Or they make arrangements to let their neighbors run stock, if they're not using it. They even got a lake three miles long up there that sits full while we're suffering down here from droughts. The Koenigs have never let anybody pass. The new one is worse than his father was."

"Thank you, Rita," DeLuca said.

"Any time," she told him. "If you ever want to get a winter place, you give me a call. Average home price in town is under sixty thousand."

"I will," he said.

"I have another idea—why don't you come over to my place and I could make you dinner?" She smiled. "I could use a fresh conversation. Everybody local has already said everything they have to say to everybody else, and the snowbirds are useless."

"No thanks," he said. "I don't think I'll be staying."

He found Ben Yutahay sipping coffee in a booth at Jose's Casa de la Waffle, recognizing his black cowboy hat from across the room. The parking lot was filled with motor homes and campers, the restaurant crowded with white-haired retirees shuffling along the breakfast bar.

"How are you, David?" Yutahay asked.

"Good," DeLuca lied, sliding into the booth opposite the Cocopah policeman and ordering coffee and a short stack of pancakes from the waitress, who had so many rings in her ears it looked as if silver caterpillars were crawling up the side of her head. "I hope you haven't been waiting long."

"I couldn't sleep," he said. "I think I got here at five, and the place was already hopping with old people here for the early bird special. I don't get it. When my people get old, we know how to spend our final moments with dignity."

"You go sit on a mountaintop until the great spirits carry you away?"

"No," Yutahay said. "We go to Florida. I have a lot of friends around the Boca area. I have to tell you, I'm worried about Marvin. Nobody here seems to have seen him. I thought maybe I'd get lucky."

"Did you learn any more about what his relationship with Cheryl Escavedo might have entailed?"

Yutahay nodded, then laid a manila envelope on the table.

"This is for you, if you want to read it," Yutahay said. "I'm afraid I was a prying old man but I went into Marvin's computer and found out that he'd saved all the instant messages that he'd exchanged with Cheryl. I can summarize for you if you'd prefer."

"I would," DeLuca said. "I'll read these later."

"They were in love all right," Yutahay said, as DeLuca scanned the pages, perhaps fifty in all. "But she was in a relationship with an older man who was very possessive of her, and very jealous. She was afraid of him because she knew he could make her life very difficult."

DeLuca came to a set of pages that were folded and stapled shut.

"What are these?" he asked.

"You can open that if you want to," Yutahay said, "but it's just my son and Sergeant Escavedo having cybersex. I think that's what it's called. Typing dirty things back and forth. I don't think it's of value and I wanted to respect their privacy, but I didn't want you to think I was keeping anything from you. It was difficult for me to read, but I suppose that's just my generation."

"I don't suppose it's necessary," DeLuca said. "Does she name this older man, by any chance?"

"She uses three asterisks," Yutahay said. "I gather she was afraid of even naming him. Do you know who it could be?"

"I think three asterisks could stand for three stars," DeLuca said. "As in a three-star general."

"That's what I thought, too," Ben Yutahay said. "Know of any around here?"

"I do," DeLuca said. "Do you think Marvin might have tried to do something foolish?"

"Marvin does foolish things all the time," Ben said. "But I don't think trying to find someone you love is foolish. I don't think refusing to believe someone you love is dead is necessarily foolish—it has a kind of nobility. I was hoping if I could have a look around at Koenig's ranch, I might be able to tell something."

"Why don't you come with me then?" DeLuca said. "Though I have to tell you something. And there are things that I can't tell you, but you should know that there could well be a high degree of danger involved, in the form of a new weapon the military has developed that General Koenig has at his disposal."

"Just don't expect any stoical Indian 'it's-a-good-day-to-die' crap from me," Yutahay said. "I saw *Little Big Man.* I liked it a lot, but when I die, I'm going to go kicking and screaming, just like my ancestors did." He opened his coat jacket to reveal a sawed-off shotgun, hanging from a sling. "I took this off a drug smuggler two years ago. It'll blow a hole the size of a garage door into just about anything."

"I welcome the company," DeLuca said.

They drove south of town on Darby Wells Road, past a dusty and desolate RV ghetto where the fattest tree trunk was thinner than a girl's wrist, across Gray's Wash and Daniel's Arroyo and past the turn to the New Cordelia Mine, closed, the sign said, up into the high country where the palo verde and saguaros gave way to scrub oak and chaparral. In the distance, DeLuca saw a pyramid-shaped mountain and thought it looked familiar, though he couldn't recall where he'd seen it. Then he remembered—the mountain had been in the background of Major Huston's hunting triptych. The truck rumbled and rattled along the gravel road.

A dozen miles from town, they turned off the main road and traveled another half mile before reaching an iron gate extending across the road beneath an arch with the words "Koenig Ranch" carved into the wood. There was a surveillance camera mounted atop a pole and an intercom by the gate.

"What were you going to say to him?" Yutahay asked him. "I was hoping you'd have a plan."

"I don't know," DeLuca said. "I never know. If you spend too much time preparing what you're going to say, you lose the ability to respond flexibly to the moment. I usually think of something."

"Do you mind if I get out?" Yutahay asked. DeLuca said he didn't mind.

He walked to the intercom and pushed the button. After a moment, a voice said, "Yes?"

"David DeLuca to see General Koenig," he said.

There was a long pause, then the lock buzzed for a moment, and the gate swung silently on its hinges, opening inward. When he returned to the truck, Ben Yutahay was crouched in the dirt, examining the pickup's front tire.

"Something wrong?" DeLuca asked.

"Not with your truck, but I didn't want the camera over there to see what I was doing, so I'm pretending," Yutahay said. "Cheryl was here. It rained here. A couple days before she disappeared. This is where the red mud we found on her tires came from. And those are her tire tracks. The sun baked the mud and froze them for us to find. Here she is, driving in, and here she is, driving out. It couldn't be plainer."

"So she went from here to her uncle's?" DeLuca said.

"Other way around," Yutahay said. "She switched cars at her uncle's, then came here, then went to Spirit Mountain. And this track at my foot is to my son's motorcycle. It's newer. Maybe yesterday. It traces over the others. He stopped here a moment, because there is his boot, and then he went to the intercom."

DeLuca looked down and saw only indecipherable ruts and grooves.

"How about tracks coming out?"

"I don't see any," Yutahay said, staring at the dirt a moment longer, then spitting. "Maybe we'll find him on the porch with his feet propped up."

The road continued for another two miles, affording at one point a view, as the road climbed, of a paved airstrip below where a twin-engine jet, a Gulfstream 2, sat on the tarmac. They passed a barn and corral where a dozen saddle horses grazed without looking up at the old truck that rumbled up the road. The house was built of logs on a stone foundation, though the structure was, to a log cabin, what the White House was to a White Castle hamburger joint. Yutahay commented that the logs used to build the house were Douglas fir and had probably been shipped in from the Pacific Northwest. The roof was cedar shake, with a massive stone chimney rising from the center, and next to it, a widow's walk where DeLuca saw that a telescope had been set up on a tripod, though it was pointing toward the horizon and not the sky, the house resting on a promontory where a table mesa dropped precipitously to the valley below. There was a large swimming pool next to the house, and beyond the pool house and patio, a large inflated white dome.

"Tennis court?" Yutahay wondered.

"That's what it's supposed to look like, anyway," DeLuca said, thinking to himself that it was also not a bad place to hide the dish array Scott said Koenig would need to command Darkstar.

"How much are they paying generals these days?" Yutahay asked. "This guy is loaded."

"His family had money," DeLuca said. "But you're right."

Beyond the tennis court, he saw a helipad where a Sikorsky S-72 sat waiting, its blades slowly rotating in preparation for flight. Koenig was on the porch, having a few words with his pilot, who saluted and moved toward the helicopter as DeLuca parked the truck. Yutahay said he wanted to wait outside and perhaps have a bit of a look around. There was a five-car garage at the side of the house opposite the pool, where DeLuca saw a black Lincoln Navigator, a World War II–era vintage Willys Jeep, and a variety of ATVs and off-road dirt bikes. Yutahay promised he wouldn't go far.

"Would your friend like to come in, Agent DeLuca?" Koenig said as DeLuca saluted.

"No thank you, sir," DeLuca said. "Officer Yutahay isn't military. He's with the Tribal Police, but he's just an old friend who wanted to take me over to the res after this." DeLuca noticed a hand-held Mark 40 grenade launcher resting across the arms of an Adirondack chair on the porch. "I hope I'm not interrupting anything. You look like you're expecting trouble."

"Trouble in the form of beavers," Koenig said. "We're flying down to dynamite a new beaver dam. Ordinarily we'd ride in on horseback but I'm in a bit of a hurry today. My wife and family are waiting for me in Colorado. Apparently the beavers have impeded the flow of water to my neighbors to the south. They're second only to man in their ability to alter their physical environment."

"You've done a nice job of altering yours," DeLuca said. "How long have you had this place?"

"My great-grandfather built it," Koenig said. "My family are seafaring people, but he wanted a piece of the West. Teddy Roosevelt used to come here to hunt. We can talk inside."

The house was decorated in a mixture of western ranch and New England antique styles, Shaker furniture, an old rocking horse, cloth dolls in a glass case, Persian rugs, nautical brass knickknacks, a massive wagon wheel light fixture in one room, a chandelier constructed of elk antlers in another. The foyer opened onto a great hall filled with the mounted heads of enough deer, antelope, elk, and mountain goats to form a small herd. The furniture was Stickney and mission style, dark wood in straight lines, leather couches, bookshelves filled with leather-bound tomes, mica lampshades, Bavarian steins, Remington bronzes of cowboys on horseback and Indians hunting bison, gold-framed Russell Chatham oil landscapes mixed with portraits of ancestors on the walls, though the main feature of the room was the fireplace, which was large enough for a man to stand upright in, built of stone with a massive slate mantel above it.

"You already know Lieutenant Carr," Koenig said, referring to the young officer who stood in the kitchen doorway with an apron around his waist, his sleeves rolled up. Carr grinned the same cocky grin DeLuca had noticed before.

"Lieutenant," DeLuca said in acknowledgment.

"Not only is Lieutenant Carr a fine aide, but he's also a gourmet chef," Koenig said. "A fine butcher, too. Ninety percent of the taste of venison is how the animal is dressed. My grandfather had a Navaho who did it for him, but I think Lieutenant Carr is as good with a filleting knife as he was."

"You flatter me, sir," Carr said, returning to the kitchen.

DeLuca ran his hand across the mantel.

"Spectacular fireplace," DeLuca said.

"That's made from stone quarried on the property," Koenig said. "We're sitting on the crest of the Tertiary Chico-Shunie basolith. We get a lot of porphyritic quartz monzonite, hematite, feldspar, quartz diorite, cuprite, malachite, pegmatites, and fanglomerates, among other more minor lithologies. A lot of people don't even know what's under their feet."

"You certainly do, sir," DeLuca said.

"I used to do a lot of rock collecting as a boy along the fractures and footwalls. My grandfather didn't believe in letting his grandchildren spend their time idly. There were usually tests at dinnertime. Can I get you something to drink? An iced tea?"

"That would be fine," DeLuca said. Koenig asked Lieutenant Carr to get the drinks. Carr returned a moment later and handed DeLuca his. Koenig drank from his own glass. DeLuca decided they probably weren't going to poison him. He sipped.

"You must get a lot of gem hunters asking you if they can collect on the premises," DeLuca said. Koenig raised an eyebrow.

"Occasionally," he said. "But you're not here for a geology lesson, and I don't have the time, so why don't you tell me why you are here? I have a pretty good idea, but why don't you tell me? By the way, after your first visit, I made some calls about you. It's very impressive. Major Huston said you put away more of Saddam's blacklist friends than anybody else. I didn't read what happened to your friend Mohammed Al-Tariq, but regardless, you should know that I'm expecting a lot from you."

Koenig was clearly unconcerned at DeLuca's suddenly showing up at his door. He'd expressed very little surprise. It was almost as if he'd been expecting him. DeLuca saw a door that opened onto a study where a laptop computer glowed on the desk. He wondered what a search of the hard drive would turn up.

"The Al-Tariq file is still classified," DeLuca said. "I'm sure you could gain access if you wanted to."

"I'm sure I could, too. Did you find the disks?"

"I did," DeLuca said.

"And what was on them?"

"I don't know yet," DeLuca said, gambling that Peggy Romano's firewall was as strong as she said it was, and that Koenig had not been able to intercept the e-mail that Walter Ford had sent. "What I mean is, I'm not sure. It looks like financial information, bookkeeping stuff, but I haven't really had time to study it yet. I was going to wait until I had more information before I showed it to anybody. As it stands, I haven't told anyone I've found them."

"Because?"

"Because I'm not exactly sure where I stand, actually, vis-à-vis Darkstar," DeLuca said. "Right now, I could either stop you or help you. And frankly, I'm not sure what I want to do. I was hoping maybe you could talk to me."

It had been his experience that most criminals were essentially lonely. It always surprised him when, interrogating a gang member or street criminal, an offer of simple friendship led to the disclosure of information. Criminals had secrets, and keeping secrets was hard for anybody—only the most deeply psycho-emotional sociopaths could do it in a prolonged way with any sense of comfort. Most people wanted to confess. The question was always how to get them talking in a way they felt safe and supported. The approach had worked for him in Iraq. Perhaps it would work here. Koenig saw himself as a man's man, a vigilante going it on his own, historically wronged but doing what he considered the right thing, even though nobody would ever agree with him. Part of him had to long to be understood.

"I don't know what you're talking about," Koenig said.

"I'm read on," DeLuca said, "but I have a feeling they didn't tell me everything. Only you would really be in a position to do that. Right now, they're looking for a non-functioning piece of space crap, or they're looking for proof that Darkstar is operational, which gives them a different set of headaches. My own team doesn't even know how I'm adding this up, but I think I have that proof. Not just the disks. How did you and Cheryl get involved?"

"We got involved because I put my personal needs in front of the country's and ended up compromising the only program we have that's going to keep this country safe, and save millions of lives," Koenig said. "When my grandfather ran the Navy during World War II, he made sure the job came before the people doing the job. People are the weak link. Always have been. Fortunately, with the new technologies, it's going to take fewer and fewer people to get the job done. When I told Cheryl the situation had gone too far, she couldn't handle it. If I have difficulty suffering fools, of either gender or whatever the rank, I'm not going to apologize. I saw in your service record that you have some of the same difficulties. First Gillette and then Reicken. You have a way of disposing of your superior officers, DeLuca."

"You make it sound like I did something illegal," DeLuca said. Gillette had been a base commander in Stuttgart who got chaptered out after DeLuca's investigation proved he'd misappropriated funds. Colonel Stanley Reicken had been DeLuca's immediate superior in Iraq, until he gave the order for his men to fire on Iraqis holding a white flag, and there, DeLuca had helped a BBC reporter gain access to the proof. "But you're right, I don't like bureaucrats. And I guess I'm not so big on rules. The

Army is exactly who I'd want with me if we needed a thousand guys to cross a field, but sometimes you need to slip through a narrow door, and then you don't want a thousand guys with you. Why Vitaly Sergelin? Was it the money or the oil?"

"Both," Koenig said. "It always astonished me, how few people understood the nature of power in the old Soviet Union. People saw a row of unsmiling men in bad hats watching May Day parades in Red Square and thought they were in charge. Vitaly Sergelin had more to do with the democratization of the Soviet Union than Gorbachev or Yeltsin ever did. China's gross national product tripled in the last five years and it's going to triple again in another two—that's a billion people who twenty years ago were riding bicycles and building houses out of bamboo. You think we're the only country that's going to want oil? You think a billion Chinese aren't going to want cars? If we can't control demand, we'd damned well better control supply. Russia has more oil reserves than all of the Middle East and Alaska combined."

"And what Sergelin doesn't have is the physical force to protect his assets," DeLuca said. "So you work together. He funded your parallel programs and in return, you provide security."

"He's part of the decision-making process, as an ally," Koenig said. "There are others. Maybe you haven't noticed, Chief DeLuca, but this little world of ours is falling apart, reverting to tribalism at its most elementary components, sometimes quite literally—look at Africa. Countries that have been stabilized either by despotism or by democracy for a quarter of a century or more are splitting at seams along tribal lines. Hutus and Tutsis. Dinkas and

Arabs. Kum and Fasori. You're starting to see it in China, Pakistan, India . . . That narrow door you're talking about is globalization. Those who manage to get through, fine, great, they're our allies, but those who get shut out and can't get inside, they're joining the barbarians."

"And the barbarians are armed," DeLuca said.

"You're goddamn right they are," Koenig said. "And I'm not just talking about a few pissant 707s flying into office buildings. I'm not talking about having to fight two wars on two fronts today and thirty wars on thirty fronts tomorrow. I'm not even talking about dirty bombs or suitcase nukes passing through airport security checkpoints manned by overweight unwed-mother high-school dropouts who couldn't find a bowling ball in a bread basket. We have eight thousand nuclear-armed cruise missiles and five thousand ICBMs on this planet and a hundred million laptop computers capable of launching them, and all somebody's got to do is write the program that lets them, and once that gets on the Internet, we're going to have eight thousand rockets launching all at the same time. And what are we going to do then? Who's going to be left to say, 'Gee, I wish we'd thought of that—I wish somebody had prepared for that'?"

DeLuca decided to play a hunch.

"And that's just the terrestrial threat," he said.

Koenig didn't say anything. Was it possible that Koenig believed in UFOs? If so, it was probably the darkest secret he had.

"I'll leave whether or not we need Darkstar to bigger brains than mine," DeLuca said, shifting the focus back to things Koenig could talk about. "But if Darkstar is a fact, then the people controlling Darkstar are going to need intelligence. I don't mean SIGINT or IMINT. I mean boots on the ground, global. I mean somebody who can walk into a village in Pakistan and ask, 'Where's Osama Bin Laden?' and get a straight answer. And tell you, this is where he goes, this is when he'll be there, come and get him. I think you're right about tribalism. And tribes have chiefs, but how do you know who they are? Who's going to go in and get you the information you need? And that's what I'm good at. That's what I'm best at. You can look it up. And that's what I'm offering you."

He thought a little megalomaniacal posturing was in order, delivered deferentially.

"Correct me if I'm wrong, but if we're talking about the virtually instantaneous projection of force, and I wouldn't deny the need for it for one second, particularly after 9/11, then isn't it imperative that that force be used wisely?" DeLuca said. "You said the problem is people, not technology. People can't make good decisions without good intelligence. You can rely on SIGINT or IMINT all you want, but you're still not going to build a machine that can open another man's mind. I make my living getting people to do just that. And I guess I'm asking you to do that, too, sir. Obviously, I came here fully aware that if you turn down my offer, you could take me out the second I step out that door, and that from your point of view, the threat I pose is well-contained. But I don't think you'd delete an asset once you appreciated the value of it. And the idea of working for somebody who could get more done in five minutes than the Army could accomplish in five years is more than a little appealing. I've got my résumé in the car if you want to see it."

Koenig smiled.

"That won't be necessary," Koenig said. "I'm aware of your abilities. You should know that when I think somebody is looking into me, I'm going to look into them. You're quite right about the advantages of intelligence. You know, General Taylor at Huachuca is a friend of mine. Had him out here hunting a while back, so I asked him. He said you were one of the best instructors he ever had. Wishes you were still there."

"General Taylor's one of the best commanders I've ever had," DeLuca said. "His good opinion always meant a lot to me."

"He referred me to the chapter you wrote on interrogation techniques," Koenig said. "Quote: 'It is often useful to find a way to make the person you're interviewing feel like you have his own interests at heart, whatever they may be. Taking an aggressive position is more likely to raise his defenses than to lower them. From a global perspective, when questioning an enemy combatant, the United States armed forces as "bad cop" is the default assumption. One might actually win hearts and minds with compassion, which can be either real or feigned. Real is better.' Did you write that, DeLuca?"

"I did," DeLuca said.

"And did you think you could play me the way you might play some third-world towelhead?" Koenig said. "Did you think you could pretend to have our interests at heart?" Apparently Koenig hadn't read the part about the value of making an angry adversary think you're stupid. "You have no idea what you're dealing with, DeLuca. None. And the funny thing is, you still found out more than you were supposed to. All you had to do was find the girl and the disks and eliminate one little intangible. I asked them to get me someone who was good but not too good, and primarily, someone who could stay within the parameters of his mission. One look at your record would have suggested you weren't going to do that. I don't like soldiers who can't stay within the parameters of their missions, DeLuca. Never have."

"I didn't come here to be liked," DeLuca said, now that the game was up. When in doubt, declare victory.

"Then why did you come here?" Koenig said. "Not that I care, but I don't know how you think."

"I came here to arrest you," DeLuca said.

"And you thought I would let you?"

"I thought you might not like it," DeLuca conceded. "Most people don't."

"You don't really have the faintest inkling of what you're dealing with, do you?" Koenig said. He called out to the next room. Carr appeared in the door, his .45 Colt automatic in his hand. "Lieutenant Carr," Koenig said, turning to leave. "Would you please take care of this? And when you're finished, see to that Indian fellow wandering around outside."

"Take *care* of this?" DeLuca said. "You can't even shoot me yourself? What kind of pussy bullshit is that?" Koenig stopped in his tracks. DeLuca wasn't exactly sure where he was going with this or what he was hoping to accomplish, beyond getting Koenig to do something stupid. He imagined Koenig had a high opinion of himself. Such high opinions were often a man's weakest link. He also wanted to stall, on the off chance that something brilliant would occur to him. "But then I haven't met a candy-assed rear-echelon motherfucker like you yet with half the balls he thought he had. You guys are great at sitting behind your plasma screens with your hot little mouses in your hands, clicking on what infantry platoons you want to send where or what village you want to target from six thousand miles away, but not one of you pissants ever had to kill a man with your own hands close enough to watch his eyes turn red or come within a hundred miles of being killed yourself. You know what the real soldiers call you? Playstation Generals. But don't stay on my account—I know you've got beaver you need to hunt with RPGs."

Koenig turned and was about to say something, then thought better of it, nodding to Carr before walking to the front door and exiting.

DeLuca turned to face Carr.

"I don't suppose if I told you you were under arrest, you'd put the gun down?" DeLuca said.

Carr shook his head, still smiling confidently.

"It looks like I'm going to have to wipe that smirk off your face myself then," DeLuca said. He circled slowly to his left. Carr responded, evidently amused anew.

"And how are you going to do that?" Carr said.

"Well," DeLuca said. "I could just let you kill me and hope that thirty or forty years of having a guilty conscience would destroy your soul. But that presupposes a level of self-reflection your generation tends to lack, so I guess I'll just have to kick your ass the old-fashioned way."

"You're going to kick my ass?" Carr said.

"I'm going to try," DeLuca said, still sizing up his opponent. "My boy Dan Sykes said you're pretty good. And I know you're not going to shoot me here because you don't want to get blood on the general's Persian rug, so why don't you put the gun down and show me some of your jujitsu shit? But I gotta warn you—I did a little boxing in college. Come on, Lieutenant—don't tell me you're afraid of a man my age? And you know I'm right about the rug."

"Your boy Sykes lasted less than a minute," Carr said, lowering the gun. "What makes you think you could do any better?"

"I have something Dan Sykes didn't have," DeLuca said.

"The wisdom that comes with age?" Carr offered.

"No," DeLuca said. "Backup."

He glanced over Carr's shoulder. Carr refused to look.

"Is this where you cleverly trick me into turning my head?" Carr said.

"I don't want to shoot you, son," Ben Yutahay said from the doorway, where he leveled the Remington pump-action shotgun at the lieutenant, "but on the other hand, I don't really care about the rug."

Carr turned his head, momentarily, but it was long enough for DeLuca to pick up a lamp with a heavy ceramic base, which he then broke across the back of Carr's head. Carr fell where he stood.

DeLuca heard the helicopter's engines revving.

He picked up Carr's automatic, nodded a thank-you to Yutahay, then ran for the helipad, which was about a hundred yards off. There was no time to think, so he didn't try. He squeezed off four quick rounds but knew the small sidearm wasn't going to stop the helicopter, so he sprinted, knowing only that if Koenig went to ground, he was going to be much harder to find. He was thirty yards away as the chopper lifted from the pad. DeLuca ran harder and managed to grab hold of the portside runner, sprinting along with the helicopter until the engine revved even higher and he felt himself lifted from the ground, at which point he realized this was one of the stupider things he'd ever done. It was not his intention to fly, and he'd never cared much for helicopters, even when he was inside them ("fifty thousand rivets flying in loose formation," a pilot friend had once called them), but when he realized he was twenty feet off the ground and rising, he decided it would be prudent to hang on.

He threw a leg over the runner and wrapped his arms around the pylon. Koenig's pilot tried to shake him off, banking sharply to the left, then to the right, while the ground below spun and whirled. The pilot pulled on the collective and the nose of the helicopter turned skyward. DeLuca felt his weight shift to the rear.

The chopper pitched left, then right, then left again. When the helicopter suddenly dived, DeLuca felt his stomach turn inside out, but he managed to wrap his other leg around the runner to straddle it. They wheeled left and circled back to the house, picking up speed.

Then a winch began to lower from the starboard port, a fat iron hook on the end of a half-inch-thick steel cable. At eight feet, it stopped.

Koenig's pilot banked sharply left, using the winch in an attempt to knock DeLuca from his perch. The first blow struck the strut, clanging loudly. The second missed by a wide margin, but then the hook whipped around and struck DeLuca in the ribs, breaking at least one of them, by DeLuca's rough guess.

He held on.

The chopper banked left and dived. The earth spun. DeLuca saw the estate below him. His head swam and he felt dizzy. The hook swung back and momentarily wrapped around the runner's pylon, pinching his right hand. He screamed as the pain shot the length of his arm. When the cable unwrapped, he tried to grab the hook and immobilize it, but as the chopper banked sharply right, he lost his balance.

He fell.

He grabbed hold of the cable to stop his fall. He tried to hang on to the runner with his feet, but the force was too much, and when the helicopter jerked again, his feet slipped.

He spiraled below the helicopter, swinging free on the winch cable, his weight sliding him down the cable until he grabbed the hook with his right hand, his flesh torn and burning. He was spinning madly and couldn't reach the hook with his left hand.

The helicopter turned sharply. He swung out wide from centrifugal force. The pilot was lowering the cable. At the same time, the helicopter descended.

He managed to grab the cable with his left hand, gaining purchase, but he was still spinning. He was bleeding, blood running down his right arm.

He hung on.

The helicopter rose, heading back toward the house.

He spread-eagled his legs to stabilize his rotation.

He saw the house below approaching. He saw Ben Yutahay standing in the driveway, the Mark 40 DeLuca had seen on the porch resting on Yutahay's shoulder, aimed at the chopper.

They were over the stables.

They were over the pool.

He wasn't going to get a second chance.

Timing was key. He estimated the chopper's forward speed at thirty or forty miles an hour, but hanging from the bottom of a helicopter by a cable, it was difficult to be certain.

He saw Yutahay fire. He saw the grenade snaking up from the ground.

He let go.

The grenade missed the helicopter, hissing over his head as he fell.

He flew through the air, dropping from what he estimated to be a height of perhaps one hundred feet. He spread his arms and legs wide to slow his acceleration. Falling free. Soaring. It was almost pleasant. He recalled a parachute jump he'd made in Iraq, a night jump from a height of over six miles. Falling from the sky might not be a bad way to die.

Maybe some other day.

His timing was good. He braced himself, covering his face and turning sideways before slamming flat against the side of the inflated tennis court dome. The blow knocked the wind out of him, and he nearly blacked out, but the ripstop nylon held, collapsing under his weight and the force of the collision like an overinflated pole vault pad but cushioning his fall.

As the dome sprang gently back into form, DeLuca slid down the side and hit the ground hard. He wanted to scream in pain—apparently the hook had struck him in the ankle, though he hadn't noticed—but he had to regain his breath first.

He limped around the end of the dome, which blocked his view.

In the distance, the helicopter was changing its vector, rising and banking left, screaming off toward the airstrip. DeLuca watched as it climbed, helpless to stop it, the sound of its engines growing fainter and fainter.

Ben Yutahay was at his side, putting his arm around DeLuca's waist to support him.

"Are you all right?" Yutahay asked.

His ribs hurt if he inhaled too deeply—something was definitely cracked where the winch had struck him—and the palm of his right hand was a bloody mess, but other than that, he was no worse for wear.

"I'm okay," he told Yutahay. They watched as, a moment later, the white jet they'd seen parked on the landing strip screamed into the sky.

"I hope you don't mind that I shot at the helicopter, but I figured you for a goner anyway," Yutahay said. "My artillery skills are a little rusty."

"I would have figured the same way. I'm only sorry you missed," DeLuca said.

He crossed to the door to the tennis court dome, testing the knob to discover the door was locked. Yutahay moved to his side, bidding DeLuca to stand back, lowering the sawed-off shotgun at the door, until he thought better and aimed ten feet to the left of the door before firing. The blast blew a six-foot hole in the fabric. The air that rushed out was cool.

DeLuca ducked his head and entered first. Yutahay followed. DeLuca'd hoped to find a satellite dish array inside the dome, but instead found only a tennis court, red clay, air-conditioned, the surface strewn with bright green tennis balls.

He found a towel and wrapped it around his hand, then went back outside. He looked at the house. A search was unlikely to turn up anything, given Koenig's thoroughness. DeLuca would have given anything to have a look at the laptop he'd seen on Koenig's desk.

He felt Ben Yutahay's hand on his shoulder as he stared off to the east. There was no sign of the helicopter anymore, no sound but the desert breeze.

"What about Marvin?" DeLuca asked. "Any signs?"

"Signs, yes," Yutahay said. "I think I don't want to agree with what they're telling me."

"What are they telling you?" DeLuca said.

"He stopped, about there," Yutahay said, pointing to the front of the house. "I saw his boot heel but not his kickstand, so I don't think he got off the bike. I think he was talking to someone at the house. Then he took off at a high speed, because you can see where his rear wheel fishtailed. He rode in that direction," Yutahay said, pointing, "and then he turned right. I found one of those circles of glass in the sand where he veered, and another where he turned. I think he was running from somebody. Then the tracks of his dirt bike lead up to the edge of the cliff. I don't think he knew it was coming because there's no sign that he hit his brakes, and I think he must have been going maybe sixty to eighty miles an hour. There's maybe a three-hundred-foot drop. I was going to climb down to see if I could find his bike or his remains when I sensed that you might be in trouble."

"We can send some men down there when we search the house. You can go with them if you'd like," DeLuca said, even though he doubted they'd find anything.

"Who do you think he was running from?" Yutahay said, looking DeLuca in the eye. "Can you tell me?"

DeLuca wished he could.

"I think Cheryl had an affair with Koenig. He wouldn't let her end it. I think Marvin came here to tell Koenig to back off. He was in love with Cheryl Escavedo."

Yutahay looked as if he was about to break down, but only for a moment. He blinked once, then took a deep breath, steeling himself.

"I'm glad that he was in love," he said at last. "It would be a hard thing, to die without ever knowing that. I don't think he ever loved his wife. He married her because she was pregnant, but I don't think he ever loved her. Maybe it's a good thing to know that you are going to die because of love. Do you think?"

Chapter Fifteen

DELUCA GOT HIS HAND ATTENDED TO AT THE Kirtland Base Hospital, telling the doctor he'd had a rope-climbing accident. He'd cracked his seventh rib with a torn costochondral joint and sustained a badly bruised medial malleolus in his right foot, for which the doctor prescribed Tylenol and rest. He could do the Tylenol part, but rest was out of the question, at least for now.

He called a full briefing in the RV, with Colonel Oswald and General LeDoux split-screened on the plasma monitor. Oswald explained the reasons why the team had been only partially read on about Darkstar. Sykes seemed annoyed, judging by his body language, but the others accepted the explanation at face value. When Oswald was finished speaking, he asked if there were any questions.

"I just don't understand how it is that we don't have the technology to find this thing," Vasquez said. "I mean, we built it, right? It's like a Klingon Bird of Prey or something."

"We built it to be invisible," Oswald said. "To radar, infrared, opticals. We did a good job. And it only changes its signature when it fires, for a few seconds. We'd have to know exactly where to look, and exactly when to look.

Other than that, this thing is a needle in a haystack as big as the sky."

"What about the danger of a matter/antimatter reaction," DeLuca asked, touching on an element that Oswald had omitted from both this briefing and the previous one. If his team was going to be read on, then they were going to be read on all the way—no more bullshit. MacKenzie's eyes widened as if she'd just seen a Kate Spade bag on sale for four dollars.

Oswald looked uncomfortable, uncertain how to answer.

"What Agent DeLuca is referring to," General LeDoux said, "is a new kind of reactor powering the laser. Do you want me to get the hard science on this or would you settle for my own understanding?"

"Yours will be fine," DeLuca said.

"My understanding is that the possibility is virtually nil," LeDoux said. "At the same time, 'virtually nil' is not the same as 'nil.' What would actually happen in a cataclysmic detonation, since we can't build an antimatter bomb small enough to test, is just theory. So far."

"So what do we do?" Sami asked. "I mean, why don't we send the Third Army into Colorado and surround Cheyenne Mountain and say, 'Come out with your fucking hands up'? Pardon my French. We don't have the resources or something?"

LeDoux shook his head.

"You're it. You are the resources," he said. "I should tell you, people at the Pentagon have their jockey shorts twisted up around their ears, thinking that the knowledge of this has gone as far as it has. I've been arguing with them from the start about your need to know exactly what it is you're dealing with, but the fight, as I understand it, goes all the way to the White House, where the feeling is that this is the biggest secret since Enigma. The op stays black, maximum discretion. I can get you all the toys you need, but as far as personnel goes, you're it."

"But Sami still has a point," Dan Sykes said. "You say Koenig's been running this through NORAD. If he wrote the codes that let him do that, why can't we unwrite the codes and reset the system? Or just pull the plug on Cheyenne? I mean, literally, take the cord out of the wall socket and watch all the lights go out and move everything to NORAD II for the time being?"

"We can lock him out, or try to," Oswald said, "but we can't pull the plug, for obvious reasons. We can't blind him without blinding ourselves. As far as NORAD II goes, General, why don't you tell them?"

"I was going to call you about this if you hadn't called me first, David," LeDoux said. "Sinkhole came online last night at 0200 hours. We had a team meet Koenig's jet when it landed at Peterson but he wasn't on it. If he's at Sinkhole, we need to get him out. Unfortunately, Sinkhole is even more secure than Cheyenne, and all the access codes have been changed. It's always been last resort, the deepest underground facility in the world and entirely self-contained. We can't break in, at least not without drawing a whole lot of attention, and we can't shut it down. Once again, this illustrates the weakness of a system designed to keep intruders out but which can apparently do very little once the firewalls are breached. Right now we can't even communicate with it, but we're assuming whoever is in there is going to pick up the phone eventually."

"And say what?" MacKenzie asked. "What does he want? That's what I don't get. His gig is blown—we know what he's doing. I mean, we do, right? So what does he have left?"

"We're not sure what he wants," LeDoux said. "Colonel?"

"Department M-3 out of DOD's PSYOPS is a watchdog unit that, since 1994, has run periodic evals on military personnel at the highest levels," Oswald said. "Basically it's a room full of Army shrinks who read reports and hopefully identify any psychological problems in leadership before they manifest themselves. They're supposed to have access to everyone right up to the Joint Chiefs of Staff, but there've been some at that level who've resisted. It's a good program, but it was originally Hillary Clinton's idea, so you can imagine how well-received that was. At any rate, one of the doctors there has been trying to flag Koenig for years. Unfortunately, we didn't listen to him. He thinks Koenig is certified paranoid-schizophrenic, possibly even to the point where he hears voices. But very special voices that tell him what to do and empower him. The doctor also thinks Koenig's managed to surround himself with true believers, something like a personality cult, within STRATCOM."

"I was planning on talking to Lieutenant Carr, to see what he knows, after he gets over his headache," DeLuca said. "I'll brief you on what I find out."

"You can cancel that," LeDoux said. "Lieutenant Carr killed himself last night." DeLuca had sent Carr to the brig at Kirtland, but he hadn't thought to post a suicide watch. "Apparently he didn't want to answer any questions."

"Apparently," DeLuca said.

"That might illustrate what we mean by Koenig's developing a cult following. What we've been trying to avoid," Oswald said, "is any sort of Randy Weaver/Jim Jones/David Koresh-type situation where the guy feels pushed up against the wall. But that's what we have, with the obvious difference that the man is holed up, literally, but instead of a guy in a cabin with a high-powered rifle keeping everyone at bay, this time the weapons are outside the cabin, and we're the hostages. We're obviously not going to make any concessions, but until we hear from him, we're working blind. The White House is very concerned. I've got a meeting later today with Carla White and with the vice president's national security adviser."

"So what we need to do," DeLuca said, "is either find a quiet way into Sinkhole, or find a way to talk Koenig into coming out. Is that the mission now?"

"You got it," LeDoux said. "Needless to say, this is time-sensitive. We'll work on it from this end, but we're open to anything you can come up with. I'll send you the schematics on Sinkhole, but as you'll see, it's pretty impenetrable."

"We'll get back to you," DeLuca said.

He asked his team to brainstorm while he paid a call on Penelope Burgess. An overcast sky had broken into a hard, driving rain that was probably snow at the higher elevations.

She lived at the end of Cliff Road, out toward Vulcan Peak and the Petroglyph National Monument, at the east end of town. The house was a log cabin, surrounded by pine trees, with a wrap-around porch that afforded a view of Tijeres canyon below, though at the moment that porch appeared to serve primarily as a woodshed, keeping her supply dry for the winter. A plume of smoke drifted up into the rain from the stone chimney at the center of the cedar shake roof.

"If it was two degrees colder, this would be snow and you wouldn't have made it up here," Burgess said from the porch, grabbing an armful of logs. "I put some Mexican cocoa on the stove when you called, if you'd care for some."

DeLuca said he would. The cabin was roomy inside, decorated in Navaho rugs and artifacts from Burgess's travels, jade carvings from China, a ceremonial headdress from Sumatra, as well as crystals unlike anything DeLuca had ever seen before, gypsum blossoms and selenite claws, cave pearls, dripstone fragments, aragonite straws and frostwork, coralloids that looked like popcorn, each protected in a glass globe and labeled in Penelope Burgess's handwriting. On a wall, he saw a poster-sized photograph of a domed chamber in Oman with a shaft of light streaming in through the entrance in the ceiling, and the dome looked like it was maybe twenty feet high, until the eye fell to a person in yellow overalls and a red helmet, standing on a debris pile at the bottom of the shaft of light, the figure about a millimeter high, which only then revealed the chamber to be perhaps five hundred feet high.

"Josh Truitt took that. Apparently the poor guy had to lug in a couple thousand old-fashioned flash bulbs to get that shot. You said when you called you wanted to talk about Sinkhole?"

"When was the last time you were there?" DeLuca asked her.

"Hmm," she said, handing him his cocoa and throwing a fresh log on the fire. "Seven or eight years ago, I guess. They pulled the funding long before that, but since I was a geologist and not a physicist, I got to stay longer. I think they closed the neutrino observatory a few years before that. They were already draining the bubble tank when I got there. The whole place smelled like dry-cleaning fluid. Of course, we were allowed in that part of it. Why?"

"There was a section of the laboratory that was restricted?"

"Oh, yeah," she said. "What we heard was that it was part of NASA's backup system. Someone else said NORAD. The big rumor that it was the Apocalypse White House. We weren't even allowed to use the elevator at the same time as those guys. We knew they weren't military because of the uniforms, but that's about it. They basically kicked us out to expand whatever it was they were doing into our space. After that, our own scientists had to go to Sudbury or Kamiokande if they wanted to finish their projects."

"And access was via an elevator shaft?" DeLuca said. "No other way in or out?"

"Most caves only have one way in or out, and few have elevators," she said. "It wasn't as scary as it sounds. If the elevator failed, you could always climb out. Though it would have been a helluva climb, even up a ladder. The place was a mile underground."

"What's at the top of the shaft?" DeLuca asked.

"The entrance is adjacent to the visitors' area at Carlsbad Caverns. You're already a thousand feet underground. There's a door that just says 'Authorized Personnel Only,' with a guard, and behind that are the blast doors. They were designed out of steel and lead to keep out cosmic rays, but what we were told was that any one of them could withstand a direct hit from the biggest bombs we had."

"And how many of them were there?"

"Three."

"So if you wanted to lock yourselves in, there'd be no way anybody could gain access without you letting them?"

She shook her head.

"And Gary worked on the Army side?"

She nodded.

"I met him in the parking lot. He thought my Saab was cute."

"I don't want to hear your Saab story," DeLuca said. "I talked to him, by the way."

"I thought you might," she said. "Where did you find him?"

"He's not far," DeLuca said. "Do you want an address?"

"Not just yet, I think," she said. "I guess I sort of feel like it's up to him to contact me. But he's all right?"

"He's all right," DeLuca said. "I think he's going to call you."

"Forgive me if I don't get my hopes up," she said, thinking. "Oh, God. I thought all these feelings were dead. I'm not soft, you know. I just need closure, one way or the other. Anyway, I need to ask—why are you asking all these questions about Sinkhole?"

DeLuca hesitated.

"I found the diskettes Cheryl Escavedo took," DeLuca said. "And I know that she passed some of that information to you. Some of her figures turned up in your speeches, and there was no other way you could have gotten them. I'm not angry with you for not telling me. I even understand why you'd think I'm one of the bad guys. I was hoping you'd at least see me as one of the not-as-bad guys, because I'm after the worse guys, and if you knew how bad they were, I think you'd help me. I'll settle for one honest answer to one question. Did Sergeant Escavedo tell you anything about the project her boss was working on?"

"She said she could give me a breakdown of space weapon program figures, including black budgets," Penelope Burgess said. "We were going to meet in person but we never got the chance. I think all I actually got was a two-page e-mail attachment. She said there was more she could tell me, but I don't know what that was. That's the truth."

DeLuca nodded.

"And I don't think you're one of the bad guys. Maybe I did at first, but I don't anymore. How can I help you?"

"I don't know that you can," DeLuca said. "Unless you know a way into Sinkhole that nobody else knows about. There's someone in there and we have to get him out. That's all I can really tell you. I came here on the chance that you might have an idea."

She sipped her cocoa, staring at the fire for a moment.

"Well," she said at last. "I might. It's almost not worth mentioning, but . . ."

"What?"

"I was thinking about the ventilation system."

"No offense, but I think you watch too much television," DeLuca said. "People crawling through big giant vents isn't exactly how it works in the real world. We don't have too many bombs with a digital clock counting down the time to detonation in big red digital numbers on the outside either, while we have to decide whether to cut the red wire or the white one."

Penelope Burgess stared at him.

"I honestly don't know what you're talking about," she said. "And if you take a look around you, you might notice that I don't even own a television."

"I stand corrected," he said. "And I apologize. But I'm serious about the ventilation system. I looked at the schematics and as far as I could tell, there isn't one."

"I know," she said. "The air is drawn from the cave itself. It's run through a HEPA filter but it's not drawn from the surface, at least not through any man-made shafts. Caves breathe through their skin. Particularly the ones in the New Mexico karst."

DeLuca could imagine what a good teacher she was.

"Sinkhole is a subsystem of Carlsbad," she continued, reaching for a book from her shelf and opening it to the central map. She pointed out the places she was talking about with her finger, setting the book open on the coffee table and sitting on the couch next to DeLuca. "Carlsbad has been a show cave for the last hundred years and it still hasn't been entirely explored. The southeastern escarpment of the Guadalupe Mountains comprises a limestone uplift that happened during the Tertiary period, about ten million years ago, but the limestones and dolomites themselves were formed during the Permian period, 230 to 250 million years ago, when the entire region was underwater and full of organic life. Part of that sea was a deeper section called the Delaware Basin, now the Chihuahuan Desert extending into the plains of west Texas, but reef limestone and lagoon limestone built up at a much shallower part on the western end of the basin. During the Tertiary uplift, the rock fractured into fissures that allowed hydrogen sulfide gases to rise from deep within the earth, and when the hydrogen sulfide hit the water table, it combined with the oxygen in the water to form sulfuric acid. Limestone is soluble both in water and in sulfuric acid, but the processes are quite different. Lechugilla cave, where I've worked, was formed by sulfuric acid slowly bubbling up, unlike most caves, which are formed by water percolating down or flowing underground to form carbonic acid."

She reached for a second book, the same book that DeLuca had found in the backseat of Cheryl Escavedo's car, and opened it to the section of cave maps, using her finger on the page to lead DeLuca through the system.

"The entrances to Carlsbad and Lechugilla are about eight kilometers apart as the crow flies, but Lechugilla starts at a lower elevation. Lechugilla is the deepest limestone cave in the United States. I'd compare it to Swiss cheese, but Swiss cheese is much more predictable and not nearly as complex. There've been theories for years that Lechugilla and Carlsbad connect somewhere. If they do connect, then they might connect to Sinkhole as well, since it would be an uphill approach and Sinkhole is the lowest part of Carlsbad."

"How many miles of undiscovered cave are there?" DeLuca asked, before he could stop himself. She stared at him. "That's a stupid question, isn't it?" She nodded.

"And you've heard it before, haven't you?" She nodded again.

"One way to estimate the size of a cave involves measuring the differences in barometric pressure changes within the cave environment, relative to changes on the surface. A cave is like a bottle, and air goes in and out depending on the air pressure outside. By those calculations, Lechugilla might be the largest by volume, and by the same calculations, we think only about 5 percent of it has been explored or accounted for. And again, parallel measurements of both Carlsbad and Lechugilla indicate a connection. Theoretically."

"Is it a passage a human being could make?"

"It would be extraordinarily difficult."

"Has anyone ever tried?" DeLuca asked. She hesitated. "Has somebody done it?"

She hesitated again.

"According to caver legend, yes. A character who calls himself 'The Mole.'"

"Josh Truitt?" DeLuca said.

Burgess looked stunned.

"How did you know?" she asked.

"Just an informed guess," DeLuca said. "Josh himself told me about The Mole. It's been my experience, as a law enforcement officer, that within the first five minutes of meeting certain types of people, if they know you're a cop, they tell you a secret. Or they hint at one to see if I can guess it, to test me. Like they have an urge to confess but not to get caught. At first I thought it was odd, but now it seems almost charming."

"What kind of people?"

"People with consciences," DeLuca said. "And moral compasses. It's like confessing to a priest, maybe. True psychopaths are different."

"Did I do that?" she asked him.

"Do you have a secret?"

"Josh Truitt and I had an affair," she said. "I wondered if you were going to find that out. A fling. Gary and I were having . . . trouble, and Josh and I were in Cuba, working in a cave there. We had to spend almost a week waiting in our beachside motel for the government permits to come through. We agreed that it would end once we got back on American soil, and it did. And we stayed friends. He told me what happened to Theresa. I had the impression he thought she was the one. I met her once. She was nice."

"Do you think he found the passage?"

"If he says he did, then he did," Burgess said. "He's got something really special. I was actually thinking of designing a way to test it. The way he describes it is a photographic memory for spatial relationships, but I think there's more to it. Animals from humpback whales and bluefin tuna to hummingbirds and monarch butterflies have internal compasses that allow them to migrate almost infallibly across great distances, using the earth's magnetic field or the stars, we're not sure. I think Josh has whatever those animals have. In three dimensions. It's funny. Not funny ha-ha."

"What is?"

"The last I spoke to him, he said he was feeling a bit lost."

"Do you know where he is?"

Penelope Burgess called Truitt on his cell. They found him in a Japanese tea garden in Rio Grande Park, protected from the rain by the roof of the prayer pagoda, the Japanese symbol for peace painted on a hanging scroll that swayed in the breeze. The rain was falling harder, filling the river below. Truitt had his headphones on, the corduroy collar of his Carhartt jacket turned up against the cold, when DeLuca and Burgess approached. He took his headphones off when they sat opposite him, but he said nothing.

"What are you listening to?" DeLuca said.

"The Brandenburg," Truitt said. "Number Three."

"Got a minute?"

"For what?" Truitt said, turning to Burgess. "You didn't say you were bringing him."

"Just listen," Burgess said.

"I know you're upset about Theresa," DeLuca said. "I wanted to offer you a chance to do something about that. Penelope tells me you have a gift. I know that you're 'The Mole.' She tells me you have a gift for orienteering and spatial relationships."

"I'm a fucking idiot savant," Truitt said. "It's people I don't do so well with."

"I didn't think you were the type to waste time feeling sorry for yourself," DeLuca said.

"Oh yeah?" Truitt said. "What type am I then?"

"The type that can't see a problem without thinking of the solution. That point in the river," DeLuca said. "What direction is that?"

"From here?" Truitt said. He glanced at the sky, then looked upriver, then down. "Due west."

"How far?"

He looked at the point of the towhead dividing the Rio Grande into two channels.

"Seventeen hundred feet," he said. "Give or take a few."

"Hang on," DeLuca said. He took out his satellite phone and dialed the number for his son, Scott, whom he'd asked to stand by. "Scooter—have you got me on your screen?"

"Milsat 14," Scottie said. "Gotcha."

"You have my GPS?" DeLuca asked.

"Loud and clear," his son replied.

"Can you see the island in the river, the upstream point?" Scott said that he could. "What direction is that from me?"

"Pretty much due west," Scott said. "North thirty-five degrees, four-point-seven-three-five-zero latitude and west one-zero-six and forty-point-three-three-zero-seven longitude."

"How far is it from me?"

"In feet or meters?"

"Feet'll do."

"Fourteen hundred exact," Scott said.

"Thanks," DeLuca said. "Say hello to your mother for me."

He hung up.

"You're right about the direction but you're off about the distance," DeLuca said.

"No I'm not," Truitt said. "Your satellite is off."

"The satellite can't be . . ." DeLuca began, then remembered that Peggy Romano had recalibrated his GPS to read a hundred yards west of true as a way of protecting him from Darkstar. "You're right," he said. "The satellite is off. And you can do that in three dimensions, underground?"

Truitt shrugged.

"Do you want to help me get the men who killed Theresa? Do you want to help me solve this problem?"

Truitt thought a moment.

"What would I have to do?"

"We need a guide," DeLuca said. "I want you to take me through Lechugilla to Sinkhole. Penelope says you've done it before. Can you do it?"

"You'd never make it," Truitt said.

"Let me worry about that," DeLuca said. "Can it be done?"

Truitt stared at Burgess, angry that his secret had been revealed.

"Yes."

"How long would it take?"

"Me, traveling alone?" Truitt said. "Forty-eight hours. One way."

"How about a team of four?" DeLuca said.

"Five," Burgess said. "You're going to need more than one experienced caver. Not to mention that a chance to explore the far reaches of Lechugilla is a chance I can't pass up."

"Six days," Truitt said. "One way. But as I said, you'll never make it."

"We don't have a choice," DeLuca said. "I want you to get us there in forty-eight hours. We're all fit and we all have rope training."

"You were limping when you walked across the parking lot," Truitt said.

"It's not a problem," DeLuca said.

"Why would I want to help you?"

"Because we think the man who killed Theresa is in Sinkhole."

Truitt looked at Burgess again, shaking his head.

"This is insane," he said.

"Like I said, we don't have a choice," DeLuca told him. "Money's not a problem—how long would it take to put it together?"

"I can help with the prep," Burgess said.

"We could leave in the morning," Truitt said. "It's going to take us four hours minimum just to drive there."

"I think I can arrange for somewhat faster transportation," DeLuca said. "Meet us at the north gate of Kirtland at 0400 hours."

"You sound like my father," Truitt said. "I'll meet you there at four o'clock."

DeLuca found an e-mail from Walter Ford waiting for him when he got back to the RV.

David,
Thought you might be interested to know. One of my students decided to look into what happened to the rest of Koenig's classmates at Decatur Acad. Where are they now, etc. Took a while. He tracked down everybody but one, Daniel Berman, also a member of the Key Club. Recall that the Key Club was an organization of young conservatives who thought the Vietnam War was just and winnable and that Nixon was just the guy to win it. Not exactly ideologically mainstream at the time, and particularly not among young people (as you may recall). Turns out that the reason we couldn't find

out anything about Daniel Berman was that he changed his name before entering Yale, seeking something "less Jewish sounding," according to his friends. The new name was Carter Bowen. If that doesn't ring a bell, Bowen is currently White House assistant national security adviser to the vice president. Same guy who tried to argue that Saddam was buying enriched uranium from Nigeria and the guy who coauthored the legal brief saying the president has the right to order the torture of prisoners if he so chooses, as long as the prisoner is from a country not signatory to the Geneva Convention. Strongly opposed the resolution banning the assassination of foreign leaders. And—served as vice ambassador at the U.S. embassy in Moscow during the time Koenig was posted there.

Don't that blow a nice breeze up your boxer shorts?
Walter

DeLuca ordered his team to get a good night's sleep, because they were going to need it. Peggy Romano told him that General LeDoux wanted to speak with him in private and that she'd be in the motel bar for karaoke night if he needed any help. In the RV, LeDoux came on-screen from a briefing room inside the Pentagon. DeLuca told his old friend what their plan was.

"I'm leaving Sami here to hold down the fort and to go bring Antonionus in while we're gone. It might be leverage. I don't know how and I know it seems strange, but something tells me they're connected. Plus, Sami doesn't have the rope training or the PT that the rest of us have."

"Agreed," LeDoux said.

"Was that what you wanted to see me about?"

LeDoux looked uncomfortable.

"I've been advised," he said, "in terms I'd have to describe as unambiguous, to relate to you the rules of engagement. I'm not exactly sure where this is coming from, and I'm trying to find out, but it's definitely the highest levels. Personally, I don't agree with it, I'm going to go on the record to say, and I've been trying to run interference for you, but it's ugly. Passing this over to you isn't something I'd do to a friend, but I guess that's what we get for fraternizing all these years."

"If it's bad news, just give it me straight, Doc,'" DeLuca said. He recalled that LeDoux had had a meeting at the White House with Carla White and with the vice president's security adviser—Carter Bowen.

"I guarantee you're not going to like this. Basically, they don't want to go to trial with this, David. They don't want publicity of any kind. They don't want a three-star general sitting in jail and they don't want the ex-head of STRATCOM giving out press statements. They don't want any book deals. They don't want any lawyers. They don't want this on *The O'Reilly Factor* or the nightly news. General Koenig has been designated for termination, by any means necessary. That goes for whoever is with him. That's what they want me to tell you."

"You're giving my team a Direct Action mission," DeLuca said. He wasn't angry, but he wasn't happy either. "Is that what you're saying?"

"Officially, Koenig has been declared an enemy combatant," LeDoux said. "Equivalent to Mohammed Al-Tariq or Chemical Ali or anybody else. Ordinarily, this would be given to the CIA, but there are reasons why the CIA can't be involved right now."

DeLuca knew it had happened before, particularly in matters where national security needs trumped the right to trial in a court of law, and he understood that since passage of the Patriot Act, restrictions on the use of preemptive termination had been relaxed. He could also imagine that the decision to execute a United States general was not one entered into lightly. He understood the rules of warfare. He wasn't so sure he agreed with how flexible the definition of war was becoming.

"And if he comes walking out waving a white flag?"

"We're not recognizing any white flags," LeDoux said.

DeLuca stared at the screen a moment.

"Message received," he said, logging off before his friend could say anything more.

He knew how difficult it had been for LeDoux to pass the order on, because he knew it was not an order he'd be able to give to any member of his team. It was, simply, an order he would have to take on himself.

He found MacKenzie at the bar, nursing a beer and staring at the bubbles. When he asked her if everything was okay, she said things could be better.

"Could be worse, too," DeLuca said. "There could be a guy up on stage singing 'Moondance' on an Ovation guitar with his eyes closed. What's wrong?"

She continued to look at her beer, as if embarrassed.

"You know I grew up in California, right?"

"Malibu," he said. "Surfer girl."

"Well yeah, but we didn't live in the rich part of Malibu."

"I didn't know there was a poor part."

"There is," she said. "The part we lived in was prone to mudslides. I got caught in one. We were in the car and my father was driving. I was six. We were crossing this bridge when it hit us. I guess just the tail end of it. It'd been raining all day. Anyway, for a second, I got covered, and then my father reached in and pulled me out. Ever since then, I haven't been so big on caves. I like staying on top of the ground just fine."

"If you want off the mission tomorrow . . ."

"That's not what I'm saying," she said. "Okay? I just don't want anyone thinking, she's just a scared girl. I surfed the big water at Waimea side by side with the boys when I lived in Hawaii. I just thought it would help if somebody else knew. Your son told me you had a fear of flying before you did the HALO jump in Iraq. You tell anyone?"

"Yeah," he lied. "The anticipation is worse than the reality. That's the whole deal, really. You going to be able to sleep?"

"I'll give it another try," she said, leaving three dollars on the bar. "Thanks."

"Don't forget, Mack," DeLuca said. "You're going to have a lot of fathers tomorrow who can reach in and pull you out."

"Good night," she said.

Chapter Sixteen

CAPTAIN MARTIN INFORMED THE BASE AT KIRTland to expect a crew of civilians from the University of New Mexico at 0400 hours, to be flown to the town of Carlsbad City, and from there, they would proceed with government survey work. The cover story was that they were going to locate a site for a new radar platform to service the White Sands missile range. The team wore orange coveralls over UNM T-shirts, shorts, and lightweight hiking boots. DeLuca had chosen a twenty-year-old Cessna for transport, as nondescript an airplane as he could find. A white University of New Mexico van was waiting for them at the Carlsbad airport. They took 62 south to Dark Canyon Road, turning left after thirty minutes onto an unimproved road that changed to gravel, stopping at the base of a canyon where Truitt parked the vehicle and got out. No sign marked the way to the cave entrance, but DeLuca trusted that Truitt wasn't lost.

They hiked in just as the day was breaking, crossing landscape that bore the approximate topology of an egg carton, all peaks and valleys with sharp declivities but rarely anything flat or moderate. If the pace Truitt set on the trail to the cave entrance was indicative of the pace he intended to set inside, DeLuca knew he was in for a grueling forty-eight hours. Atop a short ledge, Truitt dropped his pack and donned his climbing harness as the others followed suit. "Anybody who has to piss or take a dump," he said, "find a bush. Once inside, we triple-Ziploc our by-products and pack the burritos out. In about ten minutes, you're going to be soaked in sweat from the heat and the humidity, so travel in your shorts and pack your coveralls to put on when we rest. We sleep in the dirt. There's potable water inside, so we're going to camel it from pool to pool to cut down on the weight we carry. We're climbing a modified frog system. I'll do the rigging. You've got food?"

"MREs," Sykes said. "Yummy yummy."

"What we want is maximum calories per cubic gram, but that's up to you. You said you were bringing ropes?"

DeLuca dropped a pair of packs on the ground.

"That's it?" Truitt said. "That's the length I told you we'd need? That can't possibly be enough."

"That's actually twice what you said we'd need," DeLuca said, "compliments of DARPA. Tenth Mountain out of Fort Drum was testing this stuff, but it's still classified. They told me you were going to like it."

Truitt opened one of the packs and examined the rope DeLuca had brought.

"What is this? Six millimeters?"

"Four. It's a Teflon-Kevlar microweave."

"Kevlar doesn't stretch," Truitt said. "Without shock absorption, you weaken your anchor points. This takes abrasion?"

"The Teflon protects from abrasion and the braid provides the stretch," DeLuca said.

"Cool," Truitt said. "Can I keep this when we're finished?"

"I don't think I've ever seen anybody get so excited about rope," Sykes said.

The cave entrance was protected by a sealed door, much like the hatch on a submarine, at the bottom of an unmarked twenty-meter-deep pit in the earth set into a hillside. Truitt tied onto a permanently fixed bolt, and one by one, the team rappelled down through a narrow mouth, gathering around the hatch below, where Truitt punched in the code he had obtained from the Park Service, turned the handle, and the hatch swung open, revealing a corrugated tin culvert with a series of ladder rungs leading down into the darkness. A strong wind blew from the hole at what Truitt said averaged sixty but often reached eighty miles an hour.

"We leave this place the way we found it," Truitt said, looking from face to face. "I'm going to move fast and push you, but monitor your bodies and if you have to rest, don't be too proud to say so. A few years ago, a woman got careless and broke her leg, less than half a mile in, and it took fifty volunteers almost a week to get her out, so don't fuck up. Maintain body awareness. Maintain rope awareness. Check your gear. I have extra LEDs for your headlamps and extra cells but conserve your energy, biological and electrical."

Truitt was first down the culvert, followed by Sykes, Vasquez, and MacKenzie, with DeLuca and Burgess bringing up the rear. Wind roared through DeLuca's helmet as he descended. At the bottom, he found Truitt standing at the top of a fixed rope leading down into a black abyss. The lights on their helmets illuminated only the nearby rock—the abyss seemed bottomless, the darkness around them a consuming thing that was somehow both magical and terrifying.

The fixed rope led an easy hundred meters down to a ledge that Truitt identified as Boulder Falls, a vertical drop that Truitt took first, abseiling down and then calling up from the bottom, his voice distant and tinny. They followed in the same order as they had entered, but this time, when DeLuca left the rock to find himself free-pitching in a black void, he felt entirely strange and oddly alone, floating and somehow out-of-body, swinging on a pendulum without visual cues, the opposing forces of gravity and centripetal force pulling at his guts in a way that challenged his senses. Beyond the lip, the pit opened into a bell shape, until his headlamp failed to reach the surrounding surfaces. A glance below made him shiver, certain that he would reach the end of the rope and fall and never stop falling. He slid faster, the rope slipping through his gloved hand. He saw the lights of his teammates as he reached the bottom, where he disconnected from the rope and danced down a short pile of breakdown, getting out of Penelope's way as she descended above him.

"This was the easy part," Truitt said.

They hiked The Rift, a sequence of downward vertical passages that could be traversed with only the occasional use of ropes. DeLuca was aware that every step took him farther from the world he knew. He noted, with irony, that until Koenig could be stopped, this world beneath the world was safer than the one above. It was warm inside the cave, a constant seventy-two degrees, but humid. In a matter of minutes, he and the others were soaked in sweat. At a place called Snow White's Passage, they rested a few moments, drinking from a nearby pool. They were at the central nexus of the cave system, Josh explained. From here, they could turn either to the Near East, a confusing maze of passages leading to an even more convoluted spaghettilike structure of caverns, faults, and constrictions known as the Far East subsystem, or they could head into the Southwestern Branch, or they could pass through the Western Borehole into the Western Branch, the most reticulated and perforated of the subsystems, with sponge work that had stopped all previous cavers from further exploration. On a road atlas, Carlsbad Caverns and Sinkhole lay to the east-southeast. Burgess expressed surprise when Truitt got to his feet and headed toward the Western Borehole.

"West?" Burgess said. "That's a bit counterintuitive."

"Not really. You have to look at the rims," Truitt said. "If gypsum precipitates on the downwind side, then from here through to the Three Amigos, the air movement is eastward, but in the Northwest Passage it reverses. There's no way it could do that unless the pressure source was higher than in the Wild West. You can see it where the hydromag balloons curl at the eruptions—they all sag in the same direction. It took me three trips, but I finally found a breach just past Hudson Bay, where it meets Spar City. You'll see."

In some chambers, passage was a relatively easy stroll. Occasionally, the team was required to squeeze through terrifying constrictions between bedding planes where water had once flowed across horizontal plates of bedrock. For DeLuca, the squeezes were the worst, the fear of getting stuck pervasive and unshakable, even with Burgess coaching him reassuringly from behind, "a little to the left, now bend your knee . . ." At the same time, the mineral deposits they saw along the way were beyond description, words like "breathtaking" and "astonishing" failing to describe what they saw, flowstones and dripstones, gypsum blossoms and flowers and massive chandeliers the size of upside-down oak trees hanging from the ceilings of ballroom-sized chambers, aragonite bushes blooming on flat shelfstones as if on display in a museum, coralloid sheets and forms coated in frostwork glistening brightly in their headlamps, selenite crystals the size of grandfather clocks, cave pearls and button popcorn and snarls of underwater helictites and calcite-encrusted strings of organic material in pools so still and clear it was difficult to see where the surface began unless you made a ripple.

It was hard to estimate the passage of time. When DeLuca finally thought to look at his watch, he saw that ten hours had passed. He might have guessed five. They stopped for dinner, six MREs from Sykes's pack. In Iraq, "MRE" was commonly understood to stand for Meals Refused by Everyone, but DeLuca was ravenous, the turkey Tetrazzini he'd mocked in Balad as so much wallpaper paste now possibly the best thing he'd ever eaten. Truitt wanted to push ahead another kilometer before making camp for the night.

"Are you serious, man?" Vasquez said. "I'm wiped."

"You can wait here if you want," Truitt said with a smile. DeLuca tried to imagine what they would do if Truitt or Burgess were to somehow get hurt. None of them would be able to find their way out, and none of their technology would help them one bit. "Just remember the first rule of caving. Truitt's Law."

"Which is?"

"You must exit a cave the same number of times as you enter it."

The next three hours were excruciating. Every muscle in DeLuca's body ached, as did his rib where it was cracked, and his ankle, but he kept going. Finally, Truitt stopped beside a gorgeous pool that glowed in blues and oranges when he shone his light into it.

"We'll camp here," he said, turning to DeLuca. "How much sleep do you think you'll need? I usually get by on two. If you want to make it in forty-eight, I suggest no more than four."

"Four it is," DeLuca said. He felt like he could sleep for twenty-four. "Where do we go tomorrow?"

"Through there," Truitt said, pointing to the wall at the far end of the lake.

"Through the wall?" Sykes said.

"Under it," Truitt said.

"That's a water trap?" Burgess asked. Truitt nodded.

"The phreatic zone starts here," Truitt said, pointing. "You can find fluting along the sides if you dig deep enough, so it's the solution pan everybody always thought it was, but it also siphons off to the south. I was camped here one night and I felt pressure in my ears, so I knew the water was rising. I learned later that it had rained heavily that night, but only on the eastern slopes of the surface ridge. If you posit a uniform vadose zone, then the sump had to lead from west to east, which made it a through-cave."

"Could I get that in layman's terms?" Vasquez asked.

"We swim underwater," Burgess said. "Below the water table. The cave continues on the other side."

"How far underwater?" Sykes asked.

"Not that far," Truitt said. "The first time, I didn't know exactly where I was going. I probably had two or three seconds of air left before I found the pocket, but then, I was holding my breath. You guys have air, right?"

Peggy Romano had supplied each of them with a fifty-cubic-inch tank, the kind of emergency supply used by pilots forced to ditch their aircraft in the sea. Each contained fifteen minutes of air.

"How long can you hold your breath?" MacKenzie asked him.

"Five minutes," Truitt said. "But I got a bit disoriented."

"I thought you didn't get disoriented?"

"I accidentally kicked the sediment on the bottom with my foot," Truitt said. "Ten million years' worth of silt. The water turned cloudier than clam chowder, but by then I was past the point of no return. I never said luck doesn't play a part."

"Are you nuts?" Sykes said. "This guy is insane. He dives into a pool past the point of no return because he thinks there's air on the other side."

"I'm still here, aren't I?" Truitt said. "I never break the first law of caving. Tomorrow, I'll string a guideline for the rest of you to follow. Just don't lose the line."

DeLuca wasn't sure if he slept or not. He had vivid dreams of climbing through the darkness. The blackness he experienced when he opened his eyes was profound and absolute, a complete absence of visual data that magnified everything else. He heard the blood rushing in his ears. He felt his heart thumping in his chest. Surrounded by his team members, the way he'd been so many nights in their tent in Balad, he nevertheless felt an intense sense of solitude, and a strange sadness—it made little sense, but for a while, the sadness was overwhelming, until he reached for his helmet and turned on his headlight, briefly, just long enough for him to regain his bearings. He shut the light off again.

"You, too?" he heard MacKenzie whisper from where she lay next to him.

"Me, too," he admitted.

"I keep thinking this is what death is like," MacKenzie whispered.

There was a long silence.

"Wanna spoon?" MacKenzie asked.

"Love to," DeLuca said. He felt MacKenzie back into him, and he threw his arm over her side, hugging her close. "Just don't tell my wife."

"You know what I always say," she whispered. "What happens at the center of the earth stays at the center of the earth."

They slept.

Seemingly seconds later, though it was hours, he heard Truitt's watch beeping. They ate a quick breakfast. While they ate, Truitt tied green Cyalume chemlites at ten-foot intervals along a length of rope, cracking each chemlite to make it glow before moving on to the next one, the line like a string of Christmas lights where it piled up on the sand.

"Is everybody clear what we have to do?" he asked. "Any questions? I'll go first and I'll give a tug to tell you when I'm on the other side, but if for some reason you don't feel the tug, wait two minutes and then follow.

Come one at a time and keep your eye on the chemlites. If you bunch up, the chances of somebody silting it up increase. Put your pack under your stomach if you want—it'll help you float. The total swim is going to be about a hundred feet."

"I do have a question," Vasquez said. "What if the reason we don't feel a tug is that you've drowned, and then we follow you and one by one, we drown, too?"

"That would suck for all of us, wouldn't it?" Truitt said. "And try not to touch the ceiling either because it's white gypsum and the shit is nasty if you get any down your collar or in your shorts. So, see you on the other side."

"You don't need one of these?" MacKenzie said, offering him a spare oxygen bottle.

"Air is for pussies," he said. "No offense. Personally, it makes me lose focus."

DeLuca watched as Truitt disappeared into the water, his headlamp illuminating the bottom, where DeLuca saw bright orange disks and gray mineral crusts that looked like seashells or broken crockery. Then Truitt's headlamp was gone, the way illuminated only by the string of chemlites, which disappeared into the maw of the earth.

No one spoke. DeLuca looked at his watch. A minute passed. Then another. Sykes held the line, his head cocked as if he were listening for something. Three minutes passed, then four.

"I don't feel anything," Sykes said. "Time to shove off then. I'll go next . . ."

"Wait a minute," Vasquez said, his voice filled with a sudden urgency. "Hold on."

"What's wrong?" DeLuca asked.

"I've been testing my breather," Hoolie said. "It's empty. I mean, it had about tens seconds of air and then it ran out." He looked at the gauge, tapping it against a rock. "The gauge says it's full. Test yours."

Sykes put the regulator in his mouth and breathed, spitting the mouthpiece out a few moments later.

"Mine's empty, too," he said. "Shit!" he shouted, his words echoing inside the cavity.

"Hold on," DeLuca commanded. "Nobody panics. Mack, how about you?"

"Empty," she said. "So's the spare."

"The gauges must be faulty," Vasquez said.

"Stop," DeLuca said, thinking. The mission was too important to abort. They had to try. "It doesn't matter. We can do this. We just have to think a minute."

He looked to Penelope Burgess for ideas. She had none to offer.

"Hoolie," DeLuca said. "How many Ziploc bags do we have left?"

"Half the box," Hoolie said.

"Everybody fill up three or four with air and tuck them inside your overalls. That should give us enough air to get to the other side if we need it. We used to do this when we were kids on Long Island—just remember when you open the bag to get underneath it, open it, stick your mouth in, and inhale. Don't try to catch the bubbles from above—go like this," he said, demonstrating. "Okay? We go as a team, buddy system. I don't care what Truitt said—we're stronger as a team than we are as individuals, right? So we help each other, buddy system. Move quickly but no panic. We can do this."

"I'm not saying we can't," MacKenzie said, steeling herself, "but if somehow we can't . . . just on the off chance that we can't—does anybody know where we are?"

"LeDoux knows," DeLuca said. "He'll come and get us, even if he has to send the whole Third Army."

"But how will they know where to look?" MacKenzie asked. She had a point. DeLuca knelt and wrote in the sand with his finger, CI TEAM RED, then drew an arrow indicating the way they would go.

"Thanks," MacKenzie said.

She went first with Sykes, followed by Hoolie, then Burgess, DeLuca bringing up the rear. They swam as far as they could on the surface, then collectively took deep breaths and dived at the count of three.

The string of green lights led into a darkness that, because it was underwater, seemed even blacker and more complete than before. Burgess swam with a frog kick, while Vasquez chose a scissors kick. Sykes and MacKenzie were soon out of view. DeLuca held his breath, feeling the tightness in his chest increasing with every stroke. He swam down, keeping the green chemlites in view. He felt as if his eyes were going to burst from their sockets, his lungs aching, but he swam, until he needed air. He reached for a Ziploc bag, but it slipped from his fingers and was gone. He grabbed a second bag and inhaled from it. It was good, but it wasn't enough. He swam quickly to catch up to the others as the string of chemlites turned to the right. He kept going. He needed air. He kept going.

Then the water ahead of him turned cloudy. He reached up to grab the guideline just in time as the water around him turned opaque. Somebody had silted the pool. He wasn't angry. He slowed his thoughts. It was something like a habit he had, when trouble loomed, telling himself, "If I'm going to die, I'm not going to die with fear in my heart . . ."

He swam, pulling himself forward and holding on to the line, hand over hand, his headlamp illuminating only the water six inches ahead of him. He paused to pop his last air bag, inhaling.

It wasn't enough.

He kept going. He could see nothing. He had to be close. How much farther? His lungs ached. Pain stabbed at his heart, and then he realized that the line was now slack in his hands.

He slowed his thoughts. He slowed his thoughts. He slowed. Which way had he been heading? His muscles remembered which way the line had tugged, so he swam in that direction. Then, he had nothing left, could hold his breath no longer. He thought of his wife, and of his son, sorry that he'd never see them again.

Suddenly, he felt a tug on his sleeve as Josh Truitt grabbed his arm and pulled him the last ten feet.

He gasped as he broke the surface, supported on all sides by his team, their hands holding him up.

"Are you all right?" Truitt asked.

"I'm fine," DeLuca said, shaking the water from his eyes. "Where to from here?"

"Straight up," Truitt said. "Maybe two hundred feet." DeLuca looked up to see a narrow slit between two vertical walls, close enough, Truitt said, that they could chimney up without using ascenders.

"Terrific," DeLuca said. "Let's go."

"You didn't really do that when you were kids in Long Island, did you?" Burgess asked him when they had a private moment, after the others had begun the ascent.

"No," DeLuca said. "But it's exactly the stupid kind of thing we would have tried."

They rested at the top, everyone but Truitt exhausted, then pushed forward down what Truitt had dubbed the Northeastern Borehole. They passed one spectacular chamber after the next, scrambling over chockblocks and talus fields, drop passages, an open traverse across a place Josh called the Bottomless Pit, and judging from how long it took for a tossed rock to reach the bottom, he was nearly right. They walked, climbed, and roped until they came to the edge of a precipice where their combined headlights revealed nothing in front of them. When Truitt took a pocket laser and projected it into the void, a beam that should have been visible from up to half a mile revealed nothing ahead.

"I call this Gram's Canyon, after Gram Parsons," Truitt said. "I think it could be the largest underground canyon in the world. Some day I'm going to photograph it if I can figure out how to light it. The left wall is lagoon limestone and the right wall is reef limestone and I think the ceiling is the base plate of the Yates formation."

"It's strange to think there's so much beauty in front of us and we can't see any of it," MacKenzie said.

"Sort of like sitting in a bathroom stall next to Catherine Zeta-Jones," Hoolie said. "Not that I've ever done that. To my knowledge."

"That's gross," Mack said.

They made good progress, moving through forests of stalactites, stalagmites, towers, and columns, past haystack-shaped mounds of flowstone, balancing on steppingstones that shifted underfoot as they crossed shallow ponds and deep water-filled crevasses. Here the ground was red with iron, there it was a curried yellow color from sulfur, until it turned white with gypsum forming carpets of cauliflower, then a prairie of straw crystals, dropping off into an inky void.

DeLuca stopped beneath an arch to catch his breath. His legs felt as if they were turning to rubber. He let the others go on ahead while he cracked a power bar for energy. He chewed slowly, watching the headlamps of his teammates bobbing in the darkness, strung out along a relatively easy uphill trail. He turned off his own light for a moment, to save on batteries.

Then he thought he heard something, but the sound came from behind him instead of in front of him.

He froze, listening.

He heard it again, the sound of gravel falling on rock. He'd thought he'd sensed that someone was following them an hour earlier but wrote it off to his imagination. Who could possibly be following them? And if someone was, why didn't DeLuca see his lights?

From his backpack, he quietly opened a Ziploc bag and took out his NVGs. The batteries powering the goggles were only good for a few hours, and without peripheral vision or depth perception, they weren't the tool of choice for caving, but whoever was following them was evidently using them, for when DeLuca donned his, he saw a man approaching, an infrared lamp glowing from his helmet.

DeLuca took a second Ziploc bag from his pack and drew from it his Beretta, chambering a round before taking position to the side of the trail behind an outcrop. He waited. He heard footsteps, drawing closer. When the man passed him, DeLuca stepped out and put the gun to the base of the man's skull.

"Not another step," DeLuca said.

"Don't shoot," the man said, raising his hands in the air. "Please . . ."

DeLuca put the gun down.

"I hope you called your father before you came here," DeLuca said. "He doesn't know where you are."

"Agent DeLuca?" Marvin Yutahay said. He was wearing jeans, a denim workshirt and canvas high-top sneakers, a red bandana around his neck and a coil of rope over one shoulder.

"What are you doing here, Marvin?" DeLuca asked. "Your old man thinks you went over the cliff at Koenig's ranch."

"The bike did, but I got off," Marvin said. "Koenig was trying to kill me. He killed Cheryl."

"I know," DeLuca said. "That still doesn't explain what you're doing here?"

"Cheryl said Koenig had a second place near Carlsbad," Marvin said. "Some sort of control center. She wouldn't tell me any more, and she said she didn't know where, exactly, so after he tried to kill me, I went to Carlsbad to ask around. When I heard on the caver grapevine that a government team was coming to do survey work, I went to the airport and then I followed you, but I didn't know it was you. When I saw the sign you left at the water trap, I wasn't sure if you knew I was here or what, but by then I'd come too far to turn around."

"You thought we were Koenig?" DeLuca said. Marvin shrugged. "And if we were, you were going to kill him?"

"He killed Cheryl," Marvin said. "Somebody needs to kill him to make it even."

"Come on," DeLuca said. "The others are probably waiting for me to catch up. Where'd you get the NVGs?"

"E-Bay," Marvin said. "Tricks of the trade. I was down to my last set of batteries."

Marvin explained himself again when they reached the expedition party. Vasquez offered him a power bar, which he devoured. Marvin hadn't been prepared for such an undertaking, evidently, but his determination made up for it.

They rested again at the head of the canyon, pausing for a second round of MREs, during which Marvin told them how he'd navigated the water trap, using the snorkel he'd brought along, standard equipment among experienced gem hunters. Truitt, who'd described gem hunters with the less polite term "cave robbers," held his tongue. Marvin had followed the string of chemlites until he reached the end, then saw in the distance, using his NVGs, three that had floated to the top of the pool on the far side, the image faint but enough to lead him to safety.

"How'd you get through the hatch?" Sykes asked him.

"I was hiding in the entrance pit," he said. "Halfway up the wall. I was watching over your shoulder when you punched in the code."

While the others rested, Josh Truitt searched for the mark he'd made at the edge of a region he called the Bone Yard, a massive limestone maze resembling a large pile of porous bones. He returned a few minutes later to say he'd found it. The team seemed reenergized. Josh led the way, through an erratic three-dimensional webbing of shapes and forms, bridges and arches, keyholes and windows, slots and grooves. They climbed up and forward, angling this way, then that. Occasionally Truitt stopped to get his bearings. Midway through, they paused to rest.

"What exactly are you basing your decisions on?" Sykes said. "You change course but it all looks exactly the same."

"Humidity," Truitt said. "Where we're going is wetter than where we came from. The water percolates from above. We're looking for the source."

"You can sense that?" Sykes said. "Changes in humidity?"

"You can't?" Truitt said.

"My hair gets frizzy," MacKenzie said. "That's how I know. I'd kill for a shower."

"Be careful what you wish for," Truitt said, "because you're going to get one."

True to his word, they stopped where the Bone Yard met the ceiling, the air getting wetter and wetter until they could hear the sound of running water. Illumination showed a stream of water pouring out of a hole in the wall, falling through a narrow pit into a plunge pool Truitt said was five hundred meters down. By the look on his face, he seemed dismayed.

"What is it?" DeLuca asked.

"I was afraid of this," Truitt said.

"Of what?"

"We want to go through there," he said, pointing to the hole from which the water poured. "The stream is free surfaced on the other side, but with all the rain we've been having, the hydrostatic pressure might be more than we can handle. In midsummer, this thing would be dry. We'd just traverse across and zoop-zoop. It's only about six feet, but against this kind of current, that's a lot."

"You can't do it?"

"I didn't say that," he said, thinking. "I could bring a rope with me and then once I'm on the other side, I'll pull whoever's next through. Actually, I'll bring two ropes and anchor one for the next person to climb on, and they can tie off on the second rope. The traverse across the pit is a little tricky. Penny, think you can handle that?"

Burgess nodded, asking, "How are you going to get through?"

"That's a very good question. All we can do is try, right? Hey, cave robber," Truitt said to Marvin Yutahay. "Mind if I borrow your snorkel?"

"Not a problem," Marvin said, handing it to him. "Just don't get your germs on it."

It took Truitt half an hour to rig a line of bolts on the far wall, tying a rope taut between them for the others to walk on, looping the rope back around parallel, six feet higher, to serve as a hand line, both leading to the edge of the waterfall. Standing on the base rope, he reached his arms into the flow in an attempt to hammer in a piton to hold on to. His first three attempts failed. Finally he managed to set the first bolt, the water pounding against his chest and face as he worked. He emerged from the stream to catch his breath, exhausted from the effort. When he regained his strength, he began tying knots in the anchor rope.

"Once I'm through," he shouted above the roar, "I'll lower the snorkel to the next person. Leave your packs and the last person can tie them on. Watch out for the roof because that's where you could get snagged, and getting snagged is going to be fatal. Pull yourself hand over hand on the knotted rope and tie off with this one and I'll pull you up from above. There's a good foothold here," he said, reaching into the stream with his hand. "The second person is going to be the hardest—after that we'll have two people pulling. It should be someone small."

"I'll go second," MacKenzie said. "I hate waiting for men to finish in the shower."

DeLuca took Truitt aside for a moment.

"Needless to say," DeLuca said, keeping his voice down, "the Army appreciates what you've done. Am I to understand that on the other side of this is the passage that leads to Sinkhole?"

Truitt nodded.

"Then you might want to bear in mind," DeLuca said, "the possibility exists that someone armed may be waiting for you on the other side."

Truitt stared at him.

"I just thought you should know." DeLuca said.

Truitt readied himself, spending a few minutes taking deep breaths to charge his lungs with oxygen. He gave the others two thumbs up, checked his gear one last time, took a final deep breath through the snorkel, and dived headfirst into the stream, disappearing from the waist up. They watched his legs as he dug for the foothold, and then he found it, and then he was gone.

DeLuca stared at the water as it poured from the rock, glancing occasionally at his watch. Truitt had said he could hold his breath for five minutes. DeLuca imagined that was probably sitting still in a chair, not fighting vigorously to make his way upstream like some sort of subterranean salmon. The snorkel gave him a few extra minutes at best.

They watched, waiting.

Suddenly, they saw him again as the stream ejected him into the void.

Burgess screamed as Truitt fell, tumbling head over heels in the tumbling water.

Then the rope Truitt was fastened to drew taut and stopped his fall. He bounced once, until the water falling on him beat him back, pounding him against the rock face parallel to his drop line. Quickly, Sykes and Vasquez moved to grab the rope and pull Truitt up. A minute later, the caver was lying on the ledge next to the others. It took some time before he could speak.

"I'm aborting," DeLuca said. "We can't do it. It's all right. As soon as you're good, we'll head back."

Truitt shook his head.

"That was just to set the second bolt," he said, struggling to sit up, propping himself with one arm. "Now we're good. Whoever's next, give me three tugs to tell me you're coming and I'll start to pull. I'm going to pull as hard and as fast as I can because there's no turning back once you commit. I'll give you three tugs first to tell you I'm ready."

He prepared himself with deep breathing, then disappeared back into the flow. A minute later, the knotted rope came back, followed by the towrope with the snorkel attached to it. MacKenzie traversed the pit and readied herself, tying onto the towrope and grabbing the knotted rope with both hands. DeLuca gave her two thumbs up. She felt three tugs on the towrope. Then she gave three tugs and dived into the stream. DeLuca watched as her head and shoulders disappeared, then her torso, then her legs. A few minutes later, the towrope returned with the snorkel attached. Sykes went next, followed by Yutahay, then Vasquez. It got easier and easier with more people pulling on the other end. DeLuca told Burgess he believed in ladies first. When she was gone, he had a fleeting thought—what if, for some reason, the rope didn't reappear? What if they left him there? A stupid but human thought. There was no reason to think they would. Horses didn't like being alone. Deep down, humans didn't either.

Then the rope appeared. He tied on and went through.

They followed the stream above for a quarter mile, climbing a series of waterfalls, until they branched off to the right. They chimneyed up a fissure and emerged only to squeeze through the narrowest constriction so far, but by now, DeLuca felt like an old pro. They came to a grotto on the far side where, at the top opposite, DeLuca saw a faint light shining through a slit in the rock. When he climbed up and stuck his head through the slit, Truitt next to him, he saw that they'd reached the elevator shaft, the rungs of a service ladder fixed to the rails opposite and eight heavy steel cables running down into a darkness lit every fifty feet by yellow light bulbs in wire cages for as far as the eye could see. Seeing something man-made seemed strange, but also strangely comforting.

Truitt was looking at his watch.

"Forty-two hours and twenty minutes," he said. "I thought we were making good time."

"We'll pay you for the full forty-eight," DeLuca said.

"I'll jump across and tie a line," Truitt said. "You tell the others."

They climbed down the service ladder in single file, with DeLuca leading the way and the civilians bringing up the rear, descending an endless series of rungs until they saw a square of light at the bottom. A hundred feet up, DeLuca stopped to take an M-12 machine pistol equipped with a silencer from his pack, as much firepower as he could pack in the smallest amount of space. The others broke out their weapons as well. He stepped softly onto the roof of the elevator and listened.

He heard nothing.

He pried the trapdoor in the elevator ceiling open slowly without making a sound.

The elevator was empty.

He dropped in, then gestured for Sykes, MacKenzie, and Vasquez to follow. When Sykes took a charge of C4 explosives from his pack to blow the door, DeLuca shook his head and pointed to the "Open Doors" button.

He gestured to Truitt, Yutahay, and Burgess to wait in the elevator, then pressed the button.

The doors opened onto a long empty corridor. The team fanned out, guns ready, carefully searching the rooms that lined the corridor, four on the right side and three on the left, but they found only empty offices and empty desks.

The doors at the end of the corridor led to a second set of doors, marked "Authorized Personnel Only." On DeLuca's signal, they kicked their way in, Sykes and Vasquez crisscrossing low while DeLuca aimed high.

The control room was empty.

For a moment, DeLuca saw a large screen showing a map of the globe with satellite orbits represented by green lines, but when an intruder alert sounded, the screen automatically went dark.

They searched the entire compound, but it was empty. Whoever was using the computers in the complex had been doing so from a remote location. When they searched the hard drives of the mainframe, they were, to no one's surprise, blank.

"Fool me twice," Vasquez finally said.

"Where is everybody?" Yutahay asked.

"We don't know," DeLuca said. "They were supposed to be here."

They took the elevator to the top. When the door opened, they pushed through a second door at the end of the hall and found themselves in the Carlsbad Caverns underground cafeteria, staring at a rack of Coke and candy machines. DeLuca squinted at the bright fluorescent lights. They took a second elevator to the surface. The sun was just rising in the east. He was glad to see it. A nondescript van full of soldiers waited by the entrance to the gift shop. The leader introduced himself as Captain Jones, adding that General LeDoux had sent him to assist. DeLuca told him his team could head on down, but that they weren't going to find anything.

"Where to now?" Sykes asked DeLuca as a dozen soldiers scrambled from the van.

"Back to square one, I guess," he said. "Personally, I intend to see a woman about some oxygen bottles."

But when they got back to Albuquerque, the Ms. Kitty was gone.

Chapter Seventeen

SAMI HAD PUT RAINBOW AND RUBY IN A CAB and paid the driver for the round-trip fare to Seattle, where Rainbow still owned a home, even though she'd planned to sell it and give the proceeds to Brother Antonionus. She'd decided to go home after Sami played her a tape he'd made surreptitiously, interviewing Brother Antonionus. Sami had informed him he was going to have to arrest him, unless Antonionus was willing to make a deal. He played the recording for DeLuca when he got back, using the speakers on his laptop, which he set up on the bed in his motel room.

"Why should I make a deal with you?" Antonionus said. "I should have you arrested for lying to us about who you were."

"Undercover officers do that all the time," Sami had explained. "You can't have me arrested."

"And just what is it I've done?" Antonionus asked. "Is it legal now for the government to persecute its citizens for their beliefs?"

"We're not arresting you for your beliefs," Sami said. "We're not even arresting you for scamming people out of their belongings, though I'm not sure how legal that is.

We're arresting you for aiding and abetting the act of treason. That's a pretty serious offense, Malcolm."

There was a long silence on the tape.

"I don't know what you mean," he said, sounding scared. "I'm not aiding or abetting anyone."

"You're aiding and abetting your old friend Tom Koenig," Sami said. "Your old prep school chum."

There was an even longer pause.

"And just how do you think I've been aiding and abetting?" Antonionus said. "Just what is it I've been doing that's so illegal?"

"Disinformation," Sami said. "There's nothing new about disinformation, Malcolm. Hitler was great at it. You want to run a program putting radios in people's teeth, the best way to hide it might be to have some well-known wacko who no one believes go on television and say, 'The government is putting radios in people's teeth.' You wanna test-fly Stealth bombers in secret, you have some discredited wacko saying, 'The Air Force is flying invisible airplanes . . .' See what I'm saying?"

"That's crazy."

"That may be, but you're not. You've known what you've been doing all along. And if, in the meantime, you can get people to give you all their money and mow your lawn for you, all the better."

"There's nothing illegal about asking people to give you their money," Antonionus said. "If they're stupid enough to say yes, that's their problem."

"Or asking them to believe in UFOs?"

"I've never asked anybody to believe in UFOs," Antonionus said. "Every single moron who comes here is a believer before they ever see me. I just channel their beliefs into more creative venues."

"And more lucrative for you?"

"As I said, it's not illegal," Antonionus said. "Some people give a tenth of everything they make to the Church because they think it will get them into heaven. Can you prove that any of them are in heaven? Can you prove they're not? If it's not wrong to take a tenth, why would it be wrong to take it all? I'm the beneficiary of some very generous friends."

"Generous or gullible?"

"Why can't you be both?" he asked.

"If we checked your phone records, would we find any telephone calls between you and Tom Koenig? Because we can pull your call logs. There's no problem there."

"You couldn't carry Tom Koenig's jock strap," Antonionus said.

"Wouldn't care to try," Sami said. "You know he's going to be arrested for the murder of Cheryl Escavedo, don't you? The fact that you were on the scene to tell everybody it was a UFO makes you an accomplice to murder. It does bother me that you let a little girl watch it. That doesn't bother you?"

"She'll get over it," Antonionus said. "She's just a kid. You can't prove a thing."

"I don't have to prove anything to arrest you," Sami said. "We don't even have to bring you to trial if we don't want to. Maybe you'd like to see Cuba? Of course, so would the prisoners at Guantanamo—they've been sitting in the sun with bags over their heads for three years. Does that appeal to you, Malcolm?"

"You can't do that."

"I can if you don't help me."

Silence.

"What is it you want me to do?"

"I want you to tell me about Tom Koenig. I want you to go public about working for the government to mask their satellite programs all these years. If you're lucky, you can get a book deal and be on Oprah. I want you to help us get Koenig."

"I'm hardly part of his inner circle," Antonionus said, sounding hurt. "He's never so much as asked me over to his house. I think he's ashamed to admit he knows me. That's not right, is it?"

"That's not right at all. Why did Cheryl Escavedo contact you?"

"Cheryl Escavedo never contacted me," Antonionus said. "I left a message saying I was returning her call, but she never called. That was planted for you to find."

"Can you talk about the Key Club?"

"What's a Key Club?"

"At Decatur Academy. You and Koenig and Hilton Jaynes and Daniel Berman. And others, I assume. You've forgotten?"

Silence.

"You can't talk about that?"

Silence.

"Who are you afraid of? Koenig? Carter Bowen?"

"I'll talk to you," Antonionus said in a hushed tone. "Not here. You have to give me time. I'll have to get my things in order. I have a chain of businesses I have to protect. I want it on the record that I came in voluntarily. Afterward you'll have to take care of me. I'm not even sure the witness protection program is safe enough."

"We can do that," Sami told him.

Sami shut the recording off.

"I told him he could come in on his own. I don't make him as a flight risk—he needs us too much to take off."

"You played this for Rainbow?"

"Uh huh," Sami said. "I had to. I couldn't keep it from her. There's nothing on it that's classified. Is there? Should I not have done that?"

"No, no, that's okay," DeLuca said. "How'd she take it?"

"She took it hard," Sami said.

"She blame you?"

"I guess so," Sami said. "I'm not sure we were meant for each other anyway. I'm a crusty old bastard from Boston. She could do better. You know what they say—if you love something, let it go, and if it comes back to you . . . cuff it."

"You okay?"

"I'm all right," Sami said. "I'm good. I'll get over it."

DeLuca stared at the laptop.

"How did you tape the conversation?"

"I had my cell phone on in my shirt pocket," Sami said. "I dialed in to Peg Romano and she recorded it from the RV."

"Was that your idea or hers?"

"Hers," Sami said. "Why? Is that a problem?"

"It is for Malcolm Percy," DeLuca said. "Romano was playing for the other side. When did she take off?"

"She said she needed to have the transmission serviced," Sami said. "She left this morning."

DeLuca called his friend Mike O'Leary at the FBI and put out an APB on the motor home and did the same on the military side through Captain Martin in LeDoux's office, but he held out little hope. As difficult as it might be to hide a forty-foot silver motor home, he knew Peggy Romano would have prepared a way to cover her escape well in advance. He suspected the RV was either inside a semi–tractor trailer on a highway somewhere or in the belly of a C-130 under a false bill of lading.

When he called the Brethren of the Light, he was told that Brother Antonionus was unavailable. When he stopped by the Albuquerque police department, he learned that Malcolm Percy's car had been in a car accident, killing the driver and sole occupant of the car. When DeLuca pressed for details, flashing his B's and C's and identifying himself as a member of Army counterintelligence, he was told that the body had been burned beyond recognition, the white Rolls-Royce he was driving in having crashed into a bridge abutment on Interstate 25, but the odd thing was that although the car was demolished, the gas tank was intact—the fire had started in the driver's compartment before the collision itself. Forensics was testing for accelerants inside the vehicle.

"It's like the guy spontaneously combusted," the sergeant said. "Like you read about in those magazines."

"Yeah," DeLuca said, "but you can't believe everything you read in magazines."

Before returning to the motel, he stopped by the Japanese tea garden at the park by the river, pausing first at a mall to make some purchases at a cell phone store. Using a new phone, the account opened under a false name, he called his son, Scott, in Kirkuk and asked Scottie to lock on to his GPS signal and tell him, again, how far it was to the point on the river. It took his son a minute. Again,

Scott told him it was fourteen hundred feet, off by exactly one hundred yards.

"The mobile ops center we've been using . . ."

"The Ms. Kitty?" Scott asked.

"Yeah," DeLuca said. "Do you still have the access numbers we used the first time we linked with you?"

"I think so," Scott said.

"Do you think you could shut it down?"

"Do you mean blow it up?"

"Negative," DeLuca said. "I just want you to rewrite some of her software. Could you do that?"

"I couldn't personally but we've got some guys here who could," Scott said.

"Are they busy?"

"Well, there is still a war going on, but yeah, I think I could get them to help. We'd need to know her password to reach the kernel codes. We could probably get into her system without one but you'd save us a lot of time if you had it."

"I don't," DeLuca said, "but I'll bet it has something to do with women's basketball. Try all the last names of all the players in the WNBA, and if that doesn't do it, go to the colleges. Start with UConn. Here's what I want you to do . . ."

He called a team meeting at the motel bar. He'd told his team to stay low, take the batteries out of their satellite phones, not go out, not use the room phone, not watch TV in their rooms, log on to the Internet, or interact in any way with the electronic grid. He'd passed the same message to Walter Ford, who said it was winter break anyway and a good time for him and his wife, Martha, to take a little vacation.

"We can assume," DeLuca told Dan, Hoolie, Mack, and Sami, "if Romano was bad, then they know what we know. Everything we've put into our reports and everything we told each other over our so-called 'secure' phones. And anything said inside the RV, which was probably tapped and taped."

"Who's 'they'?" Sami asked. "That's what I want to know?"

"Wasn't that what you guys taught us at Huachuca?" Vasquez said. "The first task of intelligence is learning enemy numbers and locations—after that, you look at intentions. Isn't that what they say?"

"That's what they say," DeLuca said. "Romano was a private subcontractor with DIA for years. LeDoux wouldn't have used her without checking her out. The question is, who got to her?"

"And who recommended her?" Sykes said.

"Maybe, maybe not," DeLuca said. "She could have come in clean and turned halfway through. It's still a good question, but not one we need to answer right now. We have more immediate concerns. I think it's safe to say we're caught up in something bigger than we were led to believe initially. I think it's also safe to say we're being watched, and we're being hunted. I don't know how many op centers they have, but we've essentially shut down three of them. They can't use Cheyenne anymore, and they can't use Sinkhole, and they can't use the RV. I'm going to guess that each time they move, their systems get less and less secure."

"Well that's good to know," Sykes said. "They should be surrendering any minute now. On the other hand, they could vaporize any one of us the second we step out the door. I say we pull a Butch Cassidy and the Sundance Kid escape like at the end of the movie with guns blazing. It beats going like a bug in a bug zapper."

DeLuca looked at the younger man.

"That's very dramatic," he said. "But not helpful."

"Why would she mess with our oxygen?" Vasquez said. "They obviously have other means at their disposal. For our disposal."

"They wanted us to disappear," DeLuca said. "We found out more than we were supposed to. Romano knew when we debriefed the mission that we'd be doing some diving—she talked it over with Truitt. Nobody was going to find six bodies at the bottom of a lake a mile underground in a part of a cave nobody knew about. Not for a while, anyway."

"What do you recommend, then?" Sykes said. "We're cut off. We can't use the vehicles we have, we can't use the phones—we can't even use our ATMs. We can't use any of the cover identities we brought with us, and we can't leave this building. And I personally can't sing, so staying here for karaoke night isn't an option either."

"He's right," Vasquez said. "I've heard him sing. He's awful."

"Cash won't be a problem," DeLuca said. "I wasn't sure what our expenses were going to be or who we'd have to grease, but I've got about three hundred thousand dollars in my suitcase that I brought just to cover. The larger issue is going to be identities."

He set his new cell phone on the table.

"I bought a new one for each of you," he said. "But Dan's right—we can't use the covers we brought with us because they're on file. We're going to have to get new ones."

"How?"

"I'm afraid we're going to have to steal them," he said. "I registered mine to the name of a credit card carbon I pulled from the trash at the phone store. The Mormon Church has a Website where you can find people's mothers' maiden names."

"I can get what we need off the motel registry computer if somebody can get me two minutes alone in the office," Vasquez said. "I used to work the front desk at a Best Western when I was in college. All I need is somebody to distract the desk clerk."

Through the double doors, they could see the front desk, manned this afternoon by a lone young man of Pakistani origin named Bindar.

"I've got it," MacKenzie said. She held a credit card in her left hand. With her right hand, she reached inside her blouse, which was sleeveless, and unfastened her bra, extracting it from her left armhole with a tug. "Has anybody got a penknife?"

"I don't know why," Sykes said, "but every time I see a woman do that, I feel like I'm watching Houdini escape from a locked box."

"Get over it," MacKenzie said, stuffing the bra in her purse and undoing her top two buttons. "Penknife?"

DeLuca handed her his Gerber knife, which she used to alter the final digit on her credit card, an 8, into a 3.

"What are you doing?" Sykes said.

"The last digit is the validation key," she said, "using the Mod 10 LUHN formula algorithm. You double all the other digits, add them together and then subtract the total from the next highest number divisible by ten. If the last digit is off, the card reads but won't verify. You ready?" she asked Hoolie.

"Ready when you are," he said. "Why don't you give it another button, just to be safe?"

"Two is enough," MacKenzie said. "You know what P. T. Barnum said. 'Make 'em laugh, make 'em cry, but make 'em wait.' Cleavage works the same way."

The others watched as MacKenzie approached the front desk and leaned over as Bindar tried to total up her bill before checkout, his eyes moving from his computer screen to her card to her eyes to her chest and then self-consciously back to his computer screen, while Hoolie slipped quietly into the office behind him. When the young man turned his head momentarily toward the office door, MacKenzie leaned harder on the counter, lifting an arm to scratch the back of her neck.

"Poor kid," Sykes said. "Five more seconds and we're going to see smoke coming out of his ears."

A minute later, Hoolie slipped out the office door, moving quickly to the pay phones, where he pretended to make a phone call before returning to the bar. MacKenzie returned a moment later.

"I've always said that if women knew the power they have over men, they'd rule the world," Sykes said.

"What makes you so certain we don't?" MacKenzie replied.

"I can use the laptop in my room to get the maiden names and socials," Vasquez said. "I have a screen name no one knows about. What? It's not like I use it to download porn or anything."

"Of course not," DeLuca said. "When you've got it, set up new phones using the stolen identities. We should at least be able to communicate with each other, for a while, anyway. We'll reimburse the good citizens loaning us their identities later."

"Meanwhile, how do we get out of here?" Vasquez said.

"This might help," Sami said, holding up the cardboard display sitting between the salt and pepper shakers and the artificial sweeteners and on it, the motel's event schedule, including, today, an antique car show and swap meet taking place in the parking lot. The bar was full of car show aficionados, old men reminiscing about their first Fords and Chevys and young guys wearing "I Love Dale Earnhardt" or "I Hate Dale Earnhardt" T-shirts. "If you've got cash, I'm sure we could pick something up."

"To what end?" Sykes said. "Where are we going?"

"Usually there's safety in numbers," DeLuca said, "but not just now. We can't stay here. And we can't go home. We can't even call home. I'm going to talk to LeDoux, but it's going to have to be face to face. Meanwhile, we disperse. Once you get 'em set up, keep your phones off and only turn them on for five minutes on the even hours. I'll call you when it's safe. I've asked Scottie to hack Peggy Romano's system and disable her reset to default codes. That should give us the hundred-yard margin if they do find us, but it won't take them long to recalibrate. It shouldn't come to that, though. What's wrong?" he asked Hoolie.

"I'm going to have to sell my Cadillac. I spent six years working on that car."

"You can't sell it," DeLuca said. "Not without putting whoever buys it at risk. You have to leave it. You can come back for it when this is solved."

"What are you going to ask LeDoux?"

"I'm going to ask him what's going on," DeLuca said. "But I don't think he knows. I think somebody is manipulating him the same way they're manipulating us. He wouldn't run me, even if he was ordered to, so he's got to be blind, but he won't know it until I tell him."

"Are you sure?" Sykes asked.

"I'm sure," DeLuca said. "Meanwhile, think of a safe place to go and go there. And we don't tell each other. In case we're asked. I should think we'll all be home in another week or two."

"And if we're not?" Sykes asked. "Not to be paranoid, but Theresa Davidova thought she was in a safe place. Cheryl Escavedo was headed for what she thought was a safe place. We could go back to Lechugilla, but I'm not down with that."

"We'll be all right as long as nobody knows where we are," DeLuca said. "And that shouldn't be for too long. Once I reach LeDoux, I'll figure out a way to bring you in. In the meantime, pick up some fat Tom Clancy novel in the gift shop and catch up on your reading."

"I don't know," Hoolie said. "All that military/government intrigue. It's so unrealistic."

DeLuca distributed the cash in his motel room. Mingling in the crowds examining the antique cars assembled in the motel parking lot, over a thousand in all, CI Team Red resupplied itself. Hoolie bought a 1951 Ford with a grille and nose cone that made the car look like it had a face. He also purchased a massive sombrero in the gift shop, telling the others it was the same satellite defense system used by the Mexican army. When the others laughed, DeLuca told them it wasn't such a bad idea—NSA had been working hard on biometrics after 9/11, in its search for Osama Bin Laden, developing cameras and ways of identifying people from space. The others bought umbrellas in the gift shop and found them useful when a light drizzle began to fall. Sykes bought a 1970 GTO, MacKenzie a yellow 1964 Volkswagen bug with thirty-one thousand original miles on it. DeLuca bought a red 1968 Dodge Dart with a slant six in it with only eighteen thousand original miles on it. Sami was headed east, the same direction as DeLuca, and decided to ride with him. For all the years that DeLuca and Sami had ridden together as partners, patrolling the streets of Boston first as uniformed officers and later as detectives, they'd never taken a cross-country trip.

They'd decided to drive straight through in shifts. They were having a late dinner in a truck stop in Memphis when DeLuca said he felt as if there was something simple that was eluding them, something obvious.

"The information Escavedo copied was all financial," he told his old partner. "Why?"

"She needed to get Koenig to back off," Sami said. "Maybe she threatened to go public if he didn't leave her alone."

"Maybe," DeLuca agreed.

"What did Walter say about the money?" Sami asked.

"She'd isolated an account Koenig was using for home improvement," DeLuca said. "That was the last document she'd worked on, anyway. She suspected he was misusing government funds. Or covering up black-budget spending by assigning other uses to cook the books."

"Was he?" Sami asked.

"Which?"

"Using government funds for home improvements?"

"Twenty-one million dollars?" DeLuca asked. "Maybe, but what was he doing? Putting on a golden dome for a roof?"

"So what's left?" Sami asked. "What's not accounted for?"

"I don't know," DeLuca said. "He took out the DVD factory in Beijing to improve his stock portfolio. Or maybe he had other reasons. That seems thin. He took out a caravan on a glacier on the Afghanistan-Pakistan border, I'm guessing, just because the target presented itself. He didn't know Frank Pickett was with them because Pickett hadn't been able to report in yet, but as soon as Koenig learned, he took out the witness, too. He was probably targeting Fowler for the work he was doing with the House Armed Services Committee."

"But he didn't target Fowler," Sami said.

"Not after he knew we were watching him," DeLuca said. "If I hadn't mentioned Fowler's name to Koenig, I'm sure there would have been a mysterious and unexplained disappearance at sea. So all we've really got is a note Theresa Davidova found with the words 'Tom never,' but, Tom never what? Tom never loved me? Tom never told me . . . ? Tom never wanted . . . ? It's not enough."

"Is that with a capital *N* or a lowercase *n*?"

"I don't know," DeLuca said. "She mentioned it to me over the phone. I never saw the note. It wasn't in the house and apparently she didn't have it on her. Why?"

"Maybe it was a capital *N*. There's a town called Tom Never, on Nantucket. Just south of Siasconset. I've taken fishing parties out that way when they want to fish the Gulf Stream for bluefins."

"Near Siasconset?" DeLuca said.

"Yeah," Sami said. "There's a big Coast Guard Loran station there."

"That's where Koenig's house is," DeLuca said. "The family compound. I saw a picture of it on his screen saver."

"You think he'd go there?"

"Why not?" DeLuca said. "He's not afraid of us, that's for sure."

"Maybe he did spend $21 million on home improvement," Sami said. "That's gonna buy you a lot of gizmos at Staples for the home office."

"Maybe even a satellite dish or two," DeLuca said.

"Call LeDoux and tell him to have an aircraft carrier meet us there," Sami suggested.

"Except that LeDoux's office isn't secure," DeLuca said. "I don't know where the leak is or where the system is compromised, but it is. I think I'd prefer to handle this first. Who do you know on Nantucket?"

"A couple guys," Sami said. "I know a party boat captain. And a conch fisherman."

"Anybody you could ask to sail up the shore with a pair of binoculars and find out if Koenig is in residence, without raising too much suspicion?"

"Sure," Sami said. "We could check with the general store, too. If he's been in to buy a *New York Times,* they'd know. Particularly midwinter. The year-round population is pretty low. Everybody knows what's going on and who's there and who isn't."

An hour later, somewhere near Nashville, Sami's cell phone rang. His contact on the island said General Koenig had been seen in town during the last few days, and that a younger officer was with him.

They hit a bad snowstorm in Cincinnati that, according to the radio reports, represented the trailing edge of a weather system socking in the entire East Coast. They left the Dodge Dart at the airport in Columbus, caught the last flight to Boston, and managed to talk a charter pilot into flying them to Nantucket despite the weather by offering him twice his normal fee, landing in the dark just before eight o'clock. The owner of the car rental service on Church Street had left a note on his door saying if anybody wanted him, they could find him at the Cambridge Street Café. DeLuca paid him cash for a one-day rental on a Honda Odyssey. The road to Siasconset, a village on the eastern side of the island and seven miles from the harbor, was iced over by a freezing rain that blew in horizontally, and they were the only car on it.

They got directions at the Siasconset general store, where a teenage kid in a fleece sweatshirt with his cap on backward was washing muffin pans in a stainless-steel sink. The Koenig compound was a mile from town, in the dunes beyond the Coast Guard station. They left the car at the general store, certain that Koenig would be watching his perimeter, alert to any intruders and/or cars that might be approaching. Two men on foot would arouse less suspicion. They bought heavy-weather rubber Helly Hansen raincoats, rubber boots, and neoprene gloves at the general store, but even then, DeLuca was cold. DeLuca purchased a pair of binoculars, a Boy Scout compass, and a sandwich that he ate as they walked. A massive black Newfoundland dog joined them as they made their way along the coast road, oblivious to the weather in his heavy fur. DeLuca took it as a good sign—two Nantucketers out walking their dog would arouse even less suspicion than two men walking alone. DeLuca had his .38 police revolver as well as his nine-millimeter Beretta. Sami carried DeLuca's MAC-10 as well as a Glock-9. They'd passed the Coast Guard station and were walking through a pitch-black night, the freezing rain stinging against their faces, when Sami finally spoke up.

"It's probably the lights up ahead," Sami said. "On the right."

"Probably," DeLuca said. He was staring at the Loran radio tower, rising eight hundred feet into the night from the coastal plain, topped by a blinking red light. The tower was held in place by two separate sets of steel cable stays, one set fixed to the antennae two-thirds of the way up and a second set with a narrower base circumference attached a third of the way up, both sets of cables lit with smaller red warning lights. DeLuca examined the array through the binoculars.

"There's your dish," he said.

"Dish," Sami said. "Call me crazy, but I see a tower."

"The relays are rigged on the stays. The placement on the wires forms a dish shape. You want a look?" DeLuca said, offering him the binoculars.

"I'll take your word for it," Sami said. "David?"

"Yeah, Sami?"

"You know I got your back all the way, and I haven't said anything until now because it's your show, but at this point, I gotta ask. You got some sort of plan in mind, or are we just gonna wing it?"

"I thought we'd wing it," DeLuca said. "I've got a few ideas. He's got a little more firepower than we do, so there's no point going head to head."

"I guess not," Sami said. "I still like the idea of bringing in a couple thousand guys and asking him to surrender."

"That might be plan B," DeLuca said, plodding on, the going difficult in the thick wet sand. "If he fights, a thousand might not be enough, and if he doesn't, two is plenty."

"What do you want me to do?"

"Whatever happens," DeLuca said, "hold your ground and don't move."

The beach road rolled over the dunes between impenetrable hedges of beach plum and dwarf pine, stopping at a salt pond, where a mailbox in the shape of a sperm whale beside a driveway bore the house number they were looking for. At the top of the driveway, they passed through an arch of braided vines as the approach opened onto a large yard, buried under a blanket of slush. The house was a sprawling mansion of five gables and a grand porch facing the ocean, a warm and inviting light glowing amber through the windows. The siding and roof of the house were of weathered gray cedar shakes, in the grand Nantucket tradition. They made their way in the darkness, keeping away from the lights and staying in the shadows, until they faced the house, their backs to the sea, separated from the house by the vast lawn.

"So far so good," Sami said. "I don't think he knows we're here."

"Yeah, but what good is that?" DeLuca said, putting the battery back into his satellite phone. "Wait here and I'll be right back."

He walked to the house, stopping at the bottom step to the porch, where he saw an old brass telescope mounted on a tripod. He looked up a moment, looked down, then turned and walked back, stopping at the top of the stairs leading down to the beach. He gestured for Sami to join him there. Below, nestled into the dunes, he saw a pair of ancient weathered concrete bunkers. He wondered what was in them. Perhaps it was where Koenig kept his servers, behind hardened shelters.

"You change your mind?" Sami asked.

"I think I should call first," he said. "It's rude to just drop in on people."

He dialed Koenig's number and waited.

"General Koenig?" he said. "David DeLuca here. I was wondering if I could have a minute."

There was silence on the other end.

"What do you want, DeLuca?" Koenig asked. DeLuca saw a figure appear in the window, looking out with night vision goggles.

"You're aware that they might just shoot us," Sami said, fingering the MAC-10 nervously.

"I know," DeLuca said, covering the phone, "but they won't." He took his hand off the phone. "I want to talk to you, General. No playing this time. We came alone. You're not in a good position. I think we can improve it."

"I'm not in a good position?" Koenig said. "How is that?"

"If we could come inside . . ."

"Stay where you are," Koenig said, as DeLuca had expected he would say. "As I see it, you're the one whose position could bear improvement."

"I'm just cold and wet," DeLuca said. "You're up shit creek without a paddle. I don't know if you know this, but my orders are to kill you. Did Peggy Romano tell you that?"

"Is that a threat, Agent DeLuca?"

"That's not a threat, General," DeLuca said. "I wonder if you appreciate what that means. That means the ground you're holding is being sold out from under you. It means the people you thought were going to support you aren't. I know you believe in loyalty, but you're not getting any in return, General. Only a fool shows loyalty to a traitor. They're doing the same thing to you that they did to your father and the same thing they did to your grandfather. Think about it. They've been trying to get me to believe you've been doing this entirely on your own, the rogue general who has to be stopped, and I'm the guy they wanted to stop you. They don't want you testifying in front of any congressional committees. Which is exactly what you should be doing, General. I know you don't like the media, but if you want your story heard, you're going to have to go public, because you know you can't trust Congress to get you out of this. Only public opinion is going to do that. I think if the public heard your story, they'd support you."

"You think so, Agent DeLuca?" the general said.

"Look at Oliver North," DeLuca said. "Same deal. Got used as the White House's private soldier and screwed when the White House turned its back on him, but look at him now—he's got his own talk show. He pulled himself out of it. You can, too."

"Jesus, David—you're offering him a *talk show*?" Sami whispered.

"So what do you suggest, Agent DeLuca?" Koenig said.

"What do I suggest?" DeLuca said.

"He's keeping you on the line," Sami whispered to him, covering DeLuca's phone with his hand.

"I know," DeLuca whispered, taking Sami's hand from the phone as Koenig stepped out onto his porch, wearing a thick Navy peacoat and a watch cap. He recognized the man next to him as Major Huston.

"Good evening, Major," DeLuca said. "What I suggest is immunity. For both of you. I can get you that. You won't have to spend any time in prison. Either of you. I can get Warren Benjamin, Ross Schlessinger, Carla White, and Danforth Sykes behind you," he told the general, referring, respectively, to the deputy director of Homeland Security, the deputy director of the CIA, the White House's national security adviser, and the cochairman of the Senate Select Committee on Intelligence. "I work directly for them. You give us Carter Bowen, and we'll make sure you have a soft landing. We know he's the one you've been talking to." DeLuca was playing a hunch, but it was an informed one.

"You're offering me a deal?" General Koenig said.

"I have the power to offer you a deal, yes," DeLuca said. "They've already started to smear you, just in case you do go public. Did you know that? I have psych evals that say you're crazy. I know that's not true. I know that you've been following orders. You come in with me and you'll get a chance to set the record straight. What's the alternative? You made one mistake—you fell in love with a beautiful girl. I think we can even make the case that she had to be eliminated as a national security risk. They ordered me to kill you, but like you said, I've never been too good at staying within the mission. You come in with me and I'll set you up with the right people. The only people who can protect you."

He watched as Koenig consulted Major Huston.

"It's sort of amusing," Koenig finally said to DeLuca over the phone. "I have more power at my fingertips than anyone in the history of the world, and you're standing there trying to make me think I'm the one in trouble. And you make a good argument, Mr. DeLuca. I have to give you that—you're really quite persuasive. I can see why you're as good at your job as people said you were."

"We're both good at our jobs," DeLuca said. "The difference is that if I've done my job right, nobody knows I've done it. I don't have to worry about how history is going to see me. You do."

"History?" Koenig said. DeLuca knew it was a button he could push, and Koenig reacted as he thought he would. "Don't talk to me about history, DeLuca. My grandfather commanded the largest navy in the history of the world, over four thousand ships and two million sailors, and no one even knows his name. They know MacArthur, they know Eisenhower, they even know Nimitz, but the chief of naval operations is lost to obscurity forever. My father misinterprets a single ruling, a clerical error, and that's all he's remembered for—he goes to his grave because that's all he's going to be remembered for. You dare talk to me about history?"

"General Koenig," DeLuca said, "I'm trying to help you. I really am. I know this is going to sound cynical, but if your father or grandfather had accepted help, instead of trying to take it all on their shoulders and go it alone, history might have judged them more favorably. We have public relations companies these days that can take anything and turn it around. Look at the last election. We can get the truth out, General. But not by toughing it out. That's not how the rules work anymore. And you can't make it go away by pressing a button."

"That's where you're wrong, DeLuca," Koenig said. "You're standing there trying to dictate the terms to me. Do you know what your problem is, Agent DeLuca? You have an entirely overinflated ego. You're talking to me about history—what do you really know, DeLuca? I can *make* history. For the first time since this country was founded, we have the ability to really make this world safe. I don't know what you believe in, DeLuca, but I believe in my mission. There's nothing you could say that's going to shake that."

"I believe in my country," DeLuca said. "I believe in checks and balances. I believe the president should not have the power to go to war without permission of Congress."

"The president is an idiot," Koenig said angrily. "The president froze while this country came under attack on 9/11. The president sat for seven minutes reading *Pete the Penguin* to schoolchildren when he should have been protecting his country. There's a lot more we can do in seven minutes today than we could do in 2001, DeLuca. The president would let a caravan of Al Qaeda terrorists cross a glacier in Afghanistan just because they're accompanied by a half dozen so-called noncombatant Pakistani soldiers—I wouldn't. There aren't any noncombatants anymore, DeLuca. If we had Darkstar before 9/11, not a one of those planes would have killed anybody, and that's the bottom line. You know what your problem is, DeLuca? You're filled with pride. Well, you know what they say about pride."

He took a hand-held computer from Major Huston and held it up for DeLuca to see.

"Think I can't make it go away with the push of a button, DeLuca?" he called out across the lawn. "Just watch me."

"Hold your ground, Sami. Just hold," DeLuca whispered.

Koenig clicked on the PDA.

Instantaneously, the porch of the house was consumed in a column of light. DeLuca saw Koenig and Huston disappear where they stood, melting into the earth. He grabbed Sami and rolled over the edge of the dune just as a ball of heat passed over his head. He'd expected a brief flash, but instead, the column of light burned for what DeLuca estimated to be ten or fifteen seconds, sending a fountain of flame and smoke and debris high into the air, making a noise like a thousand locomotives bearing down on them. Then the night sky lit up in a massive flash, horizon to horizon, the burst of light originating at the point in the sky where the column of light ended, as if a supernova had occurred, somewhere just this side of the moon, bright enough to be visible through the cloud cover. When it was gone, DeLuca had a blue spot on the back of his retinas as bright as if a camera flash had gone off three inches from his face.

Then it was dark, save for the light coming from the fire that consumed the house.

DeLuca stood and helped Sami to his feet, climbing back over the embankment.

They were able to approach the house, cooled by the freezing rain, until they were close enough to stand at the edge of the hole made by Darkstar's directed-energy beam, a perfectly round scar in the earth. When they peered over the edge, they couldn't see the bottom, the sides as smooth as if bored by a drill. Sami found a burning timber and kicked it into the hole with his foot. The red flare disappeared into the darkness, extinguishing before reaching bottom.

"Jesus Christ," Sami said. "What just happened?"

DeLuca took from his pocket a three-dollar Boy Scout compass he'd bought at the general store and showed it to Sami.

"We were standing one hundred yards due east of the porch," he told his friend. "I paced it when I walked back. Sometimes low technology still beats high technology. The GPS signal on my phone is off by one hundred yards. This hole was meant for us."

"Somebody'd better fill it in," Sami said. "It could be dangerous if there were kids playing nearby."

"Somebody will," DeLuca said, taking out his phone to call Captain Martin. He estimated it would be thirty minutes to an hour before the Coast Guard and the Massachusetts National Guard could arrive in helicopters to seal off the area. He saw something on the ground. It was the brass telescope he'd seen on the porch. He picked it up and looked through it, pointing it at a distant light. It still worked.

He threw it into the hole.

From the corner of his eye, he saw what he thought was a black bear. It was the Newfoundland that had accompanied them on their walk. In the distance, they saw the red flashing lights of a fire truck approaching.

"Let's get down to the beach road before the Nantucket FD gets here," he told Sami. "We don't want anybody seeing this just now. When the National Guard arrives, you wanna head back or find a room on the island?"

"I wanna go home," Sami said. "I don't care how late it is."

"I'm with you," DeLuca said, tossing his satellite phone into the hole as well. "I'm with you."

Epilogue

THE NEXT DAY, THE PAPERS SAID SCIENTISTS believed the earth had witnessed the collision of two asteroids, a million miles from earth but close enough that the energy released created the flash viewed by people from Los Angeles to Moscow. A scientist from NASA said astronomers had had their eye on the two asteroids for some time but thought the likelihood of a collision was remote. He even produced a scientific paper written in 1983 predicting just such an event, a paper DeLuca knew had not existed until that morning, just part of the cover story. One lone scientist said a collision of asteroids couldn't possibly explain the massive release of gamma radiation from the explosion, but by then the public was too engaged by the cosmic and/or spiritual dimensions of a "near" miss of an asteroid collision to pay much attention. The paper said a television minidrama was already in the works, based on how the earth might realistically respond to such a threat.

A second story reported a fire on Nantucket, caused by a lightning strike that destroyed the historic home of General Thomas Koenig, who died in the fire, along with an aide. National Guard troops and local emergency crews were cleaning up the area and, DeLuca suspected, filling in a very large hole. DeLuca clipped the article and popped it in the mail to Josh Truitt, with a note suggesting he share the news with Marvin Yutahay.

DeLuca's wife had been surprised to see him arrive home at four in the morning, looking tired and limping, but she was glad to see him. She wasn't surprised when he told her, after only four hours of sleep, that he needed to go to Washington to meet with Phil LeDoux. He promised he'd be back that evening. She told him if he had to stay longer, not to worry—another day or two wasn't going to make her any more annoyed by the lack of communication than she already was. He told her he'd make it up to her when he got back.

"You can try," she said.

"I might not be able to tell you exactly what's been going on . . ."

"What else is new?" she said.

He'd asked to meet LeDoux alone. During the flight, he'd tried not to permit himself to think his friend might have betrayed him. It wasn't entirely reassuring to consider the alternative, that they'd both been duped.

"I just want you to know I'm goddamned angry," LeDoux said before DeLuca had a chance to sit down. "I've already talked to Maitland at INSCOM and DIA, and I have a call in to Warren Benjamin. Just so you know."

"My flight was fine, thanks," DeLuca said. "They had to de-ice the plane twice, but other than that . . ."

"I'm sorry," LeDoux said. "How are you? You're limping."

"I'm okay," DeLuca said. "I fell out of a helicopter."

"You want to keep that to a minimum," LeDoux said. "Sit down. Tell me your thoughts. I'll hold mine for later."

"We were used," DeLuca said. "That's what I think."

"I agree," LeDoux said. "I'm trying to find out by whom. Colonel Oswald has been transferred. I can't find out where, but I will."

"We were bait," DeLuca said. "They couldn't find Darkstar, so they needed to give Koenig a target, so that they'd know when and where to look when he fired on it. And I was it. Am I warm?"

"As far as I can tell, yes."

"What are they telling you?" DeLuca asked. "That the antimatter explosion everybody saw was caused by an overload?"

"They're not saying it but they're implying," LeDoux conceded.

"What do you think it was?" DeLuca said. "Here's what I think. I think Darkstar1 took out Darkstar2, and then when Darkstar1 decloaked to fire on me, they took it out with Darkstar3. I think there's another one up there. And they want everyone to think the program is down. Yes?"

"I think you're right," LeDoux said. "But I don't know that for sure. What else?"

"Koenig was working for the White House. Just like Ollie North. Apart from using Darkstar to clean up his own personal messes, he was only doing what he was told. Huston killed Davidova on his own, to protect his boss and curry favor. Mitch Pasternak said the bullet that went through Davidova's head came from the same kind of rifle I saw in the picture Huston took of himself with a deer he shot. And when Carter Bowen tried to rein Koenig in, Koenig wouldn't listen because he didn't like civilians trying to tell him what to do. Is Bowen going to fall?"

"Carla White is announcing his resignation today," LeDoux said. "For health reasons. How are your people?"

"They're headed home," DeLuca said. "I called them this morning. Sami's flying to Seattle, just to check in on Rainbow. Koenig wasn't crazy, was he? He was as sane as you or me."

"No," LeDoux said. "He wasn't crazy. Just inconvenient."

"We were also used as an OPFOR squadron," DeLuca said. "To test security at NORAD II. They knew it was empty."

"They suspected," LeDoux said. "They're saying they couldn't assume. Captain Martin is making inquiries. It wouldn't be the first time that was done."

"Or the last. What's the Sergelin connection?" DeLuca asked. "Was he the money, or was he the front for the money?"

"When all this began, the Soviet Union was the only country that could shoot down Darkstar," LeDoux said. "My sense is that rather than alienate them, it was better to bring them in as a junior partner."

"That explains why we got a ping from Sergelin's helicopter the night Darkstar shot down Cabrera's chopper," DeLuca said. "To avoid friendly fire."

"One of my all-time favorite oxymorons," LeDoux said. "Sergelin wasn't working outside his government any more than Koenig was, though I'm not sure Koenig knew it. We've been working with the list of Soviet scientists your friend Gary Burgess gave us, by the way. Three of them have disappeared. So far. Sergelin's been arrested."

"I'm not surprised," DeLuca said. "So who used us? Who wanted Koenig out? Bowen?"

"I think he had help," LeDoux said.

"Who?"

"Off the record, it looks like it could be Air Force," LeDoux said. "A lot of people were not happy when the STRATCOM took over NORAD. People at the Pentagon who didn't like how Darkstar's original mission changed. I'm told they hoped that if they gave Koenig enough rope, he'd shoot himself in the foot. To very badly mix a metaphor. And so he did. And then some."

In all his years in the service, DeLuca had seen rivalries and feuds between branches of the service erupt in virtually every avenue of endeavor. It was the same old shit, different day. The stakes were just higher this time.

"Why Shijingshan?"

"A demonstration," LeDoux said. "A shot across the bow. The White House has been in trade negotiations with the Chinese for a while now."

"Gunship diplomacy?" DeLuca asked.

"Except now the gunships are in orbit twenty-eight thousand miles away," LeDoux said.

"Was Peggy Romano working for Bowen or the Air Force? I handed her the disk Escavedo stole. That's what they wanted all along, wasn't it? She only gave Walter a fraction of what was on the disk, didn't she? Just enough not to tip her hand. But why try to kill us with the oxygen bottles?"

"She was working for the Pentagon. I didn't know. She was supposed to take the disks, once you found them, and make sure no one else saw them. It looks like the oxygen thing was actually an accident," LeDoux said. "There was a recall order issued on those bottles but the order hadn't reached her yet. Apparently."

"Apparently," DeLuca said. "Darkstar's mission changed from what? From antisatellite to tactical?"

"Not just that. In its original conception, it was supposed to be powerful enough to blast any asteroid that might be approaching earth into bits."

"Asteroids?" LeDoux nodded. DeLuca suddenly saw the story the newspapers were putting about about asteroids colliding as a kind of preparation. "We're in danger—do something," the public would say, and then the Pentagon could reply, "We hear you—we will."

"You're saying this is a big case of mission-creep?" DeLuca asked.

"Big case. From asteroids to satellites. To anti-UFO," LeDoux said. "I know, I know. This is something they're never going to cop to. The belief has been that the possibility of an attack from extraterrestrial forces is real enough to at least prepare for it. Too many pilots over too many years reporting too many things going zip in the night."

"You've got to be shitting me," DeLuca said. "So Mars really does need women? I saw a UFO, Phil, and then Gary Burgess explained exactly how it could happen."

"I know," LeDoux said. "Midnight on the twenty-third, right?"

"Midnight on the twenty-third," DeLuca said.

"Which was 10:00 A.M. Moscow time, which was when the rebel brigade attacking Sergelin's pipeline got vaporized in Chechnya."

"What's your point?"

"Those are opposite sides of the earth," LeDoux said. "Darkstar could do a lot of things, but one thing it couldn't do was be in two geostationary orbits on opposite sides of the earth at the same time."

"Then it was Darkstar3," DeLuca said.

"D3 wasn't launched yet," LeDoux said. "It was launched two days later. Maybe it was your imagination."

Suddenly DeLuca knew how Sami must have felt.

"Maybe," he said.

"Meanwhile," LeDoux said, "we're not going to loan you out to any joint commands again. That was my mistake. After what you went through in Iraq, I thought I was lobbing you a softball. It's my fault that it got to be more than that. We're clamping down."

"Good idea," DeLuca said. "We wouldn't want the actual sharing of intelligence resources to compromise a well-oiled military machine."

"I don't need your sarcasm," LeDoux said. "I have plenty enough of my own to go around. Where are you going next?"

"I promised my wife a vacation in the sun," DeLuca said. "She found a spa in Arizona she wanted to go to, but I'm feeling a little burned out on the Southwest. I'm thinking of maybe Key West, or the Caribbean. I feel like I've inhaled a lot of darkness lately. I need a good sunburn."

"Leave your phone on," LeDoux said. "We could be sending you to a sunny place some time in the near future."

"Where?"

"Go on vacation," LeDoux said. "Put it on your CI card. You've earned it. And kiss Bonnie for me. I'll brief you when you get back."

"I almost forgot," DeLuca said. "One last thing. There's a lieutenant somewhere named Joyce Reznick, unless she got busted in rank, too. Koenig had her transferred to get her out of the way. Tell Captain Martin to find her and transfer her back. See if there's a recruiting office in Provincetown or Northampton where we could put her to use. Okay? I'll see you around."

About the Authors

David DeBatto has served in the active-duty Army, Army Reserve, and Army National Guard as a German linguist, counterintelligence course instructor, and counterintelligence special agent. He served in Europe at the height of the Cold War in the late 1970s to early 1980s and in Iraq during Operation Iraqi Freedom in 2003 where his Tactical Human Intelligence Team (THT) hunted Saddam, WMD, and top Ba'ath party leaders. He is currently writing further books in this series for Warner Books along with Pete Nelson as well as articles for major publications such as *Vanity Fair, Salon,* and *The American Prospect.* He is also a frequent guest on major television and radio news programs giving his analysis of breaking stories in the global war on terrorism. David lives in Florida.

Pete Nelson lives with his wife and son in western Massachusetts. He got his MFA from the University of Iowa Writers' Workshop in 1979 and has written both fiction and nonfiction for magazines, including *Harper's, Playboy, Esquire, MS, Outside, The Iowa Review, National Wildlife, Glamour,* and *Redbook.* He was a columnist for *Mademoiselle* and a staff writer for *LIVE* magazine, covering various live events including horse pulls, music festivals, dog shows, accordion camps, and arm wrestling championships. He's published twelve young adult novels, including a six-book series about a girl named Sylvia Smith-Smith, which earned him an Edgar Award nomination from the Mystery Writers of America. His young adult nonfiction WWII history, *Left for Dead* (Random House, 2002), about the sinking of the USS *Indianapolis,* won the 2003 Christopher Award and was selected for the American Library Association's 2003 top ten list. His other nonfiction titles include *Real Man Tells All* (Viking, 1988), *Marry Like a Man* (NAL, 1992), *That Others May Live* (Crown, 2000), and *Kidshape* (Rutledge Hill, 2004). His novel *The Christmas List* was published by Rutledge Hill Press in 2004.

More explosive CI Action!

See below
for a preview of
David DeBatto and Pete Nelson's new novel

CI: Mission Liberty

available in October 2006.

THE CAR BOMB HEADING FOR THE U.S. EMbassy, a fifteen-year-old Isuzu passenger van carrying two sixty-four-gallon drums marked "ammonium nitrate," enough to sink an aircraft carrier, was driven by a young man wearing a vest that appeared to be packed with C4 explosives. He was joined on his mission by four men in ski masks carrying AK-47s and glancing nervously at the mobs that were throwing stones and looting stores and burning everything that had the taint of "foreigners." A fifth man rode on the roof, grabbing the roof rack for support whenever the vehicle hit a pothole or crossed one of the open sewers.

Down an alley, they saw a group of men with machetes chasing three boys who slipped through a hole in a fence. At the next corner, they were slowed in their progress when four women with babies strapped to their backs crossed in front of them, carrying portable stereos still in their boxes. The palm-lined avenue called Presidential Way was strewn with debris, the smoking shells of burned and overturned cars, the blackened armor from what used to be a military half-track with two burned bodies falling from the back, one corpse with its head intact and one without. Groups of children dressed in cast-off clothing donated by American charities, wearing T-shirts bearing logos for Georgetown University or faded images of Britney Spears, huddled in doorways, aiming toy rifles and broomsticks at the passing vehicles and laughing. Mixed with smoke and cordite and the pungent aroma of raw sewage flowing in the gutters was the faint smell of tear gas in the air, lingering in the areas where government troops had beaten a retreat in the face of the onslaught. Uncontrollable mobs now surged through the streets of Port Ivory, driven forward by rebel troops in green forest camo uniforms and red berets. Many of the regular rebel forces hadn't been paid in weeks and now took their compensation in the traditional way of conflict, seizing whatever they could load into their jeeps and trucks or carry in their arms, and in whatever pleasures could be gained along the way.

The driver of the Isuzu, an Arab man in his early twenties, slowed as they passed the British embassy, where thick black clouds of smoke poured from the former colonial governor's mansion beyond the cast-iron fence, the fire not enough to deter the gangs of looters darting in and out of the building, braving the flames in search of treasure.

The Isuzu slowed again as it approached the American embassy, on the opposite side of Presidential Way from the British embassy. Their target was Ambassador Arthur Ellis, but they feared they were too late, the grounds of the American compound overrun by Ligerians and rebel troops, the top corner of the building blown away where a shell from a seized Ligerian tank had detonated, the windows all broken, pieces of roof tile scattered across the yard. A thick black plume of smoke poured from inside the embassy, the image captured by a film crew with Belgian flags taped to their shirts. There was a large U.S.-made M-113 military transport parked in front of the gates, where six men in green uniforms and red berets fired their rifles in the air in celebration, a response that was returned by the man on the roof of the van, raising his AK-47 in the air in a gesture of victory.

A man whose uniform bore the insignia of a captain approached the van, smiling, his eyes hidden behind his wraparound sunglasses, his machine gun hanging casually from a strap over his shoulder.

"Where is the ambassador?" the driver of the van asked the captain in accented English. "We come for the ambassador."

"They moved him," the captain said. "I don't know when."

"Where did they move him?" the driver asked, at which point the captain pointed down the road with his gun.

"To the castle," he said. "They could not defend this place. We were too many. Too strong! They have their Marines, but not so many. We have them up a tree, man."

"I will see," the terrorist leader said. He made a brief inspection of the castle. In the ambassador's office, he found shredded papers, a wastebasket in which documents had been used to light a fire, and atop the fire, burned and melted CDs and videotapes. All had been destroyed. He returned to the van. The massive Castle of St. James loomed at the far end of Presidential Way, at the opposite end of the esplanade from the presidential palace, which was also under siege.

"Can you take us there?" he asked the captain. "To the castle?" The captain nodded, glancing inside the van at the drums of explosives in the back. He ran to the transport and ordered his men to take their guns and get in. The troops moved slowly, too drunk to move any faster. The leader of the car bombers saw a man dump a half dozen empty beer cans out the rear of the truck in front of them.

"We have an escort," the man in the front seat said.

"Praise Allah," a voice from the back seat added. "God is great."

They heard machine gun firing from inside the soccer stadium, an open-roofed ring of concentric concrete risers where the banks of lights already blazed white as the twilight approached. There was no telling who was being killed inside the stadium or how many, though the men in the van saw a half dozen orange schoolbuses parked just inside the gates, as well as another dozen military transports. Throngs of barefooted onlookers pressed up against the fence that enclosed the parking lot to see if they could get a glimpse of what was going on inside, with mothers crying out for their sons and wives crying out for their husbands.

The Castle of St. James loomed immense above the town, originally a trading outpost built in 1534 by the Portuguese and later captured by the Dutch and then by the British, both powers adding to its original fortifications, though in each case, the main defenses were focused inland, to protect the occupants of the castle from attack by Africans, and not towards the sea where an attack could come from rival colonial powers. It stood on a natural mount, its outer bastions and casements forming a wall that girded the fortress on three sides, its fourth side backed against the sea atop a natural rock precipice where the wild surf from the Bight of Benin pounded on the foundation and the rocks below. A barbican village had grown up around the castle, where Fasori traders did their business with the Europeans, first in ivory, then in gold, then in human beings, and now formed the oldest part of the city. Cannons from inside the fortress had destroyed the town of Port Ivory, or parts of it, on three separate occasions over the centuries, but the city was always rebuilt, brown and gray houses of wattle and daub and cinder block with red tile and corrugated tin roofs, open stalls, street vendors, shops and merchants, the air hazy and stinking of kerosene cook fires and curry, car exhausts and the open sewers that ran down both sides of the streets in shallow gutters, and everywhere, chickens, goats, sheep, donkeys, and mangy short-haired dogs with curly tails. And rats. Several shops near the castle were on fire, filling the air with black smoke and an acrid stench.

The M-113 parted the crowds, the soldiers in it occasionally firing their rifles in the air in warning. Some who saw the Isuzu van behind the transport, filled with men in masks, seemed bewildered, while others cheered and blew kisses. The truck stopped at the base of a long curving stone ramp leading uphill for fifty yards to the castle's main portcullis. The gatehouse forming an outwork at the base of the ramp had been seized, with loudspeakers set up atop one of the turrets, from which Radio Liger blared, inciting the crowd, a voice saying, "Kill them, kill them all, you have much work to do . . ."

The captain walked from the transport back to the van. He was smoking a cigar. When he offered one to the man in the van's passenger seat, the man refused.

"We have machine guns and RPGs on the roofs surrounding the castle," the captain said, "and many SAM-7s hidden. SAM-9s. We think they will send their helicopters, and when they do, we will shoot them all down."

"Where are your SAMS?" the Arab in the passenger seat said in Arabic. The captain looked confused, so the man repeated the question in accented English.

"We have one in the church steeple, there," the captain

said, pointing with his cigar, "and one is in the mayor's office, right there. And we have another in the red truck over there. That one. Yes. I chose the locations myself."

"And the men firing them, they've been trained? They're not your children warriors—they're actual soldiers?"

"Oh yes," the captain said. "They are my finest. Hand picked."

"You've done well," the Arab said. "Keep them there. Now move your truck, please."

"What will you do?" the captain asked.

"We came for the ambassador," the Arab said. "We have his family. He has said if we release them, he will take their place. Move the truck now."

The captain gave orders, and the M-113 was moved. The man atop the van attached a large white flag to the barrel of his rifle, and then the Isuzu began to inch forward up the ramp. The curtain wall forming the outer bailey was lower than the bulwark inside, allowing the American soldiers visible at the rampart's embrasures to shoot over it, if they chose to, but they held their fire. The crowd below watched in anticipation. Many backed away, expecting a massive explosion as word spread that a car bomb had penetrated the American defenses. The Arab in the passenger seat saw a pair of fifty-millimeter guns mounted atop the parapet guarding the main gate and told the driver to slow down. When the gates opened, the van drove slowly through, and then the gates closed behind it.

The driver parked in the inner ward, just in front of the castle keep, and then the men got out of the van. They were met by a pair of Marines, who escorted them into the historical museum's main exhibit room. Ambassador Ellis, wearing a helmet and a flak jacket, accompanied by a half dozen Marine bodyguards, stood in front of a large glass exhibit case, inside of which was displayed a long flowing garment called, according to the brass plaque at the top, The Royal Sun Robe, worn, historically, by a succession of Fasori kings. The man who'd been riding in the passenger seat took off his ski mask, saluted, and then extended his hand to the ambassador.

"Special Agent David DeLuca, U.S. Army counterintelligence, Team Red," he said. Some of the soldiers looking on were surprised to notice that one of the "men" in the ski masks was in fact a woman. "Thanks for not shooting us. I wasn't sure you got our message. My driver is Agent Zoulalian. This is Agent Sykes, Agent Vasquez, and Agent MacKenzie. Sorry we weren't able to visit you under happier circumstances. Your wife and kids are fine, by the way, but the cover story is that we're swapping them for you so they've been kept out of sight on the carrier."

"This is Captain Allen, in charge of my security detail," Ambassador Ellis said. "Sorry we had to leave the embassy. What's the plan? They've been jamming my goddamn SAT-phone."

"Who do you have here for staff?" DeLuca asked, scanning the massive stone walls. It was the kind of place where a few Marines with machine guns could hold off an entire army, for a while, anyway. He could hear the staccato stutter of gunfire beyond the castle walls, the voice from the loudspeakers at the gatehouse muffled, as if coming from a pair of headphones left on a pillow.

"Just my secretary," Ellis said. "Everybody else got out. What's the situation at the embassy?"

DeLuca shook his head.

"How about the British embassy?"

Again DeLuca shook his head.

"The British pulled out yesterday and lost seven men trying."

"I'm blind here, DeLuca—fill me in. Why can't I use my phone?"

"We believe they're using U.S. jamming equipment we sold the government," DeLuca said. "Where do you want me to start?"

"Where's General Ngwema? What's Osman doing? Where's LeClerc?"

"LeClerc can't move until the Security Council says he can," DeLuca said. "Osman's A.U. forces are waiting to hear from Addis Ababa, but I don't think they have what they need, even if they get clearance. Most of the city's Christians have fled. Ngwema's holding the ground west of town. We think the majority of the refugees are behind him."

"Why isn't he moving?" Ambassador Ellis said. "What's he waiting for?"

DeLuca shrugged.

"He might not be waiting for anything. He might be protecting the oil fields and letting the city fall. We're not sure just what his mind is."

"Bo?"

"President Bo is in the presidential compound, which, from the looks of it, is more strongly fortified than this place," DeLuca said. "We can debrief on the carrier if you want, sir, but I'm not sure I'm the person to do it, and I'm quite sure this isn't the best time or place."

"Why did they send you?" the ambassador said. "No offense, but there are only four of you."

"Five," DeLuca said. "We couldn't do anything until we had more intel." He turned to the Marine captain. "We want to fly in a couple of jollies for you and your men with CAS and AI but we weren't sure what your ADOCS were," DeLuca told Captain Allen.

"We lost prepositioning along with our APS grids when

the embassy fell," Captain Allen said. "I have a lieutenant who served with a COLT in Kabul as the 'lino' and a sergeant who spent a week with a FIST team, but we could use an artillery intelligence officer for the DISE. We took a G/VLDD (he pronounced it "Gee-vlad") off a hummer and mounted it at the top of the turret but it's not going to be much use without the pulse codes."

"Agent Zoulalian has the codes," DeLuca said, turning to his driver. "Run upstairs and program the laser. Number one is the church steeple, two is the mayor's office, and three is the red truck parked across from the gatehouse."

Zoulalian took off on the double. Captain Allen looked at DeLuca quizzically.

"We found a rebel captain who was only too eager to brag about where he put his SAMs," DeLuca explained. "I think the intel is good, but my only worry is that he wasn't telling me everything. That and the RPGs—what's your sense there?"

"We haven't seen much, but I'm sure they have 'em," Allen said. "The question's what we can suppress."

"Shock and awe," DeLuca said. "Works for me."

"Plain English, gentlemen," the ambassador said. "I know I'm a civilian, but I'm still in charge here."

DeLuca's orders had been to take charge if he had to, but for now he could let Ellis continue under the illusion that he was in control.

"I was asking Captain Allen if he had any deep ops coordination system," DeLuca said. "He told me he has a man who served as a liaison officer with a combat ops laser team and another man who served with a fire support team. A gee-vlad is a ground/vehicular laser locator designator—that's the laser we use to paint targets for the smart bombs. He took one off a Humvee and mounted it on a tripod on the tower.

The rebels have three Soviet shoulder-fired antiaircraft missiles, in the steeple, the mayor's office, and the red truck parked by the gates. The lasers emit a pulsed code to tell the bombs where to go. My sergeant is upstairs programming the codes into the laser. What we're going to do is blow those three things up and then fly in a couple of helicopters . . . "

"Jollies?"

"Yes sir," DeLuca continued, "under close air support and air interdiction. Noise and smoke. With minimal collateral, if we're lucky. They're going to get the Marines out, but what we don't know about are rocket-propelled grenades, which can still down a helicopter."

"It sounds risky," Ambassador Ellis said.

"It is risky," DeLuca said. "That's why we're going to take you out a safer way."

"Which is?"

"The same way we came in," DeLuca said. "You look like you're about a forty-four regular, am I right?"

Deluca pulled the abaya he was wearing over his head. Beneath it, he wore his "second chance" ballistic body armor, but beneath that he wore dress pants and shoes and a white shirt (soaked with sweat) with a red bowtie of the sort that Ambassador Ellis was famous for wearing, his identifiable trademark. Back home, the only time DeLuca ever wore suits was when he had to testify in court in the trial of somebody he'd arrested. He asked the ambassador if he could borrow his sport coat. The ambassador complied. Over the sport coat, DeLuca donned the bomber's vest that Zoulalian had rigged from a Kevlar flak jacket, a spare set of distributor wires, and six cans of black Play-Doh, but it looked real. DeLuca bade Ambassador Ellis to don the flak jacket, the abaya, and a ski mask and then handed him an AK-47.

"Is it loaded?" the ambassador asked.

"It is," DeLuca replied patiently to an incredibly stupid question. "But if we do this right, nobody's going to fire a shot. In fact, they're going to cheer you as you leave. I'll bet you weren't expecting that."

"We're done setting up the Mark-10s," Mack reported, referring to the oil-drum-sized smoke bombs that had been disguised as explosives in the back of the phony car bomb, one in the near corner of the inner bailey and the second in a bartizan upwind from the keep. "Dan's setting the delays."

"We've got a J-STAR zeroed with a Hellfire on the jamming gear they're operating, in a building about a block from here," DeLuca told Allen as he climbed onto the roof of the van. "Once that goes, your comms should work. You'll hear it when it does. Fire support will call you at that point. It's going to happen fast." DeLuca saw Zoulalian returning at a quick jog. "You all done upstairs?"

"Roger that—locked and loaded," Zoulalian said, turning to Vasquez, who'd resumed his position atop the van. "You wanna drive?"

"I'm good here," Hoolie replied, raising his AK-47 and setting the safety, testing the trigger to make sure the safety had engaged. "How often do I get the chance to take my team leader hostage?"

DeLuca turned his back to Hoolie and placed his hands together. Hoolie used a pair of flex cuffs to bind DeLuca's hands behind his back, but with the plastic teeth filed off so that the cuffs were only on tight as long as DeLuca pulled on them. Hoolie threw a knit ski mask over DeLuca's head with the eyes in back, though the fabric was of a wide enough mesh that DeLuca could see through it.

"Make sure the bowtie is visible," DeLuca said. "Mr. Ambassador, if you'll take a seat in the back next to Agent MacKenzie, we'll be on our way. We have a SEAL team with a fastboat waiting about a mile down the beach and a pair of Predators watching our every move, but we're still going to need a bit of deception until we get there, so just keep your mask on and wave your rifle and look angry and we'll do the rest. Do you know any Arabic?"

"Allah akbar," the ambassador said.

"That'll do," DeLuca said. "We armored the sides and the doors but not the windows, obviously, so if somebody starts shooting, stay low. Dennis, let's not give anybody too much time to think. Captain Allen, the jollies will be here in ten minutes, so get your men ready. See you on the *Johnson*."

Zoulalian started the car, with Sykes now in the passenger seat and Mack and the ambassador in the back. DeLuca knelt on the roof with a black mask over his head while Hoolie held a gun to his neck, lifting the loose folds of the mask with his rifle to make sure the red bowtie was visible. The image was going to be a compelling one when it was shown on Al Jazeera later that night, a U.S. ambassador with bombs strapped to his chest being led from his stronghold at gunpoint by a brave band of terrorists.

They breached the portcullis and were halfway down the ramp when Zoulalian was forced to step on the brakes. At the base of the ramp, the M-113 was parked across the drive to block the way. The rebel troops had dismounted and had their guns pointed at the van. The captain, his cigar still in his hand, shook it in the air and gestured for the van to come forward.

"What the fuck?" Vasquez said under his breath.

"Easy everybody," DeLuca said into his transmitter. "Remember Mog'. Dennis—commence ranting and gesticulating."

Zoulalian got out of the car and screamed at the rebel captain, gesturing with both arms to get out of the way and let them through. When the captain waved him forward, Sykes got out of the car and walked down the ramp to speak with the man in the red beret and the wrap-around sunglasses.

"You have to move your truck," Zoulalian said in accented English. "We have to get through. Now!"

"Give the prisoner to us and we will take him," the captain said. "We can provide security for him."

"We don't need security," Zoulalian screamed. "We have more than enough of that. We have to get to the soccer stadium."

"Inducements, Mr. Dan," DeLuca transmitted.

"Perhaps you could lead the way," Sykes said to the captain, reaching into his pocket beneath his abaya and pulling out ten hundred-dollar bills, American. DeLuca always found it charming, the way people who hated America still liked our money. "Of course, we would want to pay you for the overtime. One hundred for each of your men and three hundred for you. Does that sound fair?"

The captain saw the money and moved his body so that his troops couldn't see the cash while he considered his options.

"Give the money to me, and I will pay the men," the captain said. Sykes handed him the cash, which the captain pocketed surreptitiously. "You will follow me then."

He turned and ordered his men to get back in the truck.

Zoulalian followed in the van, inching through the crowd. Hoolie did his best to block the things the people in the crowd were throwing at "the ambassador" to express their dislike for U.S. foreign policies, mostly fruits, vegetables, cassavas, one man picking up and flinging a piece of dog shit that struck DeLuca in the arm.

"Tell that guy he's going to hear from my cleaner," DeLuca said.

"What do you care? It's not your suit," Hoolie said.

"Sorry for the delay, *Johnson*," DeLuca told the mission controllers on the aircraft carrier, who he knew were watching them, both from an INMARSAT view and from a UAV-borne camera closer in. "What are you seeing?"

"It's going all to hell between you and the extraction point," the voice in DeLuca's earpiece came back. "But we expected that. Make time if you can."

"I don't think our escort is going to let us pass him," DeLuca said. "We'll do our best. Meet you on the sands of Iwo Jima."

They were three blocks from the castle when they heard the first explosion behind them, a JDAM-5 destroying the building where the rebels' communication-jamming equipment was operating. The decision had been made to use laser-guided ordnance first, because of the greater accuracy, but DeLuca understood that the destroyer USS *Minneapolis* was cruising eight miles offshore, ready to deploy six- and eight-inch guns that were nearly as accurate, should the first round of smart bombs fail to do the job. Within seconds, they heard another explosion as a missile struck the mayor's office. Hoolie took the hood from DeLuca's head in time for DeLuca to see the church steeple disintegrate in a ball of flames, and then a fourth missile hit the red truck, flipping it and lifting it thirty feet in the air. The crowd dispersed and chaos quickly followed, men firing their rifles into the air or towards the castle, where a pair of CH-47 Chinook helicopters coming in low over the water climbed the seawall and descended on the courtyard, supported by a half dozen Apaches, swarming over the city like very angry bees. A pair of F-14 Tomcats screamed over the area, a mere fifty feet above the rooftops.

"Hit it!" DeLuca shouted to Zoulalian. He lay down atop the van and braced himself against the roof rack. Zoulalian floored the accelerator and turned right down a side street. DeLuca saw, briefly, the look of surprise on the face of the rebel captain from the back of the truck.

"LBJ—can you cut enemy radio traffic?" DeLuca asked, aware that the E-6 Prowler in the air high overhead carried communication-jamming equipment.

"Not without doing yours too," the answer came back. "They're using our stuff. It's your call."

"You getting SIGINT?" DeLuca asked.

"Negative," mission control came back. "Our Ligerian friend here says they're not speaking Fasori. It's some northern tribal dialect he doesn't know."

"Might as well keep the channels open then," DeLuca said, dismayed that the mission had already crept beyond what had been intended, but then, he'd long considered "military planning" something of an oxymoron. "Loose the dogs of war" wasn't even the right metaphor, because loose dogs at least run in the same direction. "Shit hitting the fan" failed for the same reason—war was Brownian motion, chaos and anarchy, and it changed every five seconds. "We'll just have to outsmart them."

"You being ironic?"

"Nothing personal," DeLuca said.

As the van sped towards the sea, DeLuca turned and saw that the troop transport had backed up and was following them. He opened fire, as did Vasquez beside him, but the Isuzu was veering and careening around or across potholes at a speed that prevented firing with any accuracy.

"Anytime, Pred' One," DeLuca said into his radio. "Let's lose the tail."

The AGM-114B Hellfire was a laser-guided solid propellant missile, five feet four inches long, seven inches in diameter, with a weight of about one hundred pounds and a warhead capable of defeating any tank made. The M-113 following the van was no match for it, the subsonic rocket penetrating the front windshield on the passenger side, where the captain in the red beret was sitting, before blasting the vehicle into a million flaming particles.

"I'll bet that lit his cigar," Hoolie said.

Zoulalian, taking directions via his headset, turned left when the falcon view from INMARSAT told him the street connecting to the beach road was blocked up ahead by an overturned vehicle that was burning. He was instructed to turn right at the next intersection, but when he did, he stopped when a pair of "technicals" came into view, two Toyota pickup trucks, one green, one white, with .50 caliber machine guns mounted in the back. A rebel in the green truck opened fire as Zoulalian hit the brakes, backing up to speed forward again on the street he'd tried to turn from. The green truck followed while the white truck raced parallel to them, firing at them whenever there was a gap between the houses, doubtless causing serious collateral damage with rounds that didn't make it through the gaps. DeLuca shot at the truck behind them, though the road was so uneven with potholes, exposed cobblestones, and eroded excavations that it was impossible to steady his aim, and he knew he was firing more for demonstration than effect. The rebel soldier manning the machine gun looked to be no more than fifteen or sixteen years old, but for all DeLuca knew, he'd been fighting half his life.

"What do we have?" he called to support. "Taking fire."

"Stay your course," command and control came back. "*Minneapolis* has it."

He estimated their speed to be fifty or sixty miles an hour. As the next intersection loomed, he turned towards the sea. With the green truck bearing down on them from behind, slowing down was not an option. At the intersection, beyond the corner house, he looked down the street, his weapon ready. He saw the sea, and then he saw the white truck appear, and then he saw it launched into the sky when a shell from one of the destroyer's six-inch guns struck it. The van was through the intersection before DeLuca had a chance to see the truck land.

"Nice shot, *Minneapolis*," he said.

"We'll give the computer an assist on that one," a voice in his headset said. "Apache Three at your back door." He turned in time to see the AH-64D Longbow attack helicopter descending on the green truck, closing the distance rapidly. A burst from the Apache's M230 chain gun, mounted beneath the fuselage, sent a stream of .30mm rounds down the center of the green Toyota, which veered suddenly into a wall before flipping and barrel-rolling on its side a half dozen rotations before coming to rest on its collapsed roof.

The Apache climbed quickly, at low altitudes an easy target for shoulder-fireds and RPGs.

"You're three blocks beyond the take-out point," DeLuca heard in his headset. "Come back, come back three!"

Zoulalian turned right, then right again onto the street that paralleled the beach, racing past a row of fish vendors and an open-air bar, speeding another block before turning left at a marine repair shop when the way ahead was barricaded by a pair of overturned cars. He threaded his way between overturned brightly colored fishing boats and turned right again once he hit the beach, the van fishtailing and slowing as the sand grabbed at the tires. The way ahead was clear, until DeLuca saw a man rise from the sand and wave his arms at them to stop.

"Navy SEAL, Navy SEAL!" he heard in his earpiece as Zoulalian hit the brakes. "Claymores directly in front of you—do not proceed!"

Team Red spilled from the van, MacKenzie staying by the ambassador's side, while DeLuca gazed seaward, where he saw the destroyer USS *Minneapolis*, and closer in, the LST from which the helicopters had launched. The USS *Lyndon Johnson*, the aircraft carrier that was their final destination, cruised beyond the horizon.

The SEAL stood in the sand, pointing to a spot at his feet and gesturing with his arm for the team to approach.